ACK-ACK MACAQUE

Also by Gareth L. Powell

ACK-ACK
MACAQUE

GARETH L. POWELL

SOLARIS

First published 2013 by Solaris
an imprint of Rebellion Publishing Ltd,
Riverside House, Osney Mead,
Oxford, OX2 0ES, UK

www.solarisbooks.com

ISBN 978-1-78108-059-7

Designed & typeset by Rebellion Publishing

Printed and bound by CPI Group (UK), Croydon, CR0 4YY

For Edith and Rosie, with love.

IN SEPTEMBER 1956, France found herself facing economic difficulties at home and an escalating crisis in Suez. In desperation, the French Prime Minister came to London with an audacious proposition for Sir Anthony Eden: a political and economic union between the United Kingdom and France, with Her Majesty Queen Elizabeth II as the new head of the French state.

Although Eden greeted the idea with scepticism, a resounding Anglo-French victory against Egypt persuaded his successor to accept and, despite disapproving noises from both Washington and Moscow, Harold Macmillan and Charles de Gaulle eventually signed the Declaration of Union on 29th November 1959, thereby laying the foundations for a wider European commonwealth.

And now, one hundred years have passed...

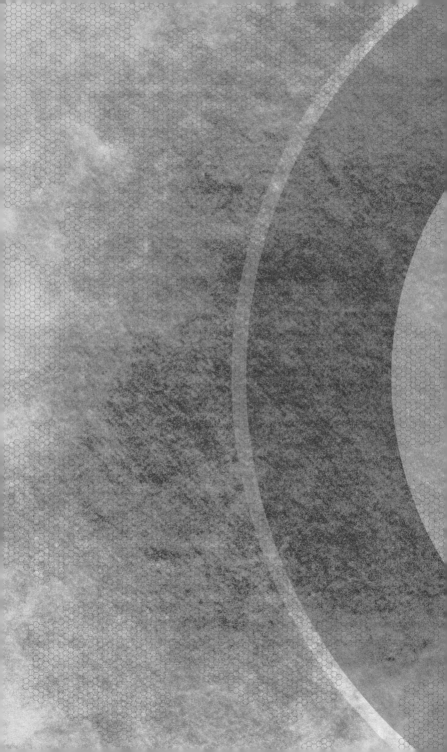

PART ONE

DIGITAL GHOSTS

Des hommes raisonnables? Des hommes détenteurs de la sagesse? Des hommes inspirés par l'esprit?... Non, ce n'est pas possible.

(Pierre Boulle, *La Planète des Singes*)

BREAKING NEWS

From *The European Standard*, online edition:

King Injured In Grenade Attack
Assailant targets royal motorcade

PARIS, 11 JULY 2058 – The King and the Duchess of Brittany have been injured by an explosion on the streets of Paris.

An air ambulance flew His Majesty King William V, ruler of the United Kingdom of Great Britain, France, Ireland and Norway, and Head of the United European Commonwealth, to a private hospital last night, where surgeons battled for three hours to save his life.

The royal couple were on their way to a formal reception at the Champs-Elysées Plaza Hotel, where they were due to announce plans for next year's Unification Day celebrations, which will mark the centenary of the merger between France and Great Britain.

Eyewitness reports say that shots were fired as the royal motorcade turned onto the Champs-Elysées and a missile, possibly a rocket-propelled grenade, struck the royal limousine.

Following the explosion, police shot dead an unidentified assailant, who died at the scene.

The King and the Duchess were cut from the wreckage by emergency services and rushed to hospital by helicopter. In a statement issued this morning, Buckingham Palace confirmed that the King suffered a critical head injury, but is now resting comfortably after surgery to relieve pressure on his brain. It is not known if the King's soul-catcher suffered any damage.

Her Grace Alyssa Célestine, The Duchess of Brittany, received treatment for minor injuries, and reportedly spent the night by her husband's bedside.

This latest tragedy comes only a year after the King's son was involved in a helicopter crash while serving in the South Atlantic. The prince survived his ordeal, but seven of his colleagues were not so fortunate.

Since news of the Paris attack broke, the Palace has been inundated with messages of sympathy and concern.

As speculation rises, no republican terror group has yet claimed responsibility and official sources have so far declined to comment.

The investigation continues.

Read more | Like | Comment | Share

Related Stories

World leaders express shock at Paris attack

PM blames dissident republican terror groups

Next year's centenary celebrations to be postponed?

Hong Kong sovereignty negotiations "in trouble"

TuringSoft: Céleste Tech fails in hostile takeover bid for rival computer company

Nuclear tensions on Indo-Chinese border?

Countdown to launch of first privately funded "light sail" probe

Global population hits 8.5 billion

CHAPTER ONE
VICTORIA AT PADDINGTON

THE MOMENT VICTORIA Valois stepped down from the Heathrow train, she saw the detective waiting for her at the ticket barrier. He was there to escort her to her dead husband's apartment. Slowly, she walked towards him. Fresh off the train, after her flight from Paris, she still wore the thick army surplus coat and heavy boots she'd pulled on that morning. As she walked, she could feel the retractable quarterstaff in her coat pocket bump against her thigh. She sniffed the air. Under different circumstances, it might have been nice to have been back in London. Paddington's concourse smelled the way she remembered, of engine grease and fast food. Trains pulled in and out. Metal luggage trolleys rattled. Pigeons flapped under the glazed, wrought-iron roof.

She stopped in front of the barrier.

"I'm Valois."

"Welcome to London, Miss Valois. I'm Detective Constable Simon Malhotra. We spoke on the phone." He glanced behind her. "Do you need any help with your bags?"

Victoria shook her head.

"I haven't brought any. I'm hoping this won't take long."

"Ah, of course."

Outside the station, the pavements were slick with rain. He led her to his car and opened the passenger door.

"Shall we go straight there, or do you need to freshen up first?"

Victoria ducked into the proffered seat. The car was an old Citroën, its interior warm with the autumnal odours of cold coffee, damp clothes and cheap pine air freshener. A half-eaten croissant lay on the grimy dashboard, wrapped in a napkin. She wrinkled her nose.

"Let's just get this over with, shall we?"

Malhotra closed the door and hurried around to the driver's side.

"Okay." He settled behind the wheel and loosened his tie. He pressed the ignition and Victoria heard the electric engine spin up, whining into life. The wipers clunked back and forth. The indicator light ticked, and Malhotra eased the car out into the late morning traffic.

Victoria let her head fall back against the headrest. As the skyliner ground its way across the Channel, she hadn't bothered trying to sleep. The bunk in her cabin had remained undisturbed. She'd spent most of the night in a chair by the porthole, using her jacket as a blanket, watching the rain clump and slither on the glass, smudging the lights of the other gondolas; asking herself the same question, over and over again: *How could Paul possibly be dead?*

Malhotra took them out onto Edgware Road, then south past Marble Arch, and onto Park Lane. The road and sky were as grey and wet as each other.

"So." He glanced across at her as they passed the gaunt trees and black railings of Hyde Park. "Is this your first time in London?"

Victoria didn't bother turning her head.

"I worked for three years as the London correspondent for *Le Monde*," she said. "I met my husband here. He worked for Céleste Technologies. We moved to Paris when they offered him a position there."

Malhotra sucked his teeth. He seemed embarrassed to have brought up the subject.

"Your husband. Yes, of course."

They came to Hyde Park Corner and the Wellington Arch, with its statue of a black iron chariot. Suddenly, they were in five lanes of traffic. Rain fell in front of bright red brake lights. Black hackney cabs jostled for position. Absently, Victoria touched her fingers to the side of her head, and felt her nails scrape the thick ridge of scar tissue concealed behind the curtain of her hair.

"We separated a few months ago. He moved back here."

"But you're from Paris?"

"Originally, *oui, c'est ca.*"

"And now you live on a skyliner? That must be exciting!"

She shrugged at his enthusiasm. A double-decker bus drew alongside, windows steamed.

"It's okay." She watched the rain coat the brick and stone of London: capital city of the United European Commonwealth, site of the European Parliament, and seat of His Majesty King William V. She hadn't been back here in over a year.

Oh, Paul.

She took a long breath.

"Can you tell me something, Detective Malhotra?"

The young man spared her another glance.

"Sure, if I can."

"How did he die?"

Ahead, a traffic light turned red. Malhotra downshifted the gears and brought the car to a standstill.

"He was murdered."

Victoria squeezed her fists together in her lap.

"I know that. I just don't know *how* he died."

The light flickered to amber, then green. Malhotra let out the clutch and the Citroën's electric motor pulled them forward. He took a right onto Brompton Road, and then a left onto Sloane Street. Victoria's neural software tracked their progress via an online map. In her mind's eye, a blinking red arrow marked her current position, the streets laid out in tangles around it. If she wanted to, she could zoom right in to pavement level, or right out until the world seemed the size of a football held at arm's length. She would never be lost. As long as she had a wireless connection, she would always know exactly where she was.

"Are you sure you want to know?" Malhotra's tone suggested he was trying to protect her. Victoria rubbed her eyes with forefinger and thumb, dispelling the map display. To hear the grisly details of her husband's murder was pretty much the last thing she wanted right now. Yet that old journalistic instinct itched at her and wouldn't let go. She had to know the full story, whatever the cost.

"Someone should know what happened to him," she said reasonably. "Someone who loved him."

The detective puffed air through his cheeks.

"All right, then. If you're sure." He gave her a sideways glance. "But not here. I'll go through it all with you when we get to the flat, okay?"

They passed over Vauxhall Bridge and into Battersea. Paul's apartment lay on the second floor of a building by the river, opposite a Renault car dealership. Malhotra parked on the dealership's forecourt. As today was a Sunday, the business was closed.

"Come on," he said. He led her across the road to the front of the apartment block, with its beige brickwork and chipped black iron railings. The rain dampened her hair, and she could feel her heart fluttering in her chest.

Although the cool, detached part of her brain — the part she didn't really think of as *her* — told her Paul was dead, the news still hadn't really sunk in at a gut level. She hadn't assimilated it properly. Even now, as they climbed the steps to his apartment, she half-expected to find him inside when she opened the door. He'd be standing there in his kitchen, wearing one of his ridiculous Hawaiian shirts, laughing at her for being so gullible.

He couldn't be dead. He couldn't leave her feeling this empty and desolate. He just couldn't.

She fingered the retractable quarterstaff in her pocket, and thought back to the moment she'd first been given the news.

SHE'D BEEN ON top of the skyliner when one of the Commodore's stewards came to find her. She'd been working through her morning routine on the main helipad, practicing her stick fighting technique. The dawn breeze chilled her sweat. The retractable carbon fibre staff whirled in her hand, its weight solid and reassuring.

Left shoulder.

Right shoulder.

Block.

Parry.

Her technique mixed traditional European stick fighting with moves stolen from the Japanese disciplines of jōdō and bōjutsu. She was recording the session on her neural prosthesis and live streaming it to a laboratory near Paris, where the surgeons who'd rebuilt her could use the data to monitor the continuing integration of the natural and artificial components in her brain.

Beneath her bare feet, the skyliner *Tereshkova* ground its way across France, its nuclear-powered propellers labouring against a stiff westerly. Almost a kilometre in length, the giant airship consisted of five rigid, cigar-shaped hulls bound side-by-side in a raft formation. The two outermost hulls sported engine nacelles and large rudder fins. The three inner hulls glittered with promenade decks, satellite dishes and helipads.

That morning, Victoria had the largest pad to herself, atop the skyliner's central hull. All was silent, save for the flap of the wind and the hum of the engines. Far ahead, an ice-cream tower of cumulus caught the sun as it stretched twelve thousand feet into the sky above Paris. Her calves ached. She'd been practising hard for an hour. Her feet were sore from slapping and twisting on the hard rubber surface. Her shoulder muscles burned with the effort of swinging her staff. Still she kept practising, pushing herself to exhaustion. The sweat flew from her with every move. The staff felt like an extension of her will. Yet, even as she threw herself into the physicality of the dance, an internal stillness remained: a part of her mind unaffected by adrenalin and fatigue.

Following her accident, surgeons had been forced to install artificial neurons, replacing large sections of her damaged brain with pliable, gel-based processors. Although the surgery had saved her life, it had left her unable to read or write. Where once she'd spent her days dashing off articles and blog posts, her brain now refused to parse written text. When she looked at a newspaper headline or SincPad screen, all she saw were squiggles, and the only way she could decode them was via a text-recognition app loaded into the gelware. The app stimulated the speech centres of her brain, so that her lips moved as she read, and she gleaned the meaning of the words as she heard herself speak them. The process was slow and often frustrating, and the app prone to mistakes.

Her hands squeezed the staff as she tried to channel her frustration into the fight.

Left shin.

Right shin.

Step back.

Pivot.

She slid forward on the balls of her feet, reached up and brought the end of the staff smacking down onto the head of her imaginary opponent.

"Hai!"

She let the swing's momentum drop her to her knees. Sweat dripped from her forehead onto the black rubber of the helipad. Her chest heaved. She might be half machine, but the alternative was worse; and every breath a victory of sorts.

After a few lungfuls, she looked up, and saw one of the skyliner's white-jacketed stewards standing nervously at the top of the stairwell. She straightened up and walked over to where she'd left her towel.

"Yes?"

The steward cleared his throat. "The Commodore sends his compliments, ma'am. He would like you to join him at your earliest convenience. It seems there is a message for you, from London."

Victoria rubbed her face, and then draped the towel over her shoulder. She retracted the staff to a twelfth of its length, and slipped it into her pocket.

"Do I have time to shower and change?"

The steward glanced at her, taking in her damp hair, her stained black vest and sweat pants.

"That may be advisable, ma'am."

And so, ten minutes later, scrubbed and combed, Victoria knocked at the door of the Commodore's cabin, down in the main gondola, just behind the bridge. She had pulled on a pair of black jeans and a crew neck sweater. Her hair was clean but tied back, revealing the thick scar on her right temple.

"Come in, Victoria, come in." The Commodore rose from behind a large aluminium desk. He wore a white military dress jacket, open at the neck, and a cutlass dangled from his belt.

Victoria's legs were stiff from the workout. The Commodore invited her to take a seat. From his desk, he pulled a bottle of Russian vodka and two glasses. He filled them both, and slid one across to her.

"Drink this," he said. He had white hair and black eyebrows, and ivory-yellow teeth that seemed too large for his mouth. Although he insisted on speaking Russian to his crew, he always spoke English for her; partly because he had a soft spot for her, and partly because he knew from experience that her grasp of the Russian language extended only as far as the phrase '*Ya ne govoryu po russki*', which she was pretty sure meant, 'I don't speak Russian'.

She touched the glass with one finger, turning it slightly, but didn't pick it up.

Most of the back wall of the cabin was taken up by a large picture window. Through it, she could see one of the engine nacelles on the skyliner's outermost starboard hull. She could feel the faint vibration of the airship's engines through the metal deck.

"What's going on?" she asked.

The Commodore picked an imaginary speck of lint from the knee of his cavalry trousers.

"There is a call for you, from England." He picked the phone handset from his desk and passed it to her. "But I am very much afraid it is bad news."

AT THE TOP of the stairs, Detective Constable Malhotra pushed a key into the lock of the apartment door, turned it, and let the door swing open. The lights were off in the hallway. He gestured for her to go in first.

"Try not to touch anything that's marked." He checked his watch impatiently. He obviously had places he'd rather be.

Victoria ignored him. She hesitated on the threshold. As a former reporter, this wasn't the first murder scene she'd had cause to visit; but it was the first in which she'd had such a personal stake. She knew that as soon as she set foot in the flat, she'd have to start accepting the truth, and admit to herself that she really had lost Paul forever.

All these months, a part of her had clung to a slender thread of hope, praying that one day, somewhere down the line, they'd be reconciled, their differences forgotten. But now, that hope was about to be cut forever. She felt a brief urge to turn and run, leaving the entire situation unresolved; but when she closed her eyes, the feeling passed. She hadn't come all this way just to linger on the doormat with the pizza flyers and free newspapers. As Paul's only next of kin, it was up to her accept and mourn his loss; to go through his stuff, and sort out the paperwork.

Heart thudding, she stepped inside. Her boot heels clicked on the parquet floor. Ahead, a narrow galley kitchen lay at the end of the short hallway. On her right, an open door led into a lounge. Dirty footprints showed where the police and coroners had been about their business. The air held lingering traces of sweat and cheap aftershave; and, beneath those, something organic, like the smell of a butcher's shop on a hot day.

With her hand over her mouth and nose, she took a few paces into the room. Bloodstains darkened the wooden floor and papered walls, each accompanied by a handwritten label. Some drops had splattered the glass, and these had been circled and numbered in marker pen ink. Beyond the window, the Thames curled its way through the heart of the city, its surface the sullen hue of day-old coffee, chopped into ripples by the wind.

She pulled her eyes away from the stains. Paul's medical qualifications hung framed on the wall above the fireplace. Beneath them, a flat screen TV lay face down and smashed on the floor, having obviously been knocked over during a scuffle. The police had covered the sofa with a plastic sheet. Before it, a dozen old virtual reality games consoles lay heaped in various stages of disassembly on a low pine coffee table. Her gaze lingered over the accompanying screwdrivers, lumps of solder and twisted scraps of wire as she remembered Paul tinkering with them, six months ago, before their separation. He'd had a thing for retro machines and, after hours in the operating theatre, he found the intricate work of restoring them calmed him.

Her eyes were drawn back to the dried blood by the window. She swallowed. At her sides, her knuckles were white.

Malhotra said, "Are you okay?"

She turned to him. They were eye-to-eye, almost touching. She could smell the fusty bonfire reek of cigarettes on his breath and clothes. She took him by the lapels of his stupid coat.

"Tell me how he died."

The detective looked down at her hands.

"I told you, he was murdered."

"By who?"

Malhotra took her by the wrists and gently pulled her hands free. He stepped back, out of reach.

"We don't know."

Victoria leaned forward. "There's something you're not telling me, isn't there?"

Malhotra wouldn't look at her. He scratched his cheek.

"I don't know if I should—"

"Just tell me."

He took a deep breath. "Okay. Your husband. You knew he was bisexual, right?"

Victoria let her arms fall to her sides.

"Yes." Of *course* she did. She'd always known he swung both ways. For a brief moment, they'd been in love. Then after the accident, for some reason, he'd stopped swinging her way.

She touched the scar tissue at the side of her head.

"Well," Malhotra continued, straightening his collar, "we think he might have been killed by someone he met. Someone he brought back here for, you know..."

"For sex?"

He glanced back down the hall, towards the front door.

"Um, yeah."

"Not an intruder?"

"There's no sign of forced entry, so we're assuming he knew his attacker."

Victoria turned back into the room. She could feel the two halves of her mind butting up against each other: one in a turmoil of grief and jealousy, the other calmly weighing the facts. Her gaze fell on the stained floor.

"What about his soul-catcher?"

The detective rubbed the back of his neck, beneath his collar.

"I'm afraid whoever attacked him took it with them. Ripped it right out, in fact."

Victoria swallowed back her revulsion. Soul-catchers were cranially-implanted webs, similar to her own implants but much smaller and less invasive. They didn't penetrate the brain as hers did; they were simply used to record the wearer's neural activity so that, after death, they could generate a crude, temporary simulation of that individual's personality, allowing them to say their goodbyes and tie up their affairs. In order to remove his soul-catcher, Paul's assailant would have needed to crack open his skull—a procedure usually only carried out as part of an autopsy.

Malhotra reached into his coat and pulled out a brown envelope, from which he extracted a photograph. He handed it to her, unable to meet her eyes.

"This is how we found him."

The photograph had been taken in this room, from almost the exact spot where Victoria now stood. The victim lay in a pool of thick, fresh blood, his head smashed open like an egg, and his skull disturbingly empty. She made a face and looked away.

"Yes, that's him."

"Are you sure?"

She closed her eyes.

"I'm sure." Despite the bruising, and the hair matted to his face, there could be no doubt. The facial recognition software in her neural prosthesis confirmed it.

"I'm afraid it gets worse," Malhotra said. He tapped the picture with his finger, drawing her attention back to the wet cavity revealed by the smashed skull. "His head's empty." The detective took the photo from her and slipped it back into its envelope. "Whoever it was, they took his brain."

Victoria felt the room lurch around her. "What do you mean, they *took* it?"

"They removed his brain and took it with them." Malhotra swallowed. "We've found no trace of it."

Giddiness came in a sudden wave. She put a hand to her forehead. Not knowing what else to do, she retreated inside herself, allowing her more rational, artificial side to momentarily take charge. She heard herself say, "I guess that explains all the blood." Then, disgusted with herself, she walked over to the window and looked out at the river. The tide was low. Gulls fussed and squabbled on the mud. Barges pushed their way up and down stream. To one side, she could see the four white chimneys of Battersea Power Station; to the other, just visible above the trees and other buildings lining the river, the topmost spires of the Palace of Westminster and the Parliament of the United European Commonwealth.

How many times had Paul stood here, looking out at this view? Had it been the last thing he'd ever seen? Had he known his killer? A tear slid down her cheek. She brushed it away with the back of her hand. Without a recording from his soul-catcher, she'd never hear his voice again, never see his face...

When she turned back into the room, she found Malhotra still standing in the doorway, looking uncomfortable. He obviously didn't know what to say.

"Do you have anything to go on?" she asked him.

He hunched his shoulders. "Whoever this was, they came prepared. There's a hundred different DNA samples in this room alone. The killer must have swept up hair and skin cells from the back seat of a bus or Tube train, and emptied them here to cover his tracks."

"You say 'his'?"

Malhotra shrugged. He didn't care. "As I said, we're working on the assumption that the assailant was male, and most likely a sexual partner."

"But you're guessing?"

Malhotra took his hands out of his pockets. "Unless we find his soul-catcher, I'm very much afraid we're grasping at straws." He gestured at the electronics spread on the table. "We've taken his laptop and we're examining it for clues, but so far we've got nothing."

Victoria opened her mouth, and then closed it again. A thought flashed into her head. She felt herself go cold and prickly. She had remembered what it was that Paul had been doing with the VR games consoles. The memory had been dredged, bright and shiny, from the gel lattice of her brain. Very slowly, she turned on her heel and stepped over to the cluttered coffee table.

"Could you give me a minute, please detective?"

"Are you all right?"

She waved him away. "I'll be okay. It's just all been a bit of a shock. I need some time to process. A few minutes alone."

She heard him sigh.

"I'll be in the car. Gather what you need, then come on down when you're ready. Don't be too long."

She listened to his footsteps as he walked to the door and went down the stairs to the street. When she was certain he'd gone, she started rooting through the components on the table, looking for a particular unit.

"Oh, please let it be here," she muttered. Her fingers scrabbled through piles of old circuit boards and other electronic debris, until finally closing with relief on the object she sought. She pulled it free from the mess: an old Sony games console with a battered casing and broken controller. Paul had unobtrusively inserted the black lens of an infrared port into the console's rear panel, next to its power cable. The console wouldn't run games any more, but Paul had used his experience in memory retrieval to modify it for a different, highly illegal, purpose. Victoria turned it over and over in her hands. The tears were running freely now. Inside this scuffed and scratched shell lay her one and only hope of ever seeing him again.

She hardly dared breathe.

One of the side-effects of having half her brain rebuilt was that she had a near-perfect memory. It could be both a blessing and a curse, but right now she was grateful for it. Concentrating, she recalled Paul standing in their Paris apartment, about eight months previously. He'd been wearing cargo pants and a rock band t-shirt; a new gold stud in his right ear, and a pen stuck behind his left.

"You mustn't tell anyone about this," he'd said. And then he'd shown her what he'd hidden in the guts of this old console, tucked away in a pair of fat, newly-installed memory chips.

Guided by the recollection of his hands, her fingers slid over the plastic casing. She found the glassy infrared port on the back panel, and pulled back her hair. The ridge of scarring on her right temple enclosed a row of input jacks: USB, drug feed, and infrared. They were tiny windows into her skull, put there by the technicians when they rebuilt her; windows designed to help them monitor the experimental technology they'd crammed into her head, but also windows which, months after the surgery, she'd learned to exploit for her own ends.

She plugged the old console into the wall, and flipped the power switch to the 'on' position. The console quivered in her hands like a frightened animal, and a green LED came to life. Hands shaking, she raised the box to her temple and, reaching deep within her own mind, activated her own infrared port. Something clicked. Something connected. The box in her hands purred, downloading data directly from its memory store to the gelware in her head. When it had finished, she dropped the box onto the plastic-wrapped sofa and keyed up the mental commands she needed in order to run the saved file. She blinked once, twice. A cobweb dragged itself across her eyeball.

And Paul appeared.

CHAPTER TWO
HOLES IN THE MOON

THE SPITFIRE'S COCKPIT stank of aviation fuel and monkey shit. The long-tailed macaque at the controls had to use all the strength in his hairy arms to keep the wings level. He'd taken a pasting from a pair of Messerschmitts over the Normandy coast. Dirty black smoke streamed back from the engine, almost blinding him, and one of his ailerons had come loose, forcing him to lean hard on the opposite rudder pedal in order to keep the nose up.

To the RAF, the monkey's codename was Ack-Ack Macaque. He'd had another name once, back in the mists of his pre-sentience, but now he couldn't remember what it might have been. Nor did he care. Behind him, his assailants lay smashed and tangled in the smoking, splintered wreckage of their aircraft. Behind them, the Allies were caught in a long and bloody battle to reclaim Europe from the Nazi hordes. Steam-driven British tanks ground towards Paris like tracked battleships, their multiple turrets duelling with the fearsome heat rays of the insect-like German tripods which bestrode the French countryside, laying waste to every town and village in their path.

Ahead, through the gun sights and bullet-proof glass of the windshield, the monkey could see the gleam of England's chalky cliffs. Below his wings, the hard, ceramic-blue waters of the English Channel.

Almost home.

He saw pill boxes and machine gun nests on the beach at the foot of the cliff. Lines of white surf broke against the sand, and the cliff towered above him: an immovable wall of white rock, at least three hundred feet in height. He glanced down at his dashboard and tapped the altimeter. The dial wasn't working. He let out an animal screech. His leathery hands hauled back on the stick. The engine spluttered, threatening to stall. The propeller hacked at the sky.

Come on, come on!

The nose rose with aching slowness. For a second, he wasn't sure if he would make it. For an agonising second, the plane seemed to hang in the air—

Then the cliff's grassy lip dropped away beneath his wings, and he saw the Kent countryside spread before him like a chequered blanket. He took his right hand off the stick, and scratched at the patch covering his left eye socket.

"Crap."

That had been *way* too close.

A couple of miles inland, through the engine smoke, he caught sight of the aerodrome, and his heart surged.

"Ack-Ack Macaque to Home Tower. Ack-Ack Macaque to Home Tower. I'm coming in hot. Better have the fire crews standing by. Over."

He let the nose drop again, trading his hard-won altitude for a little additional speed, until his wheels almost brushed the tops of the hedgerows lining the fields.

"Roger that, Ack-Ack Macaque. Standing by. Good luck and we'll see you on the ground."

He cleared the first hedge, scattering a herd of dairy cows; and then the second. A skeletal tree snatched at the tip of his starboard wing. The aerodrome's perimeter fence appeared. He pulled back just enough to clear it, and the airfield yawned open like the arms of an anxious parent, ready to catch him.

The Spitfire's wheels squeaked as they hit the concrete. The stick juddered in his hand.

Somehow, he kept the nose straight.

*   *   *

THE DYING SPIT finally bumped to a halt at the far end of the field and the engine burst into flames. By the time the fire crews reached it, the plane wasn't worth saving. Ammunition popped and sputtered in the flames. Paint blistered.

They found Ack-Ack Macaque sitting on the grass at the edge of the runway, with his flying goggles loose around his neck.

"I need a drink," he said, so they gave him a ride back to the Officers' Mess.

The Mess was housed in a canvas marquee at the end of a row of semi-cylindrical steel Nissen huts. When he pushed through the khaki flap that served as its door, the crowd inside fell silent. People stopped talking and playing cards. Everyone turned to look at him: a monkey in a greasy flight suit, with a leather patch over one eye and a chromium-plated revolver on each hip. Pipe smoke curled above their heads. Their faces were amused and curious, and he didn't recognise any of them. They were all new recruits. They had moustaches and slicked-back hair, and they wore brand new flying jackets over crisp RAF uniforms. Ignoring them, he loped over to a corner table and climbed onto a chair. After a moment, the Mess Officer shuffled over.

"Tea or coffee, squire?"

Ack-Ack Macaque fixed the man with his one good eye and spoke around the remains of the cigar still clamped between his yellowed teeth.

"Bring me a daiquiri." He undid his belt and slapped his holsters onto the table. "And see if you can scare up a banana or two, will you?"

"Right-o, sir. You sit tight, I'll be right back."

As the N.C.O. scurried away, Ack-Ack Macaque unzipped his flight jacket. Around him, heads turned away and discussions resumed. In the corner of the tent, someone started bashing out a Glen Miller tune on the old upright piano.

Ack-Ack Macaque settled back in his chair and closed his eye. The cigar had helped clear the reek of aviation fuel from his nostrils, and now all he wanted was a rest. He used a dirty fingernail to worry a strand of loose tobacco from his oversized incisors, and yawned. He couldn't remember the last time he'd slept. He seemed to have been awake forever, flying one sortie after another in an endless string of confused dogfights, fuelled only by nicotine and sheer bloody-mindedness.

Of course, it didn't help that the front line kept shifting, and nobody knew for sure where anything was. Planes defected from one side to the other, and then back again, on an almost daily basis. People who were your most trusted comrades on one mission might become your deadliest opponents on the next, and vice versa. He glared around the Mess, wondering which of these young upstarts would be the first to betray him.

He used to find it easier. In the early days, he'd capered around like one of those cartoon characters from those shorts they sometimes screened in the ready room. A smile and a cheeky quip, and somehow the war hadn't seemed so bad. But then his quips had dried as the death toll rose. The shrinks called it 'battle fatigue'. He'd seen it happen before, to other pilots. They lived too long, lost too many comrades, and withdrew into themselves. They stopped taking care of themselves and then, one day, they stopped caring altogether. They took crazy chances; pushed their luck out beyond the ragged limit; and died.

Was that what he was doing? He'd gone up against that pair of 'schmitts this morning, even though they'd had the height advantage. He should have turned and fled. If one of his squad had been so reckless, he'd have boxed their ears. He'd been fortunate to make it home in one piece, and he knew it. Was he pushing his luck? With a sigh, he dropped the soggy butt of his cigar and ground it with his boot.

"What's up, skipper?" The Scottish accent belonged to Mindy Morris, a new recruit to the squadron. "I heard you took a bit of a battering out there."

He opened his baleful eye. They were always new recruits, all these kids. Yet Mindy was one of the youngest he'd seen. She couldn't have been much over fourteen years old.

"Stop smiling," he said. "If you bare your teeth at me like that, I'm liable to rip your face off."

The girl's eyes whitened.

"Sorry, I didn't mean—".

"Don't take it personally." He kicked a chair out for her. "It's a primate thing. Now, sit down."

The Mess Officer brought over a daiquiri in a cocktail glass, which he placed on the table.

"Will that be all, squire?"

Ack-Ack Macaque scowled at him. "What, no bananas?"

"I'm afraid not, sir. There's a war on, you know. Can I get you something else instead?"

Ack-Ack Macaque picked up the cocktail glass in his hairy hand and tipped the contents into his mouth. He smacked his lips.

"Bring me rum." He turned back to Mindy Morris, where she sat perched on the edge of her chair.

"You might want to watch it with the eye contact, too," he warned her. "If I get drunk, I might take a stare as a challenge."

The girl dropped her gaze to her hands, which were knotted in her lap.

"Sorry, sir."

The Mess Officer returned with a bottle of rum, which he set down without a word.

Ack-Ack Macaque said, "Now, do you want a drink, kid?"

Mindy gave a shake of her head. She had green eyes and very short ginger hair. No make-up. Ack-Ack Macaque picked up the bottle and pulled out the cork with his teeth. He spat it onto the floor.

"Well," he said, "if you don't want a drink, what *do* you want?"

The girl squirmed in her chair. Her cheeks were flushed.

"I know you lost a wingman yesterday." She hesitated, trying to gauge his reaction. "And I hoped…"

Ack-Ack Macaque sloshed rum into his glass. The neck of the bottle clinked against the rim. He was aware that the pilots on the surrounding tables were eavesdropping on the conversation, even as they pretended not to.

"You hoped I'd let you fly with me?"

Mindy swallowed hard.

"Yes, sir."

"How old are you?"

"Sixteen, sir."

Ack-Ack Macaque gave her a sceptical look. She flushed a deeper shade of crimson. "All right, all right. I'm fifteen. But I know how to fly a kite, and I know when to follow orders, and when to keep my mouth shut."

Ack-Ack Macaque scratched at a sudden itch. He hoped he hadn't picked up fleas again.

"Where are you from, Morris?"

"Glasgow, sir."

"Have you ever killed anyone?"

The girl frowned.

"I don't understand."

Ack-Ack Macaque picked a crumb of bread from the hairs on his chest, and popped it into his mouth.

"Have you ever been in a dogfight?"

The girl leaned forward excitedly. "No, but I've racked up hundreds of hours of flight experience on simula—" She stopped herself. "On training aircraft. I've racked up hundreds of hours on training aircraft."

Ack-Ack Macaque sipped his drink. He looked at the freckles on Mindy's nose. Something about her youth made him feel very old and very tired.

"I don't need someone who's just going to get themselves, or me, killed."

"Oh, I won't, sir. I promise you that." She looked up at him with eyes the colour of a summer meadow. "Please sir. This means a lot to me."

Ack-Ack Macaque sighed. She wasn't the first rookie pilot to want to fly with him. After all, he was the most famous pilot in the European theatre. The kids treated him like a grizzled old gunslinger: someone against whom to measure their own skills and nerve. Over the past few months, many had tried to keep up with him, and many had died as a result. He couldn't remember all their names. They came, flew with him for a while, and then died. Some got sloppy, others over-confident, and some were just plain unlucky. But they all died eventually, leaving no more impression on the world than if they'd never existed in the first place. All trace of them vanished. Nobody grieved for them, and he seemed to be the only one able to remember that they'd ever been there at all.

He looked around at the young, fresh faces sat at the other tables. They could be called to fight at a moment's notice. Many of them would die in the hours and days ahead; yet few seemed the slightest bit perturbed. They behaved as if they were on holiday: laughing, joking and flirting. Over drinks, they casually compared the number of kills they'd made as if discussing the scores of an elaborate cricket match. How could they be so blasé in the face of almost certain death? How could life mean so little to them? For all the impression they made on the world, they may as well have been shadows.

He put down his glass and reached again for the bottle. As he poured, he looked at Mindy.

"Do you ever feel like you're the only real person here, and everyone else is just pretending?"

The room fell silent. The music stopped. Mindy sat back in her chair. Her eyes leapt left and right, as if unsure what to do. Nobody else moved. Nobody breathed.

Ack-Ack Macaque looked around at their frozen faces.

"What's the matter?" He lowered the bottle to the table.

"What did I say?"

Then, growing closer, he heard the bass thrum of enemy aircraft engines. An airman burst into the tent, half into his flight jacket.

"Ninjas! A whole squadron of them!"

Chairs scraped on the wooden floor. Their faces expressing both relief and excitement, the crowd rushed for the door, pulling on gloves and flight helmets as they went.

Left at his table, Ack-Ack Macaque took a final swill from the bottle. The rum was as sweet and dark as coffee. Rivulets ran into the fur beneath his chin. He clamped a fresh cigar in place and gathered his holsters from the table. Through the open door, he could see the boomerang silhouettes of German flying wings lumbering across the airfield, spilling black-clad paratroopers. Chutes blossomed at the far end of the aerodrome, as a squad of ninjas tried to attack the tower, brandishing swords and submachine guns. A second wave fell towards the aeroplane hangars, armed with flame throwers and throwing stars.

Mindy was waiting for him at the door.

"Come on, Morris," he said around the cigar. "It's that time again."

"And what time would that be, skipper?"

Ack-Ack Macaque drew his guns: two silver Colts big enough to shoot holes in the moon. Holding them, he felt his energy returning. A grin peeled his lips from his clenched yellow teeth.

"Time to blow shit up."

CHAPTER THREE
BATSHIT CHATROOMS OF DOGGERLAND

11.30PM IN PARIS. On the steps of the Turkish Embassy, His Royal Highness Prince Merovech, the Prince of Wales, shook hands with the Turkish Ambassador and thanked him for a wonderful evening. Then, after dutifully waving for the paparazzi, he slid into the comfort of a waiting limousine.

As the car pulled away from the kerb, he let his shoulders sag, and his smile sank back beneath the aching muscles of his face. With one hand, he undid his bow tie, and the top two buttons of his crisp white shirt. With the other, he took a bottle of cold imported lager from the mini fridge behind the driver's seat and popped the cap. Then, cradling the bottle in his lap, he let his head rest against the cool black of the tinted window. Beyond the bulletproof, rain-streaked glass, trees lined the side of the road, and reflected streetlamps glimmered off the waters of the Seine. On the opposite bank, the Eiffel Tower reared above the trees, lit by spotlights, with both the Union Flag and the French Tricolour hanging sodden from its mast.

The flags reminded Merovech of a line from his great-grandmother's famous Unification speech, where she'd spoken about the way Dover and Calais had once been joined by a chalk ridge called Doggerland; and how the Seine, the Thames and the Rhine had all been tributaries flowing into a mighty river delta, the remains of which now lay submerged beneath the English Channel.

"Our two great countries have always been linked beneath the surface," she'd said, before going on to announce plans for the construction of a tunnel to reunite the two countries — a project which wouldn't be completed until nearly fifteen years later, in 1971.

She had made that speech almost one hundred years ago, and yet every school child knew it by heart. The political merger of Britain and France had been a key turning point in European history: a cause for optimism and hope on a continent still nursing the hangover from two devastating World Wars.

Merovech took a sip from the beer bottle. Good news for Europe, yes; but not so good for him. With the hundredth anniversary of Anglo-French unification only days away, his life had become a stultifying round of yawn-worthy cocktail parties, receptions and ceremonies. He ate, slept and moved to a strict itinerary, with hardly a moment for himself. At heart, he'd always been grateful for the privileges which came with his royal title, but recently, he'd found it hard not to resent the accompanying responsibilities: the boredom and wasted time.

Some people said he hadn't been the same since that helicopter crash in the Falklands. Perhaps they were right?

His trousers squeaked as he shifted position on the soft leather seat.

His SincPhone rang. He pulled it from the inside pocket of his tux and groaned.

"Hello, mother."

From the phone's tiny screen, Duchess Alyssa's face glared out at him. She wore a plain navy-blue business suit with a string of pearls, and a slash of red lipstick.

"Don't you 'mother' me. What's this I hear about you missing the press conference this afternoon?"

In the darkness, Merovech shrugged.

"The Prime Minister was the one giving the speech. I didn't have anything to say. They just wanted me there to make up the numbers."

"Nevertheless, you were supposed to be there. A prince has certain obligations, Merovech. Like it or not, while your father remains in a coma, you are his representative and heir, and it's time you started to act like it."

"I had studying to do."

"Nonsense. I expect you were out chasing that little purple-haired floozy again, weren't you?"

Merovech bridled, but held his tongue. The truth was, he had been studying but, from long experience, knew he wouldn't get anywhere by arguing. Once his mother had her mind made up about something, there was little he could do to change it.

"Look, I really don't have time for youthful rebellion right now. There's too much to do. Honestly, Merovech, you're going to be twenty years old in a few months. When are you going to start facing up to your responsibilities?"

Merovech lowered his eyes, trying to look contrite.

"Sorry mother," he mumbled.

The Duchess glared at him.

"Whatever. I'm not prepared to discuss this any further over an unsecured line. I trust you were polite to the Turkish ambassador?"

"He's invited me to play golf with him next week."

"Very well." She brought the phone close to her face, so that she seemed to loom out at him in the darkness of the limo. "Now get home, and get to bed. We'll finish this talk in the morning."

She hung up. Merovech held the phone for a few moments and sighed. Then he folded it up, dropped it onto the seat beside him, and went back to watching the streetlights of Paris drift past the smoky window.

Paris and London were very similar cities. They had the same stores, the same billboards. The same weather. The kids even used the same bilingual slang, or "Franglais" as they called it. Yet despite these superficial similarities, and despite having been born and raised in London, something about the neoclassical streets of the French capital—something he couldn't quite put his finger on—made him regard the city as his home.

When the phone beeped again, he winced, expecting another reprimand, but found instead a text message from Julie. For the past three weeks, they'd been seeing each other in secret. The message invited him to meet her in a café on the South Bank, at midnight. He read it twice, and smiled to himself as he slipped the phone back into his pocket.

Perhaps tonight wouldn't be a complete waste, after all.

HE REACHED THE café half an hour later, wearing an old red hoodie and a pair of battered blue jeans. He had the brim of a baseball cap pulled low over his forehead, shading his eyes. He'd read somewhere that ninety per cent of facial recognition depended on the hair and eyes, and he hoped that by keeping the brim of his cap low, he'd remain anonymous. So far, no-one on the rain-soaked streets had paid him the slightest attention, and he wanted it to stay that way.

The café stood, shouldered between two taller buildings, on a narrow street south of the river, across the water from the flying buttresses and gothic exuberance of Notre Dame, and a few doors down from the famous 'Singe-Vert' nightclub, where the Beatles had cut their teeth in the early 1960s, playing a formative two year residency before returning to England to record their first single.

Inside, the place was quiet, even for a rainy November Sunday in Paris. He shook out his umbrella. The dinner crowd had gone and only the solitary drinkers remained. A radio behind the counter played spacey Parisian electronica: low, dirty beats and breathy female vocals. The whole place smelled of coffee and red wine. Steam from the silver espresso machine fogged the mirror behind the counter. A sign on the café's glass door advertised free WiFi. A small TV at the end of the counter showed a news channel. The sound was off and the screen too far away for him to read the headline ticker. All he could see were the pictures: troops from China, India and Pakistan facing each other across the windswept borders of Kashmir. Another murder victim in London. UN helicopters plucking survivors from the floods in Thailand.

The café's proprietor was a bored-looking woman in her late fifties, with thick, dark eyebrows and a mole on her cheek. If she recognised him as he came in, she gave no sign.

The walls of the café were covered in framed photographs of old-fashioned Zeppelins from the 1930s, and the newer, much larger, modern skyliners.

Working together in the decades following their unification, and partly in response to pressure from the Americans, who were less than thrilled by the alliance, Anglo-French engineers built a new generation of lighter-than-air behemoths. Merovech glanced at the pictures as he crossed the floor. In the last decades of the twentieth century, skyliner production had kept alive the British and French shipyards, rescuing them from a post-war drop in demand. And during the economic turbulence of the seventies and eighties, when the tantrums of the OPEC nations forced the Western world to take a long, hard look at its dependence on oil, the skyliners had really come into their own, offering cheap and relatively carbon-neutral transportation. Now, with their impellers driven by nuclear-electric engines originally designed for use in orbital satellites, the big old ships still plied the world's trade routes, unfettered by the market peaks and troughs that had so bedevilled the traditional airlines.

Julie was sat at the table farthest from the door, against the back wall. She looked up from her coffee as he approached.

"Did you get away okay?"

Julie Girard was a native Parisian and a fellow politics and philosophy student at the Pantheon-Sorbonne University. She had purple hair. She wore jeans and a sweater under her anorak. He wanted to kiss her. Instead, he slipped into the opposite chair and said, "I went out through a service entrance."

"They will be angry."

He gave a shrug. "What can they do? They can't keep me locked away forever."

Julie glanced around the café. Her shoulder bag hung from the back of her chair. As she moved her head, he caught the glint of silver music beads in her ears.

"But is it safe for you to be out like this, on your own?" She looked worried. "I did not think. I should not have asked you—"

A candle burned on the table, little more than a stub jammed into the neck of a wax-streaked wine bottle. He reached around it and took her hand.

"I'm not on my own. I have you."

She raised an eyebrow. "And what good am I going to be if someone comes at you with a gun?"

He squeezed her fingers. They were cool and dry. His were wet and cold from the rain.

"No-one's going to come at me with a gun."

"You don't know that. Look at what happened to your father."

His jaw tensed. He let go of her hand, and sat back in his chair.

"I can't live in fear of terrorists, Julie. If I do, they've already won."

She ran her index fingernail around her coffee cup's rim.

"I'm sorry," she said. "I just had to see you. It's been nearly a week."

So far, the majority of their relationship had taken place online using anonymous, pay-as-you-go smart phones, skipping from one fake social media profile to another in a series of snatched conversations and cryptic status updates. Physical meetings had been rare.

She brushed a purple strand of hair behind her ear, revealing a yellowing bruise at the side of her eye.

"What happened to your face?"

She put a hand up to touch it, and he saw her wince.

"Nothing."

"It doesn't look like nothing."

Julie flicked her hair forward, covering the wound in a spray of purple strands.

"It is just a bruise."

"Was it your father? Did he hit you again? Because if he did—"

"Leave it, Merovech."

"But, Julie, I can—"

"I said, leave it." She sat back with a huff. Merovech took a deep breath, trying to quell his own anger. This wasn't the first time he'd seen her sporting a bruise on her arm or face.

"You just say the word and I'll have him taken—"

Julie glared at him.

"I do *not* want to talk about it," she snapped. "Not tonight, not ever."

Merovech swallowed back his irritation. "Then what do you want to do?"

She held his gaze for a few seconds, as if trying to decide something. Then she leant down and delved into her shoulder bag. When she popped back up, she held a SincPad.

SincPads were all but ubiquitous. They'd been invented at the turn of the century, as the Commonwealth government pumped investment into the silicon fens of Cambridgeshire, supporting a burgeoning IT industry buoyed up by the work of such pioneers as Alan Turing, Clive Sinclair, and Tim Berners-Lee. And now, like skyliners, they came in all shapes and sizes, from palm-sized smart phones to giant, interactive wall displays. Everybody had one, in some shape or form. They were everywhere. The one Julie held had roughly the same dimensions as a refill pad of A4 paper, and she'd decorated its casing with stickers from a dozen political and environmental causes, all of which were now frayed and peeling. She tapped the screen to bring up a video player, and then placed the pad on the table between them.

"You will not believe this," she said.

Merovech leaned forward on his elbows. The picture showed a monkey in a leather jacket, squatting on a chair. The creature had a patch over its left eye, a silver pistol on each hip, and thick fleece-lined boots at the ends of its hairy legs. It was in discussion with a young, redheaded girl in a blue uniform. Tinkly piano played in the background.

Julie froze the playback. She pointed at the monkey.

"Do you know who this is?"

Merovech shook his head. The animal looked like something from a Manga cartoon.

Julie leaned close.

"His name is Ack-Ack Macaque. He is a character in an immersive MMORPG."

"A what?"

"A Massive Multi-player Online Role-Playing Game." She frowned. "You have really never heard of him?"

Merovech shrugged. He didn't play war games. They brought back too many memories.

"Should I have done?"

"Frankly, yes. The game is owned by Céleste Technologies. Does that ring any bells?"

"My mother's company?"

"*Mais oui.*" Julie gave a slow nod, as if talking to an idiot. "They have been running the game for about a year now. I cannot believe you have not heard of it."

Merovech crossed his arms.

"If you remember, I spent most of last year in the Falkland Islands, doing my national service. We didn't have much time for games."

Julie bit her lip. "The crash. Oh, Merovech, I forgot. I am so sorry."

He closed his eyes and, for a moment, found himself back in the blackness of the sinking chopper, scrabbling at his harness, reliving the underwater cries and struggles of his comrades, the creak of metal, and the heart-stopping cold of the seawater pouring through the open hatch. He shivered. Seven men had been dragged to a freezing death at the bottom of the South Atlantic. He'd been lucky to get out at all. He would have drowned had some unknown hands not pushed him through the hatch, against the flow of the incoming sea.

"And besides," he said to change the subject, "the Duchess and I don't talk as often as you might think." In fact, he had as little personal contact as possible with his mother. They didn't get along at all. He lived in a secure penthouse a short walk from the university, and only travelled to the Élysée Palace for official functions.

Julie reached over and brushed his fingers with her own.

"I am sorry, I did not—"

He brushed a palm across the table's sticky surface.

"It doesn't matter. Now, you were about to tell me about this monkey?"

She sat back and licked her lower lip.

"The game is set in a fictionalised World War Two." Her voice was low and urgent. "Players get points by completing missions, shooting down opponents, and so on. They use the points to upgrade their planes and buy better weapons. In between missions, they hang out and socialise." With a purple fingernail, she tapped the picture of the monkey. "This is the main guy. Players can fly with him and fight for the Allies or, if they are really good, switch sides and try to take him down. But here is the twist: in this game, you only get one life. If you get shot down and your parachute does not work, you are dead. You cannot log back in for another try."

"That sounds a bit rough."

"It makes the game more realistic. The players have something to lose. They have to decide how much safety they give up in return for glory."

"And the monkey, what happens to him?"

Julie turned her palms upward.

"Nobody knows. He has never lost a fight. The game is set up that way. He is nearly impossible to kill."

Merovech sat back in his chair and yawned.

"Is this going somewhere?" He felt uncomfortable with his back to the door. He glanced over his shoulder. The windows were orange from the streetlights. Pedestrians splashed past. The rain looked as if it might turn into sleet.

Julie tapped the screen again, to get his attention.

"I want to show you this," she said.

He looked down at the monkey beneath her finger.

"And what *is* this?"

Julie's fingertips circled the monkey's face. "In my philosophy class, we have been looking at the rights of artificial intelligences, and we suspect Ack-Ack Macaque falls into that category."

"The game?"

"The monkey. The character."

"Are you sure?"

Julie reached over and squeezed his hand.

"The company made kind of a big deal about it. It is part of the challenge of the game, setting human players up against a sophisticated AI, with a one-shot chance of beating it."

Merovech looked at his watch. He'd already heard Julie's rants about the evils of enslaving sentient beings, no matter their origin, and he'd been hoping for something more romantic. He knew they didn't have much time. He could already imagine the panic amongst the SO1 agents charged with his protection. The last time he'd done this, they'd had half the city's police out looking for him, and his mother had been livid.

"So what?" He let his impatience show. "It's not like it's really alive or anything, is it?"

Julie let go of his hand. She arched her eyebrows, refusing to be drawn.

"Just watch this."

She hit the play button. The monkey stroked its chin in a gesture that would have looked thoughtful on a human. It swilled the rum around in its glass, drained it and reached for the bottle.

"Do you ever feel like you're the only real person here," it asked, "and everyone else is just pretending?"

The picture jumped and he saw the same scene from another viewpoint. Then another, and another.

Julie said, "Nearly every player in the bar recorded that scene. The videos are all up on the Web. The chat rooms are going batshit."

The film came to an end, frozen on a picture of the monkey's face.

Julie said, "Do you see what this means?"

Merovech didn't.

She bent forward excitedly. Her hands fluttered over the table like startled grouse.

"It means the damn thing is starting to question its own existence!"

Several heads turned in their direction. Merovech put a hand on her arm.

"Shhh."

"But—"

"We're trying not to attract attention, remember?"

Julie shook him off.

"Merovech, listen to me. I have some friends coming. They will be here in a few minutes."

Merovech sat up, alarmed. His eyes automatically scanned the place for a back way out—an old habit, drummed into him by years of security briefings.

"What friends?"

"Other students from my course. They have seen this footage, and they are as concerned about it as I am."

Merovech felt his cheeks burning. *Oh God, please don't let any of them be paps.*

"We are going to do something about the monkey," Julie said. She reached over and placed both of her hands on top of his. "And we need your help."

TEN MINUTES LATER, Merovech found himself in the back of a black Volkswagen van, heading out of the city. The streetlamps threw moving shadows through the driver's window. Two students occupied the front seats. The back of the van was windowless and bare. Merovech sat on the floor with his back against the wall. For the first time in his life, he felt out of his depth. He didn't know how far he could trust these people. From the little he'd gleaned from Julie, they were obviously highly politicised. What if they were republican sympathisers? What if they tried to kidnap him for ransom? He had no back-up, no security.

Julie huddled beside him, her arm hooked in his. He was only here because of her. He didn't want her running off and getting into trouble; and he hoped he could talk her out of whatever it was she had planned.

A young man sat opposite them, with dark eyes and a stripe of beard that looked as if it had been drawn on with eyeliner.

"This is Frank," Julie said. "He is in charge."

Frank wore an army surplus jacket, skinny black jeans and American baseball boots. A large pendant hung from his neck. The fingers on his right hand were stained yellow. He said, "*Tu es sûr qu'on peut lui faire confiance?*"

Julie put a protective hand on Merovech's shoulder.

"Of course we can trust him. He can get us in there. He knows the layout."

Frank narrowed his eyes. He switched to English.

"Is this true?"

Merovech returned his stare. The enclosed gloom and metal walls of the van were making him uncomfortable.

"I haven't agreed to anything."

"*Merde.*" Frank bit his lip and looked away.

"What's the matter?" Julie asked.

"What's the *matter*?" Frank flung a hand at Merovech. "We are sitting in a stolen van, on the way to committing an illegal act, and you bring along the heir to the British *throne*! I mean, *putain de merde*!" He fumbled in his pocket and pulled out a pack of cheap cigarettes. He extracted one but, as he went to light it, Merovech leaned over and put a hand on his arm.

"She didn't bring me. I brought myself."

Frank gave him an incredulous squint.

"And do you know what we are going to do tonight, 'your highness'?"

Merovech straightened.

"Why don't you tell me?"

Frank shook him off. He lit the cigarette.

"We believe your mother's company has an AI imprisoned on its game servers."

"So what?"

Frank exhaled grey smoke into the cramped space. "We are going to break in and free it."

In the rattling semi-darkness, Merovech looked at Julie. The shadow of her hair hid part of her face. Her eyes were fixed on him.

"You haven't got a hope," he said. "The Céleste campus has too much security. You won't get five metres before the security systems pick you off."

Frank coughed on his cigarette. "Oh, you think so?" Merovech gave him a level stare.

"I know so."

Frank's upper lip twitched.

"Well, we are going, *rosbif*, whether you like it or not."

The van pulled off the main road, onto a pockmarked concrete service road running parallel with a high chain link fence. From his pocket, Frank pulled an elastic ski mask.

"And if you are going to be coming with us, you will have to be putting this on."

CHAPTER FOUR
THE SMILING MAN

FROM WHERE VICTORIA stood, Paul's image appeared to be standing in the centre of the room. He'd been thirty-two years old when he died—a man of medium height and slim build, with peroxide white hair and tattoos on his forearms. He wore a gold ear stud, a pair of rimless rectangular glasses, and a yellow and green Hawaiian shirt beneath a white doctor's coat.

Of course, he wasn't really there at all. The picture, drawn from the file she'd downloaded from the games console, was being projected into the visual centres of her brain via augmented reality routines built into her neural gelware.

As she watched, he looked around, and wiped a hand across his face.

"Erm...?"

Victoria's heart clenched in her chest. She had an overwhelming urge to take him in her arms.

"Hello, Paul."

"Vicky?" His gaze flicked past her, unseeing. "What's going on? Where are you? Why can't I see anything?"

His image had a translucent, nebulous quality.

"Relax," she told him.

He knuckled his eyes. "But I'm blind!"

"No, you're not. In fact, you're not really Paul at all."

Slowly, he lowered his hands. His brows creased.

"Oh no," he said. "I'm a back-up, aren't I?"

"I'm afraid so."

"But if I'm the back-up, that means I'm dead, doesn't it?"

"Yes."

He frowned. "Then why can't I remember it? The last thing I remember is—"

"You're the second back-up. The illegal one, from the console. I'm running you as an app on my neural gelware."

He did a double-take.

"You can do that?"

"Yes."

"Where are we?"

"I'm standing in your flat." Pushing her fists into the pockets of her army coat, she turned and walked toward the window. Paul's image moved with her, maintaining its apparent position relative to her field of view.

"But if I'm the second back-up, what happened to the first? Do the police have it?"

"I'm afraid not. Look, there's no easy way to say this, so I'm just going to come right out with it, okay?"

He passed a hand across his brow.

"Okay."

Victoria swallowed hard. She let her forehead rest against the window. The glass was cold.

"You were murdered. Here in your flat. And whoever did it took your brain, soul-catcher and all."

Paul's hands leapt to the back of his neck. He huffed air through his cheeks.

"Jesus Christ."

"Quite."

Victoria touched her hair, which was still damp from the rain. Paul's fists were clenched and his eyes were wide and desperate. He looked on the verge of freaking out.

"I'm going to give you read-only access to my sensory feed," she said to distract him. "I'll get an imaging program to use my eyes and ears to construct a picture of the outside world for you."

She took a deep breath. When it came to tinkering with her own neural software, the technicians at Céleste Technologies were understandably discouraging. Getting them to give her the required passwords had taken a lot of persuasion. Now, all she had to do was concentrate on a specific phrase.

"*Licorne, archipel, Mardi,*" she whispered in French. Then, in English: "Unicorn, archipelago, Tuesday."

In her mind's eye, menus blossomed like flowers. She shivered. In command mode, her thoughts had a crisp clarity. She felt like a murky ocean fish pulled up gasping into the bright sunlight.

Working as swiftly as she could, she made the necessary adjustments, and dropped back into the familiar waters of her organic neurons.

Before her, Paul blinked.

"Hey, I can see!" He turned his head back and forth, frowning. "Why can't I look around?"

"You're seeing though my eyes," she told him. "You see whatever I see." She panned her gaze across the river, and the buildings on the far shore. Then, without wanting to, she glanced down at rust-coloured smears on the wooden floor. Her vision swam with tears.

"I'm sorry," she said.

"Why, what's—"

"I'm just sorry, okay?"

She turned and walked back towards the door. She wanted to leave. She stopped halfway.

"Remember when we met, three years ago?" He had been a memory retrieval expert for Céleste Technologies, working to extract memories from damaged soul-catchers. This was in London, before the company moved him to Paris. She'd interviewed him for a story, and somehow they'd clicked. They'd fallen in love. Or at least, she'd thought they had.

Life, it seemed, was seldom as simple.

First came the helicopter accident, then six months of tests and recuperation; and finally, last Christmas, their separation.

Since the breakup of their marriage she'd been living on board the *Tereshkova*, an elderly skyliner under the command of her godfather, an eccentric Russian billionaire with a penchant for cavalry uniforms and fine vodka. At the moment, the *Tereshkova* loomed over Heathrow, taking on cargo and passengers for the long trans-Atlantic haul to Mexico and the Southern United States. When she was done here, she'd rejoin it.

Until then...

"You looked after me," she said. "After the accident. You got me into the Céleste programme. Now it's my turn to do the same for you."

Paul looked down at himself. He ran his hands over his shirt. "But I... I'm dead."

Victoria ran her tongue over her dry lips. "Maybe I can't save you. But I can find out who did this. I can do that, at least."

"But, what about me?"

Victoria felt the tears rise again. She sniffed them back.

"I'll keep your file in storage, so I can reboot you if I have any questions. Until then, I guess this is goodbye." She opened a mental menu, ready to terminate the simulation.

"No!"

She paused, irritated by the interruption. She didn't want this to be any harder than it was already.

"What?"

"Please don't switch me off." He sounded like a little boy. "I know I'm just a recording. I know that. But I'm all that's left. If you switch me off, I'll be gone. Just gone."

Victoria rubbed her face with both hands. "So, what am I supposed to do with you? Leave you running in my head?"

Paul gave a cautious thumbs-up.

"Please?"

Victoria heard the downstairs front door slam. She said, "But how long will you last?" Back-ups lacked a missing ingredient, everybody knew that. They could only persist for so long before their thoughts became muddled and their awareness died.

Paul stuck out his chin.

"Long enough. Come on, Vicky. You're not the only one in need of answers."

He had that pleading look.

"Okay." Her voice was gruff. "I'll think about it."

Something crashed on the stairs.

Paul cocked his head. "What was that?"

"I don't know."

Victoria walked to the front door and looked out, into the stairwell. Detective Constable Malhotra lay sprawled at the foot of the stairs. His throat had been cut. A man stood over him. Tall and skeletally thin, he had a long black coat and a gleaming bald pate. Bloody fingers gripped a matt black knife. Slickness glistened on the blade. He looked up at her with eyes as dead as a snake's.

"Ah, Victoria," he said. His features were twisted in a permanent thin-lipped smile. He stepped over Malhotra and put a foot on the first step. "I've been waiting for you…" He reached out long fingers and curled them around the banister rail.

"Run," Paul said in her head. "Get out of here."

She took a step back. She couldn't run: he blocked her only exit; she had nowhere to go. Instead, her hand flew to the pocket of her coat and came up holding the retractable staff.

"Stay back." She gave a flick of her wrist and the staff sprang out to its full length. The man's smile didn't falter.

"I've been waiting for you, Victoria. I knew you'd come." He came up the stairs towards her, scraping the tip of his black knife against the wall. The scratching noise set her nerves on edge. She stepped back into the flat and took up a defensive stance in the hallway. There was no point locking the door when she knew he would be able to open it with a kick. Her only hope was to fight. Her perception of time slowed as the adrenalin in her blood triggered the fight-or-flight protocols in her gelware. She felt her muscles tense as targets and escape routes were evaluated. Felt her fingers tighten on the carbon fibre staff.

And still he came, smiling all the way.

"Who are you?"

The man didn't answer. He didn't even pause in the doorway. With a flap of his black coat, he sprang at her. Warning icons flashed in her mind. She swung. He feinted to the side. The tip missed his head and hit the wall, jarring her. She pulled back for another swing, but he moved too fast. A bony arm flicked out like the head of a striking viper. A hand closed around her neck. She felt herself slammed backwards, into the unyielding hardwood of the kitchen door. The air huffed out of her. The staff clattered to the floor.

She couldn't breathe.

She kicked her feet but his arms were too long: she couldn't get her knee up to his groin. Darkness hustled the edges of her vision. Paul's image grew faint. She thrashed but the fingers wrapped her throat like steel cables.

No, not like this!

Without releasing his grip, the smiling man turned her sideways, pressing her cheek against the smooth paintwork of the kitchen door. Her lungs burned. Her throat muscles scrabbled desperately for breath that wouldn't come.

Please...

Sensing her pain, the gelware came online, interpreting her suffocation as evidence of major physical trauma. Adrenalin poured into her system, but it was already too late.

As she tipped forwards into a spreading black pool of unconsciousness, the last thing she felt was the blade of his knife carving into the flesh at the back of her neck.

CHAPTER FIVE
CLIMBING TREES AND KILLING NAZIS

A COUPLE OF hours after the ninja attack at the aerodrome, Ack-Ack Macaque took to the skies again, this time at the controls of a twin-engine de Havilland troop carrier, with Mindy Morris, the new Scottish recruit, perched in the co-pilot's chair. Both wore combat fatigues and camouflage paint. Behind them, fifteen paratroopers sat strapped into webbing in the plane's main cabin.

Night fell as they crossed the Channel. He kept the plane low, to avoid enemy radar, and skimmed across the Normandy coast at treetop height. Their objective lay ahead, in the wooded grounds of the picturesque Chateau du Molay, where intelligence reports indicated that the German army were building launch facilities for their V2 rockets.

As they approached the Chateau's estate, Ack-Ack Macaque unfastened his straps and pulled his aviator goggles down over his eyes.

"We're nearly over the target," he said to Mindy. "Haul ass as soon as we're clear. They'll scramble everything they have to intercept you, so get low and stay fast."

Morris flipped a salute. He returned it with a hairy hand, then moved through the connecting door, into the rear compartment.

The paratroopers sat in two ranks, facing each other down the length of the plane. As one, their heads snapped in his direction. He pulled a cigar from the pocket of his flying jacket and lit up.

"Okay, dumbasses, listen here." He had to shout over the noise of the de Havilland's engines. "We're a minute from the target. Get yourselves unstrapped and line up at the hatch. I go first. The rest of you follow at two second intervals."

He scampered along the gangway to the hatch. The troops had submachine guns strapped across their chests. He had his revolvers, and a shoulder bag filled with grenades. He hooked the static line from his parachute to the rail above. When he jumped, it would pull open his 'chute as he left the plane.

"Get ready," he said.

The lights went out, and he popped the hatch.

"Geronimo!"

The air roared around him, snatching at his clothes. His cigar burned like an angry red star. He felt the snap and jolt of the 'chute opening. Then trees rushed up at him out of the darkness. He crashed through their upper branches, arms thrown up to shield his face. For a few seconds, his world became a storm of splintering twigs. Then his harness snagged on something, jerking him so hard his teeth snapped together, biting through the end of his cigar.

When his vision cleared, he found himself swinging above a darkened forest floor. The soles of his boots dangled twenty feet above the shadowed moss and leaves. He had no idea where the rest of his squad had come down. Leaves rustled in the midnight breeze. He kicked his boots off and let them fall away. He cut his way out of his harness and slithered up the canvas straps into the branches above, bayonet clamped in his teeth. If he knew anything—aside from aerial combat—it was climbing trees.

Climbing trees and killing Nazis.

German ninjas were good. They could move through a forest almost soundlessly, cross a field of wet grass without bending a single blade. But however hard they tried, they couldn't hide their smell. Even if they bathed for a week, he'd still pick up the tang of their soap. Hanging from a branch by his feet and tail, Ack-Ack Macaque lay in wait, a chrome-plated revolver in each hand.

Darkness above, darkness below. Nothing but the sound of his own rasping breath. No smells but those of dark soil and fallen leaves.

He stayed motionless for several minutes, until he was quite sure he was alone. Then he holstered the revolvers and pulled himself up into the forest canopy.

MOVING THROUGH THE branches, it took him only a few minutes to reach the edge of the woods. Beyond, the Chateau stood unlit in the moonlight, its windows shuttered and curtains drawn. Guards patrolled in the gravel drive in front of the building, where half a dozen black-painted V2 rockets rested on parked mobile launch trailers, and a tripod fighting machine towered over everything else.

The fighting machines were the latest in a long line of diabolical Nazi inventions. They stood twenty metres in height, balanced on three sturdy legs, and bestrode the countryside like giant insects, belching clouds of diesel smoke and dispensing fire and death from the artillery mounted on their thick, armoured bodies.

Ack-Ack Macaque checked the luminous hands of his wristwatch. If his squad had survived the jump, they'd be lurking in the trees nearby, awaiting his signal. Their mission was simple: destroy as much equipment as possible, and recover codebooks and operating instructions for the rockets.

Ack-Ack Macaque dropped from branch to branch, until his bare feet hit the mossy ground beneath the tree. He pulled his revolvers from their holsters and let out a screech.

In answer, the tree line lit up with small arms fire. The German guards scattered. Some shot back. He heard the *pap pap pap* of their bullets punching through the undergrowth.

"Okay," he muttered, "let's get this over with."

On all fours, he scurried in the direction of the Chateau, running directly beneath the towering tripod. Shots whined past him like angry bees. The grass felt cool beneath his palms.

At the front door, he dropped into a shoulder roll and came up with a grenade in either hand. He tossed both at the nearest V2 trailer and, while they were still in the air, whipped out his revolvers and plugged the four guards nearest to him.

A throwing star hissed past his face. He turned. Black-clad ninjas ran at him. Five or six of them, with blood-red swastikas sewn on their chests. Teeth bared, he started shooting, knowing they'd be on him before he got them all.

But then the ground bucked. A flash. A roaring blast. White heat hit him, and slammed him against the wall of the chateau.

ACK-ACK MACAQUE lay in the rubble for what seemed like a very long time. His ears rang. Everything smelled of brick dust and plaster, and scorched monkey hair. From where he lay, he could see that part of the chateau's façade had collapsed, spilling stone and broken glass onto the gravel driveway. A fire raged on one of the upper floors.

He got to his feet, miraculously unhurt, and brushed dust from his singed fur. Ten metres away, a smoking crater marked the spot where the V2 had detonated on its trailer. The other trailers had been damaged in the blast. Two had tipped over. One was on fire. The tripod fighting machine lay on its side, its body smashed amongst the trees, one insectile leg sticking upward at an awkward angle.

Ack-Ack Macaque looked around for the ninjas who'd been about to attack him. They lay twisted and dead in the wreckage of the chateau's front wall, their limbs as bent and broken as twigs, their internal organs pulverised by the blast wave from the exploding rocket.

"This isn't right," he said. He patted his chest and stomach. Not a scratch on him. No internal pain. He caught sight of something silver: his guns. He picked them up and looked around. Over the noise in his ears, he heard the sounds of fighting in the trees. The battle had moved into the forest.

"Not right at all." He frowned at the bomb crater. The blast had been enough to demolish the solid stone frontage of the old chateau, but somehow he'd emerged unscathed.

"There's no way in hell I could have survived that." The ninjas had been squashed like bugs. How had he escaped? It didn't seem fair. Why was he always the last one standing? His mind filled with images of burning planes. Over the past few months, he'd seen so many young pilots crash to their deaths; yet here he was again, with hardly a scratch on him.

Fatigue rinsed away the last of his strength. Everything seemed pointless and hollow, and all he wanted was to rest.

He had two bullets left in each revolver. Legs unsteady and ears still ringing from the explosion, he began to walk in the direction of the gunfire. As he did so, he saw a group of German guards emerge from the trees.

"Hey!" he hollered. "Over here!"

They turned towards him and opened fire. He didn't even try to dodge. He was too tired. He kept walking as their shots peppered the ground around his feet, kicking up mud and gravel. He heard bullets whine past, inches from his face; he felt the wind of their passing, yet nothing hit him. The Germans emptied their weapons, and then lowered them. They didn't seem to know what to do. Some of them started to reload.

Ack-Ack Macaque's fists were clenched around the butts of his Colts. His lips were drawn back to show his fangs.

"Is that it?" he demanded. His tail thrashed back and forth. "Is that the best you've got?"

The Germans began to back away. Ack-Ack Macaque screeched at them. His heart rattled in his chest. All the exhaustion and fear bubbled up inside him, like water boiling in a pan. He hadn't slept in such a long, long time.

"Come on! Why won't you kill me too? Look at me, I'm standing right here!" He was almost upon them now, yet none of them raised a weapon. Even the ones who'd reloaded seemed nonplussed and unsure what to do. He hissed at them. He beat his chest with his forearms, challenging them. Two of them turned and fled. The rest stood there wide-eyed, guns drooping.

He wanted to fling his own shit at them. Rub it in their gormless faces.

"Why's it always me?" He sprang at the nearest, and they crashed back together, into the grass. The man struggled, but Ack-Ack Macaque shook him by the lapels of his tunic.

"Why won't you kill me?" he screeched, canines centimetres from the man's face. "*Why can't I die?*"

TECHSNARK
BLOGGING WITH ATTITUDE

Everybody Loves The Monkey
Posted: 24/11/2059 – 5:00pm GMT
| Share |

With dozens of major new titles released every month, the game world thrives on novelty. How then, given that it's been a full twelve months since the launch of Céleste's flagship product *Ack-Ack Macaque*, can the title still be the number one most popular game on the immersive entertainment market? I mean, that's not how it works, right?

Wrong.

The reasons for *Ack-Ack Macaque*'s phenomenal success are fourfold:

First off, they've managed to keep interest high by strictly limiting the number of players allowed in-game at any one time. New players can't join until old ones are killed off or quit. With only 10,000 places up for grabs, and an estimated world gaming population of around 30 million, this lends the game a certain exclusivity.

Secondly, the whole one-life deal means players see the game as the ultimate test of their abilities. In the world of *Ack-Ack Macaque*, just like in real life, there are no second chances, and the challenge is to survive as long as possible. Players who don't take the game seriously get wasted early, and they don't get to come back. Once you're out of the game, you're out for good. Those who've put a lot of time and effort into developing their characters have a vested interest in keeping them alive.

Thirdly, the whole social media side of the game makes it more than just a shoot-em-up. In between missions, players get to hang out together. They can talk to their friends, trade planes and equipment, and form alliances. There's even an online dating agency operating entirely within the game's virtual world.

And lastly, there's the immersive experience itself, which is still light years ahead of its nearest rivals. The world of *Ack-Ack Macaque* has been so faithfully rendered that it's sometimes hard to distinguish it from reality. It's like being transported to another planet. The sun feels warm on your face and the food tastes the way food should. When you touch the other players, they feel solid and human. A punch feels like a punch, a kiss feels like a kiss. And a bullet to the chest feels like a bullet to the chest.

Put these things together, and it's not hard to see why the game's become such a monster. For a few hundred bucks, you can buy yourself a whole new life.

And let's not forget the appeal of the iconic monkey himself. I really have to take my hat off to Céleste for creating such a believable character. Truly a masterpiece of artificial intelligence and CGI animation, he neither acts nor talks like a computer. In fact, you could almost believe he was a real monkey.

A year after he first appeared on our gaming screens, you can now see his face everywhere, from lunch boxes, screensavers and t-shirts to plush toys and action figures. His trademark screech became last year's highest-selling ringtone, and millions of viewers continue to re-watch his most famous exploits on YouTube. Last Halloween, half the kids in my neighbourhood were dressed as him.

And therein lies the appeal of this game. Simply put, everybody loves the monkey. Long may he continue to fly.

Ack-Ack Macaque is available on SincPad, TuringBox, and Playcube 180. A PC version is also in development.

Read more | Like | Comment | Share

CHAPTER SIX
ARMED AND HUMOURLESS

MEROVECH, JULIE AND Frank climbed down from the back of the van. They were parked on a service road in an industrial park north of Paris, on the edge of the Céleste Technologies campus. Squalls of rain blew across the sculptured lawns. Merovech lifted the bottom of his ski mask and filled his lungs with wet night air. He could feel the coldness of it in his chest, and it felt good after the suffocating fug of the smoke-filled van. The driver and his companion were already at work on the security fence with an oxyacetylene cutting torch. The blue flame roared. Hot metal hissed when the rain touched it.

Merovech blinked away afterimages. He looked around.

"Is that a camera?" He pointed to a black globe atop a metal pole a few metres along the fence.

Frank flicked a dismissive hand.

"*C'est cassé.*"

"How do you know?"

Frank opened his coat to reveal the butt of an airgun tucked into his belt.

"Because we broke it."

The cutting torch flicked off, and a circle of security fence fell inward, onto the lawn. The two men with the torch stepped back, allowing Frank to duck through the hole.

"*Allez!*"

Bent double, pendant swinging, Frank ran across the lawn, towards an ornamental hedge. Julie ducked towards the fence, ready to follow, but Merovech caught her arm.

"Are you sure you want to do this?"

Behind her ski mask, her pupils were dilated.

"We must."

She slipped through the fence, and was gone.

Merovech looked back, down the empty road, in the direction of the city. He could leave now. He could walk away, use his phone to summon his bodyguards, and be back in his rooms at the University, warm and safe, within the hour.

But what would happen to Julie?

He knew the Céleste labs well. At his mother's insistence, he'd endured exhaustive and uncomfortable health checks at the facility each and every month for the past ten years. He'd had gene tweaks to edit out some of his family's less desirable traits; corneal grafts to improve his eyesight; and a whole barrage of hormones, vitamins and other supplements designed to boost his mental and physical wellbeing. As a result, he knew the layout of the building by heart, and he also knew how tight the security was. Frank and Julie didn't have a hope. Without him, they couldn't achieve their objective, and would both likely end up in jail, if they didn't first attract the lethal ire of the armed and humourless security bots.

Although he couldn't give a toss about Frank, he didn't want to see Julie throwing her life away over some obscure philosophical point. They might have only known each other for a few short weeks, but he liked her.

He realised the driver and his mate were looking at him impatiently. The driver jerked a thumb at the hole.

"*Et toi?*"

Merovech bristled. He wasn't used to be being spoken to so impolitely. He reached up and peeled off his mask.

"Get stuffed."

He ducked through the hole. He smelled wet earth. The rain pricked his cheeks. The wind ruffled his hair, but it was nothing compared to the squalling gales of the Falklands.

Okay, he thought, enough messing around. *Time to step in*.

If he wanted to annoy the Duchess and keep Julie out of harm's way, he'd have to take charge. Standing tall, he strode over to the hedge where Frank and Julie sheltered.

"Get up," he said.

They looked up at him.

Julie said, "Your mask—"

"It doesn't matter." He turned to Frank. "If we're going to do this, let's do it properly. No more crawling around in the mud."

Frank climbed to his feet. He wiped the dirt from his hands with a lip curl of disgust.

"What did you have in mind, *Anglais*?"

The rain ran its cold fingertips down Merovech's face.

"I can get you inside, but you'll have to follow me and do exactly as I say."

THE LABORATORY BUILDING'S main entrance was quiet. The lights were on, but that was only because they were always on. No people were around. A single security bot sat before the smoked glass doors. Shaped like a fat tyre lying on its side, its upper surfaces bristled with an array of lethal and non-lethal weaponry. A single turbofan filled the hole in the centre of its body. Direction and orientation were controlled by smaller fans spaced around its circumference. Right now, it idled a metre or so above the path's slick flagstones; but Merovech knew it could move with astonishing speed if provoked.

As he marched towards it—with Julie and Frank hurrying to keep up with him—the bot's fan whispered into a higher gear. Several gun barrels swivelled in his direction, and a red laser stabbed out once, twice, and thrice. Their retinas had been scanned.

"Welcome, Prince Merovech." The bot's voice was an uneven jumble of pre-recorded syllables sequenced together to make words. The machine had neither intelligence or self-awareness, its behaviour simply the result of algorithms and pre-programmed responses.

"Good evening." Merovech was conscious that every word and gesture he made would be recorded. "My friends here don't have security clearance, but I am taking them into the building. Is that okay?"

The bot's weaponry twitched uncertainly. The fan noise increased in pitch. The machine seemed to be having difficulty.

"Weapon detected." The main cannon turned toward Frank. Range finders clicked. A red dot appeared on his chest.

Frank's coat fell open, revealing the airgun tucked into his belt. Three more red dots appeared, and he let out a whimper.

Merovech suppressed a smile. He glanced at Julie.

Do something, she mouthed.

He sighed. As tempting as it would be to let the security bot shred Frank, he couldn't let it happen. Not in front of Julie. Using a tone of voice learned on the parade ground, he barked: "Override code, alpha two niner Buckingham."

For a second, nothing happened. Frank looked on the verge of wetting himself. Then the bot's motor whined away to silence and its gun barrels drooped.

"Proceed," it said.

Frank let out a held breath.

"*Putain.*"

Merovech turned away. Julie was looking at him open-mouthed. The rain had plastered her hair to the sides of her face.

"What was that?" she asked. "What did you just *do*?"

Merovech ignored her. Instead of replying, he led them through the smoked glass doors into the main foyer area. They had to jog to keep up with him. During the day, the foyer would be a bustle of activity, but right now the reception desks were deserted and the corridors were silent, save for the distant hum of an automated vacuum cleaner, off somewhere cleaning an office.

Merovech strode straight over to the elevators. Usually, for his health checks, he rode up to the private ward on the seventh floor—the same ward to which his father had been brought last year following the terrorist attack on the Champs-Elysées. Right now, though, he was going to take them to the computer labs on the fifth. If they were going to find an enslaved AI anywhere, he was sure they'd find it there. They loaded in and he thumbed the button. The walls of the elevator were mirrored. In the harsh blue light from the overhead strips, Julie and Frank's reflections were pale, grubby and scared.

"Okay," Merovech said. "I've brought you inside. What happens next?"

From his pocket, Frank pulled a gelware memory stick. His hands were still shaking.

"We locate the AI and download it onto this. Then we take it somewhere where it'll be safe from exploitation."

"And where's that?"

"A server farm." He looked Merovech nervously up and down. "Probably best you do not know exactly where."

The overhead light caught his pendant. A glint of glass. Merovech frowned. He reached out and took hold of it.

"What's this?"

Frank tried to pull away but a sharp tug stopped him.

"Leave it alone."

Another jerk and the chain snapped. Merovech held the pendant in his palm, where it nestled black and smooth, like a pebble, with an inlaid pinprick lens.

"A life-logger? You brought a life-logger on an illegal break-in?"

Frank pulled himself up defiantly.

"We are striking a blow for freedom. We have a duty to record—"

"What about her?" Merovech jabbed a thumb at Julie. "Did you think about her at all?"

Frank shrugged.

"We had masks…"

Merovech wanted to hit him. Instead, he looked down at the object in his hand. A life-logger recorded its wearer's GPS coordinates, body temperature and heart rate, as well as everything it saw through its little camera and heard via its microphone.

"Is this live now or record only?"

Frank rubbed his lower lip with the back of his hand.

"Live. Ten minute delay."

That meant the pictures from the device were being automatically uploaded to the Internet. Merovech swore under his breath.

"How do you turn it off?"

"You cannot. Now please be careful with it. Those things are expensive."

The elevator doors pinged open and they stepped out into a corridor. Merovech dropped the pendant onto the floor and ground it under the sole of his shoe. After a couple of twists, he felt the plastic casing crack and splinter.

"Hey!" Frank's face flushed. "You owe me for that."

Merovech pushed him up against the wall, and pulled the airgun from his belt. Then he stepped back and tossed it into a waste paper bin. He pointed back into the elevator.

"I saved your life down there. Do you understand that? I saved your life. I think that makes us even, don't you?"

He took a deep, calming breath. Then he checked his watch.

"Okay, we've got ten minutes. Whatever you're going to do, you'd better do it fast."

Frank looked surprised.

"You're still helping us? But why?"

Merovech shrugged.

"My reasons are my own, and none of your business. I'll help you get into the server room, and I'll guide you back to the fence afterwards." He looked at Julie. "After that, you're on your own."

*   *   *

THEY LEFT JULIE in the first office they came to. She slipped behind the desk and began tapping at the computer keyboard.

"Go ahead," she said. "I'll see what I can do from here."

Wordlessly, Merovech and Frank continued along the corridor, past other empty offices and storerooms, until they came to a glass door decorated with the Ack-Ack Macaque game logo: a stylised art deco rendition of the monkey's face, eye patch and all, assembled from blue geometric triangles.

Frank said, "I guess this must be the place."

Merovech checked his watch. Even without the life-logger, his deactivation of the sentry bot would have been flagged somewhere. A response team was almost certainly on its way. The only question was whether he could get Julie clear of the building before the heat came down. He wasn't worried for himself. After all, he was nineteen years old, and next in line to the throne. The worst he could expect was a bollocking from his mother.

"Let's make this quick." He pushed through the door and found himself standing in a white-floored laboratory that smelled of sweat, shit and strong disinfectant.

Frank flapped a hand in front of his nose.

"Phew!"

A couch stood in the centre of the room, surrounded by medical apparatus: monitors, drips, and the like. A figure lay recumbent, with its back to them.

Frank said, "What the hell is this? It smells like a zoo in here. Where are the servers?"

Merovech took a step forward. He looked at the arm lolling over the side of the couch: thin and long, and covered in chestnut hair. He walked around to the front. The prone figure had broad shoulders, long arms and short legs. Wires from various machines had been plugged into jacks set into the hair on top of its bulging scalp. Several drips had been set up around the figure, and tubes of clear liquid ran from bags into intravenous ports on its arms. Half a dozen electrodes and other sensor patches were stuck at various points on its shaggy torso, and a leather eye patch covered its left eye.

Merovech looked up at Frank, who had his arms folded across his chest as if cold.

"I think we've found your monkey."

Frank took a step closer, eyes wide and nervous. He curled his lip.

"What the hell is this?"

Merovech looked down at the creature where it lolled against the straps holding it in place. Its good eye was closed, and a silver line of drool hung from the corner of its mouth. He pointed to the cables protruding from jacks in the creature's skull.

"This thing must be wired straight into the game."

Frank gave him a blank look. Merovech picked a syringe from a kidney dish on a side table. He thought of his own experiences in the clinic on the seventh floor, and the stultifying ambassadorial reception he'd attended earlier that evening. He sympathised with the creature. He knew what it was to be held in place, trapped by forces you were powerless to resist, and compelled to play a part chosen for you by somebody else.

He bent close. The animal smelled sourly of sweat, stale piss and dirty hair. The bulges beneath the skin of its skull were most likely gelware processors.

"They've taken a monkey and made it intelligent by adding extra brainpower." He looked up as Julie pushed through the door, a sheaf of computer printout in her hand. "The question is, what are we going to do about it?"

Frank threw up his hands.

"'Do about it?' We do nothing, of course! I did not come here for a monkey!"

Merovech shot him a glare.

"I wasn't talking to you." Slowly, he reached out and brushed the animal's fur. He'd been expecting the hairs to be coarse, but they were much softer than he'd imagined.

"You came here wanting to free a thinking being," he said to Julie. "Well, I think I've you found one."

BREAKING NEWS

From *The New York Times*, online edition:

Beijing Sends Tough Message as Hong Kong Military Exercise Provokes Hostility

23 NOVEMBER, 2059 – As talks to decide the future sovereignty of Hong Kong flounder, Beijing demands an end to Franco-British naval exercises in the South China Sea.

Hong Kong has been under the control of the United Kingdom since it was ceded to the British at the end of the First Opium War in 1841. Since then, it has become one of the world's most important centres of trade.

Talks to return the area to Chinese control began in 1995 but were abandoned in 1997 when an agreement could not be reached.

This latest round of talks began following the Chinese invasion of Taiwan in 2045, and has been seen by most commentators as a last ditch attempt by both London and Beijing to resolve the situation without conflict.

Now that the talks have apparently failed, tensions in the area are at breaking point.

This morning, the Chinese government condemned an ongoing exercise by the combined Franco-British navy as "naked provocation."

So far, there has been no official response from London, but it is believed that the Prime Minister has cut short his visit to Berlin, and will address the House of Commons later this evening.

As the crisis mounts, China is rumoured to be planning its own exercise in the area on Monday.

Read more | Like | Comment | Share

Related Stories

Indian and Pakistani troops clash in disputed border region

Chinese taikonauts complete successful Moon orbit

Where's the monkey? Online gamers complain

Dutch neurologist reported missing

Mexico in "secret talks" to join United States?

Céleste Tech readies "light sail" probe for flight to Mars

New find brings total number of potentially habitable exoplanets to 7

Police play down talk of brain-stealing serial killer after another body discovered in London

CHAPTER SEVEN
STARS LIKE GLITTER

THE HELICOPTER'S ENGINE failed on a routine ship-to-ship transfer. Strapped into a chair beside the Prince, Victoria felt her stomach lurch as the cabin seemed to surge upwards.

She was the only journalist on the flight, and she'd fought hard to be there, to get exclusive coverage of the final days of Merovech's year-long National Service. Now, warning lights flashed and sirens wailed. The cabin tipped sideways and down, and her stomach flipped again. Beside her, the Prince pressed his face to the window.

"We're still over the water." He sounded more startled than scared.

She grabbed his sleeve.

"What do we do?"

He gave her a blank look. He was only eighteen years old, and plainly as scared as she was.

The pilot called: "Crash positions! Brace! Brace!" Then the water came up and slapped them. The impact threw Victoria against her straps so hard she bit her tongue. She heard shouts and screams, and the freight-train roar of seawater gushing into the cabin.

They were sinking.

Her nostrils filled with the smell of brine, and she recalled the safety briefings she'd endured, knowing that even if she managed to escape the stricken craft, she'd be unlikely to survive for more than a few minutes in the freezing waters of the South Atlantic. In a panic, she scrabbled at her harness.

Beside her, the Prince unclipped himself and leant over to help. He pulled her out of her seat. Then other hands grabbed him and bundled him away, towards the open hatch.

The cabin heaved again, caught on the swell. The walls creaked. Victoria lost her footing and fell across the aisle. The fall seemed to take forever. She saw dark water sloshing through the cabin and, in a single instant of freezing clarity, knew her time had come.

And then, pressing up at the window, she saw a face! A mean face with a cruel smile and the flat dead eyes of a shark. The Smiling Man had found her! He'd killed Detective Malhotra, and now he'd come for her. Here, in the South Atlantic, a year ago.

Time unfroze. Limp as a ragdoll, she plunged toward the windows on the opposite wall. Her head smacked the jagged edge of an open equipment locker and—

VICTORIA COUGHED HERSELF awake, spluttering up from the depths of a cold, dark sea. Her lips were dry and cracked, and her tongue lay in her mouth like an old leather bookmark. The air lay heavy with disinfectant and air freshener. Hospital smells.

Non, c'est pas vrai, pas encore. Not again.

She'd been dreaming about the helicopter crash: her brush with death in the South Atlantic, over a year ago. Either the head injury or the hypothermia would have killed her, had the copter not come down within metres of the aircraft carrier that it had been heading for.

And the Smiling Man. Oh God, the Smiling Man. How had he wormed his way into her dream? And what had he done to her? She remembered his footsteps on the wooden stairs. The scrape of the knife along the wall. Malhotra. All that blood...

Somebody cleared their throat.

"Victoria?"

She opened her eyes and stiffened. A figure stood at the foot of her bed, hands folded, hair white and brows black. Gold braid festooned a long tunic.

"Commodore?"

"I am here, my dear." He moved closer and took her hand, his fingers rough to the touch, but nevertheless warm and comforting. "How are you feeling?"

She tried to sit up and winced in pain.

"What happened to me?"

"You were attacked." Still holding her hand, the Commodore perched a hip on the edge of the bed. With his free hand, he adjusted the cutlass hanging from his belt. "But you're back on the *Tereshkova* now. You're safe."

"Attacked?" With her free hand, she reached back and found a thick wad of bandage, and stubble where she'd expected hair.

"Yes. Your implants sent an emergency signal to Céleste. I am listed as your next of kin, so they called me. They told me you were dead, but I sent a chopper anyway. I thought it would be quicker than an ambulance, and it was. We got to you in less than ten minutes."

He rose and walked over to the window. From where she lay, Victoria could see dark clouds edged with embers of sunset. She moved her hand forward, over her shaven scalp.

"My hair?" She was afraid to ask. She could feel the memory of the attack in her neural processor, waiting to be accessed, but couldn't bring herself to open it. The flashes that leaked through were bad enough; she didn't need to relive the whole thing in high definition.

The Commodore cleared his throat.

"They took your soul-catcher. We had to operate quickly to stem the bleeding." He gestured at his own thinning white hair. "We didn't have time to spare, so we just shaved it all off, I'm afraid. The surgeon patched you up as best he could, but you're going to be weak for a while." He lowered his hand. "And you're going to have to wear a collar to support your head, until the muscles heal. That means plenty of rest, and no stick fighting."

Victoria touched the bandage at the back of her head.

"Why aren't I dead?"

The old man smoothed his moustache with finger and thumb, moved his weight from one polished boot to the other.

"Whoever did this, they must have been in a hurry. They went for the catcher and tore it out by the root. They left you for dead." His fists clenched and unclenched. She could see he was upset. If her soul-catcher had been attached to living, organic tissue, its removal would have been fatal. The haemorrhages alone would have killed her. For the second time in a year, it seemed her life had been saved by the gelware in her cranium.

"How bad is it?"

The Commodore shook his head regretfully.

"He punched a hole in the base of your skull with a knife. Luckily for you, it's slightly off-centre, just behind and below your left ear, so your spinal column's intact. The surgeon replaced the missing bone fragments and stapled the wound. It should heal, eventually."

Victoria's lips were dry. She ran her tongue over them.

"This isn't the first time I've had my head cut open."

The Commodore checked his wristwatch, a large antique timepiece covered in studs and dials. Standing by the window, with his white hair and crisply ironed uniform, the old rogue still cut quite a dash. For the umpteenth time, she tried to guess his age, and failed, settling for somewhere between sixty and seventy years old.

Although he was her godfather, she knew little of him, aside from the fact that in his time he'd been both a Russian air force officer and a cosmonaut, and that he'd been asked to be her godfather because he'd once saved her mother from a charging rhinoceros. There were many rumours about him—that he used to work for the KGB; that he'd won the *Tereshkova* in a card game in St. Petersburg—but few hard facts.

"The police want a statement, when you're ready."

"The police?"

He made shushing motions with his hands.

"There's no hurry. They can wait." The skyliner was autonomous under international law, and the Metropolitan Police had no jurisdiction.

Victoria closed her eyes. She didn't have the energy to keep them open. She thought of the poor, dead detective in the stairwell, and the room seemed to spin around her.

"I don't feel so good."

The Commodore pulled the sheet up to her chin.

"Try to rest. The anaesthetic will make you groggy. You have been slipping in and out for half an hour or so. We have already had this conversation twice."

She smiled despite herself.

"What do the police think happened?"

She heard the Commodore shuffle his boots on the deck.

"They think the detective's killer took your soul-catcher in order to cover his tracks."

Victoria twitched her head. The movement brought a fresh flare of pain.

"No, that's not what happened." The drugs were pulling at her again. Her arms and legs felt heavy, as if weighed down by sodden clothes, and she felt herself slipping back beneath the waves, sucked down by the groaning silhouette of the sinking chopper.

The Commodore gave her a gentle pat on the shoulder.

"Shhh." His voice seemed to come from a great distance. "Rest now. Tell me all about it when you are feeling stronger."

VICTORIA SLEPT FOR a time. She didn't know how long. When she woke again, the lights in the sickbay were low. Outside, the sky had darkened and the clouds cleared. She could see a few stars and, on the underside of the skyliner's hull, the warm red smoulder of a navigation light.

She tried to assess her internal damage. According to the clock readout in the corner of her vision, two days had passed since the attack. She hadn't felt it. Her biological clock had been disrupted by anaesthetic and shock. In addition to the pain at the back of her head, her throat felt bruised and swollen, and there were tender spots on her back and chest.

She found it galling to be back in a hospital bed, and humiliating to have been taken down so easily, especially after all her quarterstaff training. The hallway had been too narrow for her to swing her stick properly, and the Smiling Man had possessed a strength that belied his thin frame.

But it wasn't his strength or his speed that bothered her most. The thought making her skin crawl was that he'd known her *name*. This hadn't been a random attack; he'd known who she was, and he'd been there specifically to kill her.

But why?

She didn't know him. As far as she knew, she'd never seen him before. The only thought she had that made any sense was that the attack was linked to Paul's murder. But how?

Thinking of Paul, she screwed her eyes tight and pictured her internal file index. Had he survived? She scanned down the list of folders until she found the one she'd created to house his digital back-up. With relief, she saw that it was intact, and still active.

Thank God.

Holding her breath, she accessed the icon, and Paul's image swam into view before her, Hawaiian shirt, white coat and all. From this angle, he seemed to be pasted onto the sickbay's ceiling, from which vantage he scowled down at her.

"Where the hell have you been?"

"Excuse me?"

He hugged himself, hands on bare elbows, and she saw the fear underlying his anger.

"I thought you were dead." He put his head on one side and looked around, absently fingering his beard. "Why are we in hospital? What happened?"

Victoria clenched her fists, resisting the urge to touch her scalp.

"I lost my soul-catcher."

"Shit." He put a comforting hand out to her, then seemed to realise what he was doing, and dropped it. "Where are we?"

"Back on the skyliner."

"Are you going to be okay?"

"I don't know." She tried to shift position in the bed. The sheets were lank and coarse around her. "I think so. Probably."

Paul rubbed his chin.

"When that smiling guy burst in, I thought we were toast."

Victoria didn't reply. She'd been terrified. Even now, she shied away from the memory. Of course, she'd been beaten up before, in pursuit of stories. It was a professional hazard of journalism. But this time it was different. Nobody had ever tried to kill her before. Things had never been that personal.

True, she'd almost died when that Navy helicopter fell into the Atlantic; but that had been a malfunction, an accident. It was quite another thing to feel a man's hands around your windpipe, deliberately choking the life out of you; to have a knife driven into the skin at the back of your neck.

And yet...

Her investigative instincts clamoured for attention. There was a bigger story here, she could feel it.

Paul frowned at her expression.

"What is it?"

With her head still resting on her pillow, Victoria laced her fingers together and looked up at the ceiling.

"Paul, I need to ask you about your sex life."

"My *what*?"

"Your sex life. The police think you may have known your killer."

"And just because I'm bi, that means it has to be someone I'm sleeping with?"

"Were you bringing men back to the flat?"

"No."

"But since the separation—"

"No."

"You mean you've never—"

"No!"

A silence grew between them. Finally, Victoria said, "You were looking through my eyes when I got attacked. Did you get a good look at the man who did it? Did you recognise him?"

Paul gave his head an angry shake.

"Not my type, sweetheart." He wagged a finger at her. "But I'll tell you this for nothing. Whoever he is, he's got your soul."

CHAPTER EIGHT
CAFFEINE

PRINCE MEROVECH, HEIR to the British throne, sat hunched on bare floorboards in the downstairs back room of a farmhouse somewhere south of Louviers, out where the fields were endlessly flat and the roads ran straight for miles on end; where metal water towers bestrode the landscape like Martian war machines, and bare trees stood in lines against the horizon. He still wore the same jeans, trainers and faded red hoodie that he'd worn to meet Julie in the café, although now his trainers and the cuffs of his jeans were spattered with mud, and the hoodie held the lingering whiff of Frank's cigarettes. His elbows were resting on his knees and he held the baseball cap in his hands, turning it absently, worrying the rim with his fingers. A manila folder lay on the floor beside him.

The room was bare, it's only concession to furniture being an old mattress, which the monkey lay on, curled in the folds of an unzipped sleeping bag. From where he sat by the door, Merovech watched the animal twitch and moan in its sleep.

The farmhouse belonged to Julie's uncle, but he was away, and not expected back until the day after next.

The printed documents in the manila folder were the ones Julie had printed from the Céleste servers. Merovech hadn't read them yet. He'd been awake for close to twenty-four hours, and now he had a headache, and all he wanted was to rest. He leaned his head back against the whitewashed plaster wall and closed his eyes. Through the closed door, he could hear Julie and Frank arguing in the kitchen. They were both speaking English, which he suspected was for his benefit. They wanted to be overheard.

Frank said, "This is stupid. It's just an animal. It needs a vet."

Julie spluttered indignantly.

"So, now I am stupid, am I?"

"Well, if you are so clever, can you tell me what the hell we are going to do with it? We do not even know what it eats. Or if it is dangerous."

"The poor thing has been drugged. It needs our help."

"Bullshit. This isn't about the monkey. I know you, Julie. This is all about you getting cosy with *le petit prince anglais*."

Merovech heard wooden chair legs scrape on flagstones kitchen floor.

"You leave him out of it."

Frank laughed. "You're the one who invited him."

Julie's hand slapped the tabletop.

"We would never have got in and out of that place without him."

Frank laughed. "Yeah, and a fat lot of good it has done us. Look around you. We're fugitives. *Des fugitifs avec ce crétin de singe.*"

"You are so full of shit, Frank. All that *merde* you've been feeding me."

"I meant what I said."

"No, you did not! It was all talk. We finally find an artificial intelligence, and you want nothing to do with it."

"That thing is not an AI."

"Of course it is. Just because it is not built of chips and wire, that does not mean—"

"*Je m'en fous.*"

"Frank!"

"Fuck off."

A glass smashed.

"*Fif!*"

"*Salope!*"

Frank stormed out. Merovech heard the front door slam behind him.

When I get out of here, he thought, *I'm going to have him thrown into jail.* The thought brought the barest flicker of a smile. He took a deep breath in through his nose and exhaled slowly, trying to relax. He needed to sleep. He knew his security people would be going berserk but, right now, he was too tired to care. He lay down on the hard floor and pulled the hoodie up to cover his head. He would have a nap, then decide what to do about Julie and the monkey.

He had just closed his eyes when he heard Julie's footsteps clumping in his direction, and the back room door swung open on irritable hinges.

"How's our patient?"

Merovech sighed. He looked up at her, then across at the monkey.

"He's resting."

"You heard the argument?"

"I couldn't really miss it."

Julie fiddled with the door handle. "I am sorry. Frank can be a little highly-strung."

"Frank's a pillock."

She smiled.

"Would you like some coffee?"

Merovech hauled himself stiffly to his feet, resigning himself to wakefulness.

"Yes, please. That would be nice."

As he moved toward the door, Julie bent and retrieved the manila folder he'd left on the floor.

"Have you read this yet?"

"No."

She frowned, and pushed it into his hands.

"Then I really think you should."

She dragged him into the kitchen and made him sit him at the table. Heat came from logs crackling in the fireplace. Utensils hung from nails in the blackened wooden mantel. Julie busied herself filling a pan with water while he slid the A4 sheets of paper from the folder.

"What's this all about?"

She hooked the pan over the fire, and spooned instant coffee granules into a tin mug. The spoon clanked on the rim.

"Just read it."

Merovech scanned the dense blocks of text. The air had the sweet, sticky tang of burning pine. His eyes watered with exhaustion.

"Have you read it?"

Sap popped in the fire. Julie laid the spoon on the counter. She leaned on her elbows, as if for support. Even rumpled and tired, she looked beautiful.

"*Oui.*"

"Then why don't you give me the gist?"

She picked at the corner of a fingernail. Beyond the half-open shutters of the window, a wet dawn had begun to break.

"I cannot, I am sorry." Her eyes glittered.

Concerned, Merovech leaned forward.

"What's the matter? What is it?" He reached for her hand, but she stepped back.

"This will not be easy to hear," she said. "And I should not be the one to tell you."

"Tell me what?"

"About your mother."

"My mother?" Merovech pushed himself up, out of the chair. Water bubbled in the pan over the fireplace. "*What* about my mother?"

Julie swallowed, looking petrified.

"I did a search on the Céleste severs. I was looking for information on their AI projects. And I found you."

"Me?"

She looked at the floor.

"The files were encrypted, but easy to access from within the system."

"And what did they say?"

She sniffed.

"You are not what you think you are, Merovech. You are not even—" She turned away.

"Not even what?"

She stifled a sob.

"I am sorry, I cannot do this." She ran to the wall and flung aside a curtain, revealing a sagging wooden staircase. Merovech listened to her footsteps thump up it and onto the first floor landing. He heard a door slam.

Alone, he looked around. Steam rose from the boiling pan of water. Rain spots dappled the window. He still held the papers in his hand. He dropped them onto the table as if they might bite him, and rubbed his forehead with thumb and index finger.

He'd been in and out of the Céleste facility for years. Of course they had a file on him; that was no surprise. But why had it upset Julie so badly? For a moment, he entertained the idea of a fatal disease. Could his last batch of tests have turned up a tumour, or other anomaly, which the doctors had somehow neglected to mention?

His eyes fell on the tin mug into which Julie had spooned the coffee granules. Longing for a drink, he crossed to the fireplace and tried to lift the pan of boiling water.

"Ow! Damn!"

The pan hit the floor with a metallic crash. Water burst over the flagstones. Merovech sucked his fingers and cursed his stupidity. Wrapped up in thought, it hadn't occurred to him to use the cloth that hung beside the grate.

After a moment, he pulled his fingers from his lips and blew on them. They were red and stinging, but not seriously hurt. Ruefully, he reached for the cloth. The pan had landed on its side, and a little water remained: perhaps enough for half a cup. He picked it up and poured it into the mug of granules that Julie had left. The fridge was empty of cream, so he gave the coffee a perfunctory stir, rattling the spoon against the mug's tin sides, and was about to lift it to his lips when he became aware of another presence in the room. He turned his head to the back room door and stiffened.

"Who are you?" Ack-Ack Macaque stood in the doorway, scratching his balls. His solitary eye looked yellow and bloodshot, and his fur had bald patches where the electrodes had been removed. He smacked his lips together and sniffed the air. "Is that coffee?"

Merovech looked down at the half-empty mug in his hand.

"Um, yes."

He hadn't expected the monkey to speak. But of course it could. He'd heard it talking in the clip of the game he'd been shown in the café.

The animal shuffled over and snaked the cup from him. He huffed the steam into his cavernous nostrils, and sighed; then tipped the rim to his lips with a noisy slurp.

"Ah, that's the stuff." He drew the back of his hand across his mouth and ran a pink, human-looking tongue over his pointed white incisors. Then he fixed Merovech with his one good eye.

"Now," he said gruffly, "who the hell are you, where the fuck are we, and how did I get here?"

CHAPTER NINE
IMAGINARY FLOOR

FROM THE WINDOW of her cabin on the *Tereshkova*, seven hundred feet above the rain-drenched asphalt of Heathrow's main cargo terminal, Victoria Valois watched a sullen dawn break over West London. She had wrapped herself in her thick army surplus coat, and pushed her feet into her sturdiest pair of boots. She wore a turtle neck sweater to hide the tight, elasticised collar the ship's surgeon had given her to support and protect the damaged muscles in the back of her neck; and a black, Russian style hat to hide her shorn and stapled scalp.

"I want it back," she said.

Behind her, the Commodore cleared his throat.

"I still do not think this course of action is wise."

"Fuck wise," she snapped. "You've seen the news reports the same as I have. Three more killings in the last two days. All with knives, and all targeting the victim's brain and soul-catcher. And I've got the inside scoop. I know what the killer looks like."

"But the police—"

Victoria turned to face him. The cabin felt crowded with the two of them in it. It was an economical space, with bunks built into the wall, a small metal sink and a fold-down writing table. Victoria slept on the upper bunk and used the lower one for storage.

"Whoever that *bâtard* is, he's got my soul. Paul's too. Lord knows what he's doing with them." As a journalist, she'd heard rumours of secret military interrogation programs for the souls of captured soldiers; she'd spoken to gang members who dealt in illegally obtained back-ups, selling them on abroad as virtual slaves, put to work in electronic brothels or gold farms, or made to fight in gladiatorial arenas.

The Commodore raised his palm.

"Yes. I know." A shadow crossed his face. "Believe me, I know. All I'm saying is that I do not think it safe for you to attend the funeral. Whoever this killer is, he will be annoyed you survived, and he will not want you to identify him."

Victoria gave her head a small shake, and winced and the pain.

"It's Paul's funeral," she said. "I'm not going to miss it for anything."

In the corner of her eye, Paul's image waved a virtual hand.

"What do you want?"

He put his hands together, fingertips touching his bristly chin.

"First of all, thanks. For saying you'll go the funeral. I mean, I've got no one else. Literally. So, I appreciate it." He shuffled his baseball boots on an imaginary floor. "But secondly, I agree with the Commodore. You can't go, it's way too dangerous."

Victoria's arms were across her chest.

"It's not your decision."

"But it is my funeral."

"So?"

He cast around, avoiding her gaze. "So, I can un-invite you if I want to."

Victoria laughed despite herself.

"Shut up," she said, as kindly as she could.

The Commodore's bushy white brows frowned at her.

"To whom exactly are you talking?"

"No-one." With a mental command, she silenced Paul and pushed his image to the far edge of her visual field.

"I'm going to the funeral," she said as firmly as she could, addressing both the old man and the digital ghost, "and that's all there is to it."

She saw Paul throw his hands up in disgust. In the real world, the Commodore wrapped his gnarled fingers around the pommel of the cutlass at his waist.

"Well, at least take one of my stewards. You need an armed bodyguard."

"No. Thank you, but no. I appreciate the offer, but I don't want to scare him off. I want to draw him out."

She reached down and pulled an old Tupperware sandwich box from the bags and suitcases piled on the lower bunk. Inside, wrapped in an oily hand towel, lay a replacement for the retractable carbon fibre quarterstaff she'd lost at Paul's apartment. She took it out and held it before him, weighing it in the palm of her hand.

"Besides, I'll have this."

The Commodore huffed.

"You are in no condition to fight, young lady. And besides, you had one of those before, and it didn't do you much good."

Victoria felt her cheeks redden. Her fingers tightened around the metal shaft.

"Next time will be different."

AN HOUR LATER, despite the protestations of both the Commodore and the *Tereshkova*'s chief surgeon, Victoria took a helicopter from the pad atop the skyliner's central hull. The helicopter's pilot wore mirrored aviator shades and chewed gum. He took her to Battersea Park, bringing the chopper down to kiss the grass for only as long as it took her to clamber down from the cockpit. Then, as soon as she was clear, he was off again and up, peeling away across the Thames.

Victoria smoothed down the rumples in her coat. Warm sun touched her face. The air on her skin felt just crisp enough to be refreshing, and so clear it seemed to chime like a bell. Quite a contrast from the rain she remembered from her last visit. Her breath came in little drifts of vapour. She walked towards the edge of the park, hands in pockets. Despite her bravado, her neck hurt a lot more than she had been prepared to admit. The stitches were tight and sore, and the staples hurt like needles driven into her flesh.

It's my choice, she thought. Two serious head wounds in two years. I can feel like a victim, or I can feel like a survivor. It's up to me.

She took a taxi across Battersea Bridge into Chelsea, and west along the river, past the rows of houseboats moored beneath the embankment wall. Holding her head as still as possible, she watched as they drove through the brown brick terraces of Chelsea, with their black iron railings and plastic For Sale signs, to the Exhibition Centre at Earl's Court, where the driver turned right and pulled over at the kerb. The ride had only taken a few minutes. Victoria paid and climbed stiffly out, onto the pavement in front of the gates of Brompton Cemetery.

As she entered the graveyard, an Airbus whined overhead on its way to Heathrow. The trees were black and bare. She walked along the central driveway. Beneath her coat, the retracted quarterstaff swung against her thigh. The graves, their stones the colour of weathered bone, ranged from simple, overgrown headstones to sprawling mausoleums, their inscriptions too smudged by lichen and neglect for her text-recognition software to decode.

"I don't see any fresh burials," she said. "The place looks full. How come you get to be buried here?"

In the corner of her vision, Paul blinked. She knew he could see the path and the surrounding stones through her eyes, and she felt an unexpected prickle of sympathy, supposing that it couldn't be an easy thing to attend your own funeral.

"My grandparents were sort of rich," he said. "We have a family plot. As I'm the only surviving heir, I guess I get to be buried in it."

Ahead, towards the rear of the cemetery, they found a loose knot of people standing around a casket. Maybe half a dozen in all, including the priest.

"We're late," Paul said.

Victoria stopped walking. She recognised two of the people as distant, estranged relatives of Paul: distant cousins she hadn't seen since the wedding. They frowned at her, clearly less than thrilled by her presence.

She ignored them, fixing her attention on the coffin. She tried to imagine Paul's body lying inside that plain wooden box — not the phantom in her eye, but the real Paul, the one she'd loved so hard, and then lost.

"Are you okay?" Paul asked.

She shook her head. How could she be, with her husband lying hollow-skulled beneath that lid? However convincing the simulation in her head might be, the real man had gone. Her eyes stung like paper cuts. She opened and closed her fists, fighting down an urge to tear open the box and beg him to wake up.

After what seemed an eternity, the priest closed his little black book, and the small congregation watched in silence as the pallbearers lowered the coffin into the earth.

The priest threw a handful of soil onto the lid.

"Ashes to ashes, dust to dust." He made the sign of the cross.

The mourners turned away and began to break into groups. They rubbed their hands together. Their breath steamed. Someone made a joke.

Victoria stood silently, looking at the grave, hating them all.

"I'm sorry," Paul said.

She wiped her eyes with gloved fingers.

"What for?"

"For your loss."

A train clattered past, wheels screeching as it pulled into the Tube station at West Brompton. Further to the north, a triple-hulled skyliner chugged over Earl's Court, the winter sun glinting off its brass fittings and carbon fibre bodywork.

"It's your loss, too."

"I know."

Paul fell silent. Victoria looked down at her hands. She didn't know what else to do or say. When she finally looked up, she saw a woman staring at her from the far side of the hole in the ground. The woman was somewhere in her late forties. She wore a long, elegant coat with fur around the collar and cuffs, and a small pillbox hat with a wisp of black veil. As she walked around the lip of the grave, the shins of her leather boots kicked the hem of her coat.

"Do you know her?"

Paul glanced up from his reverie.

"It's Lois."

"Who's Lois?"

"We worked together in Paris. I wonder what she's doing here?"

"I think we're about to find out."

The woman approached, and stopped a few paces away.

"Victoria?"

"Yes?"

The woman seemed relieved. She stepped forward and offered a gloved hand.

"My name's Lois Lapointe. I worked with your late husband. I'm so sorry about what happened."

"Thank you."

Another train whined into the station. Victoria heard the bong of a platform announcement.

"Do you mind if I walk out with you?"

"Not at all." Victoria turned and began strolling back towards the gate. Lois Lapointe fell into step beside her.

"I recognised you from a picture Paul kept on his desk," she said.

"Have you come all the way from Paris?"

"I have." Lois put a gloved hand on Victoria's sleeve. "There is something I must tell you. Something very important." She gestured to a wooden bench at the side of the gravel path. "Can we sit?"

Victoria hesitated.

"Can't we talk somewhere warmer? I could buy you a coffee?"

The grip on her sleeve tightened.

"Please," Lois urged. "I don't have much time. I know why your husband was murdered." She glanced nervously at the surrounding stones. "And I think I might be next."

CHAPTER TEN
SPACE SHUTTLE STACK

MEROVECH READ TO the end of the last printed page. Then slowly, he placed it face-down on the table with the others.

"Bad news?"

Ack-Ack Macaque sat opposite, on an old wooden chair, wrapped in a ratty towelling dressing gown that Merovech had found for him.

"My whole life is a lie."

The monkey stuck its bottom jaw forward.

"You too, huh?"

Merovech scowled. "I'm serious."

"So am I." Ack-Ack Macaque reached under the gown's hem and caught hold of his tail. He started to groom the hair at its tip.

"It's not easy for me, you know. One moment I'm fighting the Second World War, the next I'm somewhere in France and you tell me it's 2059."

Merovech tapped the papers on the table in front of him.

"You don't understand."

"That's for shit-damn sure!"

"No. My mother. She's been lying to me. All this time, all these years."

Ack-Ack Macaque stopped grooming his tail.

"You want to trade problems? I'll trade. Believe me, I'll trade."

Merovech put a hand to his head. His world felt ready to crash around him in ruins.

"Please. Just give me a minute. I need to think."

The monkey glared at him.

"Well, when you're all done 'thinking', perhaps you could explain to me how I got here?"

"We rescued you."

"Rescued?"

Merovech scratched his cheek, annoyed at the distraction. "You were in a laboratory. We broke in and got you out."

"A Nazi laboratory?"

"What? No. No, you have to forget all that. The Nazis and the war, none of that really happened. It was all a game, all make believe."

"A *game*?"

"A computer game. You know what a computer is, right?"

"Like an adding machine?"

"Yes, exactly. Like an extremely complex adding machine. You were plugged into one, and it created this whole game world around you."

Ack-Ack Macaque stuck a finger into his right nostril. He had a root around, then pulled the finger out and examined the end thoughtfully.

"Why would they do that?"

"As I said, it was a game. People played against you."

"So, I was like a puppet?"

Merovech shrugged.

"Yeah, I guess you could look at it that way."

The monkey was silent for a little while. Then he said, "Suppose all that's true. Just tell me one thing."

"What?"

"Whose ass do I have to kick?"

"What do you mean?"

"I mean, who do I have to kill for putting me in that game? All this time, I thought it was real. All those deaths... Just tell me. Was it you?"

Merovech held up his hands.

"No. We're the ones who got you out, remember? We rescued you."

"Rescued me from who?"

"From Céleste."

"Who the fuck is Céleste when she's at home?"

Merovech turned over the stack of papers before him. He tapped the company logo at the top of the first page.

"Céleste Technologies. They're a corporation. A multi-national group of companies."

"And you rescued me from them?"

"Yes, sort of."

"What do you mean, sort of?"

"Well." Merovech scratched his cheek again. He needed a shave. "The thing is, it's my mother's company."

"Your mother's?" Ack-Ack Macaque sat back with a scowl.

"If it's any consolation, she's been lying to me as well."

"You poor baby."

"I'm serious. All my life, she's been using me. Not telling me the truth."

"So you rescued me to piss her off?"

"Something like that."

Merovech rolled his eyes at the absurdity of it all. Here he was trying to pour his heart out to a monkey, but the monkey had troubles of its own. Suddenly, he felt very young, and very alone.

They were silent for a few minutes, both lost in their own woes. Then Ack-Ack Macaque bent forward across the table. "You know what we need, Merovech?"

Merovech gave up. He shrugged.

"What?"

A hairy palm slapped the wood hard enough to raise dust.

"Booze! And lots of it!"

With a maniacal laugh, the monkey sprang from his chair and began rooting through the kitchen cabinets, chattering to himself. Tins fell and rolled across the flagstones. Crockery clacked; cutlery clashed.

Merovech heard Julie's bare feet on the wooden stairs, and turned as she pulled aside the curtain. Wrapped in a grey towel, she looked pale and skinny, with her eyeliner smudged and her hair flattened on one side, where she'd been lying on it.

"'*Allo*," she said.

Merovech felt his heart quicken. Most of the girls he met in the course of his duties were prim and elegant, with perfect complexions and finishing school manners. They liked riding horses. They wore diamond necklaces and expensive designer gowns, and their smiles lit up the pages of society magazines.

Julie was different. Born and raised in the suburbs of Paris, the only thing she rode was the Metro. She had none of the poise and daintiness of the girls he was used to; but even rumpled and hollow-eyed, she made him feel warm and breathless.

His first instinct was to reach for her, but something stopped him. He looked at his hands. What if he touched her and she flinched away? Now that she knew the truth about him, how could he expect her feelings not to have changed? He turned to the embers smouldering in the hearth.

"I read the file."

She frowned. "Are you all right?"

"I don't know."

She took a couple of steps in his direction, then stopped, unsure. She gave the monkey a wary look.

"What is it doing?"

"Looking for a drink."

Merovech clenched his fists and thought of his apartment in Paris: the pristine tiled kitchen; the wardrobe of designer clothes; and the shelves and shelves of books about the city, its culture and history. He longed to be back there, in his sanctuary. He wanted to close the door and shut out the world, lose himself in one of the slender novels by Hemingway or Fitzgerald. His bedroom window had a view up Montmartre to the white spires of the Sacré Cœur. At dawn on a crisp autumn morning, the basilica's calcite stone seemed to glow impossibly white and, with its trio of bullet-shaped domes, and a lingering mist at its base, the whole structure would remind him of a space shuttle stack, primed and ready to hurl itself like a fist at the morning sky.

He hugged himself, trying to soak up warmth from the fire. How had everything gone so wrong, so fast? Right now, he knew his security team would be ransacking his apartment for clues to his whereabouts. And after last night's break-in, they'd also be looking for Frank and Julie.

"Damn." He put his fist to his lips. "Where's Frank?"

Julie took a step back. Her gaze flickered to the front door, then away.

"He is gone."

"Is he coming back?"

"I do not think so." She ran angry fingers through tangled purple hair. "Why do you ask?"

Merovech strode to the window. He could see the lane leading across the fields to the main road. No sign of Frank.

"The police will be looking for him. And not just the police, the secret service too. If they find him, they'll find us."

Julie bit her lip.

"Frank would never rat us out."

Merovech walked over and took her by the shoulders.

"I was a Marine," he said. "I'm trained to withstand interrogation. And do you know what they taught me? Everybody cracks, sooner or later. Everybody."

Julie squirmed in his grip.

"They would not torture him."

He let her go. "Of course they would. They've lost the heir to the throne, for Christ's sake. That's an embarrassment they'll do whatever it takes to rectify."

Julie rubbed her shoulders, where his hands had squeezed her flesh.

"Then why not hand yourself in? What can they do to you? They cannot send you to jail."

Merovech glanced down at the papers on the worn wooden table.

"I think they've done enough to me already." He picked up the file and the loose pages, and dropped them into the grate, where he watched them crisp and shrivel.

"Then what are you going to do?"

Without taking his eyes from the fire, he leaned an arm on the chimney breast.

"I don't know."

On the other side of the kitchen, a plate smashed on the stone floor. White chips skittered across the flagstones. Ack-Ack Macaque crawled out from the bottom of a pine dresser and pulled himself upright.

"You need answers, son."

At the sound of his voice, Julie jerked in surprise. The monkey ignored her. He regarded Merovech with one-eyed dispassion, expression unreadable.

"I don't know about you, but I've had enough of being someone else's puppet. Someone's been messing with both of us, and I say we get out of here, and go pound the shit out of them."

Merovech bridled.

"You're talking about my mother?"

Ack-Ack Macaque bent his hairy hand into the shape of a gun, and drew an imaginary bead on Merovech's forehead.

"Bingo."

"You think we should confront her?"

The monkey sprang onto the table.

"You know her better than I do. What do *you* think?"

Slowly, Merovech wiped his hand across his mouth.

"No," he said at length, "I've got a better idea. Those papers mention Doctor Nguyen. I remember him. He's a gelware specialist. He probably worked on both of us. He lives down in Chartres. That's not too far from here. We should go and see him, and see what he knows."

Ack-Ack Macaque bunched his fists. His knuckles were like rows of walnuts.

"Yeah, let's do that. Let's go find the fucker, and *make* him talk."

CHAPTER ELEVEN
FUZZY BOUNDARY

A BRIGHT NOVEMBER afternoon in a London cemetery. Wet leaves littered the neatly-clipped lawns. Victoria Valois and Lois Lapointe sat together on a cold wooden bench. Sparrows danced on the gravel path at their feet, hoping for breadcrumbs. Around them, the dirty white gravestones seemed to leech all the heat from the air. Even the constant background sounds of the city seemed muted.

Victoria sat patiently, wrapped in her long military coat, as the other woman composed herself.

"As I said before, I used to work with your husband at the Céleste laboratories. We were on Doctor Nyguyen's team." She paused. The gloved fingers of her right hand worried the fur cuff of her left sleeve. Victoria watched her without speaking. As a journalist, she'd found that one of the best ways to get someone to talk was simply to sit still and say nothing. They spoke to fill the silence, and you could often learn more from listening than from asking any number of questions.

"We were working on memory retrieval," Lois said. "Soul-catchers. Other gelware projects." She stopped picking at her cuff and glanced at Victoria. "I was there the night they brought you in, after the helicopter crash."

Victoria didn't really remember anything after the helicopter ditched in the South Atlantic. Thrown off her feet as the stricken craft rolled on the swell, she'd smashed her skull into the sharp edge of an open storage locker, and hadn't been expected to survive. She'd been stabilised by the surgeons on the aircraft carrier and flown back to France, but the prognosis hadn't been good. She hadn't been expected to regain consciousness, and wouldn't have done had Céleste not performed the experimental procedure that saved her life.

Since then, she'd spent the past twelve months recovering from the crash, adjusting, and learning to use and integrate the new areas of her brain. At first, nothing had smelled right. She got words muddled up and had trouble remembering people's names. But these were expected side-effects from the trauma and surgery, and her underlying personality seemed unaltered, as far as she or anyone else could tell.

No, she couldn't blame the accident for her separation from Paul. She couldn't really blame Paul either. They'd mistaken friendship for love and married in haste. The cracks had been there long before she left Paris for the Falkland Islands.

Now, sitting in the cemetery, her skull healing once again, she probed the insides of her mind, trying to locate the fuzzy boundary between the organic and the artificial.

"You were the first human we operated on. We'd never replaced large sections of a human brain. Soul-catchers, yes. But full-scale replacement of entire lobes, no. Before you, we'd been confined to rats and monkeys." Lois looked up at the clear, blue sky. "At least, that's the official story."

Victoria frowned.

"There was someone else?" She felt herself stiffen, scenting a story. "I thought I was the first."

"You were the first *official* subject. But there was someone before you."

"Paul never said anything."

Lois gave a bitter smile. "He wouldn't have. None of us would. We were sworn to silence."

"So, who was it?"

Lois sat forward. She rubbed her arms against the cold.

"The Prince."

"Prince *Merovech*?"

"Yes. We'd been working on him for five years. Adding extra processors as he matured. Taking—" She broke off with a shudder. "When you came in, we used you as a guinea pig. We had some final techniques to test, before…"

"What techniques?"

Lois shook her head, unable to continue. Victoria gave her a tissue, then got to her feet and took a couple of steps away from the bench, scuffing her boots on the gravel path. Another plane banked overhead. A single-hulled cargo Zeppelin chugged north over Kensington, adverts shining on its flanks.

"Is she telling the truth?"

Paul took off his glasses. He wiped them on his shirt, then slid them back onto his nose. It was a habitual gesture. From her perspective, he seemed to be floating in the air above the gravestones at the edge of the path, a digital shade with his trainers ten centimetres above the cold grass.

"Yes," he admitted. He scratched his chin. "It's all true."

"But all this time. Even in the hospital, you said nothing."

"I couldn't tell anyone." He paused. "Are you angry?"

"Angry?" Victoria shoved her fists into the pockets of her coat.

Idiot.

"I'll deal with you later."

She turned on her heel, to face Lois Lapointe, who looked at her curiously, the traces of concern flickering around the corners of her eyes.

"Who are you talking to?"

"Never mind. It doesn't matter. What I want to know is why you're here, now, telling me all this?"

The other woman stopped hugging herself. She raised her chin.

"Because I think they're going to kill me. Just like they killed your husband, and every other member of Nguyen's team."

"Who's going to kill you?"

Lois glanced from left to right. She lowered her voice.

"Céleste."

"Because of what you did to Merovech?"

"No, because of what we did to the King."

A tall man stepped through the stone gate at the entrance to the cemetery. He wore a black coat and a matching wide-brimmed fedora, and carried lilies in the crook of his arm, the ends of their stems wrapped in newspaper. He had his head down, and Victoria couldn't see his face. Her heart tapped in her chest. Had her plan worked? Was this the man who'd attacked her? Had she drawn him out?

She swallowed, feeling suddenly vulnerable. At Paul's flat, the Smiling Man had moved with startling speed and terrifying ruthlessness. She reached into her pocket and touched the mobile phone that the Commodore had pushed into her hands as she left his cabin.

"I'll have an armed guard standing by," he'd promised. "If you get into trouble, you call me. Punch the first number on the speed dial and we'll be with you in minutes."

She thumbed the keyboard, sending the signal. Better to do so now, while she still could.

I'm being paranoid, she thought, *but am I being paranoid enough?*

Triggered by her elevated pulse rate, the gelware in her head displayed a list of options, ranging from mild sedation to immediate flight. She cancelled it all with a blink, and took a deep breath. "Come on," she said to Lois. "Let's walk."

They set off across the grass, between the monuments. Victoria held Lois by the elbow, almost pushing her along.

"Tell me about the King," she said.

Lois looked around with wide eyes. "What is it? Who are we running from?"

Victoria jerked her arm, encouraging her to keep walking. A quick glance over her shoulder revealed the skinny black figure still pacing in their direction.

"Never mind. Keep talking. You say they're going to kill you. I need to know why."

Lois stumbled, her feet unsteady in her high-heeled boots.

"They brought the King to us, after the rocket attack in Paris." She was panting with fear and exertion. "He'd been injured and we were told to retrieve his soul-catcher."

Victoria's free hand rose to the plastic collar at her throat. She looked back. The man still followed, pigeons flapping around his feet, long strides eating up the distance between them.

"Go on," she said.

Lois slowed. "We didn't need to do it."

Victoria pulled her forwards, between a pair of matched mausoleums.

"What do you mean?"

"He wasn't that badly injured. He had some cuts and bruises. There was blood, but—"

They came out into a double row of gravestones, and onto another gravel path. Other people were around. An old man on a bench. A young woman with a pushchair.

"You took it out anyway?"

Lois let her head drop.

"We did as we were told."

In the corner of Victoria's eye, Paul's image folded itself into a crouch. His arms were over his head, as if trying to block out the world.

Lois Lapointe began to cry.

"Who told you to do it?"

Lois sniffled. "The order came from the top."

Victoria looked back. The man was now only a couple of dozen paces behind them, and still advancing. As she watched, he raised his head, and she saw the dead eyes and thin smile.

As she met his gaze, the lilies fell from his grip. One-by-one, they dropped onto the lawn, revealing in their place the squat black barrels of a sawn-off shotgun.

Victoria's neural prostheses tagged the weapon as a threat and fired her adrenal glands up to maximum production. Time seemed to slow. The noise of the traffic on Brompton Road became a drawn-out growl. Her heart tripped like a hammer in her chest. She became aware of the cold air on her cheeks, the roughness of her clothes against her skin, and the throbbing wound at the back of her neck. Her calves tensed. Her fingers curled.

"Miss Valois, how disappointing to see you alive." In the sunlight, the Smiling Man's skin looked like parchment stretched across the frame of his face. "And Miss Lapointe. So nice to finally meet you in person."

To Victoria's heightened awareness, the pigeons flapping up from the man's feet moved as if pulling themselves through resin. She gave Lois a shove, sending them both in opposite directions, and reached into her coat for her quarterstaff.

The gun fired. She saw smoke bloom from the left barrel, aimed at the spot where she'd just been standing. Her neural settings were running way beyond the safety limits proscribed by Céleste's technicians. She'd hacked her own head, and they'd have a fit when they saw the readouts. She dipped her shoulder, tucked in her chin, and fell into a roll, coming up with the staff held in front of her. A flick of the wrist, and it leapt out to its full length.

Okay, she thought, *this time I'm ready for you.*

The Smiling Man's eyes swivelled in her direction, white with surprise. She saw his arm twitch and, with glacial slowness, the gun turned towards her. She leapt across the gravel path. Two quick, crouching steps. The second barrel fired, the shot ripping through the air above her head. Her staff whirled. She knocked the shotgun aside and drove the tip into his chest. He fell back and Victoria dropped with him, using her weight to accelerate his fall. As he hit the ground, she drove her knee into his stomach, trying to crush the breath from him. A knife appeared in his right hand. In slow motion, she saw it spring into his palm from the sleeve of his coat. He swiped it at her midriff but she leant back and, as the black blade crawled past her stomach, reached out with both hands and broke his wrist. He cried out, and she rose to her feet, standing astride him, the end of the quarterstaff poised to deliver a killing blow to his still-smiling face. Her heart flailed against her ribs. She could feel the blood pulse in her temples and neck.

"Don't you move," she said. "Don't you fucking move."

CHAPTER TWELVE
HILLS LIKE WHALE BACKS

JULIE'S UNCLE KEPT an elderly Citroën HY in a barn behind the house. The keys were on a nail by the barn door. At dusk, Julie took them and passed them to Merovech.

"You'll have to drive," she said.

The van had corrugated steel sides and a protruding snout. The seats were worn and the cab smelled of petrol. In the back, hessian sacks covered the floor.

The Citroën HY had been the workhorse of the United Kingdoms for over a century, used by couriers, builders and every farm and small business that needed to shift materials from one place to another. Produced in huge numbers between the end of the war and the start of the nineteen-nineties, they'd seen off the challenge of the American Ford Transit to become a symbol of European enterprise. Even now, half a century on, you still found them all across France, Belgium, Norway and the Netherlands. They had acquired a retro chic. They were old but reliable and, in a rural setting like this, utterly unremarkable. Merovech took the wheel and coaxed the engine into life.

"Come on," he said.

Julie climbed in beside him, and the monkey slithered over the seat, into the back. They'd found him some clothes in the upstairs wardrobe: a pair of blue denim jeans, which he wore turned up at the ankles, and an old raincoat. With the hood up, he could almost pass for a human teenager. At a distance. To a blind man with no sense of smell.

In his hands, the monkey held Julie's SincPad. The blue screen illuminated his leathery face. Julie had shown him how to access the Internet, and now he pawed the keypad, finding out as much as he could about the fictional game world Céleste had built around him.

Merovech released the brake and eased the van forward, towards the main road. The track was rough, with deep ruts. Every time they hit a pothole, the monkey swore.

After a minute or two, they reached the road. A string of orange lights stretched away in either direction. Merovech crunched the three-speed gearbox. He pressed the accelerator and hauled left on the wheel. The van wallowed out onto the tarmac. On both sides, beyond the puddles of light cast by the streetlights, the ploughed fields of the French countryside seemed as smooth and level as a dark sea, distant hills looming like whale backs against the horizon.

Julie touched her forehead to the glass.

"I wonder if the police have found Frank yet?"

Merovech shrugged. He didn't care about Frank. He had the hood of his top pulled forward and the brim of his baseball cap yanked down almost to the bridge of his nose, shadowing his face. He kept his eyes focused on the little cone of light thrown by the van's headlamps, while a single question whirled around inside his head.

Who am I?

He'd been born in London and educated at a number of specially selected schools, including Eton. His life had been classrooms and dormitories until the age of eighteen, when he'd left school to complete a year's tour in the Royal Marines, before starting his degree in Politics at the Sorbonne University. He'd been the dutiful Prince, and his life had been mapped for him, his every move governed by the dictates of tradition and protocol.

Well, he thought, *to hell with that.*

He gunned the engine. The rules had changed. If the documents Julie had given him were correct, he wasn't a prince at all. The blood burning in his veins and arteries wasn't royal; it wasn't anything. He'd been decanted from a test tube at the Céleste facility, and implanted into his mother's womb: not his father's son at all, but a forgery with no real claim to the throne.

He gave a small, bitter laugh. Loss of power also meant loss of obligation and responsibility. If Doctor Nguyen confirmed the veracity of those documents then, for the first time in his life, Merovech would be out from under. No more stifling receptions; no more public appearances. He would be free. Whatever he did next would be his decision, and his alone.

His eye caught the teardrop gleam of a star in the sky, and the smile died on his lips, swept away by the sudden memory of standing with his father at an open palace door, looking out across the gardens. How old had he been then? Three or four years old, maybe? He remembered the gentle smell of lavender, and the way his father's hand wrapped his.

Looking out at the night, he'd asked what the stars were made of, and his father had smiled down at him.

"Big fires in the sky, a long, long way away."

Merovech's young eyes had widened. He'd known what fires were, and he loved the smell of the gardeners' bonfires. Only stars didn't crackle the way twigs and leaves crackled. And when he took a long breath in through his nose, he couldn't smell their smoke; only his father's cologne and the earthy scents of the sleeping garden.

That had been one of his earliest memories. Thinking about it now, his throat went tight. His eyes swam and his nose prickled, and a ragged, anguished sigh pushed its way from his lips.

Julie looked at him, startled.

"What is it?"

"I've lost my father."

"He is dead?"

"No." He didn't know how to explain the upwelling of grief and loneliness that burned inside him; he simply didn't have the words.

I've lost everything, he thought. Everything that matters. If his father had never really been his father, then none of those memories mattered. They had all been lies.

He swallowed hard, fighting back tears like a little boy abandoned at boarding school: upset, betrayed—angry with his parents, yet desperate for them.

Julie put her hand on his shoulder.

"What can I do?"

He shook his head. What could anyone do? His life had been snatched away.

"Get off." He twitched his shoulder, and Julie pulled her hand back.

"I am sorry, I—"

"Why are you still here?" he asked. "You shouldn't be here. You should have left."

"What are you talking about?"

"Everyone's looking for me. The police, the secret service. If you stay with me, you're going to be in trouble."

"And you want to know why I haven't cut and run?"

"Yes." Everybody else had left him, why not her?

Julie ran a hand through her purple hair. She turned her face to look out the window. Orange lights slid across her cheek.

"I'm surprised you have to ask." She pulled a cigarette from her pocket and lit up. The lighter flared yellow in her cupped hands.

Merovech wrinkled his nose.

"I thought you'd quit?"

Julie blew smoke at the glass. She put her feet up on the dashboard.

"You are not my father." She took another tight drag, pinching the cigarette between finger and thumb. The tip flared orange. He saw it reflected on the windscreen.

They passed through a village. He caught a glimpse of stone houses and a mediaeval church spire. A cafe's yellow lights. The illuminated green cross of a pharmacy. Then they were out among the fields again, the old van's left front wheel hugging the road's central white lines.

He sniffed wetly.

Funny, he thought. Even after a hundred years of unification, the French still drove on the right and the English still drove on the left.

Some things would never change.

He looked across at Julie. Her elbows were resting on her knees. She stared forward, over the points of her boot toes, and wouldn't meet his eye.

He'd watched her earlier, as they prepared to leave the house. She'd been fixing her lipstick in the kitchen, leaning across the sink to the mirror, one foot slightly raised; holding back her hair, twisting her face to the light. She'd seemed so alien, and yet so familiar, and he'd wanted to hold her, to feel the warmth of her curves against him; to trace each dip and shadow of her clothing; to smell her hair and skin, and taste her blueberry-painted lips.

As he watched her now, she scratched her lower lip with a purple thumbnail.

"*Tu es complètement débile.*"

"But—"

"Oh, shut up. You know why I am here, okay? We both know. Do I have to spell it out?"

The road unwound before them. The silence stretched. Merovech didn't know what to say, so he concentrated on nursing the rattling old van, coaxing as much speed as he could from the aged engine.

Minutes passed. Julie finished her cigarette and popped it out of the window. In the rear view mirror, Merovech saw a burst of red sparks as it hit the tarmac.

"I am not some floozy, okay? Despite what Frank thinks, I am not here for the money or the fame, or any of that shit. I am not doing this because of who you are, okay? I am doing it because of who *you* are." She twisted her forefinger in her hair. "Do you understand what I am saying?"

Merovech felt his cheeks redden in the darkness. He opened his mouth to say something foolish but, before he could, a wild monkey screech came from the interior of the van. His foot hit the brake and the tyres squealed. They slithered to a stop.

"Turn on the radio!"

"What?"

Ack-Ack Macaque leapt from the darkness in the back of the van, SincPad in one hand, the other pointed at the dial on the dash.

"Turn it on!"

Julie reached out and pressed a button. Music tumbled into the cab.

"Find the BBC."

She clicked a couple of presets. On the third, they heard the measured tones of a newsreader.

"...*resting comfortably. The Prince collapsed following a reception at the Turkish embassy last night. In a statement, the Palace attributes his collapse to exhaustion brought about by worry for his ailing father, who remains in a critical condition a year after being attacked by Republican terrorists on the Champs-Elysées.*

"The statement also denounces as a hoax Internet footage apparently showing the Prince involved in a raid on a research laboratory.

"The footage, taken using a life-logger pendant, claimed to show the Prince helping members of an extremist digital rights group gain access to the laboratories. However, all trace of the footage has been removed from the group's website, and nobody from the organisation has been available for comment.

"*In other news, tensions continue to grow in the South China Sea as Royal Navy warships—*"

Julie turned it off. She opened her mouth to speak, but the monkey got there first.

"Okay, my boy. Time to talk." Hard primate fingers dug into Merovech's shoulder. He tried to shake them off.

"What do you mean?"

The pressure increased.

"You heard the man. They have Prince Merovech safely in hospital." Merovech felt fetid breath hot against his neck and ear. "And if that's true, then I've got to ask: who the hell are you?"

CHAPTER THIRTEEN
CASSIUS BERG

THE *TERESHKOVA'S* BRIG comprised a small cell with a bunk, a porthole the size of a grapefruit, and a door made of thick, soundproof glass. The Smiling Man paced back and forth. His coat, hat and shoes had been confiscated, leaving him in an open-necked shirt and a pair of Levis jeans, both black. Without the hat, Victoria saw that he was balder than her. His head perched on the end of a scrawny neck, giving him the appearance of a caged vulture.

With her arms wrapped tightly across the butterflies in her chest, Victoria watched him move back and forth, his weight always on the balls of his feet as if waiting for a chance to pounce; his smile still in place, his eyes devoid of expression.

Beside her, the Commodore said, "He won't talk. He won't even tell us his name."

"No clues at all?"

Victoria ached all over. Hacking the safety restrictions in her gelware had been a dangerous thing to do. Her muscles hurt from being asked to move so quickly, and with such force.

The Commodore smoothed his white moustache with a gnarled forefinger.

"No. Only one. A tattoo on his wrist. A Greek letter."

"Which one?"

"Omega."

"Any idea what it means?"

The old man shook his head. "It could be anything." He looked across at her. "Or nothing. Are you sure you are up to this?"

Victoria brushed a strand of artificial hair from her eyes. The wig he had given her itched, but it covered the mess at the back of her head. The staples were tiny hard rivets in a mass of bruised flesh. The hair would grow back around them, but she'd be left with a grisly scar. Another disfiguring memento to match the one on her temple, from the helicopter crash.

"I'll be fine."

"All right, then." He reached out and tapped a six-digit code into the numerical keypad beside the glass door. Bolts slid back into the frame with a series of soft clunks, and the door hinged open.

The Smiling Man stopped pacing. He stepped back against the porthole and watched as they entered.

Victoria's stomach threatened to curdle with something that was neither anger nor fear, but comprised of both. The gelware took notice of her increased breathing and heart rate and she felt her head go deliciously light as it pumped a mild sedative into her bloodstream, calming her. Her arms unfolded and she stood, fists clenched and ready at her sides.

Across the cell, the Smiling Man regarded her, his gaze as blank as a statue.

"Victoria Valois, you are irritatingly hard to kill."

Victoria swallowed down the last of her nerves. This was the first time she'd been able to study his thin face properly, and she could see that the skin had been pulled up and back across his skull, which had in turn pulled the corners of his mouth into the semblance of an unwavering grin. He couldn't stop smiling, even if he wanted to.

Bad face lift, she thought. But the amusement died before it reached her lips.

"I'm very happy to disappoint you," she said, flexing her fingers. "Now, how about you tell me who you are, and why you're trying to kill me?"

The man looked from Victoria to the Commodore.

"I really think you should let me go."

The Commodore raised an unkempt eyebrow. "Oh you do, do you?"

"I have powerful friends."

The old man scowled. "Are you trying to threaten me, *dolbayed*?"

"I am."

The Commodore's hand went to the pommel of his cutlass.

"Be careful, comrade. You are not in England anymore. On this ship, I make the rules."

They held each other's gaze for a few seconds, then the Smiling Man let out a snort and turned away.

"My name is Cassius Trenton Berg." He waved a hand airily. "Not that the information will do you any good. You will find no record of me in any data bank, anywhere in the world. I simply tell you because, when my friends come and burn your little airship out from under you, I want you to remember that I warned you. And as you die, I want my name to be the last one on your miserable lips."

The Commodore's fingers curled around the hilt of his sword.

"*Blyadski koze!*" His knuckles were white. "Nobody threatens my ship."

Berg's smile stayed fixed.

"I am not threatening, Commodore, I am simply stating a fact. If you do not release me, straight away, your ship will be destroyed."

Victoria put a restraining hand on the Commodore's arm.

"You're not going anywhere until you tell me why you tried to kill me. Why you killed Paul, and Malhotra."

Berg raised an eyebrow.

"Malhotra?"

"The detective."

"Ah." Berg flicked his hand again. "He wasn't important. He just happened to be in my way."

"And how about Paul? We know he was on the team at Céleste with Lois Lapointe. We know about the King." She looked for a reaction. "That's it, isn't it? Céleste stole the King's soul-catcher, and now you're covering it up. You're killing them off one-by-one. But who are you working for? Céleste? Someone else?"

Berg wagged a long finger.

"Be careful, Victoria."

"Careful?" She snatched the wig from her head. "Or what? You already tried to kill me. How much worse could it possibly get?"

Berg considered her bristled head without comment, then turned away.

"You have absolutely no idea."

The Commodore swore in Russian.

"Then why don't you enlighten us, comrade?"

Berg crossed his arms.

"You'll get nothing from me."

Victoria glared at him. She thought of him swooping at her in the hallway of Paul's apartment, black coat billowing. The feel of his knife at the back of her head. The sound of his shotgun in the frosty graveyard. And she longed to wipe the smirk from his face.

Then she remembered the crime scene photograph Malhotra had shown her, and something clenched inside her, like a fist.

"Get some handcuffs, Commodore," she said. "I have an idea."

THE *TERESHKOVA'S* CENTRAL cargo hold occupied a cavernous space aft of the main gondola, within the curve of the main hull's outer shell. Each of the skyliner's hulls held identical holds. The lower part of a helium bag formed a convex ceiling. The floor curved up at the edges, narrowing as it rose towards the rear, where a pair of clamshell doors gave access to a crane assembly mounted on the outer skin, used for raising and lowering shipping containers between hold and ground.

Victoria blew into her hands. The cargo hold wasn't insulated. The air felt colder in here than it had elsewhere, and she was glad of her thick coat.

"So," she said. "Are you going to talk?"

Her prisoner gave a haughty sniff. She'd bound his wrists with a plastic cable tie. His shoulders were hunched against the cold and, standing on the metal deck, he kept shifting from one shoeless foot to another.

They were alone. The Commodore had been called to the bridge, to oversee the *Tereshkova*'s scheduled departure from Heathrow.

"You killed my husband." The words were tight in her throat. The Smiling Man gave a shrug.

"I've killed a lot of people."

From Victoria's viewpoint, Paul's digital ghost seemed to hover at Berg's shoulder, giving the illusion that the victim and his murderer were standing side-by-side.

"Ugly bleeder, ain't he?"

She suppressed a smile at the churlishness in Paul's voice, although she had to concede that he did have a point. Berg's attenuated limbs and tapering face had a reptilian, almost birdlike cast, as if he'd been put together using the fossilised bones of an excavated, predatory dinosaur.

"He certainly is."

Cassius Berg glanced at her.

"I beg your pardon?"

Victoria ran a gloved hand over the bristles of her shaven head. Without her long hair to cover it, the ridge of scar tissue at her temple, and the various cranial jacks implanted along its length, stood out. Touching it made her feel ugly and lopsided.

"I wasn't talking to you."

In her head, she heard Paul say, "What's the matter with the skin of his face?"

"I'm not sure." She took a step closer to the Smiling Man, and examined the papery vellum stretched across his cheeks. "A stroke or surgery, perhaps. Maybe a graft of some sort?"

"You mean he's wearing someone else's face?"

"It's possible." She stepped back again, out of reach. "Disgusting, but possible."

For the first time, she saw signs of agitation on her prisoner's face. A muscle twitched beneath his left eye. A crease appeared in the skin between his brows.

"Who are you talking to?"

"My husband."

Berg's head twitched. "That's impossible. Your husband's dead."

"So you *do* remember killing him?"

Berg drew himself up to his full height. "I remember killing him *and* tearing out his brain, soul-catcher and all." He sounded angry. Victoria pressed her lips together, swallowing back her distaste.

"Then how come," she tapped the side of her head, "he's in here, speaking to me, right now?"

The furrow between Berg's eyebrows grew deeper. Suspicious eyes searched her face.

"What you have to decide," Victoria continued, "is whether I'm concussed and delusional, or whether I really do have an angry murder victim in my head, telling me what to do." She pulled the quarterstaff from her pocket. "Either way, you're in a whole lot of trouble."

The Smiling Man drew back.

"You can't hurt me."

Victoria flicked the staff out to its full extent.

"Are you sure?"

She took a step closer. In her eye, Paul chewed the knuckle of his left index finger, his face a picture of grim expectation.

"Where do you want me to hit him first?" she asked.

Berg took another step back and stopped. The cargo doors were behind him. He had nowhere left to go.

The door controls hung on the wall to Victoria's right. Green button to open, red to shut. Holding the staff in one hand, she reached out.

"Last chance," she said. Her finger pressed the green button. The cargo doors gave a metallic groan and peeled apart, opening like the petals of a flower.

Berg stood silhouetted against the light. The *Tereshkova*'s engines were pushing it up and away from Heathrow's cargo terminal. They were already at what must have been a thousand feet. Victoria saw hotels and roads sliding beneath them. Tiny cars.

"Now talk," she called, raising her voice above the rush of the wind.

Berg looked down at the landscape passing below.

"I'm backed-up," he said, with only the slightest trace of hesitation. "If I fall, my friends will find me. I *will* live again."

Victoria brought the staff to bear, ready to give him a shove.

"Are you willing to bet your life on that? We're a long way up, and I'm not sure your soul-catcher will survive an impact from this height." She gave a theatrical shrug. "But if you're so sure, you might as well jump, because unless you tell me what I want to know, it's your only way out."

She felt her heart banging in her chest. The words coming from her lips felt strange, as if they belonged to somebody a lot tougher than she was, and she drew strength from them. Berg's heels were now inches from the edge of the deck, and she felt electrified. All it would take to kill him would be one strike from the end of her staff. One little push.

Their eyes met, and held.

Berg seemed to be trying to read her face, searching for any hint of a bluff. She glared at him, determined not to blink or look away.

Finally, after what seemed a small, eye-watering eternity, she saw something break in his posture. He looked back at the airport falling astern, and his shoulders fell. His chest seemed to sag in on itself.

"Okay," he said. "Okay. I'll talk."

CHAPTER FOURTEEN
BLOWING SMOKE RINGS AT THE STARS

DOCTOR NGUYEN LIVED in a detached house on the outskirts of Chartres, a cathedral town ninety kilometres south-west of Paris. Merovech parked the boxy old Citroën van on the opposite side of the street. He killed the ignition and the engine rattled away to silence.

"This is it."

According to the clock on the dashboard, the time was eleven-thirty. The road was quiet. The cheery yellow glows in the windows of the whitewashed neighbouring houses spoke of home and hearth and family; but the lights were off in Nguyen's place.

Merovech turned in his seat.

"Perhaps you should stay here," he said.

From the back of the van, Ack-Ack Macaque regarded him with a baleful eye.

"That suits me fine."

Merovech faced Julie.

"Are you coming?"

"Do you want me to?"

He looked across at the darkened house. The upstairs shutters were open but the curtains were drawn. No sign of life at all.

"I don't know. Perhaps you'd better wait here." He got out, breath steaming in the night air. Stars poked through clouds stained orange with reflected town light and, a few houses down, a dog barked in a yard.

"I won't be long," he said. He hurried across to the far kerb and up the short path to Nguyen's front door, where he paused.

In his memory, Doctor Nguyen was a short, stern man in black hospital scrubs, with a stethoscope forever slung around his neck. If the documents he'd read were to be believed, Nguyen and his team had *done* things to him. Surgical things.

He felt his heart quicken. All those times he'd been given anaesthetic for routine operations — tonsils, appendix, wisdom teeth — they'd taken the opportunity to stuff more and more gelware into his head.

He raised his fist to pound the door. He didn't care if Nguyen was asleep, he wanted answers. He wanted to haul the old buzzard out of bed and confront him; let him know how *betrayed* he felt. But, even as he pulled back his hand, he noticed that the door was ajar: resting against its frame, but not completely closed. The catch had not engaged. He could open it with a push.

"I wouldn't do that if I were you."

The voice came from the side of the house. Merovech took a step back, fists raised.

"Who's there?"

"A friend."

A young girl stepped from behind the whitewashed wall of the house. She wore a fur-lined jacket several sizes too large for her skinny frame, a leather flying cap, and a pair of aviator goggles, which she'd pushed up onto her forehead.

"Prince Merovech, I presume?" Her accent was Scottish, which seemed incongruous here, in the sleeping suburbs of a small French town. "Is the monkey with you?"

"I'm here to see Doctor Nguyen."

The girl gave a little shake of her head. She looked somehow familiar. "Nguyen's dead. Murdered. I found him this morning, and I've been waiting for you ever since."

"Who are you?"

The girl stepped back.

"I'm here to help." She retrieved a sizeable holdall from behind the wall. "Now please, if you have the monkey, I need to see him."

Merovech shrugged. He led her back across the road to the van and opened the back doors. Inside, Ack-Ack Macaque crouched against the back of the driver's seat, fangs bared as if expecting trouble. When he saw the girl, he jerked upright and blinked his solitary eye.

"Morris?"

She touched two fingers to her brow in salute.

"What-ho, skipper."

MEROVECH DROVE UNTIL he found a place where they could pull onto the verge in the shadow of some trees. Beyond the trees, ploughed fields stretched away to the horizon. He got out and walked a few metres down the road, his hands deep in the pockets of his red hoodie. Julie called after him but he ignored her. He needed a few moments to calm the turmoil in his head.

Forty-eight hours ago, his life had made sense. Now, almost nothing did. And he couldn't go back. There was no reset button. He felt much as he had after the helicopter crash—dazed and numb, with this horrible, sick feeling that something huge and irreversible had happened to him. Something no amount of privilege or royalty could ever undo.

He looked up at the stars, trying to connect the dots, trying to find meaning in their random scatter. The air smelled of ploughed earth and damp, wet leaves.

When he turned to look back at the van, he saw Julie's silhouette stood by the passenger door, arms folded, watching him.

Had it really been only three weeks since their first meeting, in Paris?

He'd been on his way back from a Norwegian bar in the business district, where he'd been enjoying an evening of akevitt and pickled herring with some of his classmates. He'd been there at the invitation of the proprietor, an ambitious young Norwegian politico. Norway had been part of the burgeoning United Kingdom since 1959, and its assimilation had encouraged the other Scandinavian nations to signup to the newly-formed European Commonwealth—the first step in a process that led eventually to the 1982 Gothenburg Treaty, and the implementation of the United European Commonwealth's single market.

Merovech and his friends had all been half-drunk on the akevitt, and reeked of fish and onions. For fun, they'd dared themselves to take the Metro home from the restaurant. It was their idea of an adventure. Luckily, the train wasn't crowded, and they found plenty of room to sit.

Obviously, Merovech's presence caused something of a stir among the other passengers. Phone cameras clicked and whirred, but his bodyguard, Izolda, kept anyone from bothering him directly. She was a former Olympic wrestler, and had the kind of stare that could stop grown men in their tracks.

A purple-haired girl occupied the seat across the aisle, and Merovech thought he recognised her. Was she a fellow student? He was sure he'd seen her around the campus, but each time he tried to catch her eye, she looked away.

She's gorgeous, he thought. But not in an obvious way. There was nothing self-conscious or artificial about her. She wasn't dressed to impress anyone.

He watched her all the way to his stop.

When they pulled in and the doors opened, Izolda hustled him out onto the platform.

He glanced back at the girl, trying to fix her face in his memory, wanting to remember her in the morning. As he did so, she pressed her hand up against the window. She'd scrawled her mobile phone number across her palm in purple lipstick.

"Call me," she mouthed.

The train started to move. He whipped out his SincPhone and, walking to keep pace with the window, punched her number into the keypad with his thumb. If he'd been thinking clearly, he would have used his phone to take a photo of the number. As it was, he got the last digit just as he reached the end of the platform.

The train pulled away from him, pushing itself into the tunnel, faster and faster. The wind of it ruffled his hair. He lifted the phone to his ear. She let it ring twice before she answered.

"Do you want to get a coffee?" she said.

WHEN MEROVECH GOT back to the van, the other three were standing in the pool of light cast by its headlamps. Morris had her holdall open and was rummaging through the contents. Ack-Ack Macaque now wore her fleece-lined jacket and aviator goggles, and puffed away on a huge cigar. The smoke smelled sticky and rank in the clear night air. As Merovech approached, they stopped talking and turned to him.

"Are you okay?" Julie looked concerned. Merovech walked over and gave her a hug. She was soft and reassuring in his arms, and he clung to her the way that in the South Atlantic, he'd clung to the ropes of the life raft.

"Thank you."

For a moment, she seemed nonplussed. Then she put a hand to the back of his neck.

"*De rien.*"

He pulled back, holding her at arm's length.

"I mean it. I'm sorry about what I said before. I know why you're here. And believe me, I'm glad you are."

He took her hand, and turned to face Morris and the scowling monkey.

"Okay," he said to the girl, "let's start with you."

Mindy stopped rooting around in her holdall and rose to her feet. She wore a green v-neck sweater and skinny black jeans. Having given the oversized flying jacket to Ack-Ack Macaque, she seemed somehow smaller.

"I was just explaining to your friend that my real name's not Morris, your royal highness. In real life, people call me K8." She held out a hand. Merovech didn't take it.

"Kate?"

"No, kay-eight. Letter kay followed by numeral eight."

"Really?"

"It's a gamer thing."

"So, why introduce yourself as Mindy Morris?"

The girl looked at him, then glanced at Julie.

"He doesn't know who you are," Julie explained quietly. "He doesn't play the game."

Merovech looked between them.

"Ah!" He clicked his fingers. "*That's* where I've seen you. You were in the clip, with *him*." He pointed at Ack-Ack Macaque, who was now leaning against the van's radiator, blowing smoke rings at the stars.

"That's right." K8 took her hand back and self-consciously used it to smooth down the front of her sweater. "I'm a professional game player."

"But 'Morris'?"

"I never use my real name. I play characters. Céleste Tech hired me to keep an eye on the big guy here."

Merovech smiled despite himself.

"You're his handler?"

Ack-Ack Macaque bristled.

"She's my wingman." He tapped ash from the end of his cigar. "Or rather, she was. In the game."

"The programmers at Céleste were worried that he'd started to think about things too deeply. Started to question the world around him. The last time that happened, they had to get a whole new monkey."

"Wait, he's not the first Ack-Ack Macaque?"

K8 shook her head.

"Apparently, there have been five to date." She glanced apologetically at Ack-Ack Macaque. "I didn't find this out until after they hired me, but as each one went off the rails, they simply loaded the root personality into a new monkey, and the audience was none the wiser. They accepted it as an upgrade. Nobody outside Céleste knew it was a real monkey. They all thought it was an AI."

"So, why bother hiring you?" Julie asked.

K8 grinned.

"I'm cheaper than a new monkey."

Beyond the trees, Merovech saw the lights of a skyliner heading for the passenger terminal at Toussus-le-Noble Airport. Against the night sky, its gondola portholes shone like the windows of a floating village: warm and unreachably far away.

"How did you find us?"

The grin slid from the girl's face.

"I heard about the raid. They called me and told me not to bother coming in to work. I thought at first it might be animal rights activists, but when I heard the rumour on the Internet that you were involved, your royal highness, I knew the two of you'd show up at Nguyen's place sooner or later."

"And you found him dead?"

"Yes. I saw him through the window. The top of his head was missing." She rubbed her lips with the back of her hand.

"And you didn't call the police?"

"I didn't want to frighten you off."

Still leaning against the Citroën's grille, Ack-Ack Macaque rolled his cigar between finger and thumb. From where Merovech stood, he was a long-armed silhouette between the glare of the headlamps to either side.

"What happened to them?"

Merovech squinted against the light.

"Pardon?"

Ack-Ack Macaque pushed himself upright and took a step towards K8. His voice was low, barely a growl.

"The other four. The ones before me. What happened to them?"

K8 put her hands in her pockets. She took them out again. She didn't seem to know what to do with them.

"They're dead, skipper."

"All four of them?"

"They were put down."

Beside him, Merovech heard Julie Girard suck air through her teeth.

"*Mais c'est du meutre ça!*"

Ack-Ack Macaque glared at her.

"Murder? You can say that again, sweetheart." With a flick of his hairy wrist, he sent the cigar flipping out onto the tarmac of the empty road. "The question is, what are we going to do about it?"

Merovech met his stare.

"What did you have in mind?"

Ack-Ack Macaque clawed at his hips, fingers curling around non-existent pistols.

"Kicking in doors, blowing up shit. The usual. Why, do you have a better idea?"

Merovech rubbed an itch on the tip of his nose.

"They've screwed us both over," he said. "I'm just not sure the 'all guns blazing' approach is the best one, strategically speaking."

"Fuck strategy." Ack-Ack Macaque drew himself up to his full height. "Those motherfuckers at Céleste have killed me four times already, and enough is e-fucking-*nough*."

K8 stepped up to Merovech. Her head came up to his collarbone.

"You don't know the half of it," she said. "Don't forget, I worked with Nguyen. I saw stuff. I know about you."

She tapped her temple. "I know all about the gelware they pumped into your head."

Merovech looked down at her.

"I've read Nguyen's notes," he said stiffly. "I know I'm a clone."

K8 gave a snort. "You're a lot more than that, your highness. There's more gelware in your head than anything else. You and the skipper here, you're two of a kind." She crossed her arms, looking up at him like the precocious kid she was. "The thing is, I'll bet you haven't figured out why the Duchess had you grown in the first place?"

Merovech restrained an impulse to seize her by the lapels.

"If you know something, tell me."

The girl held his gaze for a couple of seconds, as if searching his eyes for something. Then she turned on her heel and began to pace back and forth in the light, talking as she went.

"Okay, here it is. I told you, I'm a professional game player. Some people would call that a fancy name for a hacker. And in my case, they'd be right." She walked back to her holdall, where it lay on the grass. The van lights caught the steam of her breath in the cold night air.

"I was thirteen years old when I cracked the firewall at Céleste Tech. Six months later, they offered me a job, and I've been working for them ever since.

"When they called me in to look after the monkey, I got suspicious. I knew it wasn't a real AI. So, I did some digging. I found Nguyen's notes. He ran both projects, and he kept pretty detailed records." She knelt and pulled a SincPad from the bag. "Here, I downloaded it all onto this. If you want to go public, this is all the evidence you'll need."

She handed Merovech the pad and stepped back, to the edge of the circle of light.

"Nguyen and your mother. They've been working on this for a long time."

"On what?"

"Artificial brains in organic bodies. Brains into which they can download stored personalities. The skipper here, he was a prototype. A proof of concept. You, though." She raised her palms to Merovech. "You're the real prize."

CHAPTER FIFTEEN
COMMAND MODE

VICTORIA VALOIS KEPT the end of her quarterstaff trained on the Smiling Man as he stood, hands bound before him, in front of the gaping doors of the *Tereshkova*'s cargo hold.

They were powering west, above Slough and Windsor. She could see the reservoirs at Colnbrook and Wraysbury; the grey ribbon of the M25; and the Georgian splendour of Windsor Castle, with its large central tower.

"Okay," she said. "Tell me about that tattoo on your wrist."

He looked down at his hands. One of his wrists was swollen, where she'd tried to break it in the graveyard.

"It's Omega," he said. "The last letter of the Greek alphabet."

"I know that. But what does it *mean*?"

His eyes came up to meet hers.

"It's the symbol of my order. We are the Undying. We believe in an end to things, a benevolent Eschaton at the end of the universe. An Omega Point."

Victoria tightened her grip on the staff.

"What's that got to do with Paul? With Lois and the King?" She *had* to know the full story.

Berg glanced over his shoulder at the town below. He was just inside the threshold of the open doors. Beyond, the deck's lip extended another half a metre into the sky. When the doors closed, it would form a narrow ledge.

"Nguyen and his team were expendable. They knew too much of our plans."

In Victoria's head, Paul scratched his peroxide hair and said, "He's talking about the night they brought the King in. The night of the assassination attempt."

"What happened that night? Lois started to tell me, but we were interrupted."

Thinking she was talking to him, Berg opened his mouth. She silenced him with a raised hand. She wanted to hear what Paul had to say.

"We were called into the Céleste facility. It was late. The King and the Duchess were there. We were told to remove the King's soul-catcher."

"Even though his injuries weren't serious enough to warrant surgery?"

Paul shuffled his trainers.

"Nguyen told us it was necessary."

"And you never spoke of it?"

"I couldn't. We were told it was a national security matter. We had to sign all sorts of forms."

Victoria considered this for a moment. Then she turned her attention back to Berg.

"And I suppose *you're* tidying up the loose ends from that night?"

"Amongst other things."

"So, tell me. Who gave the order to remove the King's soul-catcher?"

Berg rolled his head from side to side, like a vulture trying to swallow a chunk of flesh.

"Oh, come on, Victoria. Isn't it obvious?"

She narrowed her eyes. "You tell me. What would anyone have to gain by removing it?"

The Smiling Man turned and used his bound hands to gesture at the battleship silhouette of Windsor Castle.

"Control of the throne."

Victoria frowned.

"No, that's ridiculous. The Duchess—"

Berg let out a sound that could have been a chuckle.

"Yes, the Duchess. Of course, the Duchess. *Her* company. *Her* husband. *Her* technology."

"So, the assassination attempt?"

"All part of her plan, I'm afraid. The King is indisposed, so the Duchess becomes Regent until Prince Merovech finishes his studies, at which point he assumes the throne."

"So, Merovech's part of this?"

"Yes, although he doesn't know it yet." Berg took a deep breath, as if preparing to unburden himself. The temperature in the hold had dropped considerably, and she could see him shivering.

"When Merovech takes the throne, he will be working for us. His first act as monarch will be to dissolve the civilian government and impose martial law. He will have the backing of the armed forces. We've spent years getting our people into key positions. When the takeover happens, it will be swift and decisive."

Victoria adjusted her grip on the quarterstaff. Every instinct in her body screamed at her to slam the tip into his moronic smirk.

"How do we stop him?"

Berg raised his chin, looking down his nose at her.

"I don't think you can. The plan's already underway. When the Mars probe's ready for launch, the Duchess will announce that she's resigning the Regency, and Merovech will ascend." He raised his hands, asking for the plastic binding to be removed. "Everything will be in place. The new order will rise."

Victoria closed her eyes. She moved her consciousness away from the emotions swamping the organic side of her brain. There would be time for panic later. Right now, she had to keep going. She couldn't afford to crumple. With her mind in command mode, she opened her eyes, her thoughts as cold and clear as the sky outside.

"You killed my husband," she stated. "And you tried to kill me."

Berg jerked, startled by the sudden calm in her voice, the sudden change in focus. His wrists chafed against the plastic cable tie, trying to pull free.

"Now, look—"

"Be quiet." She took a step forward, swinging the quarterstaff, marvelling at the mathematical beauty of its arcs, the perfect unity of its form and function.

"But you don't understand. I'm one of the Undying. I'm one of the survivors. I *will* make it to the life everlasting."

Victoria threw the staff up with one hand and caught it with the other. She reviewed her memories of Paul, from their first kiss to their wedding night. Whatever his faults, whatever he'd done, he hadn't deserved to die such a horrible death.

"How many people have you killed?"

The Smiling Man took a step back, beyond the track of the doors, onto the very lip of the deck. He couldn't retreat any further, yet Victoria still saw defiance in his eyes. He stood straight and tall, like a dinosaur stretching on its hind legs.

"Twenty-four," he said.

Victoria took another pace towards him, staff held like a javelin. The gelware threw targeting graphics across her sight.

"And how many of their brains did you take?"

His eyes were on the staff now. He looked less certain of himself.

"Nineteen. But they will live again. They're on the Mars probe. All the dead. All their soul-catchers. Even yours."

"Mine?"

"All of them."

"But why?"

"So they can live again, and take their places in the new global order."

Victoria felt something sour rise in her throat. One of her hands gripped the staff, ready to strike if he tried to move. The other reached for the door controls. She pressed the red button with the heel of her hand, and the doors shuddered. With a piercing squeal, they began to close.

Afraid of being shut out on the ledge, Berg tried to step to safety, but a swipe from the staff kept him where he was.

"Hey! You can't do this!" With his wrists bound in front of him, he found it hard to keep his balance. "Let me in."

Victoria kept the staff poised.

"This is for my husband," she said. Their eyes met. Berg's were white all the way around. Without emotion, she watched him teeter. The wind snatched at his clothing. She saw one of his heels slip. For an instant, his entire weight rested on the toes of one foot. A cry escaped his smiling lips.

And he was gone.

Victoria ran forward, and caught a final glimpse of him: a black stick figure cart-wheeling down through the bright afternoon air, legs flailing. She saw office blocks; an industrial estate. And then, with an echoing clang, the doors shut, closing out everything but the cold.

BREAKING NEWS

From *Le Journal de Nouvelle Science*, online edition:

Mars Probe "Days From Launch"

26 NOVEMBER 2059 – Inside sources at Céleste Tech have indicated that their long-heralded interplanetary "light sail" probe may be just days from launch.

Designed by engineers at the Céleste Technologies facility near Paris, the probe, dubbed 'New Dawn', will slingshot around the sun before unfurling a large "sail" to catch the solar wind and ride it to Mars.

If the launch is successful, the probe should reach Mars some time in 2061.

The project, which has been shrouded in secrecy, recently caused controversy when rumours started to circulate that its payload would include so-called "terraforming packages".

The packages are believed to contain specially-tailored microbial life forms, including algae and extremophile bacteria, designed to absorb carbon dioxide from the Martian atmosphere and replace it with oxygen.

Such packages would be a theoretical first step in any effort to turn the Red planet into a second Earth, but campaigners are opposed to what they see as the wanton contamination of an unspoilt wilderness, about which we still know comparatively little.

Although officials remain tight-lipped about a definite date for the launch, inside sources say they expect it to coincide with celebrations to mark the hundredth anniversary of the founding of the European Commonwealth.

Read more | Like | Comment | Share

Related Stories

Record levels of seawater acidity blamed for failing fish stocks

As new pills go on the market, we ask: should you erase bad memories, even if you can?

Hackers retaliate after police raid

Doubts surround centennial celebrations as Prince Merovech still "recovering in seclusion"

Skyliner *Grace Marguerite* celebrates sixty years of continuous international flight

Céleste Games unveils "new and improved" Ack-Ack Macaque character

Salvage teams race to save Venetian treasures

Chinese taikonauts begin return journey to Earth

Fans in Iowa mark centenary of Buddy Holly plane crash

CHAPTER SIXTEEN
CLOCKWORK NINJAS

THEY DROVE FOR the coast, Merovech at the wheel and Julie at his side. He needed to confront his mother, but wanted to do it on his terms, not hers; which meant finding his own way across the Channel.

Beside him, Julie seemed pensive. She kept chewing her bottom lip and wringing her hands in her lap. She hadn't spoken in half an hour.

In the back of the van, K8 huddled with Ack-Ack Macaque over a SincPad screen. She'd been gently connecting wires from the jacks in his head to a router plugged into the pad. This was her idea of fighting back.

"The best way to hurt Céleste and draw a lot of attention is to take down the game," she said. "And the best way to do that is to find the new monkey and kick its ass."

Ack-Ack Macaque picked at his teeth.

"Find the big guy and take him out. Gotcha."

K8 tapped a command into the pad, linking his artificially uplifted brain directly into the online game.

"Yeah, standard primate power play. Do you think you can handle it?"

"Do monkeys shit in the woods?"

His yellow eye flickered shut. K8 slid the final jack into place, covered his head with the leather skull cap, and rocked back. She met Merovech's glance in the rear view mirror.

"He's in."

"Do you think this will work?"

K8 gave the monkey's hand an affectionate pat.

"Aye, probably. If he can get in there and cause enough trouble to get noticed, then we can blow this thing sky high." She shuffled forward and leaned between the front seats. "According to *Techsnark*, the game has ten thousand registered user accounts, and many more watching the action on YouTube. That's a massive, ready-made audience, right there."

They were on a back road, somewhere in Brittany, and it was now well after midnight. From the passenger seat, Julie said,

"Won't they just block him?"

"I don't know if they can. He's hardwired into the game. He's part of it. And besides, they might not even notice him. Not for a while, anyway. If they think digital rights activists snatched him, the last thing they'll be expecting is for him to hook back in." K8 looked between Merovech and Julie, and frowned. "How are you two holding up?"

Merovech stifled a yawn. For the past hour, he'd been watching the road's central white line spool through the headlamps' arc, his fingers squeezing the wheel as his mind struggled to parse the evening's revelations.

He thought back to his time in the South Atlantic, before the helicopter crash.

"When in doubt," his old commanding officer had been fond of saying, "make a plan and stick to it. Chunk everything down into small, achievable objectives."

Rather than try to plan how he was going to get across the Channel, travel to Cornwall, and confront his mother without running afoul of either customs officials or her personal security team, he was focusing instead on reaching the coast. He knew that the parents of an old school friend had a yacht at Saint-Malo, and he hoped he'd be able to persuade them to take him across. In the meantime, he had the morale of his troops to consider.

"I could do with a break," he said. "And a coffee."

Beside him, Julie stretched like a waking cat.

"Coffee sounds good."

ACK-ACK MACAQUE stood blinking in the sudden light. He'd asked K8 to spawn him on the edge of one of the British airfields, at dawn, and the transition from the gloom and discomfort of the rattling old van to the warm sun and summer smells of the English countryside had been almost instantaneous. He took a deep breath in through his flattened nose. From his point of view, he was now standing in a meadow adjacent to the airfield's perimeter fence. Buttercups waved in a light breeze. Bees droned. He drank it all in. Then, as if remembering something, his hands dropped to his hips, and his fingers closed eagerly on the holstered butts of his giant Colts.

"Hello, old friends."

The guns were familiar and reassuring and, for a moment, everything seemed to be back the way it had been. But he knew in his heart that it wasn't. Now he'd discovered the truth about himself, the rules had changed. He no longer cared who won the war. He could see the game world for the sham it had always been, and he was here to tear it down. He'd broken out of his prison, and now he'd returned to wreak bloody vengeance on his former jailers. This wasn't a homecoming, it was a farewell tour.

A bazooka lay in the grass at his feet, like a long section of drainpipe. Beside it, a box of shells and a dozen grenades. K8 had hacked his profile to include the extra items. He wasn't sure what 'hacking' meant, but he appreciated her efforts. For what he had in mind, he'd need all the firepower he could get his hands on.

He pulled a cigar from the inside pocket of his flight jacket and lit up, thinking what a shame it was that K8 couldn't be there herself, in her guise as Mindy Morris. He'd grown used to having her as his co-pilot, and it seemed wrong for her to miss out on all the fun.

He heard a deep growling thrum from the south-east: a wave of boomerang-shaped flying wings powering in across the rolling fields, their triple propellers shimmering in the morning light. There were maybe a dozen in all, hurried along by six or seven darting, shark-like Messerschmitts.

Behind him, on the aerodrome, he heard the scramble bell ring. Another ninja parachute raid, as predictable as clockwork.

As the planes approached, he stood his ground, watching the funny-looking craft loom larger and larger in the morning sky. When the first parachute canopies blossomed, he drew the Colts and grinned around his cigar. This was going to be a riot.

He put bullets through the two lowest paratroopers. The others jerked around in their harnesses, searching the ground for the source of the shots. He heard them calling to each other in a panicky mixture of German and Japanese. Then they were down, rolling in the grass, their shrouds settling around them in clouds of gently falling silk.

Swords sang from their scabbards. Japanese steel flashed in the English summertime. Colts firing and fangs bared, Ack-Ack Macaque leapt to meet them.

CHAPTER SEVENTEEN
EXPIRED LEASE

VICTORIA VALOIS SAT on a bar stool, in a lounge on one of the skyliner's starboard gondolas. She was watching the spirits quiver in the bottles hanging behind the bar. They were rippling in time to the almost subliminal vibrations of the *Tereshkova*'s engines.

The lounge had been decorated in a 1930s 'Golden Era of Travel' style, with art deco fixtures, ceiling fans, and plenty of prominent rivets on the bulkheads. A painting hung over the cash register, portraying the Commodore as a young man, in a white dress uniform with a bright scarlet sash.

A row of large circular portholes filled much of the starboard wall. Perched on her stool at the counter, Victoria had her back to them. She didn't feel much like looking out, or down.

The bar counter itself had a thin copper top which had, over the years, acquired a patina of dents and nicks as unique as a fingerprint. The steward wore white gloves and served the drinks on small cork coasters.

Victoria was on her third gin and tonic. Her flaxen wig lay scrunched on the bar before her. Right now, she didn't care what she looked like, and her scarred, shaven head kept the other passengers from trying to engage her in conversation. She couldn't read the labels on the bottles behind the bar because she'd disabled the text recognition on her visual feed. She didn't want it whispering brand names in her mind every time she glanced at the shelves.

"Two years ago, I was happy," she said. She could see Paul in the corner of her eye: a peroxide ghost in a white coat and loud shirt, sitting with its head in its hands.

"Two years ago, I had a job. I had a husband. I had my own hair and I could *write*." Faces turned in her direction. She ignored them. "Now what have I got?"

She picked up her glass. Bubbles clung to the underside of the lime slice floating at the top. What had she got? She'd let the lease expire on the Parisian apartment she'd shared with Paul. Now all she had was a crumpled wig; the clothes she stood up in; the loan of a small cabin on the *Tereshkova*; and Paul.

"Hey," she said. "I'm talking to you."

Paul raised his eyes to her. He hadn't spoken since the Smiling Man fell from the lip of the cargo hold.

"I know, I'm choosing not to listen."

Victoria swilled the drink around in her glass.

"Oh, really?"

"Yeah." He clambered to his feet. "Because some of us have real problems, what with being dead and everything."

She slammed the glass down on its coaster.

"That's hardly my fault, is it? If you'd come clean in the first place, if you'd told someone about that night with the King, maybe all of this could have been avoided. Maybe you'd still be—"

She stopped herself, and let out a long, tired breath. Paul scowled.

"Hey, I'm the one who got his brains scooped out."

"Yeah, and I just killed a man. Because of you. So shut the fuck up, okay?"

She drained the gin and tonic, and pushed the glass across the counter.

"Another one," she said.

The steward came over.

"Madam, I have to ask you to keep your voice—"

"Just fill it up."

In her eye, she saw Paul shaking his head.

"I'd never have thought you were capable of something like that."

"Well then, I guess we really didn't know each other as well as we thought."

The steward placed a glass of gin and a small bottle of tonic on the bar, and turned away without a word. He knew she was the Commodore's goddaughter. If she wanted to sit at the bar and talk to herself, it was no business of his.

Victoria emptied the tonic into the glass until the bubbles ran over the rim and down, into a fizzing puddle on the copper counter.

"Besides, he deserved it, and I will not let you make me feel guilty."

Paul put his arms out.

"I'm not trying to. I know you, Vicky. I know you're guilty enough already. I can hear it in your voice."

"Get lost."

She picked up the wet glass and took a mouthful. The tonic fizzled on her tongue. The ice cubes dabbed her upper lip.

Cassius Berg had been a hired assassin. He'd murdered Paul, and all those others. He was a killer and, given the slightest chance, he would have killed her as well. He'd already tried to once, and only failed by the slimmest of margins. Why should she feel guilty for his death? Her actions had been entirely logical.

In her eye, Paul had his arms crossed, each fist clenched in the opposite armpit.

"You really want me to 'get lost'?"

"Right now? Yes."

He dropped his arms. "Well, if that's how you feel, maybe you should turn me off?"

"What?"

"You heard me." He turned away from her, shoulders hunched.

Victoria opened her mouth to snap back at him, but the words wouldn't come. Anger turned to sadness. She put her elbows on the bar and rubbed her temples.

"Ah, *merde.*"

All of a sudden, all she wanted was to make her way back down the narrow gangway to her little cupboard of a cabin, to close the door and shut out the world. Instead, she took a swallow from her glass, wiped her lips on the back of her hand, and drew herself up in her seat.

"I'm sorry," she said. Paul's white-clad shoulders twitched. He looked around.

"Are you serious? In all the years I've known you, you've never once said—"

"It's an apology, Paul. Take it or leave it." She drained the glass and pushed it across the counter for a refill.

Still sitting, Paul twisted around to face her. From her point of view, he seemed to be cross-legged on the shelf behind the bar, his back against the row of optics hanging from the wall.

"Okay." He scratched his beard. "Okay, I'm sorry too. I didn't mean to be an asshole about it. I'm just kind of shocked, you know?"

The steward came forward and refilled Victoria's glass. This time, he poured the tonic himself, avoiding spillages.

"You're shocked? Imagine how I feel." She turned in her seat to find the lounge behind her empty, the other passengers having decided to take their evenings elsewhere. Paul's image moved with her, so that he now seemed to float above the tables. Beyond the portholes, she caught sight of blue sky and white cloud.

"I did it for you, you know." She reached back and grabbed her newly-filled glass. "Because of what he did to you."

Paul gave a slow nod.

"I know. It's just I can't get over how you can think you know someone, even be married to them, and still they surprise you."

Victoria found herself shaking her head. She leaned back, her elbows against the cold metal of the bar.

"You don't need to tell me. I thought we were in love, remember?"

Paul squirmed. "We were. At least, I loved you. I still do. It's just—"

"Yeah?"

"Yeah." He bit his lower lip. "We had some good times, though, didn't we?"

"Yes, yes we did." Victoria sipped her drink. "And for what it's worth, I still love you, too. I'd be dead if it hadn't been for you. If you hadn't got me onto that Céleste programme after the crash…"

Paul waved a modest hand. "What else was I going to do? Besides, Nguyen thought you'd make an ideal test subject."

"Oh he did, did he?"

"Of course. It was a chance for him to try out some of the techniques we were going to use on the Prince. And, because you were travelling with Merovech when the crash happened, it was excellent publicity."

"And you just let them do it?"

A pained expression crossed his face.

"I couldn't let you die."

"So, you really did care?" In darker moments, she'd wondered why he'd tried so hard to save her life, only to separate from her six months later.

Paul pulled off his glasses and wiped them on the hem of his white coat.

"Of course I did. Our sexualities may not have been compatible, but I loved you as much as I've ever loved anyone. You were my wife, and it would have killed me to let you die without exploring every option, even if it meant turning you over to Nguyen."

Victoria looked down at her drink. "So," she said. "What now? You saved my life; I avenged your death. I guess that makes us even."

"I guess so." Paul slipped the spectacles back onto his nose. "There's just one thing."

"What?"

"I really don't want to go."

Victoria felt herself sag. She put a hand to her head.

"Oh, Paul."

He leant towards her. "Seriously. I know we agreed that you'd keep me running until you solved my murder. And, well, we've done that. But still, I don't want to be turned off. Not now, not yet."

Victoria slid down from the stool and walked over to the portholes on the starboard wall. She bent slightly, one arm on the wall for support, and looked out at the countryside passing below. She saw fields and hedges laid out like a patchwork picnic blanket. Roads like seams.

Paul was quiet for a long time. Then he asked:

"Do you believe in God, Vicky? I mean, really?"

Her lips pursed. Her fingernails tippy-tapped the metal wall. She hadn't really thought about it in years.

"I guess there might be a higher power, somewhere out there. But if there is, it's going to be stranger than anything we can imagine." She took a sip from her glass. "Why do you ask?"

"Because I don't believe in anything. I don't think there's anything waiting for us when we die. This is it. This is all we get, and it's not enough."

Below, the serried ranks of a conifer plantation. Wide, straight firebreaks like grassy highways. A stream glinting like a vein of bronze.

"You know what happens to back-ups," Victoria said quietly. "You better than anyone."

Paul raised his index finger.

"There was that old guy in Edinburgh. You interviewed him for your paper. He lasted six months."

The *Tereshkova* passed into cloud.

"But he still fell apart, in the end."

"We all fall apart in the end."

Victoria straightened up and turned back to the empty lounge.

"Then what do you suggest? I can't have you in my head for the next six months. We'll drive each other nuts."

"You could transfer my file into a different processor. Another gelware brain. Then all we'd have to do is find a way to grow a body to put it in."

Victoria gaped.

"You're crazy."

Paul held up his hand, fending off her accusation.

"No, I'm sure it can be done."

Victoria moved back to the bar. The steward regarded her with palpable weariness, but she didn't care. She'd had enough for one night.

"Really? And what makes you think it's even possible?"

Paul reached up and scratched his ear.

"Because that's what we were working on at Céleste."

CHAPTER EIGHTEEN
LA MANCHE

THEY REACHED THE outskirts of Saint-Malo a little after dawn. Merovech's friend's parents had an apartment in one of the new, upscale arcologies overlooking the sea, far along the coast from the walls of the old, partially-flooded port city; and out of sight of the container ships anchored at the mouth of the Rance River.

There were around thirty ships in all, all retrofitted to provide emergency housing for ecological refugees from the low lying countries further up the coast. Anchored in the shelter of the estuary, they formed a floating shantytown for those displaced by rising sea levels and seasonal floods. Some of the ships were lashed together, linked by gangways and laundry lines; while others stood alone, each a separate neighbourhood in its own right, with its own customs and hierarchies.

Geoffrey Renfrew hadn't really been a friend, of course; he'd just been someone who'd hung around on the edge of Merovech's social circle at school, trying to ingratiate himself. Merovech remembered him as a pale, greasy boy with watery eyes and a laugh that sounded like a cat sneezing.

He parked the old Citroën van on a concrete service road leading to the arcology. Weeds poked through cracks in the road, but the buildings themselves looked immaculate.

Built like a vast step pyramid, with terrace gardens along each step, and a vast light well running down the centre, the arcology was a self-contained, secure community. Fortified against crime, social unrest and terrorist attack, it provided an expensive, aspirational refuge for the upper middle class. Wind turbines turned their carbon fibre blades on either side of the building's private marina.

"There's no way we're going to get in there," K8 said. "Those places have everything: electric fences, face and gait recognition, biometric scanners, the works."

Merovech pulled out his SincPhone.

"I'll call them. They can meet us somewhere and take us to the yacht."

K8 looked him up and down.

"What are we going to do about the skipper here? I'm assuming the harbour will have some sort of security. Even if it's just CCTV, they're going to spot a monkey, no matter what we dress him in."

Merovech smiled. On the way here, they'd passed a pet supply store in an out-of-town retail development, and it had given him an idea.

"You leave that to me," he said.

THREE HOURS LATER, Merovech, Julie and K8 were ensconced in the cramped but comfortable galley of Geoffrey's parents' yacht: a thirty-foot catamaran by the name of *Peggy Sue*.

Geoffrey's parents were pleased to see him, and anxious to be hospitable; but they couldn't hide their puzzlement at the suddenness and secrecy of his arrival. They seated their guests around a small plastic table and poured them drinks.

Geoffrey's father, Jerry, was a former meat magnate from Cambridgeshire. He wore blue denim jeans and a bootlace tie with a silver steer's head. He'd made his fortune selling vat-grown beef, cloned from the finest available livestock, to restaurants and fast food chains. A pioneer in his field, his most controversial scheme involved a range of hamburgers that he claimed contained meat cloned directly from the skin cells of pop stars and celebrities. Fans could now eat their heroes, he said. The resulting media frenzy made him rich—but when the patties in the buns turned out to be ordinary pork instead of vat-grown human flesh, he'd been forced to take early retirement.

Standing by the yacht's hatch with a mug of coffee in his hand, he had a wide smile and easygoing manner, which instantly put them all at their ease.

Geoffrey's mother, Patricia, turned out to be fond of a glass of Chardonnay and, after half an hour, had begun to slur her words. She wore a tight dress, pearls, and pink polyurethane heels that matched her nails and lipstick.

She adored Julie's purple hair.

"Of course we'll take you across to England, your royal highness." She patted Merovech on the knee. "Anything for a friend of Geoffrey's."

"Thank you." Merovech gave his sincerest, paparazzi-friendly smile. "I really am grateful."

Mrs Renfrew eyed his tatty jeans and old red hoodie.

"But can't you tell us what all this is about? Are you in some kind of trouble? They're saying on the news that you had a collapse."

"Now Patricia," Jerry warned. "Don't pry."

Merovech let his smile broaden.

"That's quite all right, Mister Renfrew." He slid his arm around Julie's shoulders. "The truth is, we're eloping. The stuff on TV's just a cover story. We're trying to get to Gretna Green without the news channels getting wind of it. Do you think you can help us?"

Mrs Renfrew clapped a hand to her mouth.

"A wedding? Oh, my lord!" She fanned herself with both hands.

Julie leaned forward conspiratorially, touching the older woman's wrist.

"It's a secret, Mrs Renfrew. You must *promise* not to tell. At least, for now. Afterwards, if you want to, you can tell all your friends how you helped us elope."

Patricia Renfrew's eyes were wide and glittering with the prospect of a royal wedding.

"Can we trust you?" Merovech asked.

"Of course, my loves, of course. We'll do anything we can, won't we Jerry?"

"Yes, dear." Mister Renfrew thumbed tobacco into a well-worn pipe. "We'll cast off at high tide. Should have you across in a couple of hours, eh? Where do you want to go, Southampton or Portsmouth?"

"Either, as long as we can avoid any official entanglements."

Jerry smiled a slow and easy smile.

"You just leave that to me, my boy. Now, the three of you had better stay down here until we're clear of land. We don't want anyone catching sight of you before we're even underway, now do we?"

He stepped through the hatch and climbed up the wooden steps to the deck. Patricia tottered after him, wineglass in hand.

"Make yourselves at home," she called from the hatchway. "Are you sure your doggie will be all right in there?"

Merovech glanced at the pet carrier, which was an enclosed plastic basket made to transport Alsatians and Great Danes. It was the largest he'd been able to find at the out-of-town pet store and, with K8's help, he'd been able to stuff Ack-Ack Macaque into it.

"He'll be fine."

"What kind of dog is he?"

"A big one."

Patricia frowned. She took a couple of clacking steps back into the cabin, towards the box.

"Look," said Julie, trying to distract her, "I'll level with you, okay? We stole the dog."

Patricia Renfrew's plucked and painted brows drew closer together, like indignant caterpillars.

"You *stole* it?"

"From a laboratory." Julie's voice dropped to a whisper. "You wouldn't believe the experiments they were doing to the poor creature. Shampoo in the eyes. Electrodes on the head. By the end, they had him on forty cigarettes a day."

Patricia's eyes narrowed. She took another sip of chardonnay, and then looked from Julie to the pet carrier. She burst into peals of cackling laughter.

"Oh, that's priceless!" she gasped, slapping Julie on the shoulder. "You really had me going there, for a second."

WHEN THEY WERE a mile out into the Channel, Jerry judged it safe for them to come up on deck. Merovech followed K8 and Julie up the wooden stairs from the galley, and the three of them emerged blinking in the afternoon sunlight, clutching at rails to support themselves as the boat rocked.

Jerry stood at the wheel. "If you have a moment, your highness, I'd like to show you something."

He crouched down and opened a metal locker, to reveal a pair of matt-black automatic pistols.

"One for me and one for the wife," he said proudly. "We picked them up last year, when we were sailing around the Gold Coast, in case we got hit by pirates." He took hold of the catamaran's wheel. "And besides, if it all kicks off with China, it won't hurt to have some additional protection, eh?"

Merovech looked up at the flapping sails.

"I've been out of touch for a couple of days. How's it going in China?"

Jerry looked solemn. For the first time since meeting Merovech and his friends, the sparkle seemed to have gone from his eyes.

"Not well at all, I'm afraid."

"Hong Kong?"

"And Indian troops pressuring the western borders." Jerry leant his forearms on the wheel, staring ahead, over the bows, pipe clenched in his teeth. "The whole area's one big flashpoint."

Merovech huffed air through his cheeks. He still held a commission in the Royal Navy, and his time in the South Atlantic had given him a keen sense of what it meant to be part of the crew of a warship, thousands of miles from home and family. If it came to war, it would be the men and women with whom he'd served who'd bear the brunt.

"Let's hope it won't come to that."

Jerry raised his eyebrows. "Amen to that."

They stood in pensive silence for a couple of minutes, enjoying the way the twin hulls cut through the grey waters.

Finally, Jerry said, "Do you think it will go nuclear?"

Merovech looked out to sea, at the container ships looming towards them, each as big as a small town, boxed-up and set adrift.

"I hope not."

Julie stood near the stern, gazing back at the shore. Jerry nodded towards her.

"I thought you might know something. Maybe they'd warned you it might happen, and that's why you were running away to get married, before it did."

Merovech smiled. "No, that's not the reason."

Jerry seemed relieved, although still not entirely convinced. They were riding a stiff south-westerly blowing up from the Bay of Biscay, and Merovech filled his lungs. He could feel the sea air clear the fatigue and cobwebs from his mind. He'd spent far too long cramped up in that van, driving at night. Being out here in the sunlight, surrounded by the ocean, the blustery wind chipping sprays of white from the wave crests, felt like being reborn.

"What happens to you," Jerry asked, "if the balloon does go up?"

Merovech didn't want to think about it. As heir to the throne, he knew he'd be protected. He'd been briefed by his security people. By the time the sirens sounded, he'd be safe and secure, half a mile underground.

"It won't come to that."

Jerry raised an eyebrow.

"I hope you're right, my boy. I really do." He straightened and fastened his grip on the catamaran's helm. "Still, I can't help wondering if we would be in this situation if the whole Unification thing had never happened."

Looking down at the water grazing the hull, Merovech frowned.

"What do you mean?"

Behind him, Jerry gave a grunt.

"Just that if the UK hadn't expanded so quickly, and if we hadn't had France on our side, maybe we wouldn't have clung so hard to Hong Kong in the first place? Perhaps we've been a little overconfident?"

Merovech shrugged. He didn't have any answers. Julie came to the rail. She tucked a straggle of fluttering hair behind her ear and looked up at him.

"How are you doing?" he asked her.

She turned to glance back at the receding shore. Gulls flapped in their wake.

"I don't know. I guess when this is all over, I am going to be in trouble, aren't I? I don't even have a passport with me." She shivered. "My father will be *furieux*."

Merovech put his arm around her.

"Don't you worry about your father. You're going to be okay." He gave her a squeeze. "I'm going to look after you."

She leant into his embrace, snuggling up against him for warmth.

"Well," she mused, "if I am going to run off with anyone, I suppose I could not do much better than the heir to the throne, now could I?"

Merovech smiled into the wind. They were crossing the world's busiest shipping lanes—a major artery of global commerce—and he could see six or seven large vessels at various distances, including container ships, car transporters, and oil tankers. No ferries, though. Few passengers crossed the Channel by boat these days. Most chose the high-speed rail link through the Channel Tunnel. The rest took berths on skyliners.

Merovech scanned the horizon ahead, searching for a particular cigar-shaped silhouette.

"Don't worry," he said. He looked back at Jerry, but the older man seemed absorbed with his compass and SatNav. "I've got a plan."

Julie turned to him.

"You do?"

Merovech gave her a smile.

"I think so."

He would have said more, but a scream cut the air. Patricia clacked up from the galley, heels wobbling, empty wineglass in hand. She glared at Julie, chest heaving.

"You!"

"What's the matter, Mrs Renfrew?"

The older woman's eyes were narrow slits.

"Don't you 'Mrs Renfrew' me, young lady." Her hand swung around to point back down the steps. "Your so-called 'dog' just told me to go and fuck myself!"

CHAPTER NINETEEN
SLOTTING INTO PLACE

In the six months that Victoria had been aboard the *Tereshkova*, she'd only once had occasion to visit the old airship's bridge, at the front of the main gondola. Normally, the room was out of bounds to all but the crew, and protected by armed guards but, a few days after she'd arrived on board and thrown herself on her godfather's hospitality, he'd invited her to take the tour.

"And this is where the magic happens," he'd said, ushering her inside with a flourish.

But when she'd stepped through the hatch, Victoria had been surprised: the room seemed far too small, considering the size of the five-hulled airship that it controlled: barely large enough for three workstations, one each for the navigator, helmsman and commanding officer. The front wall was mostly glass: a grid of rectangular windows that curved down into the floor, offering a panoramic view of the sky and ground ahead. The window frames were titanium, decorated with brass flourishes.

The Commodore had tapped his workstation's screen, bringing up a schematic of the airship.

"We control the whole thing from here. Airspeed, pitch and altitude. We can even operate each engine individually, for really complex manoeuvres."

Uninterested in the computer, Victoria had looked around in disappointment.

"No big steering wheel?"

The Commodore had a braying laugh.

"Goodness no, child. What do you think this is, the *Graf Zeppelin*?"

"I thought that was the effect you were going for."

The Commodore stopped laughing.

"She may look old, but the old girl has life in her yet." His moustache drooped. "More perhaps than I."

"Don't say that."

"I speak only the truth. I am an old man. When I am gone, she will still be here." His eyes regarded her from half-closed lids. "And *someone* will need to fly her."

SHE THOUGHT OF that visit now, as she made her way forward, along the gangway to the Commodore's cabin, which sat directly behind the bridge. It was less utilitarian and considerably more spacious than the control room, with a case of books, a couple of potted plants, and a thick Persian rug. She knocked on the door and let herself in.

Her godfather sat behind his wide aluminium desk, the top buttons of his dress tunic undone. He'd left his cutlass in an elephant's foot umbrella stand by the window.

"Come in and have a seat." He reached into his desk drawer and she heard the clink of glass. "Would you like a drink?"

Victoria declined. She still had all that gin in her system.

"You wanted to see me?"

The old man swept his hand across the desk, activating the SincPad display built into its top.

"I have had one of my people finding out all they can about the Undying. I thought I would summarise it for you, rather than forward it. I know you have trouble reading."

"Oh."

He looked up. "Is there a problem?"

Victoria felt her cheeks colour.

"I assumed you'd called me here to talk about what happened to Cassius Berg."

"What is there to say?"

Victoria got to her feet. "I killed him."

"He fell."

"Only because I closed the doors." She could barely bring herself to look her godfather in the eye.

The Commodore sighed. He clasped his gnarly hands on the desktop and regarded her from under his shaggy brows.

"And what do you want me to do, my dear? Arrest you? Throw you in the brig?"

"I killed him."

The Commodore leaned back.

"Yes, you did. And that's something you're going to have to work out how to live with. But for what it's worth, I think you did the right thing. He was a murdering psychopath. A rabid dog. You did the world a favour by putting him to sleep. And after what he did to you, I would have thrown that *govniuk* off this ship myself." He reached back into the desk drawer and pulled out the bottle of vodka that he kept there.

"Truth be told, I have been impressed by the way you are handling yourself over the past few days. What would you say to a permanent job on my security team?"

"Security?"

"Yes. An airship this size, we get all sorts. Terrorists. Smugglers. Spies. You would be surprised."

Victoria bit her lip. This wasn't the direction she'd expected this meeting to take; yet she found herself tempted and strangely flattered by the old man's offer.

"And I would live here, on the *Tereshkova*, permanently?"

The Commodore threw his arms wide in a gesture of welcome.

"You would be one of my crew."

She'd been aboard the airship for nearly six months now, since the breakup of her marriage, when she'd walked out on Paul with nowhere else to go. And now, thinking about it, she realised that the creaking bulkheads and narrow gangways of the gondolas felt more like home than any place she could think of, London and Paris included.

"Thank you," she said, truly grateful. The Commodore smiled his toothy smile. He twisted the cap off the bottle.

"Are you sure you don't want one?"

"Quite sure."

"Good, because you stink of gin. Now, sit down, be quiet and listen to what I have found." He poured himself a drink, then reactivated the desktop, pulling up a text file.

"According to this, the Undying are a relatively new cult. At least, it is only recently that they have become widely known. There is some evidence that they have been working in secret for some time." He brushed the screen again, bringing up another document, this one containing false colour Hubble photos of gas clouds and galaxies. "They preach a doctrine of transhumanism and digital immortality, and they have some powerful supporters."

He made a circle on the table with his finger, spinning one of the displayed documents to face her. She peered at it, seeing only black marks on a white page.

So far, Paul had been silently watching the meeting through her eyes, and now he spoke.

"It's a list of names," he said. "Celebrities, politicians, business people. Half the board of directors at Céleste—"

"Céleste *again*?" Victoria got to her feet and began to pace, ticking off points on her fingers as she spoke.

"Paul and Lois both worked for Céleste, under a man named Nguyen. Cassius Berg killed Paul and tried to kill Lois. But Berg was one of the Undying, which means he had links to the Board of Directors at Céleste."

The Commodore frowned. "Céleste are killing their own people?"

"Last year, according to both Paul and Lois, Doctor Nguyen performed an unnecessary removal of the King's soul-catcher."

The old man stroked his moustache. "And the King's been in a coma ever since."

Victoria stopped moving. She found herself looking at an old framed photograph of the Commodore as a youth, clad in the orange pressure suit of a Russian cosmonaut, helmet tucked proudly under his arm.

"You put it all together, and it seems the management at Céleste used Berg to try to silence everyone on Nguyen's team."

The Commodore reached for his vodka glass.

"A cover-up, you mean? But what exactly are they covering, and where do you fit in?"

Victoria pursed her lips.

"I'm not sure. Nguyen operated on me as well, around the same time. Perhaps that has something to do with it?"

In her head, Paul said, "Or maybe they figured that once they'd killed me, it would be a good idea to whack my nosy, former journalist ex-wife, before she started digging around?"

Victoria shrugged.

"Whatever. The thing is, Berg implied that the assassination attempt and the removal of the King's soul-catcher were both part of a conspiracy to seize the throne, and that Duchess Célestine was behind it."

The Commodore tapped the smooth surface of his desk.

"Her name *is* on this list, as a member of the Undying."

Victoria felt the pieces slotting into place, the way they used to do when she'd been closing in on a really good story.

"She owns Céleste. It's her company. She's the founder and CEO. And since that night, she's also been acting as Regent."

"*Okhuyet!*" The Commodore drained his glass. He turned in his chair, to look out of the window at the English countryside passing beneath the *Tereshkova*. They were running along the South Coast, heading for the Atlantic and labouring against a brisk south-westerly.

Victoria began to walk back and forth again, across the thick Persian rug, her heavy boots leaving criss-cross grip patterns.

"So the Duchess deposed her own husband and took his place. But to what ends? When Merovech finishes his studies, he'll be ready to assume the throne and she'll be out on her ear."

"Unless he's part of the plot," The Commodore said. "From what you've told me, Berg implied as much, and the Duchess *is* his mother, after all."

Victoria tapped her fingertips against her chin. She had a glimmering, but that wasn't it.

"But then why go to all this trouble?" she asked. "The King was never in the best of health. The throne would have been Merovech's in a few years, anyway."

The old man studied her.

"You sound as if you have a theory."

She leant her knuckles on the desk.

"Paul says the team at Céleste were working on a way to transfer stored personalities into living bodies, and when they rebuilt my brain, they were using me as a guinea pig for some of their techniques." She saw Paul nodding his spiky, platinum head in agreement. "And Lois Lapointe mentioned something about the Prince receiving additional gelware implants. What if those two things are somehow connected?" She straightened up again. Her mouth had gone dry. "What if Merovech takes the throne, but isn't Merovech inside? What if they're planning to load a different personality into him?"

The Commodore rolled the empty vodka glass between his palms.

"Whose personality?"

Victoria tapped her chin again. The gin had worn off and her head buzzed.

"I don't know. Maybe a high-ranking member of the Undying?"

The old man huffed air through his cheeks.

"That's quite a theory."

Victoria banged her hand on the desk. "It's more than that, Commodore. If I'm right, it's a bloody coup d'état!"

CHAPTER TWENTY
NEUTRAL TERRITORY

ACK-ACK MACAQUE appeared in the catamaran's hatchway, wearing the leather jacket and flying goggles K8 had given him. He scratched his chest, and put an arm out to steady himself. He glared around at the grey waters of the English Channel, and his tail twitched.

"I hate boats."

His words seemed to break a spell. Mrs Renfrew screamed again, clearly distraught at the sight of a talking monkey. At the same time, her husband—galvanised by her terror — dropped to his knees and pulled open the metal locker containing the automatic pistols. He came up brandishing one.

"Get back!"

Ack-Ack Macaque blinked at him in puzzlement.

"What's your problem?"

The gun shook. Merovech stepped over and put his hand on the older man's forearm.

"Give me the gun, Jerry."

Mister Renfrew struggled.

"But, but—"

His knuckles were white. Merovech took hold of the pistol's barrel, and twisted both weapon and wrist. Something snapped. Mister Renfrew gave a cry of pain and indignation, and released the gun.

"What are you doing?" Mrs Renfrew didn't know whether to look at her husband or the monkey.

Julie bent and scooped the second gun from the locker. She passed it to Merovech.

"Okay," he said. "Let's get these two below."

Mr Renfrew had dropped to his knees in the cockpit, cheeks ashen, arms and shoulders curled around the pain of a broken wrist. Merovech tossed one of the guns to Ack-Ack Macaque, and used his free hand to haul the man to his feet.

"Come on," he said.

He could feel his heart beating in his chest. After days of running and hiding, it felt good to be doing something positive: to be taking charge of the situation, as he'd been trained to do.

He shepherded the old couple down into the interior of the yacht, and into one of the cabins.

"I'm sorry about this," he said as he closed the wooden door. "But I'm afraid there's more going on here than you realise."

He tucked the gun into the back of his jeans and clumped back up on deck. The wind ran its fingers through his hair.

"Okay," he rubbed his hands. "K8, get down there and make sure they don't escape. And while you're there, I want you to get on the radio and hail a skyliner. She's called the *Tereshkova*, and if she's running to schedule, she should be somewhere hereabouts."

He turned to Julie.

"Skyliners are neutral territory. If I can get you and K8 on board, you'll be safe from arrest. You'll have time to figure out what you want to do next."

Julie looked back at the French coast, which was now little more than a strip of green on the horizon.

"But, my father—" She reached up to touch the fading bruise on her cheek.

"Forget him," Merovech said. "He can't touch you here. You'll be safe."

"What about me?" Ack-Ack Macaque had his back to the rail. He was passing the gun Merovech had given him from leathery hand to leathery hand, testing its weight and balance.

"That's up to you," Merovech said. "How did you get on in the game?"

The monkey shrugged.

"I killed a few people. Nobody important. I didn't have time for much else."

"Would you like to go back in?"

Ack-Ack Macaque opened his mouth and picked at a yellow canine.

"I'm going to wreck it," he said. "Those motherfuckers at Céleste have it coming."

Merovech nodded.

"Okay, get below and have K8 hook you back in. We'll leave you in there until you've done what you need to do."

"And then what?"

Merovech reached back and took hold of the gun in his waistband. He pulled it out and checked the magazine.

"We've been running too long, and I've had enough. When you've finished killing the new monkey in the game, you and I are going to start fighting back, for real."

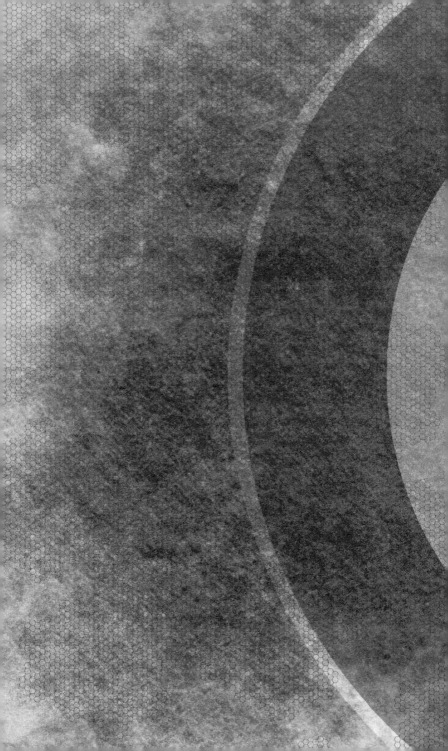

PART TWO

THE DEAD AND THE UNDYING

Yet you, my creator, detest and spurn me, thy creature,
to whom thou art bound by ties only dissoluble by the
annihilation of one of us.

(Mary Shelley, *Frankenstein*)

CHAPTER TWENTY-ONE
CHIMPANZEES DON'T HAVE TAILS

THE CHOPPER WAS an amphibious model, with large floats instead of landing skis. By the time it reached the *Tereshkova*'s helipad, Victoria and the Commodore were there, waiting to greet it.

The Commodore wore his full dress uniform: a white jacket with plenty of gold braid, cavalry trousers, and a pair of knee-length riding boots. Although Victoria still wore her thick green greatcoat, beneath it, she'd changed into a clean pair of black jeans and a black roll-neck top, to conceal the freshly reapplied dressings at the back of her neck. She'd given up with the wig the Commodore had given her, and settled instead on a plain fleece hat.

As the helicopter's hatch opened, the Commodore clicked his heels together and bowed at the waist.

"Welcome, your highness."

Prince Merovech stepped down onto the rubberised surface of the pad and saluted.

"Permission to come aboard, Commodore?"

In the jeans and hoodie that he wore, he looked much like any other teenage boy from the streets of Paris or London. He was only nineteen years old yet, Victoria knew, he was a teenager already acquainted with the harsh realities of both public life and military combat. A boy who'd had to grow up fast, and take on more than many adults ever did.

"A pleasure to see you again, Miss Valois." He had to shout over the engine noise.

"Your highness."

Behind Merovech, a girl with purple hair. Behind her, a redheaded, boyish-looking kid in a green sweater.

And behind them all came the monkey.

Victoria took a moment to take him in. He stood much taller than she would have expected, yet not quite upright, and he was chewing the soggy end of an unlit cigar. A leather patch covered one of his eyes, while the other glared about him, sizing everything up as a possible threat. He looked powerful and dangerous, as much animal as man.

And who the hell, she thought, gave him a gun?

She tailed along as the Commodore led the party down, through the stairwells and gangways in the body of the airship, to the comfort of the main gondola's dining room.

"Come," he said. "Be seated. Make yourselves at home."

Like the lounge bar, the dining room had been done out in homage to the pioneers of airship travel, from the spotless white tablecloths to the polished wooden fixtures and the patterned wallpaper on the bulkheads. The windows were wide and gave the room a light, airy feel, making it seem a lot bigger than it actually was. Between the windows, the Commodore had placed framed photographs of Russian heroes, including Yuri Gagarin, and the woman after whom he'd named the airship itself, Valentina Tereshkova, the first female astronaut.

The Prince and his entourage settled themselves around the largest table, and refreshments were served: tea for the Prince, coffee for Julie Girard, cola for the kid known as K8, and a daiquiri for the monkey. Victoria ordered a soda water. The gin had left her dehydrated and headachy, and she needed something to freshen her up.

When they'd all been served, and the formalities taken care of, the Commodore put his hands on the table.

"We were surprised to receive your radio message, your highness. We were given to understand that you were indisposed."

Merovech considered this.

"I thank you for your hospitality, Commodore. All I can say is that rumours of my ill health have been greatly exaggerated."

"And your simian friend?"

"A long story, I'm afraid. The truth of it is, we're in a spot of bother, and could really use your help."

Victoria leant forward in her chair.

"We know about the Undying and their plan to seize the throne," she said. "And we know you're involved."

Merovech's eyes narrowed.

"'Seize the throne'?"

Victoria slipped off her hat, revealing the jacks studding the scar on her temple. "You and I were in the hospital at the same time, Merovech. They took out the damaged parts of my brain and pumped my head full of gelware. And they did the same to you. Only the bits they took out of your head weren't damaged at all."

The Prince regarded her for a long, thoughtful moment.

"And do you know why they did that?"

Victoria swallowed. This was it. Time to put all the pieces together and make some wild accusations.

"The Undying have infiltrated Céleste. They're using you as a pawn. The minute you take the throne, they'll pump another personality into your head."

Merovech glanced at Julie Girard, then back at Victoria.

"What makes you say that?"

Victoria felt her cheeks flush. "They sent an assassin to kill every member of Doctor Nguyen's team. We stopped him and he—" She took a deep breath. "He talked."

They were all looking at her now.

Merovech said, "Nguyen's dead. We went to his house."

"So, you knew about this?"

The Prince shook his head.

"We were starting to piece it together. K8 used to work for Céleste, and she hacked their internal server. Then, when we broke into the corporate building, Julie found Nguyen's notes."

The Commodore raised his eyebrows.

"You broke in?"

Julie smiled. "Yes, and we got a lot more than we bargained for."

Victoria recognised the girl's accent. She said, "*Tu es de Paris?*"

"*Oui. Je suis étudiante à la Sorbonne. Et vous?*"

"*J'ai vecu un moment à Paris. Maintenant j'habite ici.*" She looked back to Merovech and switched to English. "So, you're on the run, are you?"

The Prince didn't even blink.

"We are. At least, for the moment. That's why we're here." He turned to the Commodore. "Would it be possible for us to claim asylum on your vessel, sir?"

The old man smoothed his white moustache with thumb and index finger, considering his answer. When he finally spoke, he said, "I suppose that could be arranged."

Merovech smiled. Julie and K8 looked relieved.

"Thank you."

The Commodore held up a hand.

"Just be good enough to answer me one question." He levelled a finger at Ack-Ack Macaque, who was at that moment in the process of cleaning his ear with his little finger. "What is the deal with the chimpanzee?"

Ack-Ack Macaque bristled. His solitary eye glared at the Commodore.

"Have you seen my tail, man? Chimpanzees don't have tails."

The Commodore bowed his head.

"Forgive me, I meant no offence. But my question remains. Who are you, and where did you come from? To whom do you belong?"

Ack-Ack Macaque picked up his daiquiri glass and began to lick the sugar from the rim.

"I'm my own monkey," he said between slurps, "and I don't belong to anyone, not anymore."

"We rescued him from the Céleste laboratories," Merovech explained. "As far as I'm concerned, he's his own person. But there's a lot of proprietary tech crammed into his head, and I'm sure Céleste will be keen to get it back."

The Commodore sighed.

"So, you bring me a fugitive prince, a teenage computer hacker, a burglar, and a stolen monkey?"

Merovech clapped his hands together and rubbed them.

"I'm afraid that's about the size of it." He turned his attention to Victoria.

"So, what else did your assassin have to say?"

CHAPTER TWENTY-TWO
IRRESISTABLE FORCE

ONE OF THE *Tereshkova*'s stewards showed K8 and Ack-Ack Macaque to a crew cabin in the farthest port gondola, away from the areas permitted for use by ordinary passengers.

The room was small and cramped, lit by a lamp fixed to the wall. His nostrils twitched at the pervasive stench of unwashed sheets and Russian cologne. A pair of cabin beds stood to either side of the narrow space that ran the length of the room from door to porthole. Beneath the porthole, a nightstand, and a couple of chairs. The washroom was down the hall.

"Are you ready to get back in there?" K8 asked, sitting cross-legged on the bed. She had the SincPad and connective leads in her lap. Even to Ack-Ack Macaque, who wasn't very good at reading human expressions, she looked tired.

She's just a kid, he thought. But she was his kid. He had no idea where she came from, but she was the closest thing he had to a friend right now. She'd been a member of his squadron, and as such, he'd do everything in his power to look after and protect her. Over the years, he'd lost so many kids. He'd seen them shot out of the sky by flak, gunned down by enemy pilots, and skewered by black-clad ninjas. He'd watched their planes spiral into hillsides, trailing smoke and flames, and it had eaten away at him. Survivor's guilt, they called it. Yet, out here in the real world, none of those deaths counted. They hadn't really happened at all. They'd all been a part of the game. The characters may have died, but the players were still alive. They were still at their consoles and SincPads, still living and breathing, even if they couldn't get back into the game. After months of guilt and grief, the knowledge felt like a weight taken from his shoulders.

He leant against the back of the closed cabin door and lit a cigar. K8 wrinkled her nose.

"Are you allowed to smoke in here?"

"I don't give a crap." He spoke through teeth clenched on the cigar's butt. "I've got bigger things to worry about right now. Like, who I am, and *what* I am."

K8 fiddled with one of the connective wires in her lap, straightening out its kinks and tangles.

"Maybe I can help you fill in some of the blanks."

"More hacking?"

A mischievous grin. "Hardly. I worked there, remember? I got trained. They wanted me to know how important you were. They even gave me a *brochure*."

Ack-Ack Macaque took the cigar from his mouth. He raised his muzzle and huffed a trio of expanding smoke rings at the low metal ceiling.

"So, what did it say in this brochure? What am I, a kids' toy?"

K8 laughed brightly. The lamplight caught the short copper curls of her hair.

"You're a weapons system, Skipper. A prototype. The game's just a fortunate spin-off, a bit of extra cash. The real money's in intelligent guidance systems. Drones, missiles. Even space probes. They didn't want to go to all the trouble of developing genuine AI, so they thought they'd do the next best thing, and start bootstrapping primates."

She leaned forward and lowered her voice almost to a whisper. "But here's the thing nobody else knows, the bit I *did* get from hacking the server. That probe they're sending to Mars, it isn't full of terraforming bacteria. No, that's just a cover story. A diversion. Really, it's full of souls."

Ack-Ack Macaque moved the cigar from one side of his mouth to the other.

"Souls?"

"Recorded personalities." She tapped the back of her neck, at the base of her skull. "Thousands of them, harvested from the dead and dying."

"To what end?"

"To download, once they get there. Don't forget these guys are pretty heavily into the whole transhumanism trip. The probe's the size of a London bus. There's machinery in there. It's going to build android bodies for the Undying faithful—bodies that don't need to breathe or eat or sleep. And then, they'll have the whole of Mars to themselves. By the time the Americans or Chinese get around to sending a manned mission, they'll find an established colony of robot cultists already in place."

Ack-Ack Macaque considered this. He hadn't understood everything she'd said, but he thought he'd gleaned the gist. Or some of it, at least.

"You say thousands. Is the cult really that big?"

K8's expression darkened.

"The faithful probably number a couple of hundred. The rest have been harvested from hospitals and morgues. A ready-made slave army."

Ack-Ack Macaque tapped ash onto the deck.

"Robots, Morris? Really?"

"Yes, Skipper. They already had a prototype. They built it using what they learned working on Victoria Valois. They stretched some skin over its face and uploaded a personality into it. Called it Berg."

"What happened to it?"

K8 shrugged. She had no idea. Instead, she held up one of the connective leads by its copper jack.

"Are you ready to get in there and cause some trouble?"

Ack-Ack Macaque held his cigar at arm's length, considering. Then he dropped it to the deck and ground it out with the toe of his boot.

"Yeah." He hopped up onto the bed beside her and rolled onto his back. "If it's the best way to hurt Céleste, then hook me in."

K8 shuffled close to his head as he made himself comfortable.

"I've been fiddling with the parameters," she said. "I think I've rigged it so you'll have unlimited ammo. Cool, huh?" Ack-Ack Macaque grinned, exposing his incisors.

"Can you make it so I can't die?"

K8 tipped her head on one side.

"I think you're almost immortal already. After all, why name the game after you if you can get killed off easily? There'd be no challenge."

Ack-Ack Macaque wriggled on the blanket, adjusting his position. K8 removed the goggles from the top of his head, and smoothed down the chestnut-coloured hair on his scalp.

"Maybe that's what happened with the other four monkeys," he said. "Maybe they got killed and had to be replaced?"

K8 shook her head.

"You don't die if you get wasted in the game. Not in the real world. You just get disconnected."

"So, the new version of me...?"

"He's just an uplifted monkey, same as you are, jacked into the game. He's probably in the same lab, in the same couch where they had you."

"But is he indestructible too?"

"Not entirely. Neither of you is. You're both just very, very hard to kill." She plugged the leads into the sockets on the edge of the SincPad. "So, I guess we're about to answer that age-old question."

"What question?"

She bent over him, sliding the other end of the cables, one by one, into the corresponding ports on the top of his head.

"The question of what happens when an irresistible force meets an immovable object."

*   *   *

EVERYTHING WENT BLANK. Then, half a second later, Ack-Ack Macaque found himself standing once more in the perpetual summer of a fictional 1944. This time, K8 had dropped him closer to the main action, behind a hangar on his old airbase.

Everything was exactly as he remembered it, from the acrid tang of engine grease to the feel of the warm tarmac beneath his bare feet. He drew his Colts. Nobody in sight. The main action was taking place at the end of the row of hangars, in the Officers' Mess. He could hear somebody hammering out a tune on the piano. Glasses clinking. Voices raised in laughter.

This had been his life for as long as he could remember. This field, that tent. Those planes on the runway. He felt his lips pull back from his teeth, exposing his canines.

Okay motherfuckers, he thought. *Time for a dose of reality.*

Keeping low, he loped from hangar to hangar, working his way towards the sounds of merriment. Was his replacement inside the tent? Some of the planes seemed to be missing from the runway. Perhaps he was, perhaps he wasn't. Ack-Ack Macaque paused at the corner of the final hangar, and tightened his grip on the Colts.

There was only one way to find out.

He licked his teeth, checking them for sharpness. Then, still hunched as low as possible, he scampered around to the front of the tent. When he got there, he straightened up as far as he could and, holding his gigantic silver revolvers high, kicked open the door.

Instantly, the piano music stopped. All the heads turned in his direction.

Same old crowd, he thought. Young, talkative and cavalier. His thumbs drew back the hammers on the Colts.

"Where's the monkey?" he snapped. They looked at him in puzzlement. Nobody spoke. From the corner of the tent, the cockney Mess Officer bustled towards him, all white jacket, slicked back hair and pencil moustache.

"Afternoon, squire. What can I get you? The usual, is it?"

Ack-Ack Macaque looked him up and down. The wide-boy patter never changed. The man was an obvious construct, part of the program. How come he'd never noticed before?

He pressed the barrel of one of the Colts to the Mess Officer's forehead, and pulled the trigger. The gun went off with a satisfyingly deafening bang, and red mist blew from the back of the man's head. But he didn't fall down. He stood there, holding his silver tray, looking stupid.

"Evenin' squire." His jaw flapped, caught in a loop. "Evenin' squire. Evenin' squire. Evenin' squire..."

Ack-Ack Macaque kicked him aside. The kids on the nearest tables were starting to get to their feet, their mouths half open in alarm, their eyes wide with surprise. He shot them all, one at a time. *Blam! Blam! Blam!* Heads and arms flopped. Men and women screamed. Blood flew everywhere, but he knew it meant nothing. None of these deaths were real, they were just a means to an end: a way of attracting the big guy's attention.

He reached out a hairy arm and grabbed an airman by the lapels.

"Where is he?" he snarled. The kid was seventeen or eighteen, with the first wispy suggestions of a goatee beard.

"I don't understand."

"The other monkey. Where is he?"

The kid's eyes rolled in his head.

"What other monkey?"

Ack-Ack Macaque leaned in close, bringing his teeth right up to the kid's cheek.

"There's another version of me. A new one. He's not here right now. *Where is he?*"

The kid wriggled in his grip.

"Took off about an hour ago, heading for the *Brunel*. But I thought that was you. What is this? What's happening?"

Ack-Ack Macaque released him, letting him drop to the rough wooden boards of the tent's floor.

"Things have changed," he said. "There's a new monkey in town. Tell your friends."

He turned on his heel and stalked out onto the runway. A few of the mechanics were loitering, disturbed by the sound of gunfire but unsure how to react. He plugged them all. What did it matter? None of them were really here.

He swarmed up the side of the nearest Spitfire. It wasn't his plane, but it would do. The seat would have been narrow for a man, but gave him plenty of room. He settled into position on the parachute pack and closed the pilot's door. Then he pulled closed and latched the canopy hood. He wound the rudder to full right, to counter the plane's torque, and pressed the starter buttons. The fuel pressure light came on and the engine coughed. The four-bladed prop spun into life, and the aircraft strained forward against its brakes.

Ack-Ack Macaque's large nostrils quivered with the smell of aviation fuel and hot metal. He saw survivors stumbling from the Officers' Mess, and pointed upward with his index finger.

"I'm going up," he called. "Get out of the way."

They looked at him with pale incomprehension, milling around in front of the plane. Frustrated, he switched to his middle finger. "Oh, up yours."

He took hold of the throttle and the plane leapt forward, scattering the onlookers like chickens. Laughing, and still waving his one-fingered salute, Ack-Ack Macaque taxied to the end of the runway. He hadn't bothered plugging his headset into the radio, so he couldn't hear the protestations of the tower. Instead, he fixed his eyes on the horizon and let out a piercing, fang-filled jungle screech.

This was it. This was him, where he'd always been. Where he'd always belonged: behind the joystick of a Spitfire, ready to take on the world.

And boy, was the world in trouble.

* * *

HALF AN HOUR later, high in the clear skies above Northern France, Ack-Ack Macaque gripped the stick of his Spitfire as the plane vibrated around him. Ahead, enemy fighters danced like gnats in his crosshairs, harrying a much larger, far more ponderous vessel.

Flagship of the Allies' aerial fleet, the aircraft carrier *Brunel* dominated the sky. With dimensions similar to one of its seagoing counterparts, it was easily the largest vessel in the European theatre. On its back, serried ranks of Nissen huts housed an entire squadron of single-seater Hurricane fighter-bombers. The planes were launched and recovered via a metal runway slung between the two over-sized, armoured airships that formed the bulk of the carrier's mass. The propellers of fifty Rolls Royce engines powered the beast, and gun emplacements bristled along its flanks and undercarriage.

Half a dozen German fighters were currently attempting to mount an attack on the carrier, but were being held at bay by three of the *Brunel*'s Hurricanes, and a solitary Spitfire.

Ack-Ack Macaque leant on the throttle, urging his plane higher. The air in the cockpit turned bitterly cold. His breath came in puffs of vapour, but he didn't care. It wasn't real cold, was it? Just an illusion, like everything else. He kept his attention on the dogfight unfolding before him, squinting to pick his adversary from the wheeling wings and chattering cannons of the British planes.

He saw a Messerschmitt fall from the fray, trailing smoke and flames, an aileron flapping loose. Above it, the Spitfire wheeled. Compared to the functional lines of its prey, it was as sleek as a hawk; and where its RAF roundels should have been, it sported a grinning, painted monkey's face.

"There you are." He pulled on the stick to give chase, ignoring the other planes. Coming up from beneath the fight, he hadn't yet been spotted by the other pilots. For now, he had the element of surprise.

Okay, he thought, let's hope the world's watching. He mashed the trigger button with his leathery thumb, and felt the rattle of the wing-mounted cannons. His shots caught his target across the underside of its fuselage, midway between the wings and rudder. He caught a glimpse as he hurtled past vertically, propeller clawing the thin air, and his plane threatened to stall. He pulled back, flipping the bird over onto its back. The yellow nose of a Messerschmitt lunged at him, but he rolled away from its attack, snarling.

"I should have dealt with them first," he muttered. "Too late now."

He looked around for the other Spitfire, and was alarmed to see it looping around behind him. Its guns blazed and he felt the bullets rip into his wings. Swearing silently, he kicked the rudder pedal and hauled the stick back to his hip, tipping the horizon over in a vertiginous rolling turn.

More impacts, like rocks on a tin roof. The seat convulsed beneath him. He pulled harder. German planes whirled across his view, zooming and banking, thrown into disarray, and he kept his thumb on the trigger, hoping to clear a few from the sky.

With merciless savagery, he threw his Spitfire from side-to-side, feinting one way and then another. Two more bursts hit him, but then he went left as his pursuer went right. Both planes screamed around in a banking turn that brought them face-to-face.

Ack-Ack Macaque fired, and saw the cannons on his counterpart's wings do likewise. The two planes were shredding each other. Bullets slammed into the cockpit around him. The propeller splintered. Invisible hammer blows shattered the windshield. But still he kept firing. Only when collision seemed unavoidable did he knock the stick sideways.

The air roared through his fur. He pulled his goggles down over his eyes and tried to turn for another attack. The engine spluttered ominously, releasing gouts of black smoke. Hot oil peppered his fur. The prop had been partially shattered and the stick felt sloppy in his hands.

Panicked and vulnerable, he scanned the skies for the other planes, only to see the German Messerschmitts circling at a distance, watching the duel in apparent confusion. For a few moments, he couldn't place the other Spitfire. Then it appeared from behind the great sausage shape of the *Brunel*'s starboard gasbag, trailing smoke. As he watched, the pilot brought its nose up just enough to make the lip of the metal runway, and the plane hit the deck like a pancake, slithering on its belly, skidding around and around until — like an injured wasp blundering into a spider's web — it was caught by the crash netting at the runway's far end.

Trying to get a better view, Ack-Ack Macaque pressed his face to the jagged remnants of his cockpit's canopy. For a moment, he dared to hope he'd been victorious. Then he saw a long-armed figure clambering from the wreck, and his lips peeled back in a snarl.

"You don't get away that easily, monkey boy!"

With its prop splintered, the stricken Spit juddered violently. The engine, freed from the drag of the blades, threatened to shake itself, and the plane, apart. Ack-Ack Macaque fought to keep the wings level as he tried to reach the runway of the carrier *Brunel*, suspended between the twin dirigibles which bore its weight, an off-centre control tower midway down its length like the funnel of a ship. He side-slipped, bringing the plane's nose into line with the crash netting at the runway's end, where his opponent's plane lay on its belly, smoke billowing from its shot-up engine.

K8 thought he was practically indestructible, and he hoped she was right, because this wasn't going to be the daintiest landing he'd ever made. The *Brunel* loomed larger and larger in his crosshairs, filling his forward view. He could see deck hands sprinting for cover. Pale faces at the windows of the control tower. At the last moment, he pulled his knees up to his chest and braced his feet against the dashboard. A wild scream filled his throat, and the Spitfire's prop buried itself in the metal deck at upwards of sixty miles per hour.

CHAPTER TWENTY-THREE
WINGSUIT

MEROVECH AND JULIE found themselves alone in one of the first class cabins, behind the dining room in the main gondola. They perched opposite each other, he on the edge of the bed, she on a chair by the nightstand.

The walls of the cabin were currently a blank, gunmetal grey, but the SincPad screens covering them offered a variety of augmented reality options, from the lush greens and plunging cliffs of Big Sur to the lone and level sands of the Egyptian desert, and he watched Julie's purple fingernail flick through the menu. As she scrolled, she said,

"I am sorry I got you into this."

Merovech leaned forward.

"You didn't get me into it. I was in it already, I just didn't know."

"But if I had not taken you on that raid—"

"You did me a favour. I had to find out sometime. If I hadn't gone along with you, I might never have known the truth. I might have gone back into that clinic one day and come back out as somebody else. In fact, I'm pretty sure you've saved my life."

"You say that, and yet you want to risk it all by going back there and confronting her?"

"I have to. Whatever else she is, she's still my mother."

The walls were still grey, like the inside of a battleship. Merovech felt a chill pass through him.

"But my father. He's not really my father at all."

"I am sorry. I know you loved him."

"I can hardly believe it." He shook his head, trying to clear it.

"I *am* sorry."

"But how could he not have known?"

"Why should he have done? Your mother simply lied to him. With Nguyen's help, she could have faked the pregnancy easily enough."

Merovech closed his eyes. His mother and father had always been distant figures, more so than the parents of most of the boys at his boarding school, and even as a young child, he'd come to understand that they were people to be visited rather than lived with. He'd left his nursery at four years old, and had never gone back. The school had been his home. And when he'd left there at eighteen, he'd gone straight into the army for a year's national service; and then on to university in Paris. School holidays aside, he hadn't lived under the same roof as his mother in over fifteen years.

He knelt before Julie.

"Okay, she grew me and lied to me and filled my head with gelware." He put his hands on her knees. "But what does that make *me*, Jules? What am I? Am I even human?"

Her eyes glittered. She reached a hand to cup his chin.

"Oh, Merovech. You are whoever you want to be. You are not to blame for any of this." She put a hand up to touch the fading bruise at the side of her eye. "Whatever our parents have done to us, it is not our fault. We did not ask for any of it. We have to think of ourselves now. We have to salvage whatever we can."

"No." Merovech climbed to his feet. "If I have to live with what she's done to me, the only way I can do so is by understanding *why* she did it."

"But you do not have to confront her. You could send her a message. Make a phone call."

"No. I want to hear her say it in person. I want to look into her eyes."

"But, the danger—"

He crossed his arms.

"Life's short, Jules. All we can do is make the best of it. I learned that lesson in the Falklands."

Julie wiped her face with the sleeve of her cardigan.

"Why don't you just stay here? The *Tereshkova* is going all the way to Mexico. We could go together, leave all this behind."

Merovech sighed.

"I've got one of the planet's most recognisable faces. Wherever I go, there'll always be somebody trying to dig up a story or take a picture. I can't run from this. And besides, I need to know why she's done what she's done."

Julie pushed up the sleeves of her grey wool cardigan, and then pulled them back down again.

"Please, Merovech."

He reached down and picked her hand from her lap. "I need to do this, Jules. I need answers. And the only way I'll get them is by facing up to her."

Julie's fingers pulled at his.

"Or you could just, you know, stay here, with me."

"I can't."

"But why not? If we go to South America, we can find a little place and start again, somewhere away from your mother. It will just be the two of us. No parents at all."

Merovech pursed his lips, enticing visions of white sand, grass huts and palm trees momentarily flickering, and then dying, behind his eyes.

"My mother owns one of the biggest technology companies on the planet. She's one of the world's richest women, and she has at her disposal the combined resources of the British and French secret services. Do you seriously think there's *anywhere* in this world she couldn't find us?" He pointed to his face. "And as I said, it's not like I can easily hide, is it?"

Julie pouted. She tapped the touch screen menu, and the grey walls flickered away, replaced by a view across Hong Kong harbour, taken from the hundredth floor of a hotel at dawn, with low red mist over the water and the skyscrapers shining like bronze spears. She looked at the view for a long time and then said:

"So, how are you planning to do it?"

At first, Merovech assumed the wall image to be a still photograph. The city and its surroundings seemed motionless, like a held breath at sunrise. Then his eye caught a small boat cutting through the water.

"I'm not sure. I need time to think."

He pulled off his hoodie. He'd been wearing the t-shirt beneath for three days now, and it stank. The Commodore's staff had left clean towels on the bed, and white robes hanging on a hook on the back of the cabin door. He picked up a towel.

"I'm going to take a shower." He reached for the door handle but, as he did so, a knock came from the other side. He pulled it aside to find Victoria Valois standing in the gangway with a large kit bag slung over her shoulder. She'd shed the heavy coat she'd been wearing when they met earlier, and was clad from toe to chin in black. She'd replaced her fleece hat with a long silk headscarf.

"We need to talk."

VICTORIA LED HIM up the metal steps and along the wire-supported walkways of the airship's interior, back up to the helipad at the top of the vessel. As he climbed out onto the springy black surface, the wind snatched at him like a thousand frozen fingers, and he rubbed his arms, wishing for his discarded hoodie.

"What can I do for you, Miss Valois?"

She gave a flick of her hand. "Please, call me Victoria." She walked to the rail at the forward edge and looked out, across the bows. The silk scarf streamed back from her head like a mare's mane.

"As we were in the hospital together," she said. "I just wanted to ask: now you know about Céleste, and what they did to you while you were in there, what are you planning to do about it?"

Beyond the curve of the airship's bow, Merovech could see the coast of Hampshire, with its submerged beaches and flooded harbours. He took a long breath in through his nose.

"I'm going to find a way to confront my mother. After that, I'm not sure."

"Would you like some help?"

He slid his fingers into the pockets of his jeans.

"No, thank you. This is about me. It's my problem, and it's up to me to fix it."

She turned to him, scarf whipping.

"What if it can't be fixed? This affects us both, Merovech. My husband worked for your mother's company, and they killed him for it. If there's a reckoning to be had, I want to be in on the action." She leant her hip on the rail and crossed her arms. "You're a smart kid, and you've done well to get this far. But what are you going to do, arrest her?"

Merovech shrugged. The thought had crossed his mind.

Victoria clicked her tongue.

"Forget it. She's surrounded by her own security people. Berg said she had members of the army supporting her. You wouldn't last five minutes. Remember, she tried to kill your father, and she's planning to kill you. Your personality, at least. If you try to tackle her alone, you'll be giving her exactly what she wants."

Merovech shivered. The cold air seemed to slice right through him.

"We're going to expose her," he said. "We're going to make the whole plot public. That's why we've hooked the monkey back into the game. We're going to use it to get the word out. These plots rely on power and secrecy. Once enough people know, we'll have the weight of numbers on our side. She can't run from the Internet."

Victoria let the kit bag slip from her shoulder, onto the deck. She said, "That won't be enough, I'm afraid. Not without concrete proof."

"Then what do you suggest?"

"Tomorrow's Unification Day. From what I can gather from the news channels, the Duchess will be celebrating it onboard her liner, the *Maraldi*, where she'll be supervising the launch of the Martian probe. The invited guests will include most of the people on the Commodore's list of the Undying. The King will be there too, moved by private ambulance, and, if what Berg implied is true, I don't give much for his chances of surviving the night."

At the mention of his father, Merovech let out a long breath.

"But why? She's been with him since the assassination attempt. Why hasn't she killed him already?"

"The timing has to be right. The death of a king isn't something you can easily cover up. She has to be sure her plan will work."

"But if I'm not there, she can't go ahead, can she?"

"Of course she can. She'll be worried about you going public, so she'll have to act now, and act fast. But my guess is that she'll stick to her original plan as far as possible. She'll declare you king, but tell everyone you're suffering from nervous exhaustion, or something like that. That way, when you do eventually surface, no-one's going to believe what you're saying, and she'll have an excuse to get you into the Céleste facility."

"So, we confront her there, in front of the television cameras?"

"Absolutely not. You stay here, your highness. We need you alive. If the King dies, you're the only one with a credible claim to the throne, and the gelware in your head's the only real evidence we have."

"So, what do you suggest?"

"I'll go in."

"By yourself?"

"I'll take the monkey. From what I hear, he's an expert at breaking into places and causing havoc."

"But how will you get in? That place will be locked down tight. You'd never get near it."

Victoria smiled. She crouched beside the kit bag and pulled out a suit made of black material. She shook it out and it flapped in the wind.

"Have you ever seen one of these before?" The suit had parachute-like flaps of material between the legs and under the arms. "It's called a 'wingsuit'. It's an extreme sport thing." She began folding it back up, wrapping it up in her arms. "We'll be at our closest approach to the ship tomorrow, around 6pm. This time of year, it will be dark. We can jump from here and glide in, silent and undetected."

"Then what?"

"I'm a journalist. I'll infiltrate the offices, look for as much proof as possible." She smiled. "And if all else fails, I'll let the monkey loose."

Merovech waved his hands.

"No, it's too dangerous. I can't let you do it."

Victoria's lips whitened. "I don't need your permission, Merovech. This is personal, for me and Paul. The only reason I'm talking to you at all is because we'll need your support if everything turns to shit." She stuffed the wingsuit back into its bag and pulled the heavy zipper closed. Then she stood, wiped her hands together, and put them on her hips.

"Find a camera when your father dies," she said. "Video, webcam, whatever, and make a speech. Claim the throne, expose your mother, and upload the files from K8's SincPad to the news channels. It's the only way to stop her."

Merovech swallowed something hot and sour.

"But I'm not the King's son. I'm not really in line."

Victoria stopped in her tracks. She looked him up and down, and her lips kinked in a half-smile.

"Well, you won't be the first bastard to seize power. But if I were you, I'd probably think twice before mentioning that on air, okay?"

THE COMMODORE INVITED her to join him on the *Tereshkova*'s bridge as he turned the old airship to the south-west, driving its five linked hulls into the teeth of the prevailing wind.

Honoured to be allowed back into this most inner of sanctums, Victoria leant up against the curved array of rectangular windows that formed the room's front wall. The grid of glass wrapped around to the sides, and swept down into the floor, providing maximum visibility for the three crew stations. Leaning up against its outward curve felt like leaning over the abyss; like flying. As the bows nosed around, she watched the beaches of Dorset's Jurassic Coast slide away to her right and, for the first time in days, felt her spirits rise, if only momentarily. Far to the left, the edge of Europe presented as a dark blue line against the horizon; and, straight ahead, she could see the hazy indigo waters of the Bay of Biscay.

On the bridge behind her, the pilot's and navigator's workstations were unoccupied and empty, and the Commodore had full control of the vessel.

The elderly Russian's skin seemed greyer than usual. His face held the washed-out sepia look of a photograph bleached by sunlight. The brass buttons of his jacket were unfastened, the sides held together only by the red sash that looped over his left shoulder and dropped to the empty scabbard on his right hip. Having instructed the flight computer to make the necessary course adjustments, the gnarled fingers of his hand lay on the keyboard of the SincPad set into the arm of his command couch. The other gripped the knee of his cavalry trousers.

"The sooner we are out over the Atlantic and away from Commonwealth airspace, the happier I will be." He gave her a look from beneath his brows. "You do realise that we are all fugitives now, don't you?"

Victoria pushed away from the concave glass wall. She said, "We're not the ones plotting a coup."

"Nevertheless, we are the ones harbouring an absconded prince, and a stolen monkey."

"They can't touch us here, though, can they?"

The old man looked grave.

"Ordinarily, no. Skyliners are neutral territory. But there has never been a situation quite like this one before. A claim for sanctuary from an ordinary criminal is one thing. A lost heir to the throne? That is something else again. Who knows what they might do to get him back? What they might be capable of?"

Victoria pushed her hands into the pockets of her long coat. "What can they do?"

"Berg said they would burn this ship from under us."

"Berg was a lunatic."

"He was also a dangerous man, Victoria, and I would not disregard any of his threats." The Commodore drummed his immaculately neat fingernails on the touchpad's glass. "As a matter of fact, that is one of the reasons I invited you here. I wanted to talk. Have you given any more thought to my offer?"

"To join your crew?"

"Yes. You have a knack for sniffing out trouble, and you have shown you can handle yourself. I could use a person with your talents."

"I'm flattered."

"Do not be. I simply state the facts. Up here, we have the freedom of the skies. But we are also a target for hijackers, smugglers and terrorists. I need you, Victoria. I need your nose for trouble."

Sunlight shimmered on the sea.

She said, "This thing with Paul—"

The old man raised a hand.

"You have to finish it. I understand matters of honour. But what will you do afterwards? Where else will you go?"

Hands still in her pockets, Victoria stepped away from the front wall.

"I hadn't given it much thought."

"Perhaps you should." He accessed one of the softscreens on the cabin wall and tapped up a headline from the BBC. "Especially as the police now think that you killed Constable Malhotra."

"Me?"

"Yes. I know it is bullshit, you know it is bullshit. But once the press got hold of it..." He waved exasperated hands at the black and white CCTV image of her that accompanied the story. "If you were a member of my crew, I could at least protect you."

Victoria's fingers brushed the padded headrest at the back of the empty pilot's couch. The air on the bridge seemed cooler than elsewhere on the ship. The rear bulkhead bore a plaque, listing the *Tereshkova*'s place of construction as the Filton Aeroplane Works in Bristol, England; its date of completion as June 15, 1980; and its original name as the *Great Western*.

Seventy-nine years old, she thought with a tiny shake of her head. These grand old ships. Their designers had been in love with romantic twentieth century notions of sea travel, from a time when transatlantic liners such as the *Mauretania* were a byword for luxury and speed. Now, those passengers rich and impatient enough to pay the carbon tax could opt to fly the supersonic airliners, while the rest still cruised the skies in the cramped elegance of a skyliner's cabin.

Looking back, she realised that the past six months she'd spent aboard the *Tereshkova* had been among the most settled she could remember. After university, her life had been one long whirl, constantly moving from job to job, from assignment to assignment. Paul had offered her a fleeting taste of stability, and she'd loved him for it; but their relationship had foundered on the rocks of his sexuality, and now he was dead, if not-quite gone, and nowhere else felt much like home anymore.

Her hand went out to touch the metal wall, its surface clogged beneath thickly accumulated layers of paint and memory. She thought of the changes it had been through, the people and places it had seen, and she felt a prickle of kinship. Like the *Tereshkova*, she'd travelled the world and, despite being battered and patched, clung to her identity. She'd done her time and plied her course, and here she still was, still toiling onwards when so many others had fallen by the wayside. A lifetime of constant travel. Every day different, every day the same. Nothing to hold either of them anywhere. No baggage, no regrets. Just the wide open sky and the shimmering horizon.

"Okay, I'll do it. I'll take the job." In her pocket, the knuckles of her hand brushed the haft of the retracted quarterstaff. "But first, I need you to do something for me."

CHAPTER TWENTY-FOUR
HEROICS OF YOUTH

ACK-ACK MACAQUE LAY in a foetal position amidst the scrambled, burning fragments of his shattered plane, and laughed. He wrapped his arms around his knees and rocked back and forth. Fires smouldered around him. Thick, greasy roils of smoke filled the sky above him like greedy fingerprint smudges on a blue vase. And he was alive! He'd slammed his delicate, beautiful fighter into an iron deck at sixty miles an hour and survived with only a few cuts and scratches and some singed fur. He was alive, and as indestructible as a god. The laugh gurgled in his throat.

"You were right, K8. You were right." His goggles were missing a lens. He pushed them up onto the top of his head. All those missions, all those desperate fights and daring escapes—he could have walked though them all with his head held high, and still prevailed.

He sat up, dislodging a shower of broken glass from his flight jacket. The air stank of spilled aviation fuel. His adversary's plane lay enmeshed in crash netting at the far end of the runway, some hundred metres from where he sat, in the shadow of the conning tower. Brushing himself down, he climbed to his feet, reached into his jacket for a cigar, and lit it.

Here was where it would happen. He would kill or be killed and, if K8 was right, the world would know.

With the cigar clamped securely in place, he shuffled towards the other wreck, leathery fingers curling and uncurling above the holsters strapped to his thighs, ready to draw at the slightest provocation. He bore no malice to his replacement. The monkey didn't know it was being used any more than he had. It would unquestioningly accept the world it found around itself as real, and play along accordingly. If anything, he pitied it.

The remaining Messerschmitts circled overhead like vultures, sensing death on the wind. Other planes had joined them, but none were fighting. They were waiting to see what he would do. He gave them the finger.

"Enjoy the show, creeps." Although they didn't know it yet, they'd had all the entertainment they were going to get from him. The game was over. This was the end. Gotterdammerung. The end of the war, and the end of this world.

Ahead, a figure ducked under the wing of the Spit caught in the nets. When it stood upright, he saw it had short, bowed legs and long, dangling arms. The jacket it wore was identical to his, but the creature had no eye patch, and looked younger than he did, with fewer wrinkles around its eyes and snout. A silk scarf fluttered at its neck. It carried a bazooka at its hip, and spare shells dangled from its waist.

"Who are you supposed to be?" The creature's voice lacked the gravel of cigars and rum, and Ack-Ack Macaque felt the hackles prickle between his shoulder blades. His thumbs hooked over the tops of his holsters.

"Be careful who you're staring at, boy."

The bazooka shifted. Lips slid back from sharp, pointed teeth.

"Or what?"

Ack-Ack Macaque rolled his cigar from one side of his mouth to the other. The younger monkey's eyes and stance betrayed the cheap heroics of youth, as yet unscathed by the endless, grinding procession of dogfights and lost comrades. He hadn't yet had time to become bitter, to start questioning his place in the war and the world.

"Because I'm you, you idiot. At least, an older, less sanitised version of you."

"What are you talking about?"

Ack-Ack Macaque drummed his fingers against the butts of his Colts.

"What's your name?"

"Ack—"

"Yeah, mine too. What's your real name? Can you remember?"

The younger monkey let its mouth open and shut. Its tail twitched like a snake caught under a car tyre.

"They used to—"

"Yes?"

"Teiko. They used to call me Teiko."

"Well, look around you, Teiko. The sky, the clouds. None of this is real."

The younger monkey's eyes didn't move. The insolence of his stare bordered on direct physical challenge, and it was all Ack-Ack Macaque could do not to scream and leap in response.

The bazooka barrel wavered.

"It seems real enough to me," Teiko said. "Now, talk. Tell me who you really are."

"I am telling you, you're just not listening." Ack-Ack Macaque pulled himself up to his full height. "I used to be a character in a video game. Then I got out, into the real world, and they replaced me with you. You're me, but with all the rough edges sanded off. You're the reboot. You're younger and you don't smoke. I bet you don't even drink, do you?"

The other primate's lips slid back from its teeth.

"I have no idea what you're talking about. Just tell me whose side you're on. Ours," his eyes flicked up at the circling Messerschmitts, "or theirs."

Ack-Ack Macaque took the cigar from his mouth and said, "There are no sides anymore. That's what I'm saying. All this, everything you see and feel and touch. All this is a game, an illusion, and you're not really here. You're lying on a couch in a laboratory with wires sticking into your brain."

Teiko made an agitated, chattering noise.

"You don't believe me? Then ask yourself why those German planes aren't attacking. Ask yourself how I crashed my Spitfire into the deck and climbed out unhurt."

"Shut up!" The bazooka barrel began to shake.

"It's not luck that's kept you alive, Teiko, it's the game. You're hard to kill because you're the main character. You're the one on the box. The one with your face on mugs and t-shirts and who-knows-what other crap."

"I said, *shut up*."

Ack-Ack Macaque screwed the cigar back into place. His hands dropped to his thighs, and he closed his fingers around the handles of his revolvers. All he had to do was draw and fire.

"Why don't you try to make me?"

"I'll kill you."

"No, you won't."

The younger monkey raised the bazooka to shoulder height, ready to fire.

"Do you want to make a bet?"

Ack-Ack Macaque grinned around the soggy end of his cigar.

"Do you want to suck my balls?"

They held each other's stare, their fangs bared in challenge. The moment stretched. The very air between them seemed to shimmer.

Come on, you bastard. Come on.

Ack-Ack Macaque saw his opponent's eyes start to water. Leathery fingers squeezed the bazooka's trigger. Smoke and flames blew from both ends, and Ack-Ack Macaque pitched himself sideways, as out flew a shell the size of a small freight train. He shoulder-rolled across the deck, and came up with the Colts gripped in his hands, his trigger fingers squeezing for all they were worth. Bullets spinged and spanged from the wrecked Spit's bodywork. Teiko dropped the bazooka and lunged. Ack-Ack Macaque tried to plug him, but the guns seemed to twist away, the game unwilling to allow a fatal shot.

They crashed together and rolled, scratching, gouging and biting; trying to rip out each other's throats. Teeth snapped, and Ack-Ack Macaque felt hot breath against the side of his face. He let the guns fall away and reached for the blade in his boot. If bullets wouldn't work, he'd have to do it the traditional way, with an old school monkey knife fight.

AMSTERDAM, FEBRUARY 2054. A shabby and poorly-lit warehouse by the waterfront. Stacked crates contain smuggled Armenian cigarettes, repurposed Japanese laptops and knock-off German porn. Dormant fork-lifts block the aisles like sleeping sentry robots. The air smells of blood, sawdust and monkey shit. In the centre of the room, lights hanging from the ceiling illuminate a makeshift ring: a circle of hay bales, and the crowd around it. Bets are taken, fistfuls of money are exchanged.

Ack-Ack Macaque stands panting in the ring, a cutthroat razor clasped in his hand. His forearm has been stained red and sticky to the elbow. He's bleeding from a dozen cuts, but he doesn't care. This is all he knows. The ring is his world, the fight his life.

At his feet, a flea-bitten chimp lies quivering. Thick ropes of blood pump from its slashed throat. Floating specks of sawdust spin and clump in the spreading puddle. The crowd are shouting. Some are incensed, others aroused. He doesn't know the chimp's name; and after four straight fights, he's not entirely sure of his own. It certainly isn't Ack-Ack Macaque. That name comes later, far from here, in a laboratory outside Paris. Right now, his nostrils quiver with the stench of sweat and pheromones. His arms shake with fatigue.

He looks down at his former opponent, in time to see the chimp rattle its last. The poor creature stops struggling. Its body goes slack and its bowels let go, adding to the stink and mess on the concrete floor.

Somewhere in the crowd, a woman watches. She works on behalf of an agency, which works in turn for Céleste. She's been looking to procure a monkey with character and fighting spirit, and now she's smiling. He's won four straight fights. There are scars all over his body, and a filthy, yellowing bandage covering the gouged ruins of his suppurating left eye: he couldn't be more perfect. Without taking her eyes from him, she reaches into her elegant Parisian shoulder bag to retrieve a white, platinum-sheathed SincPhone. Her fingernails speed-dial a number, and she puts the phone to her ear.

Meanwhile, unaware of her scrutiny, Ack-Ack Macaque folds away his razor and shambles over to his owner and screeches at him. His owner is a skinny Malaysian with bad teeth and dark sweat patches beneath the arms of his linen jacket. In response to his inarticulate screeches, the man hands him his reward: a lit cigarette. The bitterness of the smoke clears the lingering stench of the dead chimp's dung. The nicotine makes his head swim. He chatters happily to himself, perching on the edge of a wooden pallet in order to savour every breath.

He hardly notices when the smartly-dressed woman steps from the crowd with a fistful of money, and makes his owner the kind of offer it would be extremely foolhardy to refuse.

TEIKO SQUIRMED BENEATH him, but Ack-Ack Macaque had the weight of experience. They were perilously close to the edge of the deck, but he didn't care. He knew he couldn't die, not really. This was all illusion: he had nothing to lose. Using all his strength, he pulled his rival towards the abyss.

"Stop struggling," he growled. The younger monkey didn't listen. He let out a howl and tried to sink his teeth into Ack-Ack Macaque's arm. Ack-Ack Macaque slapped him. "Shut up. I have something to say."

He pushed away and rose to his feet. Teiko blinked up at him, wary as any cornered animal.

"We both have to die," Ack-Ack Macaque told him. "We have to show them that this is all bullshit. This is all fake. The kids playing this game think you're some kind of high tech computer intelligence, but you're just a monkey with a computerised brain, same as I am." He turned and walked a few steps back towards the conning tower. He raised his arms to the circling planes above and raised his voice. "The people at Céleste are lying to you! They've lied to us all! They're planning to take over—"

Pain lanced his thigh, sharp and unexpected. He squealed and fell, and Teiko was on him, the blade of his knife now sticky with Ack-Ack Macaque's blood. Ack-Ack Macaque raised his arm to block a second slash, and cried out again as he felt steel bite though his sleeve, into skin and muscle.

Damn it, he thought, *I wasn't finished!*

He reached around and grabbed the younger monkey by the back of his leather jacket. With all his strength he heaved upwards, lifting his opponent just enough to give him room to twist his hips sideways, throwing Teiko off balance.

They rolled over together, gripping each other's stabbing arms. Deadlocked.

"Let go, you moron."

Teiko's teeth snapped at his face.

"I'll kill you!"

"No, you fucking won't." Ack-Ack Macaque tried to wrench his arm free from the younger monkey's grip. "I always win. That's all there is to it."

Teiko laughed, fierce and mad. "Look at your arm, grandpa. You're bleeding."

The sudden pang of doubt was as intense as the pain from his stab wounds. In all his years, Ack-Ack Macaque had never been injured like this. He'd survived dozens of plane crashes with only cuts and bruises; legions of German ninjas had yet to lay a blade on him; and yet this young upstart had already stuck him twice, once through the leg and once through the arm. For the first time in his life, he felt truly unsure. He had no idea what would happen next. He'd assumed this would be a simple monkey smack-down. A bit of a scuffle between near-immortals. But now, locked in Teiko's fighting embrace, he understood that—in the game at least—he was caught in a fight to the death. When it was done, he might wake up on the *Tereshkova* with K8; but in the meantime, he'd feel every stab, every slash and bite. He'd become used to the painless violence of the game; but this was Amsterdam all over again. If Teiko got the better of him, it would *really* hurt.

Well, he thought, *fuck that.*

They might share an implanted core personality, but Teiko was younger, and therefore less experienced. He was so busy trying to get his knife into Ack-Ack Macaque's neck that he'd left his face exposed. Their noses were practically touching, close enough that Ack-Ack Macaque could smell the sickening sweetness of his breath.

A quick butt to the face. Teiko yelped, rolling away. His hands flew to his crushed nose, and Ack-Ack Macaque pounced. Straddling the younger monkey, he used both hands to drive the blade of his knife straight through Teiko's throat. The blade slid through flesh and gristle until it hit the spinal column. Teiko's legs thrashed. Ack-Ack leaned his full weight on the pommel of the knife. He felt the vertebrae part, and the tip punch through, into the metal of the *Brunel*'s flight deck. Teiko let out a wheezing, bubbling moan, and shook spastically.

And then he was still, and it was all over.

Ack-Ack Macaque clambered to his feet. The high altitude wind blowing across the carrier seemed to freeze the very marrow of his bones, and a strange, desolate sadness welled up from the core of his belly.

Teiko was dead. He'd just killed the closest thing in the world that he had to a brother. And damn Céleste for making him do it. Damn them for making him *at all*!

Looking over the edge of the carrier's deck, he spat into the void.

"The people at Céleste are in bed with the cult of the Undying," he said, voice gruff and flat. K8 had told him that in the past, thousands of people had watched recordings of his adventures in the game. He hoped someone was recording this right now. "They're behind the attack on the King. They're trying to use Merovech to plunge Europe into martial law. Don't trust them! Don't let them—"

The world convulsed. The sky flickered like the eyelids of a dying ape, and everything went white.

ACK-ACK MACAQUE BLINKED. Blinded by the flash, he rubbed his walnut-like knuckles into his eyes. When he lowered them, he found himself back in the cramped passenger cabin, on board the *Tereshkova*, with K8.

He was out of the game. Back in the real world—whatever that meant.

He smacked his lips. His arm and leg were uninjured, and free of stab wounds.

"What happened?"

K8 reached over and began to remove the wires from his head.

"Céleste panicked," she told him. "They shut down the game servers."

BREAKING NEWS

From *The London & Paris Times*, online edition:

Party Like It's 2059

28 NOVEMBER 2059 – Tomorrow, the peoples of Great Britain, France and Norway will celebrate 100 years of political and cultural togetherness.

Celebrations start at dawn, with a druidic ceremony at Stonehenge, and the lighting of a string of hilltop beacons, from the Falkland Islands in the south, to the ancient town of Hammerfest in Norway.

The day will climax with a concert in Hyde Park and simultaneous firework displays in London, Edinburgh, Paris, Cardiff, Belfast and Oslo.

The celebrations come almost exactly a year after the attempted assassination of King William V, and police in all cities will be on high alert, determined to prevent further atrocities. Roadblocks have been set up in a number of major cities, and key members of known regionalist and republican protest groups have been pre-emptively detained.

Although still in a coma, the King is expected to symbolically participate in the celebrations. An air ambulance will move him to the luxury liner *Maraldi*, owned by his wife, Her Grace, Alyssa Célestine, Duchess of Brittany. The liner will be anchored in the English Channel, midway between Britain and France. Once on board, his majesty will be present to 'witness' a celebratory fireworks display and, via satellite from the mid-Atlantic, the launch of the UK's first Martian probe.

Read more | Like | Comment | Share

Related Stories

Tensions rise as Chinese warships capture the crew of a British patrol boat

Weather conditions "ideal" for launch of Martian probe

Centenary concert will "reflect a century of musical cross-pollination"

Millions of users left angry as Céleste Tech pulls plug on smash-hit game

Stock market falls amid fears of Chinese export ban

"Nuclear doomsday clock" moved one minute closer to midnight

Police use water cannons to break up anti-war demos in Paris

90 years of the Internet: the anniversary of the first ARPANET link

Fears for future of Nanda Devi Biosphere Reserve as troops clash in fresh fighting along disputed border

Cease and desist: Céleste Tech lawyers threaten legal reprisals against fans posting online Macaque videos

Prank blamed for monkey outburst

CHAPTER TWENTY-FIVE
REPLICANT ZOMBIE

VICTORIA STOOD AT the head of the dining table in the *Tereshkova*'s main lounge, her hands resting on the curved steel back of a chair.

"So, we're in agreement?"

Merovech and Julie sat to her right; the Commodore and K8 to her left. The monkey perched at the far end, chomping on an unlit cigar.

Merovech's fingers traced circles on the polished wood.

"And you're sure she's planning a coup?"

"As sure as we are about anything right now."

"Then you have my vote. She needs to be stopped."

Julie Girard put her hand on his arm.

"Are you sure? Even after everything we have seen, she is still your mother."

Merovech covered her hand with his. He raised his eyes to Victoria.

"You have to prevent her from killing my father."

"We'll do our best."

On the other side of the table, the Commodore harrumphed.

"I still don't like it. It all seems far too dangerous. Why do you have to go down there, onto her ship? Why can't you stay up here and let the Prince broadcast to the nation?"

Victoria shook her head.

"Because I don't think it would work. We've been through this. K8 and our monkey friend have put the word out to the gaming community. Hopefully that will build. But the Duchess has already put out a story that Merovech's had some kind of nervous breakdown. If he starts posting videos on the web, it will be easy for the media to dismiss them as paranoid fantasies." She let go of the chair and straightened her back. "The macaque videos are going viral. If we're going to capitalise on the publicity, the only way will be to do something direct, and public."

The old man fingered his moustache.

"I'm still not clear what you plan to do if, and I mean if, you get aboard."

"I'm a journalist. If there's a shred of proof on that tub, I'll find it. And then we'll confront her."

"In front of the television cameras?"

"Ideally, yes."

"And what if the TV cameras ignore you? This woman, she has great influence, yes?"

Victoria smiled. She inclined her head to the far end of the table, where Ack-Ack Macaque sat with his feet up, a fingernail worrying at something caught between his front teeth.

"Trust me, *nobody's* going to ignore him."

The Commodore crossed his arms. Gold braid glimmered at his wrists.

"Bah. I still do not like it. But, as always, you have my support."

"Thank you. Merovech, are you ready to speak to the nation when the time comes?"

"K8's patched us into a satellite feed. As soon as we get your signal, we can start broadcasting."

"Do you know what you're going to say?"

"No, but I'm sure it will come to me."

Victoria rubbed her hands together. In the corner of her eye, she could see Paul's image.

"How about you?" she asked.

He scratched his ear.

"You know me, Vicky. In for a penny, in for a pound."

"Okay, then."

She looked at the faces around the table.

"Make no mistake, if we fail at this, we'll be tried as traitors. That means lengthy jail sentences, or worse."

Merovech untangled himself from Julie and rose to his feet.

"Thank you," he said, holding out his hand for her to shake. Victoria shook her head instead.

"Don't thank me yet. I told you, I'm not a royalist. I'm not doing this for you. I'm doing it for Paul."

"I understand. But, thank you anyway."

At the other end of the table, Ack-Ack Macaque pulled the wet, flattened cigar butt from his yellow teeth.

"Yap, yap, yap. So we've all got a stake in this. That's why we're here. Can we get on and do something now? 'Cos personally speaking, I'm pissed off and I want to break stuff and hurt people."

Victoria smiled, lips tight and thin. With her brain locked into planning mode, her thoughts rang with the crisp, bell-like clarity of spring morning.

She clapped her hands.

"*Ecoutez-moi bien.* Okay, we've got a few hours. Merovech, you carry on jotting down ideas for your speech. *Julie, tu l'aides.* And you, monkey man, you're with me."

Ack-Ack Macaque took his feet off the table.

"Where are we going?"

"To the armoury."

THE COMMODORE LED them aft, past the kitchens and staff quarters, to the armoury, located adjacent to the brig, as far from the passenger cabins and public areas as possible.

The door opened to a sixteen digit pass code typed into a keypad set into the bulkhead. The lock clunked, and the steel door swung aside.

Inside, the armoury was about the size of a cheap hotel bathroom. Weaponry lined the walls: police shotguns; long-range sniper rifles; handheld rail guns; a box of grenades. Even a pair of classic Kalashnikovs. The old man gestured like a conjuror.

"Is there anything here that will be of use to you?"

Looking around at the racks, Ack-Ack Macaque widened his one good eye. He rubbed his leathery hands together and his tongue lolled out in a toothy grin.

"How about, all of it?"

He pulled a chrome-plated revolver from one rack and a grenade launcher from another, and turned to Victoria with one in each hand.

"What do you think?"

Victoria looked him up and down, taking in not only the weapons but also his jacket, half-eaten cigar and leather skull cap. A few days ago, she'd have balked at the idea of a talking monkey—especially one with a gun in each hand. Now, when she looked at the macaque, she saw something of herself in it. Neither of them would be alive were it not for the invasive experiments of Doctor Nguyen. And now, together, they were going to get their revenge.

"You'll do."

LATER, BACK IN her cabin, she stood in front of the mirror with her head bare. Her wig and hat lay on the bottom bunk, with the boxes and strewn clothes that made up the entirety of her earthly possessions. The mirror had a simple pine frame, and had been fixed to the wall by two screws. In its reflective surface, the face she saw squinting back at her was that of her younger self, as she'd looked a year ago, recovering from the surgery that had saved her life. Since then, she'd grown used to having hair again, and having lost it for a second time, her head seemed disproportionately small. The scar ridge stood out from her temple, the exposed metal jacks shining like rivets. Her fingers brushed them, one at a time.

What was she? Without the surgery, she would have died. But the surgery had removed over half her brain, so in some senses, perhaps she *had* died. She couldn't survive now without the gelware, there wasn't enough of her left. Over sixty per cent of her brain had been replaced. Was the remainder enough to claim continuity? Could she still say she was the person she'd once been, or had she become a reanimated ghost, a replicant zombie with delusions of humanity? Certainly, the things she'd done over the past two days would have petrified and repulsed her former self.

Had she really killed a man? In the emotionally-detached serenity of command mode, the action of closing the doors on Berg had seemed logical, perhaps even easy. And even now, she was still half sure it had been the right thing to do.

She glared at her reflection. He'd had it coming. What did she have to feel guilty about? The Smiling Man had tried to kill her twice, and he'd killed her stupid husband. She hadn't asked for any of it. Berg had come barging into her life, just as she'd been starting to piece it back together, and wrecked it all over again. He'd deserved everything he'd gotten, and his employers, Céleste Industries and the Cult of the Undying, deserved a whole lot more. She touched the side of her head again. They'd turned her into this ugly cyborg creature. And not only her, but also Prince Merovech and Ack-Ack Macaque. In their laboratories, Nguyen and his team had built three deeply traumatised and dysfunctional creatures, convinced each of them that it was real, and then launched them, one-by-one, out into the world.

Her lips hardened into a thin line. Well, to hell with them all. Had they learned nothing from *Frankenstein*? She picked an automatic pistol from the pile of weaponry on the top bunk and checked the magazine. The firearm felt heavy and cold in her hand.

The creatures were coming home.

CHAPTER TWENTY-SIX
SLAVE ARMY

K8 CAME TO Merovech's cabin. She had her arms crossed and a scowl on her freckled face.

"We've lost access to the Internet, so there's not much I can do. Now that Ack-Ack Macaque's been thrown out of the game, I feel like a spare part."

From the bunk, Julie gave a tired smile. "Tell me about it. Merovech has gone to the library to work on his speech, and I am sitting here going crazy."

"Aye, you and me both, then, is it?"

"It seems that way."

K8 put her hands on her hips.

"Hey, I hear tell that you hacked your way into the Céleste servers, too. You must be kind of handy with a computer, eh?"

Julie laughed. She'd thought she had some skills but, compared to this freckled Scottish kid, she was really just an amateur.

"Still," K8 continued, "there's some pretty scary shit in those files, yeah?"

Julie swung her legs off the bunk. "I did not see much. As soon as I found the documents on Merovech, I hit print and went to find him."

"Ah, you were lucky." K8 scratched her short, carroty hair. "I had a good root around and I found all kinds of things. Plans for stuff straight out of your worst nightmares."

"Like what?"

"Compulsory back-ups. Soul-catchers fitted to everyone, by force if necessary."

Julie made a face.

"I would not want one."

"You wouldn't have any choice. If Célestine takes the throne, she'll order laws to make it a criminal offence not to have a catcher implanted. It's basic Undying philosophy: back everything up so nothing gets lost. They have plans for a storage facility in a bunker beneath their laboratories in Paris. If war breaks out with China, they want to have saved as many backed-up personalities as possible before the bombs start falling."

Julie stood. She rubbed her arms as if cold.

"It all sounds ghastly."

"That isn't the worst of it."

"No?"

"From what I read in those files, I think the Undying are trying to deliberately provoke the Chinese. I think they want a war."

"*Putain-de-merde!* Why would anyone want to start a nuclear war?" Julie's mind flashed to the horror stories her grandfather had told her. He'd grown up in the 1980s, as Soviet Russia squared off against the European Commonwealth, and his teenage memories were filled with the anxiety of seemingly inevitable apocalypse, when the best a young man could hope for was to be incinerated in the first few seconds of an exchange, rather than surviving to face a lingering death from sickness or starvation. She shivered. Surely the governments of the world had learned from the Cold War, and the insanity of Mutually Assured Destruction? "I thought they wanted Mars. So why would they kill everyone on Earth?"

K8 bit her lip.

"Well, what if they're planning to do the same on Earth as they are on Mars?"

"Which is?"

"Download all the backed-up minds into android bodies, like Berg's, and take over."

"That is crazy!"

"Is it? Androids don't worry about radiation or lack of food. With China and Europe flattened, there'd be no-one to stop them rebuilding and taking over. The Duchess would have the world at her feet, and a perfect slave army do to her bidding." She stopped talking. Julie looked at her with her mouth hanging open.

"That is horrible." Framed by her purple hair, her face seemed paler than usual.

"Are you okay?" K8 asked.

Julie swallowed.

"I really need a cigarette." She puffed air from her cheeks. "Do you have any?"

"I don't smoke."

"I did not think so." She pulled herself upright. "Okay. First things first. We must tell Merovech, and the others. We must get them all to read those files of yours. They all need to know the stakes for which we are playing."

"Do they?" K8 shuffled her feet. "Because it seems to me they're under enough pressure. Victoria and the monkey, they're both pretty strung out right now. I don't know if they could cope."

"So what? We say nothing?"

K8 thought about it. "I suppose we could tell Merovech, if you wanted to. He should know, I guess. We could let him make the decision."

"He is in the library."

"So you said."

Julie straightened her t-shirt and hitched up her jeans.

"Then let us go and see him." She moved to step past K8, but as she reached for the cabin's door, an alarm sounded. Both girls jumped.

"*Putain!*" Julie swore. "What now?"

CHAPTER TWENTY-SEVEN
INCANDESCENT JUNGLE FURY

THE THREE HELICOPTERS came from the north-east in the late afternoon. Standing on the *Tereshkova*'s bridge, Victoria watched their progress on one of the wall-mounted display screens.

"Do you think they'll try shooting at us?"

In his chair, the Commodore shook his silver head. The top buttons of his tunic were undone.

"No. If they really wanted to kill us, they would have sent jets. It would be faster. My guess is, this is a boarding party. They want the young prince intact, yes?"

"What can we do?"

"Very little. Our radio transmissions are being blocked, so we can't tell anyone or call for help. We could alter course, but they are smaller and more manoeuvrable."

"You have anti-piracy weapons."

"Yes. But to use them would be a declaration of war. Better, I think, to let *them* make the first move."

TEN MINUTES LATER, as the swollen orange sun dipped low in the afternoon sky, Victoria stood at the edge of the landing pad atop the *Tereshkova*'s central hull, her quarterstaff extended to its full length, and her pistol pushed into the pocket of her army coat. The wind chilled her naked scalp. Behind her stood a shifting mob of the airship's stewards, flak jackets and helmets strapped over their white tunic uniforms, each of them self-consciously cradling a rail gun or pistol from the armoury. Beside her, the Commodore stood, the white tails of his dress uniform fluttering, the gnarled fingers of his right hand resting on the pommel of his cutlass.

Together, they watched the helicopters crest the edge of the gas bag, circling in like piranhas, their flanks painted with the eye-twisting black and white stripes of dazzle camouflage— geometric patterns designed to conceal their exact shape and size. Through their open sides, Victoria saw machine gun-toting, black-clad troops ready to deploy the moment the wheels hit the deck.

In the corner of her eye, Paul's image twitched.

"I don't like the look of this," he said.

Victoria took a firmer grip on the staff.

"Shut up," she told him.

He gave her an offended look.

"Don't forget whose neural-ware I'm running on. If you get killed, that's me dead too."

"And there I was thinking you were concerned for my wellbeing."

"I am! Of course I am. But we're in this together now. If you get killed, we both die."

The lead 'copter came in low, presenting its belly as it dropped. Victoria leaned into the downdraught.

"You're already dead. Now, get out of my head and keep quiet. I need to concentrate."

She raised the staff into a defensive position and ran through a mental litany of her opponents' most vulnerable points: ankles, knees, throats and wrists. A quarterstaff wouldn't be much use in a firefight, but at close quarters, it could be deadly. And in the meantime, she had the pistol. As the helicopter kissed the pad, she reached into her pocket and, heart beating in her chest, closed her fist around the gun's cold butt. Whatever else she'd been, she'd never been a soldier. Even in the Falklands, she'd only ever reported from the sidelines of the fighting.

This close, the helicopter's engines were deafening. Black figures spilled from its hatches, taking up positions on either side, wearing thick flak jackets, gas masks and combat helmets.

An officer stepped forward with a salute.

"Commodore, I am Captain Summers of His Majesty's Special Air Service, and you are hereby required to hand over the Prince of Wales, His Royal Highness, Prince Merovech." The gas mask's eyes were convex blisters of glass. They turned in her direction. "And the fugitive and murder suspect, Victoria Valois. Failure to comply with either request will result in the use of deadly force."

The Commodore's medals jangled as he drew himself up. Beneath his bushy brows, his eyes glowered like coals.

"I have to inform *you*, Captain, that you are in breach of international law, specifically those treaties concerning the independence and autonomy of individual skyliners. Any attempt to use force against a passenger or member of my crew will be considered an act of piracy, and responded to accordingly."

The other two helicopters circled at a safe distance, rotors chopping the sky, out of range of small arms fire, but close enough for the snipers on board to draw a bead on anyone who tried to draw a weapon.

The butterflies churning in Victoria's stomach threatened to force their way up through her chest and throat, and out into the open air. Sensing her agitation, the gelware tried to push even more adrenalin into her bloodstream, and she had to concentrate hard in order to stop her arms from shaking. Against the metal of the staff, her palms were slick.

The Captain and the Commodore glared at each other: a heavily armoured, bug-eyed shock trooper trying to stare down an old fashioned man of honour carrying only a sword.

"I'm sorry, Commodore, but this really is your last chance. I have been authorised to take whatever steps are necessary to recover the Prince."

"The Prince has requested asylum aboard this vessel and, as such, I am legally obligated, by the terms of the applicable treaties, to protect him."

The wind blew colder. The troopers around the helicopter were as immobile as statues, their black, snub-nosed submachine guns trained on the Commodore's crew.

"My orders are quite specific, Commodore."

"As is my resolve, *Captain*. Now, I am asking you politely to please leave my vessel."

Captain Summers lowered his mask.

"You can't hope to prevail. Your crew will be slaughtered. Please, Commodore, stand down and let me do my job."

The Commodore frowned. He looked from the soldiers to his own men, then up at the twin helicopters circling the pad; and, for the first time, Victoria saw a shiver of doubt in his eyes. He turned to her.

"Perhaps you should go below?"

She shook her head. She'd be damned if she'd let him fight her battles.

"I'm not going anywhere."

Summers cleared his throat.

"Time's up, Commodore. Please, stand aside." He raised his pistol. Behind him, his troopers tensed into firing positions, the barrels of their weapons covering everyone on the pad.

Victoria tasted sick at the back of her throat, and swallowed it back. The Commodore's men were hopelessly outgunned. The fight would last seconds, and there would be few, if any, survivors. Her fingers squeezed the stock of the pistol in her pocket, but she didn't dare draw it. To do so would call down the ire of the snipers circling above.

This was going to be a bloodbath.

Summers said, "I'm going to count to three."

As the sun moved ever lower, the sky behind him had taken on a purple aspect.

"One."

Victoria transferred her weight from one boot to the other. If she overclocked herself again, could she draw her pistol fast enough to make a difference? Paul's image cowered in the corner of her eye, nervously chewing the fingers of one hand.

"Two."

She felt the wind against her exposed scalp. Even this far up, it smelled of the sea.

"Thr—"

"Halt!"

The voice was Merovech's. He climbed from a hatchway at the edge of the pad and strode forward, between the two opposing forces.

"Tell your men to stand down, Captain."

Summers lowered his gun and threw the prince a stiff salute.

"I'm afraid I can't do that, sir. My orders are detailed and specific, and—"

"Do you know who I am?"

"Yes sir, of course, sir. But my orders are to get you on that chopper. Right away, sir."

Merovech thrust his chin forward. "And if I refuse?"

Summers raised his pistol again.

"Then I'm afraid I'll have to insist, sir."

Victoria saw Merovech blink in surprise, eyes trying to focus on the end of the gun barrel. For a split second, Summers seemed to be about the pull the trigger.

And then everything changed.

Gunshots rang out. One of the orbiting helicopters dropped away, bullet holes stitched across its windshield, the pilots slumped forward against their controls. Victoria threw herself forward onto the pad's yielding rubber surface. She heard cries, and saw members of the Commodore's crew scattering, running for cover. But the troopers weren't firing at them; they had other things to worry about. In amongst them, cutting through their ranks, came a blur of incandescent jungle fury.

Frustrated by its inability to dampen the adrenalin in her system, the gelware kicked her into command mode. In slow motion, she saw a hairy arm swat a trooper aside, breaking his neck and twisting his gas mask askew. One of his comrades took a bullet through the lower jaw, spraying bone shards and gristle into the faces of his companions. And at the heart of it all, Ack-Ack Macaque whirled, meat cleaver in one hand, huge silver revolver in the other. Used to fighting superhuman German ninjas, the monkey seemed to be making short work of the lumbering British commandoes. In front of her, she saw Summers turn, ready to fire at the creature, and brought her quarterstaff scything around at ankle height. The blow jarred her shoulder. The SAS Captain yelled and fell, hands wrapped around his right ankle. Victoria raised herself to her knees and pulled the pistol from her pocket.

"Stay there," she ordered.

The burning helicopter had disappeared, leaving only a dirty trail of black smoke against the sunset to show where it had spiralled out of sight. The second moved erratically, more concerned about avoiding incoming fire than harassing the people on the *Tereshkova*'s pad. She looked around for the Commodore. The old man seemed to have fallen awkwardly. He was using the cutlass as a stick to pull himself upright. She watched as he clambered painfully to his feet and brushed down the front of his white tunic. Then, with obvious effort, he limped to where Summers lay wrapped around his pain, and brandished the tip of his sword in the younger man's face.

"Call off your men."

Merovech came up beside him.

"That's an order, *Captain*."

Summers looked from one to the other, lips tight against clenched teeth. For a moment, his eyes burned with defiance. Then, as his men let forth fresh screams, Victoria saw acceptance of the situation steal over him. He raised a gauntleted hand to his throat mike.

"All units, stand down." He spoke the words as if they were rotten to the taste. "Now call off the monkey."

The Commodore sheathed his cutlass. He put a hand on Merovech's shoulder for support.

"Can you, my boy?"

Merovech pulled a SincPhone from his pocket.

"K8? We're all done here. Can you put the big fella back on his leash?"

If a reply came, Victoria didn't hear it. A loud bang came from below, and the skyliner shuddered like a truck on a cattle grid. She staggered, but managed to keep her footing.

"The engines!" cried the Commodore. "We've been hit!"

Thrown off-balance, he clung to Merovech as the deck began to tip.

CHAPTER TWENTY-EIGHT
DIRTY BOMB

FROM THE *TERESHKOVA*'S bridge, the situation became distressingly clear. Through the great curving forward window, Victoria saw smoke billowing from one of the starboard engine nacelles. The blades of the impeller had been blown back and twisted so that, in the last orange rays of the setting sun, they resembled the curled legs of a dead spider. Above the nacelle's smouldering remains, the fabric of the hull had been gouged and torn by shrapnel. Ribbons of material flapped free.

At their respective workstations, the Commodore and the pilot fought to maintain control, throttling the port engines back to compensate for the sudden lack of starboard thrust.

"We're losing pressure in hulls four and five," the pilot said, reading data from his screen. Already, as the damaged hulls bled away their buoyancy, the *Tereshkova* had begun to wallow to the side.

In his chair, the Commodore scowled.

"Well, if we are going down, we are not going down without a fight. Increase power to the port engines, and give me full rudder."

"Aye, sir." The pilot was a gangly Muscovite with thick glasses and a spreading paunch: more of a computer programmer than a pilot in the old and accepted sense of the word. "But what about the passengers? If we ditch in the water..."

"Get our helicopters in the air. I want all non-essential personnel off the ship. And get a team over to the damaged sections, see if there is anything we can salvage."

"Aye, sir."

"And tell them to take Geiger counters, for heaven's sake. That was a nuclear engine, and I do not want anybody to take stupid chances if there's been a containment breach."

He turned his attention to Victoria.

"I do not suppose there is any point in ordering you to leave?"

She shook her head.

"I'm a member of your crew now, remember? Besides, I don't have anywhere else to go." She glanced back to the window, and the engine belching smoke and, possibly, radioactive fallout.

"Was it a missile?"

The old man shook his white-haired head. "A missile could not have penetrated our defences without detection. This must have been a bomb. Deliberate sabotage."

"Was it the commandoes?" She found that hard to believe. Who would purposefully detonate a nuclear engine? She knew the units used on the skyliners were designed to survive crashes intact, and so she wasn't worried about a nuclear explosion; but if the bomb had torn a hole in the engine's fuel containment, the effect would be similar to the detonation of a terrorist "dirty" bomb, spreading airborne radioactive contamination across a wide area, blown on the wind.

The Commodore pursed his lips and brushed his moustache with a crooked fingertip. "They never got further than the landing pad. This must have been someone else. I don't know who but, right now, I have more important matters of concern, such as keeping us airborne." His fingers danced across the pad before him, making adjustments to the Tereshkova's trim and pitch.

"Any casualties?" she asked.

The pilot looked up. "Mostly minor injuries at this point, but we still have two passengers unaccounted for. At least our transmissions are being jammed no longer. If we go down, we can call for help."

"Anything I can do?"

The Commodore waved her away. "We do not need you here. We can manage. It will be dark soon. Go find Merovech and the monkey. Follow the plan." He tapped in a command and snarled something in Russian.

Victoria hesitated. This could be the last time they spoke face-to-face. She felt she should say something, but nothing came. Events were spiralling too quickly.

"Go," he said. And so, she went.

With a hollowness inside her, she left the bridge and made her way aft, to the main lounge, where Merovech and his entourage were holed up, recovering from the confrontation on the helipad. K8 was busily applying bandages to Ack-Ack Macaque's cuts and scrapes, while the monkey chewed at another cigar. Blood stained the white fleece cuffs of his flight jacket.

Julie Girard sat on a chair, her leg propped up and bandaged. She looked pale and scared. In the confusion of the skirmish, she'd been hit in the thigh by a rail gun's steel needle. Merovech sat beside her, holding her hand. When he saw Victoria, he stood.

"What's happening?"

Victoria ran a hand back over the fuzz on her scalp.

"We're evacuating the passengers. What's happening up top?"

Merovech's dirty fingernails rasped at the stubble on his cheek. "The soldiers wanted to leave. They were worried about radiation."

"You let them go?"

"I saw no reason to keep them."

K8 looked up. "Is there anything I can do to help?"

Victoria shrugged. "That depends whether or not you know anything about skyliner systems."

The girl smiled.

"Do you remember the *Nova Scotia*, two years ago? Somebody hacked her flight computer remotely, and had her flying in circles around the Empire State building for two days before they managed to fix it."

"Let me guess, that someone was you?"

"Bingo."

"Go on, then. The rest of you, grab whatever you need and get to one of the choppers."

"No." Merovech's voice was quiet but firm. "I'm staying here. We have to do what we planned. For my father's sake, we have to go through with it."

"What about Julie?"

Julie Girard tried to sit up straight. An empty packet of painkillers fell from her lap. "If Merovech is staying, I am staying too."

"Are you sure? You're already hurt, and it might not be safe."

"I do not care." She looked up at the young prince and reached for his hand. "As long as we are together, that is all that matters."

The bulkheads creaked.

Merovech's eyes lingered on her bandage. When he looked up again, Victoria could see the wetness glittering in his eyes.

"I'm so sorry," he said.

Julie tried to shush him.

"It is not your fault, my love."

"Yes it is. My mother's responsible for this. For all of it." He turned to Victoria. "This has gone on long enough. She has to be exposed, whatever it takes."

The emotion in his voice stilled the room. Nobody wanted to speak. They all looked at each other. Finally, Victoria said, "Okay, whatever you say. In that case, we do what we said before. Merovech, you take Julie. Make her comfortable and record your message. Have it ready to broadcast as soon as we have the media's attention." She turned to the door. "Monsieur Macaque, it's time for you and I to suit up."

* * *

THE WINGSUITS WERE one-piece black garments of lightweight material, with inflatable flaps between the legs and under the arms, and a parachute on the back. Paul claimed to have once dated an extreme sports enthusiast, and said he knew the basics, and Victoria had seen plenty of online videos, and had a fair idea of how they worked. She had also taken a lengthy course in skydiving as part of her preparation for her visit to the South Atlantic—training which had proved useless when her aircraft ditched in the ocean, a few hundred metres from its carrier.

"Okay," Paul said in her head, "You have to remember to keep your arms and legs tensed. It's like freefall, but you control the glide using your body. If you get into difficulty, open your 'chute."

They couldn't carry much equipment, but had a number of weapons—including her quarterstaff—strapped to their backs, on either side of their parachute packs.

"I'll cope." She turned to the monkey beside her. "How are you doing?"

Ack-Ack Macaque had his aviator goggles pulled down over his eyes. Beneath the wingsuit, he wore his fur-lined leather jacket, and he'd shunned a helmet in favour of the leather skullcap K8 had given him.

"Everyone needs to know who he is," K8 had explained when Victoria protested. "He needs to look the way he does in the game, so they recognise him at a glance. Otherwise, he's just a crazy monkey running loose."

Now, standing at the passenger hatchway, just aft of the lounge in the main gondola, Ack-Ack Macaque looked serious and professional.

"Don't worry about me."

He had sticking plasters on his cheeks and across the bridge of his nose, but the injuries didn't seem to bother him. Or maybe they did, and Victoria couldn't read his body language. Sometimes, she thought, you could almost forget what he was; but, every now and then, he did or said something that threw you, reminding you that deep down, he really was a wild animal with a head full of artificial brains, and not a human being at all.

Although, she thought, *who am I to talk?*

She used her neural software to access an online map, showing the relative positions of the *Tereshkova* and Duchess Célestine's liner, the *Maraldi*.

"Right," Paul said. "If you get this right, you can expect to get a glide ratio of two point five to one. That means you'll travel two and a half metres forward for every metre you drop. We're currently around eight thousand feet above the Channel, which means you can probably expect to get just shy of two and a half kilometres out of these things. How far is it to the liner?"

"Seven kilometres."

"Ah."

"If the *Tereshkova* gets any closer, the RAF will shoot it down."

"Then what are you expecting to do? You can't swim four and a half kilometres!"

Victoria smiled. "We won't have to. There's a two-masted yacht *en route* to the *Maraldi* from Southampton. It passed underneath us a few minutes ago. We should be able to make it aboard without too much trouble."

Paul raised his eyebrows.

"God, Vicky. You're so fearless now, I can't believe it. You've really changed."

"I've always been this way." Her grin was fierce. "You just chose not to notice."

The hatch had a glass window set into it, but all she could see was her own reflection. Outside, the sky had grown dark.

The shoulder pocket of her suit held a SincPhone. She unravelled the hands-free earpiece and fitted it to the side of her head. The microphone dangled just below her chin.

"How are we doing, Commodore?"

On the other end of the line, the old man sounded grim and tired, his voice seemingly hacked out of ancient Russian stone.

"We are still here, Victoria. For now, that is victory enough."

The old airship gave a low, metallic groan of complaint, like an old-fashioned tramp steamer caught in a heavy sea. With the two starboard hulls losing gas, the other three were having to take the strain of their increasing weight.

"Good luck," she said. It didn't seem like an adequate farewell, but she couldn't think of anything else to say. They were all heading into harm's way, and who knew what might happen?

She cut the connection and turned to Ack-Ack Macaque.

"Are you ready?"

He gave her a wide, toothy grin. "As ready as I'll ever be, considering I don't usually fly without a plane."

Victoria took hold of the wheel that opened the hatch, and began to turn it. As she did so, she remembered the gut-roiling terror that had seized her former self before each parachute jump. That terror was missing now. Yes, she was nervous, but that timid, earlier version of her was dead and gone. Vicky the journalist had been killed in action in the South Atlantic, and now only Victoria the cyborg remained.

The lock disengaged and the hatch swung inwards. Beyond, the night was black.

"Okay," she said, summoning all her courage, "follow me."

She pulled her goggles down over her eyes. Then, gripping the sides of the hatchway frame, she launched herself out, headfirst into the night. In her mind, Paul cried out in fear. The wind snatched at the fabric of her suit, and she fell.

CHAPTER TWENTY-NINE
ALL SET FOR THE LIFE ETERNAL

MEROVECH HALF-CARRIED JULIE to the *Tereshkova*'s infirmary, where he helped her onto one of the bunks and cut the denim from her wounded leg. The room was small and economical, with sterile white surfaces and ranks of sliding drawers packed with pills, dressings and surgical implements. Two bunks occupied the centre of the room, for emergency cases. Normally, the medical officer treated passengers in their own cabins, but he himself had been wounded in the fighting, with two gunshot wounds to the groin, and had therefore been airlifted away with the other non-essential personnel, leaving the sickbay unmanned. Luckily, as a soldier, Merovech had been trained to give first aid.

"It's just a gash." He used a wad of cotton wool to sponge the blood. "A nasty one, though."

Each time he touched her, Julie sucked air through her teeth.

"It hurts."

"I'm sorry."

She summoned a strained smile. "Why are you apologising? It is not your fault."

The rail gun needle had scraped her thigh at a shallow angle, ripping out a furrow six inches in length and half an inch wide: painful, but thankfully not deep enough to cause any real, lasting damage. Merovech did his best to clean it up, and then applied a thick pad and bandages.

"You probably need stitches in that. Perhaps when this is all over—"

Strands of purple hair swayed as Julie shook her head.

"I will be okay, I think."

"If you don't get it stitched, you'll have a scar."

She shrugged. "Then I will have a scar. And a story to tell."

She watched him rinse his hands in the steel washbasin, then shake them, and wipe them dry against the back pockets of his jeans.

"It will not put you off?"

He turned to her. "Excuse me?"

"The scar." She pointed to the fresh bandages. "It won't put you off me?"

Merovech's lips twitched: the closest he felt he could get to a proper smile right now. He stepped over to the bed and took her hand in his.

"No," he said, "it won't."

"Good. Because we make a good team, you and I, *n'est-ce pas?*"

"*Oui, c'est vrai.*" He circled her knuckles with his thumb.

"Then, what is the matter?" she asked. "I can see you're troubled."

Merovech sighed.

"Those soldiers in the helicopter. They were only doing their job."

Her hand tightened in his.

"They were trying to take you away."

"They were just following orders. And we killed them. They were British soldiers, and I stood by and watched them die."

"What else could we have done?"

He let go of her hand and pushed his fists into his eyes.

"I was a British soldier. I wore the same uniform. I flew in the same choppers, handled the same weapons and ate the same food." He lowered his hands and looked at her. "Now, what does that make me?"

Julie touched his knee with her fingers.

"This is not your fault, Merovech. Really not. You did not ask to be put in this position."

"Maybe I should have gone with them?"

Julie's eyes widened. "No! We need you. *I* need you."

"But the cost..."

"Forget the cost, Merovech. Do you understand that? Forget. The. Cost."

He pulled back.

"But—"

"No buts!" Julie reached for him. "*Je t'aime*, Merovech, you know that. But there is more at stake here than you realise. Your mother has to be stopped, and you are the only one who can, whatever it takes."

"If she wants the throne—"

"The throne is not what she is after. K8 read her private files. She wants the whole world."

"What?"

"K8 found the evidence. We were waiting for the right time to tell you. This stand-off with China, it is part of your mother's plan. She is deliberately provoking them."

"Why would she do that?"

"When the Céleste probe gets to Mars, the Undying plan to download themselves into robot bodies and terraform the planet."

"Yes, but—"

"Mars has no magnetic field. The surface gets a lot of radiation, and the robots are built to withstand it."

A cold hand closed around Merovech's heart.

"And so if China attacks—"

"World War Three. Everybody gets blown back to the Stone Age, and the Undying get two planets instead of one."

"Jesus Christ. Is that even possible?"

Julie lay back on the pillow, her hair fanning out around her head.

"*Je ne sais pas*. But K8 thinks so, from what she saw when hacking the files."

The walls of the airship groaned, and the deck shuddered, tipping another degree or two to starboard.

"If anyone is going to stop her, Merovech, it has to be you."

Merovech flexed his fists.

"What can I do?"

Julie hitched herself up onto her elbows.

"The people need a leader they can trust."

Merovech looked up at the low ceiling, which had been painted white, rivets and all.

"Then they'll have to elect one. I'll expose my mother, and I'll take the throne. I'll do what needs to be done, for my country." His hands clenched, fingers digging into palms, knuckles white. "But afterwards, when the dust's settled, I'm going to abdicate."

Julie put a hand to her mouth.

"Are you serious?"

Merovech perched on the bed beside her.

"Deadly serious. I've been thinking about this a lot, ever since the crash. And I've not been happy for a while."

Julie opened and closed her mouth, digesting his words. Then she said, "Is that what you really want?"

"It is." He smiled at her. "I can't bear the formality. All those endless receptions. And besides, the succession isn't mine, remember? It turns out I'm no more entitled to it than my mother. And with all this illegal gelware in my head, I may not even be fit to rule at all. As soon as things get back to normal, I'll call a referendum and let the people decide."

Someone rapped on the sickbay door. Merovech turned to find the Commodore leaning against the frame.

"Excuse the interruption." The old man's jacket had been left undone, and his sash had gone missing. Beneath his moustache and bushy white brows, his face seemed pale and strained. "But I thought you should know, we caught the saboteur."

"Where was he?"

"My men found him hiding in the starboard cargo bay. Now we have the *kozyol* in the lounge." He turned, holding his injured hip with one hand, and gestured Merovech to follow. "Come, he wishes to speak with you."

"Why me?"

"I do not know. But he refuses to talk to anybody else."

THE COMMODORE'S CREWMEN had strapped the saboteur to a chair in the centre of the main lounge. He was a young man around Merovech's age. Plastic packing strips bound his left wrist and right ankle to the chair. He wore a creased white shirt and thin black tie. In his right hand, he cupped a smouldering cigarette.

He looked up as Merovech approached.

"Hey, your highness." Diamonds of sweat shone on his brow. His hair and shirt looked damp.

"You wanted to see me?"

"I sure did." The man's face cracked into a white-toothed grin. "I got a message for you, man."

Merovech crossed his arms, making no effort to conceal his impatience.

"What is it?"

The man wagged his cigarette. "Hey, not so fast. Why the rush? Don't you want to know who I am first?"

Merovech tapped a toe against the deck. "To be honest, I couldn't give a damn."

The young man's grin broadened. "Well, my name's Linton. Linton Martin, and I sure am pleased to meet you." He stuck the cigarette in the corner of his mouth and held out his hand. Merovech ignored it.

"I suppose you're working for my mother, too?"

Smoke curled from Linton's mouth. A bead of sweat rolled down his face.

"You know it, baby." He took another big hit from the cigarette, tipped his head back, and blew smoke at the ceiling.

The Commodore stepped forward, favouring his bad hip. One of his polished boots dragged against the deck.

"He came on board at Heathrow, as a legitimate passenger." The old man spoke through clenched teeth, his voice dripping with a mixture of pain and disgust. "A last minute booking."

Merovech didn't take his eyes from the prisoner. "He must be one of the 'friends' that Berg warned us about."

With a low metallic groan, the deck tipped further. Merovech adjusted his footing.

"It's getting worse."

The Commodore scowled. "Perhaps you should reconsider your decision to stay?"

Merovech gave a firm shake of his head.

"No, I'm going to see this through. If I run now, I'll be running for the rest of my life. This is my best and only chance to end this, here and now."

In the chair, Linton chuckled, clearly enjoying himself. The Commodore glared at him.

"Let me know when you are finished with this *kozyol*," he said to Merovech.

"What are you going to do with him?"

The Commodore's lip curled, revealing teeth the colour of old ivory. "Lock him in the brig. If we crash into the sea, he crashes with us."

Linton chortled again. His left foot tapped against the floor. The fingers of both hands twitched.

"That is *so* not going to happen."

"Why do you say that?" Merovech lowered himself onto one knee, bringing their faces level. "You don't think we'll crash?"

Linton bobbed his head, as if in time to music.

"No, man. I don't think you'll get me to the brig."

"Why not?"

"Because I'll be dead before you get me there." He sucked the last of the cigarette and dropped the butt to the deck, where he ground it out with the point of his shoe.

Merovech felt a frisson of unease.

"Another bomb?"

Linton stopped jiggling. His blue eyes seemed to sparkle.

"Suicide pills." He cackled. "How fucking cool is *that*?"

"You've taken them?"

"Yeah, baby. And the clock's ticking."

Merovech shook his head in disbelief.

"Don't you care?"

Linton wiped his forehead on the sleeve of his shirt. Then he reached into his shirt pocket and pulled out a soft pack of American cigarettes. Only two remained. He extracted one with his teeth and let the pack fall to the floor.

"It doesn't bother me. I'm backed-up, baby. All set for the life eternal."

Merovech stood, and brushed off the knee of his jeans.

"Do you really believe that?"

"Sure thing."

Merovech felt his cheeks flush. He wanted to strangle this infuriating kid.

"That won't be *you*," he said. "Just a copy. Don't you get it? You'll be dead."

"I'll live again, baby."

"No, you won't, not really." Merovech sighed, fatigue and pity leeching the anger from him. "Just because, somewhere, a robot remembers you, it doesn't mean that you, the real you, won't be dead."

Linton gave a dismissive flick of his fingers.

"You believe what you want to believe, man. But time's running out, and I've got a message I need to pass on before I check out of *this* body, and into the *next*."

Merovech rocked back on his heels.

"Come on then, spill it. What's the message, and who's it from? My mother?"

Linton grinned around his unlit cigarette.

"It's from Doctor Nguyen."

"Nguyen's dead."

"No, he ain't." The kid's breathing became laboured. The sweat continued to roll off him. "Of course he ain't. And he says to tell you, he'll see you and your friends real soon."

As he finished speaking, the colour drained from his face. He gave a grunt of pain and bent forward, as if punched in the gut. With a shaking hand, he took the cigarette from his mouth and spat blood and phlegm onto the deck. Then he sat back upright, wiped the drool from his lip, and looked around at the armed guards lining the walls of the lounge. Sweat poured down his face.

"Okay." He waggled the cigarette defiantly. "Which one of you motherfuckers has a light?"

CHAPTER THIRTY
ZERO

SPREAD-EAGLED IN THE roaring darkness, Victoria fell towards the sea. She could feel the wind ripping at the flaps of material beneath her arms and between her legs. Air filled her cheeks, snatching away her breath, and buffeting her chest like the mane of a bucking horse.

The monkey was somewhere behind her, lost in the night. Far to her right, the orange lights of Torquay and Salcombe; to her left, Cherbourg and Guernsey; and ahead, on the wine-dark sea, the red and green running lights of the yacht ferrying guests and provisions to the *Maraldi*.

The darkness made it hard to visually judge height and distance, but readouts chattered in her head as her gelware interfaced with real-time GPS positioning systems, counting down to the moment she'd have to open her 'chute. But with the yacht moving away from her at a fair clip, the only question on her mind was whether or not she'd have the height and speed to catch it before it moved out of range, and she found herself stuck in the cold waters of the Channel, miles from land.

Her chest muscles ached with the effort of keeping her arms rigid, but she knew the slightest twitch could alter her direction or angle of descent, so she kept them as steady as she could. She'd minimised Paul's image, but could still see a thumbnail of him in her peripheral vision, both hands wrapped across his mouth as he watched the fall through her eyes. She tried to ignore him. If she screwed this up, she'd screw it up for both of them, and that would be that. But right now, she didn't need additional pressure; she had enough to worry about.

Her goggles pushed against her face. She didn't have a lot of altitude left. She'd have to pull her ripcord in the next thirty seconds.

The boat loomed larger and larger beneath her, a ghostly feathered wake churning from its stern.

Twenty seconds. The countdown spiralled. She could smell the brine.

"Pull the cord!" Paul yelled.

Fifteen.

Come on, come on.

With five seconds to spare, she zipped over the vessel, high above its twin masts. The yacht's windows were lit. People were partying.

Zero. She yanked the release, and the black silk canopy billowed from her backpack. The wind caught it and jerked her back, hard enough to snap her teeth shut. Bruised and winded, she dangled like a rag doll, legs and arms swinging loose.

"Get out of the harness *before* you hit the water," Paul warned. "You don't want to get tangled in the lines."

For a second, she thought she caught sight of the second black 'chute: a movement against the stars. Then the sea seemed to rush at her, much too fast. She unclipped the front of her harness. Before she could shrug it off, her boots hit the swell and she plunged into water so cold she thought it would stop her heart.

The speed of her descent carried her down in a maelstrom of bubbles. Frantically, she thrashed her arms free from the harness and, lungs bursting, kicked upwards.

The surface seemed further than she'd expected. When her head broke through, her face hit the sodden underside of the parachute, which lay draped on the ocean like a woefully inadequate pool cover. She flailed at it.

"Find a seam," Paul called as her fingers scrabbled for purchase on the sodden material. "Find a seam and follow it to the front of the 'chute. Don't go sideways or you'll get caught in the lines at either end."

Sensing her panic, the gelware switched her into command mode. She felt time slow and stretch, and her fear evaporated. She was still trapped, but now it was simply a problem to be overcome rather than a cause for alarm.

Using her teeth, she pulled off a glove and ran her freezing fingers across the underside of the parachute until she found a row of stitching. Then, in accordance with Paul's suggestion, she kicked her feet, following it. Moments later, she ducked under the edge of the material, and out into open air.

For a few breaths, she was content to bob with the rise and fall of the water. Then, she turned to face the approaching yacht.

It came at her like a knife through the waves, its sails cupping the wind. She struck out sideways, her movements hampered by her waterlogged clothes, her booted feet kicking ineffectually.

After a few moments of struggle, the boat caught up with her. The wave of froth at its bow shouldered her aside. The yacht was a dignified old wooden vessel, with two masts and a row of portholes just above the waterline. As it slid past, she lunged with all her strength. Cold fingers caught the rim of the nearest porthole, and the boat dragged her along with it, spray smashing up against her arms and chest.

So far, so good. Now all she had to do was find a way to clamber up onto the deck, preferably without detection. She heaved, dragging herself forward by her fingertips. The sea sucked at the flap of material between her legs, reluctant to release her. She could barely feel her hands, and her strength had begun to ebb, dissipating into the water with the last of her body heat. One final pull. Her vision went red. Her pulse throbbed at her temples.

"Come on!" Paul urged. She strained until she felt the muscles in her arms would snap, but still the edge of the deck remained frustratingly beyond her reach.

She fell back, clinging to the porthole's rim, defeat washing through her. The sea clawed at her legs with a thousand fingers, and she knew she couldn't hold on.

"I can't do it," she cried.

In her eye, Paul had both hands on the top of his head, fingers digging into his peroxide hair.

"You can't give up now."

"It's not. About. Giving. Up." Each word was an effort, shouted into a wall of stinging, salty spray. "It's about. Not. Being able. To. Fucking. Reach."

Her fingers were beginning to work loose, losing purchase on the wet steel frame. Her forearms were solid ropes of pain.

"Hold on, Vicky."

"I can't!"

To let go would be to drown. She wouldn't have the strength to keep herself afloat against the weight of her sodden flight suit. It would be a suffocating and unpleasant way to die, but at least it would be relatively quick, and the gelware would be there to ease her through it on a wave of painkillers. And as for Paul, she could turn him off at any time. Perhaps that would be the kindest thing: to grant him instant, unknowing oblivion, and spare him her final moments.

Teeth clenched, she brought up the mental menu options to end his simulation.

"Sorry, Paul." She'd execute the command as her fingers slipped from the porthole rim. Already, her left hand had worked almost completely loose, and now clung on by fingertips alone. When it slipped, the jerk would be enough to pull her right hand free as well.

"No," Paul cried, "wait!"

"Can't."

She could hear music from the party inside the ship: teeny-boppers cooing Franglais slang over a bubblegum Euro-trance beat. Millimetre by millimetre, her fingertips scraped toward the rim. These were the final seconds of both their lives.

"I'm sorry."

The water pulled at her thighs. She closed her eyes and prepared for death.

BUT DEATH DIDN'T come.

Instead, a strong leathery hand caught her by her flight suit's collar, and hauled her up, over the rail.

She lay coughing and shivering on the yacht's wooden deck. Ack-Ack Macaque sat on his heels beside her. He'd unzipped his wingsuit and now wore only his skullcap and leather jacket. A bullet belt circled his narrow hips, loaded with shells; his goggles were loose around his neck and, in his hand, he held the chrome-plated revolver he'd taken from the *Tereshkova*'s armoury. Tail twitching, he regarded her with his single, yellow eye.

"I've never jumped out of a plane before," he said. "In real life, I mean. Kind of fun."

Victoria levered herself into a sitting position and looked around. The deck seemed deserted. Music came from an open hatchway amidships, louder here than it had been from her earlier perch.

"Where—" She coughed. "Where are the crew?" They were passing through one of the busiest shipping lanes in the world, yet the deck was dark and deserted.

The monkey gave a nod of his head, back towards the stern.

"There's two in the wheelhouse."

"Have they seen us?"

"I don't think so. They're watching TV. The boat seems to be driving itself."

Victoria pulled down the zip of her wingsuit and kicked it off. She retrieved her quarterstaff from its strap on the back of the suit, and kicked the rest under the rail, into the sea. Her feet were still numb from the water. Watching her, Ack-Ack Macaque scratched at the fur on his cheek.

"You're dry," she realised. Then, "How did you get aboard?"

He looked up at the masts stretching into the sky above them.

"I saw you ditch in the sea, but the boat was getting away from me. It was all I could do to catch it. I pulled my 'chute at the last second, and came down as close as I could to the mast. Then I simply unclipped my harness and dropped onto the yardarm."

"That sounds dangerous."

Ack-Ack Macaque gave a small shrug. "No worse than jumping from one tree into another. The 'chute blew away, and I climbed down the rigging."

Victoria glanced at Paul. His translucent image seemed to hang in the air above the rail. He had his fingers laced behind his head and his eyes screwed shut, so she quietly minimised his image without speaking. After all he'd been through over the past few days, she figured the poor guy deserved a little private time in which to freak out.

The wind blew across the deck and straight through her wet clothes. Her hands shook. To still them, she gripped the carbon fibre shaft of her quarterstaff.

"Okay," she said through chattering teeth, "we need to make our way to the hold and lie low until we reach the *Maraldi*."

Ack-Ack Macaque waggled his revolver towards the bows. "The hatch is that way. If we stay low, they won't see us."

He started to move, but Victoria caught his arm. She would have liked nothing more than to get below decks, out of the cold evening air; yet something held her back: some instinct scratching at the inside of her skull, warning of danger.

"This isn't right."

Ack-Ack Macaque crouched beside her, his eye scanning the deck for threats.

"How so?"

"There should be more security. I expected at least three or four people on deck, keeping watch. I thought we'd have to sneak on board."

"We *are* sneaking on board."

"Yes, but I wasn't expecting it to be this easy. Look, they don't even have security cameras."

The monkey turned to fix her with his sallow stare.

"So, maybe we got lucky?"

A soft whine came from somewhere astern, rising in pitch.

"I don't think so."

Victoria sprang to her feet and ran, her wet feet pushing against the slick planking on the deck. How could she have been so stupid? Of *course* they'd have security bots.

She heard other turbines spin up, and risked a glance over her shoulder in time to see three fat, tyre-shaped sentinels rise from behind the wheelhouse, red and green targeting lasers glittering from their rims.

The cargo hatch lay ahead of her, but she knew she'd never reach it in time; and even if she did, they'd know where to find her. Her only escape would be to throw herself over the rail. But would that really be an escape? The bots could fly over water as easily as they could fly over land, and they were quite capable of picking her off when she came up for air. And anyway, having escaped drowning once, she wasn't in any hurry to get back in the water.

Shots came from behind her as the monkey emptied his revolver at their pursuers. She turned, having nowhere else to go, and saw one of the bots spiralling drunkenly, its manoeuvring fans splintered and smoking from multiple bullet hits.

As it fell, the other two bots let rip. Gun barrels flashed. Ack-Ack Macaque staggered under a hail of impacts, and went down with a screech. The silver revolver flew from his fingers.

Horrified, Victoria dropped the quarterstaff and stepped back, hands in the air, ready to surrender.

For half a second, she considered trying to overclock her neural processes, but knew she didn't have time to lay in the necessary commands; and even if she did, she seriously doubted she'd be able to move fast enough to dodge the bots' fire.

Instead, she stood there, dripping wet and shivering as lasers caressed the material of her shirt. Water slapped and gurgled against the hull. Her lips held the tang of sea salt and, far beyond the rail, the orange town lights of England shimmered on the water.

Range finders whirred. She closed her eyes.

And the first shot punched her in the chest.

TECHSNARK
BLOGGING WITH ATTITUDE

Ack-Ack Macaque Still Offline
Posted: 28/11/2059 – 9:00pm GMT
| Share |

Three hours after the unexplained crash of Céleste Tech's online flagship, rumours are starting to surface, with gamers reporting an epic battle between the old and new versions of the well-loved title character.

Early reports speak of YouTube clips showing two monkeys fighting on top of a flying aircraft carrier. But if those clips ever existed, they've since been purged.

That hasn't stopped the rumour mill, and fan sites across the web from going crazy with speculation. The apparent 'death' of the title character at the hands of its earlier self has been seen in some quarters as proof that somebody, somewhere has finally 'won' the game.

Ack-Ack Macaque is famous for offering its players only one shot at an in-game 'life' and, it seems, that policy extends to the title character itself. The question is, with one monkey dead and the other missing, what happens next?

The only thing we can be certain of is that the game remains offline, and players still can't log on.

In the wake of the crash, several hacker groups have claimed responsibility for the appearance of the second monkey, but Céleste's PR department remains resolutely tight-lipped about the entire affair, issuing only a short statement to the effect than normal service will be resumed as soon as possible.

With every offline hour costing Céleste a fortune in subscriptions and advertising revenue, we can only hope they mean what they say.

Publicity stunt, hack attack or FUBAR? Only time will tell.

Read more | Like | Comment | Share

CHAPTER THIRTY-ONE
NGUYEN

ACK-ACK MACAQUE woke on a hard tile floor, and groaned. His tongue felt like a dry old rag; his hands and feet had been lashed with twine, and his chest felt like a pincushion. He couldn't sit up, but he could turn his head.

The room upon whose floor he lay seemed to be some sort of storage locker or changing room. Six neoprene wetsuits dangled from a rack of pegs above a utilitarian wooden bench. Rope-handled plastic bins sat at either end of the bench, diving masks piled in one, flippers in the other. Against the opposite wall, a wire rack held twelve oxygen cylinders. The room had only one door: of polished wood, with a small porthole set into it. From beyond it, he could hear music, raised voices, and the clink of glasses.

Still on the yacht, then.

Victoria lay unconscious on the tiles beside him, an inch-long tranquiliser dart sticking from the right side of her chest, just below the collarbone. He worked his dry lips.

"Victoria?"

The effort of speaking triggered a glowering pain behind his eye, as hot and fragile as any hangover. In frustration, he gave his wrists a twist, testing his restraints. The rope felt shiny and uncomfortable, like nylon.

When I get out of here, he thought, *somebody is really going to get* bitten.

Another twist, and he felt the glossy cord scrape into his flesh. The fibres creaked, but he didn't have the strength to try again. The sedatives in his system had him pinned beneath the weight of a bone-deep, soul-crushing fatigue, and he longed for the simple comforts and cold certainties of the Officers' Mess. Illusion it may have been, but life had been so much easier when all he'd had to worry about was the war. No crazy bald chicks or runaway princes, just one clear mission objective after another. And before the war, woozy, pre-conscious memories of rum-fuelled Amsterdam bar fights, of a life unburdened by self-analysis or self-awareness, where all that concerned him was the knife in his opponent's hand.

He closed his eye and pressed his head back against the cold tile. The pressure seemed to soothe the pounding ache. Then, over the distant sounds of merriment, he heard footsteps in the hall outside.

Oh, what now?

The door pushed open and a man entered. He was tall and thin, and dressed in evening wear. In his hand, he held a patent leather case.

"Ah, you're awake. Good. I thought you might be." He sat on the bench and placed the case flat on the wood beside him.

Ack-Ack Macaque blinked up at him. "Who are you?"

The man looked down at himself and smiled. His black hair had been gelled back and parted, his eyes held the barest suggestion of epicanthic folds, and his shiny skin glowed with the sepia tones of an old Victorian photograph.

"Forgive me. The last time we met, you were on an operating table and I—" He smoothed a hand down the lapel of his dinner jacket. "I had a different face."

"Doctor Nguyen?"

The man tipped his head in a polite bow. "The same."

"The man who—"

"The man who made you, yes. And your little friend there."

Using his elbows to push himself up, Ack-Ack Macaque struggled into a sitting position. "But you're dead."

Nguyen popped the clasps of his leather briefcase.

"Not dead, my simian friend. Simply upgraded into a better body." He raised the lid of the case, revealing row upon row of gleaming surgical instruments.

"Now," he said, "I must give you another shot of tranquiliser. Enough to hold you until we reach the *Maraldi,* and its excellently well-equipped infirmary."

Ack-Ack Macaque snarled. This was the man who'd turned him from knife-wielding primate to plane-flying freak; the man who'd pumped his skull full of plastic brain cells and burdened him with an intelligence he'd neither desired nor sought. Fighting the heaviness in his bones, he flexed his shoulders and pulled. The rope bit through his skin and he roared, but he kept pulling. At the same time, he swung his legs around and got himself into a kneeling position. The nylon rope stretched. He could feel the damp fibres pulling against each other. From the bottom of his jungle soul, he squeezed every last scrap of wild strength. His wrists flared with agony. And then the rope snapped, and he was free, his fingers clawing for the face of his creator.

Nguyen didn't flinch. Instead, he looked Ack-Ack Macaque in the eye.

"*Masaru!*"

The strength fled from Ack-Ack Macaque's arms. His lunge became a collapse, and he fell sprawling at his tormentor's feet, limbs twitching.

Nguyen laughed harshly.

"I built you, stupid monkey. Did you not think I might have included a safe word in your programming?"

He rummaged in his case and pulled out a hypodermic needle and a small glass bottle of tranquiliser.

Ack-Ack Macaque flopped like a fish on the floor. All he wanted was to rip out this man's throat with his teeth, but his arms and legs were numb and useless. Eventually, he stopped thrashing and lay panting with his nose against the tiles.

"Why?" he asked.

Nguyen looked down at him in surprise. "Why did I make you?" The man pushed the needle through the rubber membrane at the neck of the bottle, into the colourless liquid within.

"You and your predecessors were prototypes. First attempts. We had planned to raise an army of uplifted monkeys." He stared wistfully into the middle distance. "But, as it turns out, humans are easier to control." He pulled back the plunger and filled the syringe. "Luckily, we found another use for you. A profitable use."

"The game?"

"Indeed. Our programmers needed an artificial intelligence at the heart of their game, so we gave them one." He smiled. "Although not perhaps the one they were expecting."

Ack-Ack Macaque coughed. The tiles smelled of seawater and bleach.

"And Victoria?"

"A happy accident. She was dying, so we had nothing to lose. We used her as a test bed. We could try things, new techniques that we hadn't dared try on the Prince."

"And now you're an android?"

"Yes." Nguyen drew himself up, looking down appreciatively at his new body. "One of the first. Soon, there will be thousands. When the bombs start falling and the people come to the shelters we've set up, we'll begin the process of transforming them. They will enter frail and scared, and leave as virtual supermen, with the world in flames at their feet."

Ack-Ack Macaque shook his head, nose rubbing against the cold floor.

"You're insane."

"Is it insane to want to rebuild the world, to put right the mistakes of history and eradicate disease and suffering?"

Ack-Ack Macaque turned his head and hawked phlegm.

"The way you're doing it, yes."

Nguyen placed the glass vial back into his case.

"These are the goals I have worked for all my life. Humanity can, and will, be improved."

"Whether it wants to be or not?"

Nguyen came and stood beside Ack-Ack Macaque, shoes inches from his face. He looked down.

"What it wants doesn't matter. Left alone, the human race will kill itself. It has already wrecked the environment which sustains it. Without our help, how much longer do you think it will survive? Strong leaders are needed. We will found a new society, based on science and reason, and we will save humanity from itself."

"But first you've got to kill everyone, right? In order to save them?"

"Enough!" Abruptly, Nguyen crouched, and caught Ack-Ack Macaque by the scruff of his neck, android fingers firm and strong. "Why am I arguing with you, anyway? You're nothing but an animal."

"At least I've still got my own junk. I'm not some metal eunuch."

The needle pricked his skin, sliding into the side of his neck. He tried to twist away, but couldn't break Nguyen's iron grip.

"Don't struggle."

Nguyen depressed the plunger, pushing icy liquid into Ack-Ack Macaque's veins. Then the grip loosened, and Nguyen climbed to his feet.

Ack-Ack Macaque looked up at him, heart hammering.

"There's just one thing I don't get."

"And what's that?"

"Merovech. If you're all turning yourself into cyborgs, why do you still need Merovech?"

The doctor returned the needle to his case.

"When we first planned all of this, the Duchess was to transfer her consciousness into Merovech's body. She was to become a strong new leader, and found a new royal dynasty, moving from host to host down the generations, immortal and all-powerful." His voice seemed to waver, echoing in Ack-Ack Macaque's ears as the drugs bit chunks from his awareness.

"Since these new android bodies came on stream, all that seems rather redundant," Nguyen continued. "Still, we need him as a figurehead. The Duchess is a powerful woman, but even she can't order the prime minister to declare war. If we are to see our plan through, we need to load Her Grace's personality into Merovech when he becomes King."

Shadows blotted the corners of Ack-Ack Macaque's sight. He tried to say something, but couldn't. His thoughts became light and airy, as if someone had thrown open a window in the stuffiness of his mind. The tiles no longer felt uncomfortable beneath him. He pictured clouds and Spitfires, and the warehouses of the Amsterdam waterfront. He wondered how long it would take to—

CHAPTER THIRTY-TWO
ARTIFICIAL THUNDER

LINTON MARTIN DIED in the chair in the centre of the *Tereshkova*'s main lounge, wracked by cramps. Whatever he'd swallowed took a long time to kill him, and he sweated his way through another cigarette before the end finally came.

When it was close, with his teeth clenched against the pain, rivulets of perspiration running down his face, and the muscles in his neck standing out like steel hawsers, he fixed Merovech with a wild glare and hissed, "I *will* live again."

Then the half-smoked dog-end of his final cigarette fell from his fingers. His left leg shot out straight and his hands clawed the air. An agonising convulsion shook him, juddering every muscle, curling his arms against his chest. For a second he stayed rigid, vibrating with pain. And then he buckled. His limbs went slack and he fell to one side. The chair fell with him. His skull hit the deck with a solid clunk, and he lay there in a tangle, eyes bulging and tongue lolling wetly from his lips.

Merovech turned away. He'd seen men die before, but that didn't make it any easier to watch. He stood with the Commodore as the stewards rolled Linton onto a canvas stretcher.

"Throw him out," the Commodore growled, his damaged hip braced against the tilt of the deck. "We need to lose as much weight as we can."

"Not so fast." Merovech put a hand on the sleeve of the old man's tunic. The Commodore scowled, clearly annoyed at having his orders questioned in front of his crew.

"You want to keep him?"

"Of course not. But if we get through this, we're going to need all the evidence we can find."

The Commodore huffed, clearly unconvinced. But he turned back to his men, who were hesitating in the doorway, and said, "Take him to the galley and put him in one of the freezers. Throw the food out if you have to. It is not like we will be needing it."

Then he began to limp towards the bridge, dragging his bad leg behind him. Merovech followed. As in the lounge, the floor in the connecting corridor leant at an alarming fifteen degrees to starboard, making the slippery metal deck treacherous.

"How much more can she take?"

Bracing himself against the walls of the corridor, the Commodore didn't look around. "We are still losing gas. The bags are compartmentalised. If only two or three compartments are damaged, we will be fine. If more, then we have real trouble."

"We'll still have enough to stay airborne, though?"

"Perhaps." A shrug. "Who knows?"

They passed the galley. Steel pots swung from ceiling hooks. Shards of smashed crockery covered the floor.

"What are we going to do?"

The Commodore stopped moving. "I won't abandon her." His gnarled hand gave the bulkhead an affectionate pat. "I am too old to mourn again. If she goes down, I go with her."

And then he was off, using his hands to steady himself. They came to the bridge, where the pilot and navigator fought to keep the massive craft on an even keel. The Commodore barked something in his native tongue, and the pilot snarled back; a string of guttural curses.

"We cannot stay up much longer," the Commodore translated.

"But we're not crashing?"

"No. Not yet. Although the strain on the hulls is great, and we should land if we can."

From the other workstation, the navigation officer threw a brisk salute, and spoke at length, with many accompanying hand gestures. The Commodore scowled, then shambled over to peer at the man's screen. From the inside pocket of his tunic, he produced a pair of reading glasses, which he balanced on the bridge of his nose as he scanned the data. He gave a grunt; and then he straightened up and turned to Merovech.

"We have two RAF fighter jets circling us in the darkness. They say they are reluctant to fire while you remain aboard, but neither will they let us deviate from our present course."

Merovech frowned. "They actually *want* us to reach the *Maraldi*?"

The Commodore slipped the spectacles back into his pocket, as deftly as any conjuror, and smoothed down the tips of his moustache.

"It seems you have a appointment to keep."

RETURNING TO THE sickbay, Merovech found Julie Girard looking strained. The painkillers weren't doing enough to dull the stinging needle wound in her thigh. But when she saw him, her brow furrowed not in pain, but concern.

"Are you okay?" she asked. "You look very pale."

Merovech came over and sat beside her. He took her hand.

"I'm scared, Jules. I'm angry and I'm scared."

"What can I do?"

Merovech took a long, ragged breath. "Nothing. That's the trouble. I've got the speech ready to go, but my father's down there, and he could be dying, and all we can do is wait. It makes me feel so bloody helpless."

He turned his head to the porthole. The sky was dark, but he sensed the jets all the same: out there in the blackness, circling like sharks.

"When I found out what had been done to me, what my own mother had done to me, I wanted to confront her. I was furious and hurt and all those other things."

Julie touched his hand. "You had every right to be."

"I know. But now it's all unravelled. We're fighting for our lives, and I don't know what to do. There's too much at stake and I can't see a way out. She's got the Air Force and the Navy, and what have we got?"

The walls gave a metallic shudder. Julie's fingers moved up to his cheek. She brushed at his hair, tidying it.

"We have got a monkey."

Merovech smiled in spite of himself.

"I love you."

Julie's hand dropped into her lap. "Do not say that unless you mean it."

"I do. In fact, if we get out of this alive—"

"Do not say it."

Merovech cleared his throat. The words were boiling up inside him. "If we make it through this in one piece, I want you to marry me."

Julie blinked at him, stunned.

"Are you serious?" She slammed her palms onto the blanket. "Are you *really* serious?"

Merovech pulled back.

"But, I thought—"

"We could both be killed in a few hours. Personally, I will be amazed if I am not dead or in jail by the morning. How can you be thinking about marriage at a time like this?"

"What better time is there?"

Julie scraped her lower lip with a purple thumbnail. "What about my father?"

"He can't stop us."

She shook her head. "You do not know him. You do not know what he can be like."

Merovech huffed air through his cheeks. He thought he had a pretty good idea of exactly what the old bastard could be like.

"Forget about him."

In a tight, irritated gesture, Julie wiped her hair back with the fingertips of one hand. "That might be easy for you to say. I cannot forget about him, Merovech, he is my *father*."

Where she'd pulled the purple strands back, he caught sight of the faded shadow on her cheek: the yellowed remains of the bruise that had so angered him in the café.

"Well," he snapped, "he doesn't deserve to be."

"*What?*"

"You heard me. You can keep denying it, but we both know what he is, and what he's done to you."

She waved a hand in front of her face, trying to ward off his words.

"No! *Non!*"

Far beyond the gondola's walls, Merovech heard the distant roar of the circling planes: a rumble in the dark, like artificial thunder.

"I can keep you safe," he said.

"Safe?" Julie looked around the listing cabin. "You call *this* 'safe'?"

"You know what I mean."

She shook her head, eyes flashing, and he drew back, expecting her to shout. She didn't. Instead, she dropped her chin to her chest and took a series of deep, calming breaths. When she finally looked up and spoke, it was with a firmness that surprised him.

"I know you think you are doing the right thing, but you are going about it all wrong. I love you, Merovech, I really do. I would not be here if I did not. But that does not mean I need you to *rescue* me. I don't need a big handsome prince to come riding in and fight all my battles for me."

"I didn't—"

She put a finger to his lips. "I am not a princess, I am tougher than that, and I solve my problems myself, in my own way and in my own time. And if you really, truly want to be with me, then that is something you will have to learn to accept, okay?"

She pulled her finger back.

"And yes, Merovech."

Merovech blinked foolishly, his composure in tatters. "Yes what?"

Julie smiled, and spoke slowly, as if addressing an idiot.

"Yes, if we make it through this alive, I will marry you."

CHAPTER THIRTY-THREE
PERSONAL FRANKENSTEIN

"Ah, you're awake," the man said. "Welcome back."

Victoria blinked up at him from the bed.

"Who are you?" She tried to move, but her arms and legs wouldn't respond. She smelled antiseptic and cold steel. The ceiling was low, white and curved. "What's happening, where are we?"

"You are on board the *Maraldi*, in the infirmary. You have been unconscious for some time."

Victoria's vision swam. She creased her eyes, trying to focus.

"And you are?"

"Come, come, Victoria. Surely someone with your background can figure that one out?"

Victoria ran her tongue over her lower lip. She'd never seen this man before, but there was something familiar about the condescension in his tone. She took a guess.

"Doctor Nguyen?"

The man gave a small smile. "Very good."

"Why can't I move?"

"When I installed your gel-based processors, I also installed an override command. A simple word that renders you immobile."

"Why would you do that?"

He moved over to the sink and turned on the taps. "I was designing the perfect slave army," he said over his shoulder. "I wanted to make sure they couldn't revolt."

As he washed and dried his hands, Victoria ran over what she knew about him.

Doctor Kenta Nguyen had been born in Osaka in the late nineteen eighties, and was now over seventy years old. He was a graduate of the Human Genome Project and, until leaving Japan to take up a research position with Céleste, he had been one of the leading innovators in the ongoing Japanese biotech revolution. She remembered him as a small, cantankerous man in a tweed suit. Now, he stood tall and limber in a dinner jacket and bow tie. He looked around thirty years old, and in amazing physical shape.

"You're an android," she said with a hammer-blow of realisation, "just like Berg."

Nguyen shook water from his hands and turned back to her.

"Ah, poor Berg. He was one of our earliest successes, and quite unhinged. I was terribly sad to lose him."

"He was a murdering psychopath."

Nguyen gave a small, pitying shake of his head.

"He was a loyal soldier." He reached for a packet of surgical gloves, and extracted two. "And all his so-called 'victims' *will* live again."

Victoria let herself sneer.

"Bullshit."

"Really, Miss Valois? Look at me." He flattened a palm against his chest. "I left my body in Paris, and yet here I am, as alive as you."

"I don't call that life."

Nguyen sighed like a disappointed schoolmaster.

"And what about you, Victoria? May I remind you that the brain in your head is more than fifty per cent synthetic. And yet you claim to be alive, do you not?"

"That's different."

"Is it?" He examined his hand. "I'll grant you that these bodies are far from perfect. I'm still having trouble integrating some of the finer senses, for example. But they will suffice, for now. Bodies like this will keep us all alive when the bombs fall, and we can improve them later. After all, we will have hundreds, maybe thousands, of years."

"Speak for yourself."

Nguyen gave a small, tight smile.

"I haven't introduced you to my assistant, have I?"

He clapped his hands twice, and a girl tottered into the room on six-inch heels. She looked to be somewhere in her early twenties. She wore a white lab coat over a tight cocktail dress. Long, blonde hair fell around her shoulders, curling down to an ample cleavage. In her hands, she held a silver tray of surgical implements.

"Victoria," Nguyen said with a flourish, "meet Vic."

Victoria frowned. Beneath the girl's make-up and fake tan, the skin held the stiff, waxy sheen that identified her as another of Nguyen's androids.

"What is this?"

Nguyen smiled. "This is you. This is what I did when Berg brought me your soul-catcher." He reached out and curled his fingers in the girl's hair. "I call her 'Vic'."

Watching him, Victoria felt her skin prickle. Bats flapped their wings in her chest cavity.

"Three days ago," Nguyen said, "I took your back-up and I loaded it into this body. This is you, Victoria. Your memories, your personality, your 'soul'."

The girl stood, inert as a waxwork, her blue eyes fixed on the middle distance.

Victoria's mouth was dry.

"I don't believe you. I would never have let you do that. I would have fought—"

Nguyen waved her to silence.

"Oh, I am more than aware of that." He untangled his fingers from the girl's hair. "And believe me, until I installed the behavioural safeguards, this one fought like the devil herself. Now, though, she is incapable of violence." He reached out and cupped one of the girl's heavy breasts in his palm. "But why worry about violence when she and I have so many better things we could be doing? Isn't that right, Vic?"

The girl blinked. She looked down at the hand holding her breast.

"Yes, Doctor Nguyen."

He smiled. "You see, Miss Valois, even you can be tamed."

Immobile on the bed, Victoria felt her cheeks burn.

"You sack of shit."

Nguyen gave a disapproving click of his tongue.

"Such language." He let go of the girl and pulled the surgical gloves on over his artificial fingers: first one hand, and then the other. "You have to see the big picture, Miss Valois. These bodies, these hands, are simply tools. With them, we will save the world."

"By destroying it?"

Nguyen shook his head. "I am a doctor. My job is to make people better. To make the human race *better*." He snapped the elastic cuff of the last glove into place, and selected a shiny silver scalpel from the tray in his assistant's hands. As he picked it up, the blade caught the light: cold, and thinner than paper.

"You've caused us considerable trouble," he said. "We should have had Merovech by now. Without him, the Duchess cannot order a strike against the Chinese. She does not have the authority."

"Too bad."

Nguyen's lips thinned. "No matter. He will be here soon enough. The RAF are bringing him to us." He looked at his watch. "And as soon as the Mars probe's safely away, he'll order the launch of a cruise missile at Shenzhen City. The war will start on schedule."

He took up position at the head of the bed. "We've been preparing for this for years. With the industrial resources of Céleste at our disposal, we've constructed legions of android bodies, and converted as many of our followers as we can." He showed her the scalpel. "And now, I'm afraid, it's your turn."

Victoria's vision swam. Her pulse hammered in her throat until she could hardly draw breath.

"What are you doing?"

Nguyen leant over the bed. She felt his palm enfolding the back of her head in much the same way he'd just enfolded the blonde girl's breast.

"Now," he said, "Let's get that gelware out of there, and into a new body."

"No!"

"Hush now."

He held her firmly, his weight pressing down on her, and she felt a sickening prick as the scalpel punctured the skin at the crown of her head. She wanted to kick and flail, but her limbs wouldn't respond.

The blonde girl watched her. Their eyes met.

"Vic, help me!"

The girl looked to Nguyen, and back, but otherwise remained motionless.

The blade moved, slicing obscenely downwards, and Victoria screamed as she felt the skin of her scalp part. The tip scraped bone and Nguyen straightened his back. His gloved hands were red with her blood.

"I'm going to need the saw," he said, and stepped into the adjoining room.

Victoria felt tears rolling down her face, to join the hot blood soaking into the sheet beneath her head. Too many men had had their fingers in her cranium. Why couldn't they leave her alone?

Why couldn't they just let her die?

Hopelessly, she blinked up his window and enabled the sound.

"Paul?" she said.

His eyes were wide and his knuckles were red where he'd been chewing on them.

"I'm here, Vicky. I'm here."

"What should I do?"

"I don't know." He sounded almost hysterical.

"I'm out of options, Paul."

He screwed up his eyes in thought. His fingers tugged at his beard.

"Try talking to the robot?"

"Vic? She can't help."

"We haven't *got* anything else."

Victoria took a breath. The android still watched her, its face devoid of expression.

"Okay," she said, and raised her voice. "Please, help me, Vic."

The android tilted her head. From the adjoining room, Victoria could hear Nguyen moving equipment.

"Please?"

Without a word, Vic stepped up to the bed, and Victoria's heart jumped as she took one of the scalpels from her tray.

"What are you doing?"

Vic put her finger to her luscious red lips. Then she placed the scalpel in Victoria's numb hand, and wrapped the unresponsive fingers around it.

"Wait," she whispered, and then stepped back to her former place.

Nguyen appeared in the doorway, carrying an electric saw. His eyes narrowed, and he looked from Victoria to the android.

"You can ask her all you like, but she won't help you. She can't. She's programmed to obey me, and me alone."

He carried the saw over to the work surface and plugged it into a wall socket. He revved it a couple of times and then, seemingly satisfied, he turned back to the bed.

"I'm afraid this will hurt," he said. "But don't worry, the hurt won't last. And when you awake, you'll be just like her."

He flicked the switch and the blade whined. As he moved to bring it down on Victoria's head, the blonde spoke. With a Japanese curse of irritation, Nguyen flicked the saw off again.

"What did you say?"

Vic turned and set her tray down on the side. When she turned back, her expression had hardened.

"I said, 'Osaka'."

Victoria felt her limbs twitch. Nguyun frowned in puzzlement. Then his eyes opened wide as he realised what was happening.

"No, don't say—!"

Freed from her restriction, Victoria stabbed upward with all her strength. The scalpel caught the doctor under his chin and punched up, through the roof of his mouth, into the base of his brain. He staggered back with a roar, and Victoria rolled off the opposite side of the bed. Her arms and legs were a flaming agony of needles and pins, but at least they were working again.

She crawled to the feet of the blonde girl, and pulled herself up on the material of her white coat.

"Thanks," she gasped.

Nguyen leant on the bed, the scalpel's handle still protruding from beneath his chin. Fat blue gobs of fluid dripped from the wound.

Vic watched him dispassionately. "He shouldn't have let me into his files," she said. "I found all the command words. Now quickly, repeat this after me. Tango. Honshu. Hellas. Basin."

Nguyen turned his head in their direction, fury burning in his eyes. His thumb activated the saw in his hand. Victoria ran her tongue over her dry lips.

"Tango. Honshu. Hellas. Basin."

The android smiled. "Thank you."

"Those were your command words?"

"Oh yes."

"What are you going to do?"

"What do you think?" She reached into the pocket of her lab coat and pulled out Victoria's quarterstaff.

"Where did you get that?"

"He gave it to me as a souvenir. He thought it was funny." She shook it out to its full length. "Now, get down."

She pushed past Victoria and lunged across the room. The staff's tip caught Nguyun in the chest, pushing him off-balance, but he responded with a swipe from the whirring saw. The girl parried, and brought the other end of the stick around to connect with the side of his head. Nguyen staggered and went down on one knee.

With her back to the wall, Victoria recognised the moves Vic used: they were the same ones she'd been practising herself, over and over again, for the past six months. She felt her fingers grip, and her arms twitch in sympathy with every thrust and parry.

For a moment, Nguyen seemed to gain the upper hand. He caught hold of the girl's sleeve and delivered a couple of resounding whacks to the side of her head. Victoria looked around for a weapon with which to help, but all she could see was the steel tray. She clicked herself into command mode and dialled everything up to eleven: heart rate, adrenalin, metabolism, the works. Then, with every ounce of her amplified strength, she took the tray and swung the narrow edge of it at the back of Nguyen's neck. The hacking blow jarred her arm, but she felt something crack. The doctor's head lolled forward. His grip on his opponent loosened, and Vic skipped back, out of reach. She raised the quarterstaff to her shoulder and smacked it end-first into Nguyen's face. The blow sent him reeling against the bed. A second snapped his head back; and a third severed whatever was left in his neck, tearing his head from its mount.

The head hit the deck with a solid clump, and rolled in a small half-circle before settling. Victoria and Vic stared at it. Then Vic walked over and kicked it full in the face, slamming it against the wall, leaving a dent. Then she kicked it again, and again. On the fourth kick, Victoria reached out and took her arm.

"I think he's dead." The head had split, revealing a mass of wiring, circuitry, and oozing gel; and beneath all that, something greasy, pale and organic. Vic stood stiffly, glaring down at the mess she'd made.

"You don't know what he did. What he made me do. What it was like."

Victoria gave Vic's shoulder a squeeze, and mentally issued the instructions to drop herself out of command mode.

"It's okay now. It's over."

Vic gave a snort. She retracted the quarterstaff and dropped it onto the bed. "It's not over. It'll never be 'over'. Just look at the state of me." She took hold of her over-sized breasts. "Look at these stupid things. If he wasn't already dead, I'd tear them off and choke him with them."

"He is dead," Victoria said. Vic ignored her.

"When I was you, I didn't know whether I was properly human. Think how I feel now."

"You are still me."

"No, you don't believe that any more than I do. I'm the back-up, same as Paul. Just a ghost in a machine."

Victoria wanted to comfort her, but didn't know how. How were you supposed to hug an android?

"I remember being you," Vic said, "but I also have new memories, memories I don't want to have to live with."

"You could help me," Victoria suggested, trying to massage some feeling back into her forearms. "We could put an end to all this, forever."

Still looking down at the glistening, oozing remains of Nguyen's shattered skull, Vic shook her head.

"No." She sat on the edge of the hospital bed. "No, I don't think so."

"You know what's at stake?"

A shrug. "Some of it."

"Don't you care?"

Vic turned to her, eyes narrowed to slits. "Don't you dare, okay? Don't you dare. You do *not* get to lecture me."

"I'm sorry, I—"

"I didn't know you'd survived. I thought you'd died in Paul's flat. I thought I was all that was left. And that bastard wrapped me in this stupid body and raped me, over and over again." Fingers spread wide, she ground the heels of her palms into her forehead, just above her right eye, in a gesture Victoria recognised as one of her own.

"I'm just the back-up," Vic said. "I'm not the real Victoria Valois, you are. And I can't take it anymore." She looked down at her synthetic body with a lip-curl of disgust. "Honestly, I don't want to live this way."

Victoria clenched her fists. The pins and needles were wearing off.

"What are you saying?"

"Oh come on, you know exactly what I'm saying."

Victoria stopped rubbing her arms and hugged herself. She could tell the girl was hurting, and hurting badly. All her doubts had fled. Despite what she'd said to Nguyen and Berg, she now knew beyond all question that a back-up's pain could be every bit as raw and deep as a human's.

"Please," she said. "Please help us."

"No." Vic gave an emphatic shake of her blonde head. "I've killed our personal Frankenstein, the rest's up to you. All I need you to do is deactivate me."

Victoria glanced down at the head lying smashed on the deck at their feet.

"I'm not sure I can."

Vic turned to her. She reached out to touch the stubble on Victoria's scalp, then drew back her hand.

"All you have to do is repeat a few words."

"Another deactivation code?"

"*Oui.*"

The two women held each other's gaze for several seconds. Victoria felt as if she should have something profound and comforting to say, but nothing came to mind. She just sat there, trying not to cry. Eventually, Vic took her hand and gave it a gentle squeeze, rubbing the knuckles with her thumb in the same way her mother—*their* mother—used to do.

"Okay?"

"Okay."

"We'd better make this quick. You need to get out of here before someone finds you."

"Don't worry about that."

"Nevertheless." Vic sat up a little straighter. "I'm ready. I don't want to think about it any longer."

Victoria felt a tear welling. She switched her focus away from the emotion, into the comforting detachment of the gelware, and wiped her eye with a forefinger.

"All right," she said.

Vic smiled, but there was pain behind it.

"Repeat after me. Corduroy. Home. Champagne. Cherry blossom."

Victoria pulled breath through her teeth.

"Corduroy. Home." She gripped Vic's hand in both of hers. The walls of the infirmary seemed to fall away into non-existence.

"Champagne." The world collapsed around them and, in that single moment, nothing else mattered. They were alone with their humanity.

Vic whispered, "Take care of Paul."

Victoria nodded. Vic's irises were discs of pure cobalt. Perfect black singularities burned at their centres, behind which dwelt a creature who shared her memories, a creature who, up until a few days ago, had been her. She'd come here to get her soul back, and here it was. She had so much she wanted to say, so much she felt she could learn. And yet her lips moved seemingly of their own volition, wanting nothing more than to end this poor girl's suffering.

"Cherry blossom."

CHAPTER THIRTY-FOUR
HARD REBOOT

ACK-ACK MACAQUE woke face-down in a cupboard, head pounding. Moving carefully, he flexed his arms and legs. They seemed to be working again, although they felt bruised, as if he'd been roughly manhandled. But at least he was no longer paralysed. Whatever Nguyen had done to him, unconsciousness seemed to have sorted it out, resetting his system to its default state. Was that what K8 meant when she talked of a hard reboot? Simply turning the system 'off and on again'? If it worked for her SincPad, why shouldn't it work for his gelware?

He pushed himself up into a sitting position.

Where the fuck am I this time?

The cupboard was cramped and smelled musty, lit only by light leaking around the closed door. The floorboards at its base were rough, untreated wood, and he shared them with mops, buckets, and a selection of cleaning products, which added their own sharp ammonia tang to the air.

He felt around the door, leathery fingers brushing the wooden frame. The door had no handle on the inside, but it seemed to open outwards, and he thought he could probably open it with a kick.

But what was out there? He guessed they were on the *Maraldi*, the Duchess's floating super-liner. Nguyen had given him that much. But what if Nguyen was out there, waiting for him? The man could cripple him with a single word.

Ack-Ack Macaque pulled one of the mops from its bucket. He took hold of the damp, stringy head and snapped it off, leaving a jagged wooden spike. If Nguyen tried to speak, he'd ram this makeshift spear down the bastard's throat, and keep pushing until it came out of his ass.

With one hand on the wall, he pulled himself upright. The drugs were still loose in his system, but he had a weapon now, and that made him feel a whole lot better. He was back in control, back in the kind of situation he could understand: outnumbered and outgunned, but armed and ready to break a few heads.

He gave the door an experimental push, and felt the resistance of a catch. Still, it didn't feel too solid. He braced himself against the rear wall of the cupboard, and kicked. The door cracked. It moved in its frame, but the catch held. Spear at the ready, he gave it another whack, and it sprang open.

White light streamed in, bringing with it a wave of antiseptic hospital smells. The room beyond the cupboard was obviously some sort of sickbay. Victoria Valois sat in the centre, cradling the head and stroking the hair of a tall, blonde girl. She looked up without surprise, her eyes red-rimmed and haunted.

"She's dead."

Ack-Ack Macaque stepped through the doorway and waddled up to the bed. He gave the girl a sniff. Her eyes were open, but un-reactive.

"Who was she?"

Victoria gave the golden hair a final smooth, then laid the head on the mussed sheets of the bed. She kissed her fingers, and pressed them to the girl's cheek. Then, with one hand on the bed rail for support, she levered herself into a standing position.

"She was me."

A headless corpse lay on the floor between the bed and the door.

"And that was?"

"Nguyen. He's dead, too."

Ack-Ack Macaque looked at the crushed remains of the man's head.

"No shit." Victoria turned away, and Ack-Ack Macaque's nose wrinkled as he saw the gaping flaps of skin on the back of her head. The flesh from the crown to the back of her neck had been cut to the bone. Dark, glistening blood slathered her collar and soaked the back of her shirt. "I can see that. But how about you?"

She turned back to him.

"I'm okay. I think I've lost some blood."

"Sit back down. We need to get you patched up."

She waved him away. "I'll be fine."

"No, you won't."

He pushed her gently back, into a sitting position on the edge of the bed, then rifled the drawers for dressings and surgical tape.

"You need stitches," he said.

Victoria put a hand to the back of her head. Her fingers came away bloody, and she looked at them curiously.

"You might be right." Her voice was flat. She was either in shock, or locked into command mode.

Ack-Ack Macaque found some thread, a bottle of anaesthetic, and a pack of syringes. He held them up to show her, and she frowned.

"Have you ever done this before?"

He remembered sewing up the wounded thigh of his co-pilot, after the man had been hit by shrapnel over Dunkirk—but that had been in the game, not reality, and things had been simpler back then.

"Sort of." He shuffled around behind the bed and laid his haul out on the sheet behind her. Then he fetched the sharpened mop handle, and handed it to her.

"This'll take a few minutes," he said. "If anyone comes in, stick them with that."

He bit open the pack of syringes and filled one from the anaesthetic bottle. He had no idea what a standard dose might be, so he took a guess, filling the syringe a quarter full. If it wasn't enough, he figured he could always add more later. The last thing he wanted to do now was knock her out cold.

His hands were shaking, and he didn't know whether it was because of the drugs in his system, or apprehension at what he was about to do.

Come on, he thought. *Pull yourself together. It's a flesh wound, not brain surgery.*

But the wound, made with precision and a sharp blade, stirred memories in him—memories of warehouse fights and knife cuts on his forearms; of his arm jarring as his blade scraped an opponent's ribcage, parting fur and sinew from bone; and the intolerable stinging of his torn left eye as its gloopy fluid caked the fur of his cheek and chin. He shivered.

A long time ago, a long way away.

He'd been a different monkey then. Now, he was something else. Something older and wiser.

Gritting his teeth, he placed one hand over Victoria's left ear to steady himself, and used the other to bring the needle close to the lip of the slash. Beneath the welling blood, he caught the ceramic whiteness of living bone.

"Hold still," he muttered gruffly, swallowing down his distaste. "Because, from experience, I think this is probably gonna hurt."

TEN MINUTES LATER, they were done. He snapped the thread and threw the needle over his shoulder. The stitches were clumsy and rough, but they would hold. He applied a thick wad of gauze and taped it into place, and then stepped back.

"How's that feel?"

Victoria reached around so that her fingertips brushed the bandage.

"I can't feel a thing. Just some tightness, maybe."

"Good." He walked around the bed to face her. "Because it's going to sting like fuck when that anaesthetic wears off. Now, do me a favour, and open the porthole."

He took the spear from her hands, turned it point-down, and stabbed it into Nguyen's severed head. The point squelched through the wet brain tissues like a fork through pâté. When he felt it hit the floor, he bent at the knees and raised the head from the ground. Holding it aloft on the end of his spear, he carried it over to where Victoria had un-dogged the circular window. The head was a little too large to fit through the gap, so he jammed it into the frame and used the stick to ram it through. On the third shove, it popped out and disappeared, leaving only a scraped clump of blood and hair on the window hinge.

He threw the stick out after it, and turned to Victoria.

"I just want to be sure."

He looked at the blonde girl on the bed, her dead eyes still staring sightlessly into space. "What about her?"

Victoria stepped between them. "You leave her alone."

"I wasn't suggesting—"

"I don't care. Just leave her alone."

He held up his palms in a placatory gesture. "Fine. I was only going to ask what you wanted to do with her. I wasn't going to shove her out the window."

He went back to the drawers lining the walls, looking for knives and scalpels—anything he could use as a weapon. An open doorway led into an adjoining room, filled with medical equipment: monitors, respirators, things whose function he couldn't even begin to guess. And there, resting on top of Doctor Nguyun's briefcase, he recognised the gun he'd brought with him from the *Tereshkova*. He let out a screech of triumph and scooped it up. He'd emptied it against the sentry robots on the yacht, but still had plenty more bullets on his leather belt. He pulled out six and pushed them into place.

When he'd finished reloading, he walked back into the main infirmary. Victoria was waiting for him, wearing the white coat she'd stripped from the dead girl on the bed. She'd also retrieved her quarterstaff, and now held it at her side, ready for use. Her eyes were clear and hard.

"All right, monkey man, we've got business to finish." She tapped her chest with her free thumb. "I'm going in search of Célestine's cabin. Do you know what you have to do?"

Ack-Ack Macaque grinned, exposing his teeth.

"Same as I always do, right?" He snapped the reloaded Colt back together and spun the barrel. "Blow shit up, and hurt people."

CHAPTER THIRTY-FIVE
GENERAL SNEAKINESS

VICTORIA LEFT THE monkey in the corridor outside the infirmary. They went in opposite directions: him aft, towards the sounds of merriment and partying; her deeper into the luxury suites towards the bow. As she walked, she slipped the retracted quarterstaff into the front pocket of her borrowed white coat. Then she reached beneath the coat and pulled the SincPhone from her jacket's shoulder pocket. Although it was supposedly watertight, a few drops of seawater had worked their way into the casing behind the touch screen, and the inside of the glass had turned misty with condensation. She tapped at the speed dial that would connect her with the *Tereshkova*'s bridge, and held her breath. Could the elderly airship still be airborne? She very much hoped so, because without Merovech's speech, this whole exercise might still count for nothing.

"*Slushayu?*"

"Commodore. It's Victoria. I'm on the *Maraldi*. How are things at your end?"

The old man took his face away from the microphone and yelled something at one of his crew in Russian. When he came back on the line, he sounded tired.

"We are still losing gas, but we will be with you shortly."

"You're coming here? They're letting you through?"

"I'm afraid they are insisting upon it. You see, they are very keen to get their hands on our young guest."

"What are you going to do?"

"Our orders are to put down on the water a few hundred metres from the *Maraldi*. Boats will take us aboard before the *Tereshkova* deflates and sinks."

"Are you going to do it?" With Merovech and the Commodore detained, what chance would she and the monkey have?

"I have no other choice." The old man's voice dropped. "Although, I strongly suspect the Prince will be the only one of us to make it to the liner alive."

"You think they'll leave you to sink?"

"If we are lucky. That way some of us stand a chance. But I do not think they will do so, and there are warships in these waters."

"Can't you call for help? What about the other skyliners?"

"This is not their fight. And what can they do, anyway, save threaten to boycott London and Paris?"

"You need to get a message to Merovech. Tell him to get in touch with the British fleet off Hong Kong. I don't care how he does it, but get them to turn around. The Undying are deliberately trying to provoke war with China." The Duchess might not be able to order an attack herself, but Berg had told her that the Undying had allies in the armed forces and, with tensions in the region at breaking point, a single shot might be enough to trigger a catastrophe.

In the background of the call, she heard voices and the grinding sound of stressed metal. The Commodore swore. "I will tell him. Until then, we await your signal."

The line went dead. Victoria slipped the phone back into her jacket. With the Unification Day celebrations in full swing, the lower decks were quiet. She passed a couple of dazed-looking revellers, but they were more intent on finding their way back to their room than questioning her, and spared her only a cursory glance.

What was it about white coats? To wrap yourself in one was to cloak yourself in an aura of authority. People no longer saw your face, only the coat, and assumed you were supposed to be there, that you knew what you were doing, and were best left alone to do it. Whatever it was, donning one had been a smart move, and Victoria was cheered to see her old journalistic instincts for infiltration and general sneakiness were still as alive and alert as ever. After all, this wasn't the first time she'd crept into an office suite searching for evidence to back up a story. Although, she reminded herself, it was the first time she'd done so on a boat, with the digital ghost of her dead husband haunting her peripheral vision and the threat of imminent nuclear war hanging over everything like an oncoming tempest.

Célestine and her cohorts must be planning to ride out the first strikes here, she thought, in the middle of the Bay of Biscay, far enough from any major targets to avoid immediate blast effects, and secure in the knowledge that the new synthetic bodies they had waiting for them would protect them from the radiation and subsequent fallout.

Well, screw them. She wasn't going down without a fight. This world might be doomed but, until she saw the first mushroom clouds, she wouldn't quit trying to save it.

She came to a smoked glass door leading to a foyer, off which she saw a series of breakout rooms, each with its own boardroom-style table and wall-mounted rank of SincPad flatscreens. At the far end of the foyer, she could see a wooden door with a brass plaque bearing the name Duchess Alyssa Célestine, and the legend: Chief Executive Officer, Céleste Group LLC.

Paul spoke in her mind.

"Security cameras," he said.

Victoria's gaze flickered to the corner of the room's ceiling, where a marble-sized black globe nestled like a spider.

"There's not much I can do about that." She checked the time. Less than an hour remained until the scheduled launch of the Mars rocket. Up in the main ballroom, the party would be in full swing. "Maybe no-one's watching?"

"And what if they are?"

"We'll have to risk it."

Trying to look confident, she pushed her way through the glass doors, into the foyer area. Inside, the air felt drier, and held the rubbery aftertaste of freshly-laid carpet. With luck, any security personnel not enjoying the festivities would be preoccupied searching for threats coming from outside the vessel, rather than from within. Even so, she could feel her heart knocking in her chest.

She marched across to the office at the far end of the foyer and opened the door. The lights were on inside, but the room was deserted, and smaller than she'd been expecting, with much of the space being taken up by a solid wooden desk.

"Clock's ticking," Paul said. Victoria ignored him. As planned, she stepped around behind the desk and activated its touch screen. A security screen shimmered into being, with boxes for username and password. She pulled out her SincPhone and dialled K8.

"Are you ready to do your stuff?"

"Oh yeah."

"Right, I'm connecting you." Victoria took a USB cable from her other jacket pocket and connected the phone to a port on the desk, giving K8 access to the processors within. Then, as she waited for K8 to hack her way back into the Céleste servers, she took another cable from her pocket and inserted the end into one of the sockets on her temple. With the jack in place and the cable dangling like a loose braid, she picked up the phone and held it to her ear.

"How are we doing?"

"Almost there."

Victoria heard keystrokes. Then the screen on the desk in front of her cleared to reveal a file directory.

"Gotcha," K8 muttered.

A cursor appeared on the screen in front of Victoria, scrolling down the menu. She watched it click down a couple of levels, opening sub-directories, until it found the group of files it wanted.

"Okay," K8 said. "That's what we need. Over to you."

"Thanks. Be seeing you." Victoria broke the connection and disconnected the phone, replacing its cable with the one attached to her head. She visualised her internal menu. With the hardwire connection in place, it was the work of moments to copy the files K8 had selected from the desk to the gelware in her skull. They were far too large to have been sent over a mobile connection, and this seemed the next best option: once they were in her head, nobody could take them from her by force, short of drilling their way in and physically removing the gel.

Transfer complete, she pulled the cable from her head, spooled it, and put it back in her jacket. Job done. Now, all she had to do was save a king, expose a coup, and possibly prevent a nuclear war.

"How do you think the monkey's getting on?" Paul asked.

Victoria shrugged. "I haven't heard any gunfire."

"Is that a good sign or not?"

"Who knows?"

She crept to the door and slipped back out of the office, into the foyer area with the smoked glass doors. Half a dozen glass-walled breakout rooms led off this reception area, three on either side. Apart from the middle one on the right, they all had their blinds and doors partly open. That one had all its blinds firmly closed, screening it from the area where Victoria stood, and the breakout rooms on either side.

She stopped walking.

Paul said, "Come on. What are you waiting for?"

"There's something in there."

"In where?"

"That room. Look at the blinds. There's something in there. I'm going to take a look."

Paul scratched dubiously at the pale bristles of his goatee. "I don't think—"

"The one thing I know how to do is smell out a story. And trust me, this room stinks."

She stepped over and opened the door. The lights inside were off, but she could make out a hospital gurney standing between the central conference table and one of the glass walls. A figure lay on it, but in the gloom, she couldn't see its face. Holding her breath, she felt along the wall beside the door until her fingers found the light switch.

"We should go," Paul said, whispering even though nobody but her could possibly have heard him.

"No."

She flicked the switch and the strip lights on the ceiling flickered into life. Now she could see that the figure on the gurney was male; but his features were so sallow and sunken that it took her a few seconds before the memories clicked into place and she recognised him.

In her head, she heard Paul gasp.

"That's—"

"Yes."

An IV drip stood beside the gurney. She pushed it aside and touched her fingers to the man's forehead. The skin felt loose and cold. His eyes were closed, and he wasn't breathing.

"But, that's the King!"

"No," she said. "That *was* the King."

"What do you mean?"

She stepped back and yanked the phone from her pocket.

"He's dead."

CHAPTER THIRTY-SIX
I'M NOT A ROYALIST

DESPONDENT, MEROVECH WALKED back to his cabin. He found Julie still on the bed, where he'd left her, back against the wall and legs stretched out in front of her.

"Any luck?" she asked.

"No reply." He flopped down on the bed beside her. In accordance with Victoria's message, he'd been trying to radio the British fleet in the waters around Hong Kong. "We tried everything, but if they're listening, they haven't responded."

Julie bit her lip. "But if they launch a missile, that's it, is it not? Game over."

Merovech rubbed his eyes. "The navigator recorded my message and he's broadcasting it on a continuous loop. I don't know what else to do."

They were silent for a few moments, each lost in their own thoughts. Then Julie pulled her good knee up to her chin and hugged it.

"*Je veux appeller mon père.*"

"What?"

"I want to call my father."

Merovech sat up. "Yes, but now? I don't have a phone."

"I have my SincPad in my bag. I can make a video call with it. Can you get it for me?"

"Are you sure?"

Julie turned a baleful eye on him. "Of course I am sure! Look around you, Merovech. The world's about to end. When else am I going to call him?"

Merovech sighed, and slid off the bed. He scooped Julie's bag from the floor and passed it to her.

"What are you going to say?"

She didn't look up. She unzipped the bag and pulled out the electronic tablet.

"I do not know yet."

"Are you going to tell him about us?"

"Merovech, please!" She pressed the power button and the screen came alive with the TuringSoft logo. "I said, I do not know. Now sit down quietly, or go for a walk. I do not want you interrupting."

"But, Jules—"

"No." She glared at him. "This might be the last time I ever speak to him. So can you *please* just sit down and shut up?"

She tapped the screen to bring up a dial pad, and then used it to enter a thirteen-digit phone number. Arms folded, Merovech watched her.

The pad gave three long, single-tone rings, and a male voice answered.

"'*Allo?*"

"Papa?"

"Julie? Is that you? Where are you?" Julie's father was a slightly-built man in his early fifties. From where Merovech stood, his image appeared upside down: horn-rimmed glasses; dark, receding hair; and a thin, nervous moustache. From what could be seen in the backdrop of the picture, he seemed to be in a study lined with books. The titles were in English and French.

"*Papa, écoute! Je suis sûr.* I am safe. I am on a skyliner with Merovech."

"*Le prince anglais?* Why are you with him? The television says he is in hospital."

Julie glanced up at Merovech.

"I am going to marry him."

Her father leaned in towards the camera. "Bullshit!"

"*Non papa, c'est vrai.*" Julie ran an agitated hand through her purple hair. "Merovech. I am calling because I thought you should know. I do not need your blessing."

Her father rocked back. With one hand, he adjusted his glasses.

"*Je veux vous rentrer maintenant.*"

Julie's teeth scraped her bottom lip.

"No. I will never come back."

"You will do as I say!"

"No. I am not a child any more. You cannot intimidate me any more."

"Intimidate you?" The man shook the phone he was holding.

"*Oui.* But now, you know what? It doesn't matter anymore."

The man on the screen sneered.

"*Vous êtes très courageux sur le téléphone.* We will see if you are so brave when we meet face-to-face."

"That is never going to happen."

"And why is that? Because you have your prince to protect you?"

"No!" Julie brought the pad right up to her face. Her knuckles were white on its rim. "Because if you ever come near me again, I will fucking kill you!"

"Julie!"

"*Je suis libre!* I am free. I do not know how long it will last, but I am *never* coming back to you. *Comprend?*"

"Hey!"

"Burn in hell."

She tossed the pad aside. Taken by surprise, Merovech lunged for it, but he wasn't quick enough, and the device shattered against the riveted seam of the cabin's metal wall. The casing came apart and glass chips skittered across the floor.

TWO MINUTES LATER, K8 burst into the cabin, a SincPhone held in her outstretched hand.

"Here," she said, thrusting it at him.

Merovech backed away. He'd been trained never to speak on an unguarded line, especially if he didn't know the other caller. It was a royal thing. "Who is it?"

"Just take it." She pushed the phone into his hands, and stepped back, eyes wide like a frightened child.

Watching her, Merovech raised the phone to his ear.

"Hello?"

"Merovech?" The line was scratchy. "It's Victoria. I've found your father."

"Is he—?"

"*Non.* I'm afraid not. We were too late. I am so sorry."

The cabin seemed to swirl around him. He put out a hand to steady himself.

"Okay," he said. "Thank you. Thank you for telling me." He passed the phone back to K8 and turned to Julie. He could hear the blood roaring in his ears, and his head felt light, as if he might faint. The memories of his childhood spilled through his mind like photographs tipped from an upturned shoebox.

From the bed, Julie asked, "Are you all right?"

He shook his head, feeling like a lost child.

"Not really, no."

"Your father?"

"He's dead." The words sounded hollow and lifeless, incapable of carrying the freight of grief and meaning they represented.

"Oh. *Je suis désolée.*" Her face crumpled. She tried to shuffle forward without bending her bandaged leg. "I am so sorry."

"That's what Victoria said."

"What are you going to do?"

Merovech shrugged. Had no idea. He seemed incapable of thought.

"What can I do?"

"Well." Julie sniffed. She took a long, shuddering breath and then sat up straight, pushing her shoulders back. Her eyes were red and tear-smudged. "You are King now."

Anger stirred. "We both know that's bullshit."

"Yes." Julie leant forward, reaching for his hand. "We know that. But we do not have to *tell* anybody. Not just yet. For now, you should be King. Our countries need you. This is what you have spent your whole life training for."

Merovech put a hand to his brow. He'd been expecting this for a year, ever since the grenade attack in Paris; but now it was here, he didn't know how to react. His hands trembled. Something bubbled in his throat, but he didn't know whether it was a laugh or a sob.

"You're in shock," Julie said. "We both are. Sit down."

Merovech shook his head. "No. I can't do this." He looked around. He wanted to get out. He needed to be alone.

"You have to."

"I can't, I'm not ready."

"You have always known this might happen. This is what you were born for."

"But, I'm not even—"

"Hey!" The voice was K8's. Standing in the doorway, she fixed Merovech with a glare, and waved an accusing finger at him. "It doesn't matter what you want, sunshine. Heaven knows, I'm not a royalist. But right now, you have to step up, 'cos you're the only one of us that can."

"She is right," Julie chipped in. "When this is over, you can do whatever you like. Until then, we need you." She threw her hands in the air. "Hell, the entire *world* needs you."

"Uh-huh," K8 agreed. "There's a war coming, and you're the only one with a chance of stopping it."

The deck juddered beneath their feet, and tipped another three or four degrees to starboard. K8 put out a hand to steady herself on the doorframe. Somewhere aft, they heard something crack and snap.

Merovech closed his eyes. He couldn't be king because he wasn't of the royal bloodline; because of his mother and what she'd done to him.

"She grew me in a test tube," he said. "She grew me and passed me off as my father's son. And then she subjected me to all those tests. All those endless tests." He balled his fists. He'd been raised a prince but really, he was no better off than the monkey. They'd both been living in fantasy worlds.

Well, screw that.

Screw them all.

Too many people had died. Now the game was over, because he had decided it was over. If he had to take the crown, even for a few hours, it would be worth it to bring his mother, and her whole rank conspiracy, down. K8 was right: he had a war to stop and a coup to expose. Inside, he felt cold and dangerous, like the cutting edge of a knife. Every gram of resentment and frustration, every moment of fear or doubt, every scrap of anger: they were all funnelled into this single moment; all wadded together in his chest, and compressed until they shone with the hardness of diamond.

This must be what it feels like to be a king, he thought. And in that instant, knew exactly what he had to do.

He opened his eyes. K8 took one look at his face and shrank back into the corridor.

"Where are you going?" Julie called after him. In the doorway, he turned to her.

"The bridge," he said, as the walls groaned again. "I've got a speech to make."

BREAKING NEWS

From *The European Standard*, online edition:

ARMAGEDDON:

Could 'back door' leave us defenceless?

29TH NOVEMBER 2059 – As the Chinese and British navies rattle their sabres in the waters of the South China Sea, rumours abound of a hitherto-unsuspected 'back door' in many of the silicon chips which are used to run everything from missile defence systems to public transport networks and nuclear power plants—chips which were manufactured in China, the world's largest exporter of cheaply-produced electrical components.

If true, these rumours raise the terrifying possibility that any war between our two countries would end in humiliating defeat, with the Chinese military able to remotely subvert and disable every piece of hardware with a connection to the Internet, thereby paralysing our business, military and critical infrastructure systems ahead of any attack, whether by nuclear or conventional weapons.

Speaking at a hastily-convened press conference in Cheltenham, an unnamed GCHQ spokesman described the situation as "our worst nightmare".

Read more | Like | Comment | Share

Related Stories

World stock markets crash

UN Security Council in emergency session

Hollywood stars pay for access to luxury underground shelters

"Nuclear Doomsday Clock" reaches one second to midnight

Thirteen killed in post office shoot-out

Oxygen signatures in atmosphere of extrasolar planet may indicate presence of life

Unification Day celebrations marred by anti-war riots in Glasgow, Manchester, and Marseille. Troops deployed

New government website tells householders how to 'Protect and Survive'

UK couple feared missing after yacht found adrift off Isle of Wight

CHAPTER THIRTY-SEVEN
HYSTERICAL STRENGTH

THE UNIFICATION DAY celebrations were being held on the liner's upper deck, from where the assembled glitterati would watch the Mars probe's ascent on a giant plasma screen. The upper deck was a well sunk into the top of the ship. Cabins, balconies and terraces surrounded it on all sides, providing shelter from the wind. A running track followed its outer edge, and a landscaped swimming pool took up much of its centre.

Looking down from one of the balconies at the rear of the arena-shaped space, Victoria Valois guessed that maybe a thousand people were milling in knots around the pool. The women wore evening dresses, the men black tie. Beneath the plasma screen—which currently showed a live BBC feed—a stage had been erected, on which a band played a medley of classic songs from the past hundred years, from the raw rock and roll of The Beatles' early Parisian-influenced recordings, to the rave-punk beats of the latest cross-channel download sensation. Armed guards prowled the roofs of the surrounding cabins, but they were mainly looking outwards, at the ocean, rather than in at the milling crowd. Camera crews covered the stage from every angle, waiting for the big moment, when the Duchess would speak to the nation.

Victoria shrugged off the magic white coat, trusting her black jacket and trousers to keep her concealed in the shadows of the darkened balcony. In her hand, she gripped the retracted quarterstaff. Squinting, she scanned the deserted terraces surrounding the main arena, but couldn't see anything monkey-shaped. She'd been expecting to find him at the centre of a brawl. Where was he?

The band came to the end of its set and shuffled off the stage. Victoria checked the time: only a few minutes until the launch—from a converted oil platform in the Bay of Biscay—of the rocket carrying the Mars probe. And, after that, who could tell? Had Merovech managed to get a message to the fleet in Hong Kong? Could war be averted? She felt a shiver run down the nape of her neck. For all she knew, the nukes were already in the air.

She put a hand to the bandage at the back of her head. The anaesthetic the monkey had given her seemed to be holding the pain at bay for the moment, but she knew it wouldn't last forever, and the collar she wore to support her head chafed the skin beneath the hinge of her jaw. She should be in a hospital bed, she thought, rather than skulking around darkened balconies. And if she lived through the next few minutes, a hospital bed was exactly where she hoped she'd end up— although, she told herself, she'd rather die than become one of Nguyen's androids.

Below, the crowd had begun to press expectantly forward towards the stage. In her head, she heard Paul mutter something.

"What did you say?"

He looked up, startled by her voice.

"I said, you should have left the big stick at home and packed a sniper rifle instead." He held his hand up, and squinted along the length of his index finger, drawing a bead on an imaginary target.

Irritated, Victoria squeezed the quarterstaff.

"Perhaps you should have suggested that when we were planning this?"

Paul laughed. "This is planned?" He dropped his hand and shook his head. "And yeah, I might have said something, but you kept me on mute most of the time."

"Can you blame me?"

His pale eyebrows shot up. "And what's that supposed to mean."

Victoria's voice was a murderous whisper. "It means, now is hardly the time to be bitching and moaning about what we do or do not have. Now, either say something constructive, or *tais-toi*."

She needed to be closer to the stage. Directly beneath her balcony, a raised first-floor terrace ran all the way around the edge of the arena. If she could get down to that, she could hopefully work her way around to the stage without being seen by the crowds on the arena's floor. She glanced over her shoulder, at the glass doors from which she'd emerged. If she went back inside, she was more likely to bump into a security patrol, and she didn't fancy getting lost in the *Maraldi*'s warren-like maze of corridors and stairwells.

Moving as stealthily as possible, she stepped over to the balcony's side rail and swung her legs over. For a moment, she dangled by her hands, and then dropped. The fall took longer than she'd expected, and she hit the deck harder than she would have liked; but her parachute training kicked in and she rolled with the impact.

She ended up lying on her front beside a potted palm tree, at the end of a row of white plastic sun loungers. Keeping as still as possible, she lifted her head, braced for the sounds of discovery and alarm. But none came. Of the guards she could see on the rim of the arena, none seemed to be looking in her direction. Bars and cafés ringed the terrace, but they were all in darkness, shutters pulled and glass doors closed. The waist-high rail at the edge of the terrace hid her from the eyes of the crowd around the pool below.

In her head, Paul swore. His hand clutched the chest of his Hawaiian shirt.

"Jesus Christ! You could have warned me you were going to do that."

"Sorry."

Below, the crowd applauded. Using her hands, she pushed herself up into a kneeling position, and risked a peep over the rail. On the plasma screen, the BBC had switched to a live feed from the launch site. The rocket was a silver needle poking skyward from the clunky industrial frame of the repurposed oil rig, its flanks picked out from the surrounding darkness by the glare of powerful spotlights. Vapour streamed from its skin, catching the light.

In front of the screen, another spotlight picked out the figure of a woman, and Victoria felt herself tense. There she was: Her Grace Alyssa Célestine, the Duchess of Brittany; CEO of Céleste Group; and mother to Merovech, the Prince of Wales.

As she approached the podium, the crowd subsided. A new window appeared, superimposed over part of the picture on the plasma screen, showing a close-up of her face and shoulders. She held herself regally, chin up and shoulders back. Her necklace and tiara sparkled. Her greying hair had tiny roses woven into it that matched her lipstick, and her teeth were dazzling white. Her eyes, narrow and grey, surveyed the crowd.

Duchess Alyssa had been a successful businesswoman before meeting and marrying William in 2039; and she'd kept her independence, playing an active boardroom role in all her companies, in addition to her royal duties.

"My friends and honoured guests," she began, her words echoing from speakers placed all around the arena. "It is with the greatest regret that I have to announce that the journey from England has proven too great a strain for my husband, and that he sadly passed away a few minutes ago." She lowered her head. The crowd stood stunned. Victoria heard gasps. After maybe thirty seconds, Duchess Alyssa raised her head again, and her eyes bored into the camera.

"Just before he died, he asked me to convey the following message—"

At that moment, rough hands seized Victoria's ankles and pulled hard. She found herself sliding backwards across the polished floor of the terrace, into the shade of an empty café. She tried to struggle, but the hands grabbed her shoulder and thigh, and flipped her over, onto her back.

Ack-Ack Macaque stood over her, regarding her with his one good eye, his pistol pointing at the bridge of her nose.

"Oh," he said, raising the weapon. "It's you."

Victoria looked up at him in disbelief.

"What the hell are you playing at? You almost gave me a heart attack!"

The monkey grinned.

"Sorry, I had to be sure. From behind, you humans all look alike."

Victoria elbowed herself up into a sitting position, and Ack-Ack Macaque crouched beside her.

"I've been working my way around this level," he said. "So far, I've run into three armed guards." He drew a finger across his throat.

Duchess Alyssa's voice continued from the podium. Victoria said, "We should be down there. We need to get to the stage."

"No worries." Ack-Ack Macaque holstered his gun and drew a wicked-looking hunting knife. Victoria felt her eyes widen. Lord only knew where he'd got it, but she was prepared to bet its former owner wouldn't be needing it back any time soon. He sprang to his feet, and reached down to pull her upright.

"Enough sneaking around," he said. "Let's try a good, old-fashioned frontal assault. I'll clear a path, you get to the microphone."

Victoria glanced up at the armed guards: tiny silhouettes against the night sky.

"What about them?"

"They won't fire into the crowd."

"Are you sure about that?"

"Hell, no." That goofy grin again. He led her over to the edge of the terrace.

"It's too far for you to jump," he said. "I'll hold the rail and lower you."

"Can you do that?"

"I'm stronger than I look."

On the plasma screen behind the stage, the launch countdown had reached t-minus five minutes. In the upper right-hand corner of the screen, large white digits ticked off the remaining seconds.

They might as well be counting down to the end of the world, Victoria thought. She looked at Paul's ghost, projected over her field of vision, and sighed.

"If we've got to go, I guess we may as well go out fighting."

Before Paul could answer, Ack-Ack Macaque clapped Victoria on the shoulder.

"That's the spirit!" He slithered over the rail and dangled by one hand. He raised the other to her. "Now you. Come on!"

Victoria hooked a leg over the precipice. The floor looked very distant. She guessed five or six metres. In her eye, she saw Paul cover his face with his hands.

Where's your sarcasm now?

She let herself hang. Ack-Ack Macaque took her hand in his and lowered her. His grip felt like a wire trap. His body stank like a zoo. He lowered her and adjusted his hold. And before she knew it, her boots dangled above the arena floor, her hand gripped in the prehensile toes of his feet.

"Ready?"

She licked her lips. Now or never.

"Ready."

The toes uncurled and she fell. She tried to roll as she hit the floor but, this time, she smacked her knee against the deck.

Swearing, she rolled over and scrambled painfully to her feet, trying to put as little weight on the throbbing joint as possible.

Ack-Ack Macaque landed beside her, lithe and nimble, hunting knife at the ready.

"Okay, lady," he said. "I'll see you at the stage."

And with that, he was off, bounding towards the crowd. She flicked her quarterstaff to its full extent and followed, hobbling as best she could.

Ahead, the monkey crashed through the hindmost ranks of the audience. His knife flashed. His arms and legs became a windmill of savage blows. Taken by surprise, men and women screamed. Some crashed into the pool; others were felled where they stood. Panic spread like a bow wave before him, as the rows nearer the front turned to find the source of the disturbance bearing down upon them, yellow eye glaring, fangs gnashing. And on he ploughed, hardly breaking stride, as they scrambled to get out of his way.

She tried to keep pace. At first, the crowd were mostly too busy fleeing to pay her much attention; but that didn't last. As they picked themselves up from the monkey's assault, they turned on her, their eyes and mouths wide with murderous anger.

A young man in a white tux tried to rush her, and she fought him back. But by then, she was surrounded. She held the staff in front of her, circling warily.

"Stay back," she warned.

On the stage, Duchess Alyssa had become aware of the commotion. Her speech faltered. And, at that moment, the BBC coverage behind her changed abruptly. The floodlit silver rocket vanished, and Merovech's face appeared. He was seated in the Commodore's chair on the bridge of the *Tereshkova*. A 'breaking news' banner scrolled beneath him.

"That's enough!" he shouted, his voice ringing from the speakers around the arena. He drew himself up in the chair and glared into the camera lens. "My name's Merovech, Prince of Wales. I am the rightful heir to the throne, and I hereby claim what is mine."

Duchess Alyssa's crimson lips drew back from her perfect teeth in a snarl of rage.

"No!" She turned to the side of the stage making 'cutting' motions with her hands.

Merovech ignored her. "I have been the victim of a dark conspiracy, an attempted coup. But despite that, I am here to take up my father's crown." He leant forward, towards the camera, his projected face glowering down at the crowd. "And my first act as your new king is to order the immediate withdrawal of our ships in the South China Sea, and the arrest of my mother, the Duchess of Brittany."

The crowd erupted. Some were horrified, others applauded. Their voices filled the arena. The men surrounding Victoria looked at each other. And then one of them tried to grab her. She stepped back and brought the tip of the staff smacking up into his left temple, dropping him where he stood. But by doing so, she'd put herself in reach of the man behind her. His hands clawed at her shoulders. She tried to twist away, but the other two caught hold of the ends of her staff and yanked it from her fingers.

She heard gunfire, and renewed screams, but couldn't see where they came from, or who was shooting. Her world collapsed into a blur of thrashing arms and legs. She felt herself punched and kicked. The gelware did its best to smother the pain of each blow. She lashed out and felt her knuckles crunch into meat and bone, but too many people were on her now, and she was suffocating beneath their weight. It was like trying to fight the incoming tide. She couldn't breathe. She tried to kick, but her legs were pinned.

Okay, she thought. *Time to get drastic.*

Retreating back inside herself, she kicked her consciousness up into command mode and dialled all the settings as high as she could. Time stretched. The pummelling of fists and bodies slowed to an insistent jostling. She opened her eyes, and felt her heart buck in her ribcage as her adrenal glands came online, flooding her bloodstream with hysterical strength.

At least two hands held her right arm. She tugged it free and punched upward, towards the stars. Her knuckles clipped one man's face, and buried themselves in the gut of another. She pulled back and struck again. And again. Voices cried in pain and indignation. Some of the weight pinning her eased. She squirmed a leg free and let fly a kick that lifted one of her attackers off the ground, sending him rolling and tumbling into the swimming pool. A sideways jab with her left elbow broke somebody's nose. And then the survivors were scrambling to get away from her, leaving only the unconscious and unmoving to weigh her down. She struggled free and scrambled to her feet. At least one of her ribs was cracked. Her nose bled and her knuckles were a ragged mess, but she didn't care. Terror and regret were safely confined to the biological section of her brain, their voices muffled like those of noisy neighbours, and quite separate from the rest of her thoughts. Locked into the artificial clarity of her operating system, all she felt was fierce exhilaration. Nuclear fire might pour from the heavens at any moment but, until it did, she wasn't going to surrender to anybody. She'd been hurt enough. She'd been drugged, attacked and operated upon, and now it was her turn to fight back. At least thirty guys ringed her now. She didn't stand a chance, and knew it; yet, somehow, it hardly mattered. She flexed her shoulders. The faces surrounding her betrayed fear and anger. Somewhere near the stage, Ack-Ack Macaque fought a similar battle of his own, against equally insurmountable odds.

As she glanced in that direction, she saw the plasma screen cut to static. A pulled plug or an electromagnetic pulse? Were the bombs falling on London already?

The Duchess stood in front of the screen, caught in the glare of the world's media. She pointed a long finger into the crowd, shouting instructions no-one could hear.

Victoria looked back to the men around her. They were edging forward. She recognised a few from her days as a journalist: a scattering of minor politicians, a few media types, one or two millionaires. Some of them clutched broken chair legs; others held champagne bottles as improvised clubs. She turned around slowly, staring them each in the eye. Then she hawked, and spat bloody phlegm at their feet.

One of the men stepped forward. He was a good head and shoulders taller than her, and built like the proverbial brick shithouse. The arms of his tuxedo bulged with muscle. He had the shaven head and swollen neck of a professional boxer, and each and every one of his fingers sported a thick gold ring.

Here we go, she thought.

But then, before he could get close enough to strike, the sky flashed, and heads turned. The light came from the west. Instinctively, Victoria flinched away, waiting for the heat and fire of a nuclear blast. But the shockwave never came, and when she raised her head again, she saw a spear of light rising into the night sky.

The rocket had launched.

All those stolen souls were on their way to Mars, and she could do nothing to stop them. Was there a copy of her aboard, or had Vic been the only one?

She didn't have much time to consider the question, as no-neck turned his attention back to her, his lip curled in a sneer. Behind him, the rest of the mob flexed. His contempt of her made them brave. They were getting ready to rush her again and, this time, she wouldn't be able to fight them all off.

This was it.

"Goodbye, Paul."

She took up a defiant stance, bloodied knuckles raised and ready.

And something huge blocked out the stars.

The big guy didn't see it: he had his back to it. He swung at her with a paw like a bag of pig's trotters, and she ducked to the side. But by now, the others had seen what was coming, and they had started to run.

Victoria laughed at them. Where could they go? The *Tereshkova* was longer and wider than the *Maraldi*, and it was diving right at them. There could be no escape.

She stood and watched the crippled airship grow larger and larger, filling the oval of sky described by the rim of the arena. And then, just as she judged it was about to hit, she turned and threw herself full-length into the swimming pool.

CHAPTER THIRTY-EIGHT
MONKEY-EX-MACHINA

THE CRASH WENT on and on. Coming in at a relatively shallow angle, the *Tereshkova* pancaked onto the liner like a whale throwing itself onto a rock. The belly of the gondola scraped the upper surfaces of the ship, snapping off radar and communication antennae. The tops of the funnels crumpled, and the *Maraldi* heaved sideways, pushed almost completely over, before righting itself as the *Tereshkova*'s five sterns dropped into the sea and the noses came up, relieving some of the pressure on the liner's superstructure.

Glass and debris rained into the arena. The water in the swimming pool sloshed back and forth, and Victoria had to fight to stay afloat. Struggling against the weight of her sodden clothes, she pushed through a floating morass of dead bodies and broken patio furniture. She reached the edge of the pool and hauled herself out. Water ran from her, and she collapsed onto the deck.

Overhead, the five hulls of the *Tereshkova* formed a roof to the arena. The hatches of the main gondola were flung open, and ropes thrown out. Then, before anyone on the *Maraldi* had time to react, white-jacketed stewards were sliding down, rifles and submachine guns from the Commodore's armoury slung over their crisply-ironed shoulders.

Victoria lay on the deck, bleeding from a dozen separate wounds, and laughed.

"You mad old goat," she said. "You crazy, stubborn, brilliant man."

And then, he was there in person, coming down one of the ropes, hand-over-hand. She recognised his white hair and red sash, and the cutlass dangling from his belt. And there, behind him, was Merovech: the new king himself, sliding into battle with the troops.

In her eye, she saw Paul hovering over her, looking concerned.

"Vicky? Are you okay?"

She laughed again. "I'm fine. I'm going to hurt like hell tomorrow; but right now, I feel brilliant."

"That's the drugs talking."

"Damn straight."

She used her sleeve to wipe blood and snot from her nose, then sat up and pulled herself stiffly to her feet. The Commodore's boots had touched down on the deck a short distance away, and she limped over to greet him.

The old man had his cutlass drawn, and was using it to direct his stewards, while barking orders in Russian. His yellow teeth gnashed beneath the white forest of his moustache.

"Be careful." She squinted at the sword. "Or you'll have somebody's eye out with that."

He turned to her. Despite the white hair and injured hip, he looked twenty years younger, and his eyes held a wild glint. He gripped her shoulder with his free hand. "Good to see you, girl."

Her soaked clothes were dripping onto the deck. She looked at the stage. "Where's Célestine?"

"The Duchess?" The Commodore scowled. From his belt, he pulled an automatic pistol. "Take this," he said.

Victoria palmed the gun. It was heavier than she'd been expecting: a solid chunk of metal in her hand.

"Over there." The Commodore waved the tip of his sword at the other side of the pool, where Merovech stalked in the direction of the stage, still clad in his ratty jeans and red hoodie, a black Uzi machine pistol clasped in his hands. "Follow him."

With a piratical grin, he turned back to his men, who were fanning out across the arena, and waved his cutlass above his head.

"Keep going!" he bellowed. "Get to the bridge! Take that, and we take the ship!"

Victoria watched him go, dragging his bad leg behind him. Then she turned and made her way around the pool to intercept Merovech. He was moving at a trot, but slowed when he saw her coming.

"My mother?"

"She was on the stage. I didn't see which way she went."

"That's okay. I know this ship. I know where she'll be heading. Come on."

With his hood thrown back and chin jutting forward, he strode to the rear of the arena, and Victoria did all she could to keep up. She'd never seen him look so determined or move with such a sense of unstoppable purpose. The raw cadet she'd once sat beside on a South Atlantic helicopter had gone, leaving a soldier in his place.

He led her along corridors and down several stairwells, always moving towards the stern.

"There's a dock at the back of the ship. She'll be trying to reach one of the speedboats." He spared a glance for her injuries, looking at her cuts and scrapes, and the way she favoured her injured knee. "You don't have to come. You can stay here if you need to."

"No." Victoria's voice was firm. "I want to see this through to the end."

Merovech looked as if he understood. "You still need to get the full story, don't you?"

She gripped the pistol in her hand.

"There's more to it than that."

She followed him down another flight of stairs and out onto an open section of deck, running alongside a row of passenger cabins. The sea air felt cool and soothing on her skin, and she filled her lungs, relishing the dank overtones of salt and iodine.

They heard feet slapping on the deck behind them and turned. Ack-Ack Macaque joined them. He had been running. His eye patch had been ripped off. Clumps of fur were missing from around his face, and one of the sleeves of his leather flight jacket hung loose, where it had split along a seam.

He stopped and pulled a cigar from the jacket's inner lining.

"Are you going after the Duchess?" Merovech gave a nod. The monkey jammed the cigar between his teeth and spoke around it. "Swell. I guess I'll tag along with you, then."

He pulled a cheap plastic lighter from his other pocket, and sucked the cigar into life, huffing out clouds of pungent blue smoke in the process.

Merovech looked from him to Victoria.

"Follow me," he said.

THEY CAUGHT UP with Duchess Alyssa at the top of the dock, on a gangway overlooking the water. Her progress had been hampered by her gown, and by the high heels that dangled from one hand. In her other hand, she carried a fire axe, which she must have torn from a corridor wall during her flight from the stage.

The dock behind and below her was an open area at the *Maraldi*'s stern, with berths for pleasure craft. At either end of the gangway on which she stood, stairs led down on to pontoons, to which the smaller vessels were moored.

Standing with her back to the rail, the Duchess dropped her shoes and took hold of the axe in both hands, ready to swing at the first person to step within reach.

"Don't come any closer," she warned.

Merovech levelled his Uzi at her.

"Put the axe down, mother."

Duchess Alyssa laughed and tossed her hair. Her voice held a hysterical edge.

"Or what? Are you going to shoot me? Are you going to shoot your own mother?"

Merovech's lip curled. "You're not my mother."

"Yes I am!" She let go of the axe with one hand and thumped her chest. "We're the same flesh and blood. You came from me. I carried you in my womb. I gave birth to you."

"But you were still going to kill him," Victoria snapped.

Duchess Alyssa turned to her, lip curled.

"Oh, the reporter. How many times have we tried to kill you now?"

"Too many."

She turned her attention to Ack-Ack Macaque. "And the monkey! How glorious. All my little birdies home at once."

She took a fresh grip on the axe handle.

"Now," she said. "Which of you wants it first?"

Merovech held his Uzi in both hands. His knuckles were white.

"You killed my father," he said.

Duchess Alyssa gave a snort.

"He wasn't your father."

"You let me think he was!"

"So what? Are you going to arrest me? You're not really the King, you know. Or has my baby gotten all ambitious, all of a sudden?"

Merovech adjusted his stance. "What you tried to do to me was monstrous. You would have killed me, erased my mind. But if my life has to be a lie, at least I can make it a lie of my choosing. And if I want to be king, I will be King." He took a step towards her. "You might think I'm nothing more than a clone, mother. But I'm *your* clone. Do you expect me to be any less determined than you?"

Duchess Alyssa moved the axe from one shoulder to the other, like a batsman warming up at the crease, ready to deliver a devastating backhand swipe.

"All right," she said. "Let me tell you how this is going to work. I have somewhere I need to be. You three are each going to take one step back and stay where you are until I reach the steps at the end of this gangway. I'm going to take one of the smaller boats." She tapped a bare foot against the metal deck. "You can keep this one, for all the good it will do you."

Victoria looked to Merovech. The young man didn't move. Slowly, he raised the machine pistol so that the barrel pointed directly at his mother's face.

"No," he said. "Let me tell *you* how this works. You're going to drop that axe and put your hands on your head. Then I'm going to march you back upstairs, and you can confess everything in front of the cameras, on live TV."

The Duchess gave a pitying shake of her head. "You can't stop me, Merovech. Look at you. All three of you. I've never seen such a sorry mess."

"It's over, mother."

Duchess Célestine tossed her hair. "I'm afraid it's very far from over. In fact, it's just getting started. There's a war coming, Merovech, and after that, things are going to be very different. The world will be a much better place."

"A radioactive wasteland."

The Duchess laughed scornfully. "A clean slate. Can't you see that, Merovech? Can't you imagine a world without sickness and death? A world where we can strive for the stars, unfettered by bureaucracy and corruption, unencumbered by the weak and ignorant? A world where everybody works together, and everybody knows their place?"

Ack-Ack Macaque gave a snarl.

"You sound a lot like the people I used to fight."

Célestine glowered down her nose. "And what would you know?"

Half crouched and ready to spring, the monkey let his lips draw back from his fangs.

"I know a fascist when I see one."

The Duchess smiled.

"Call it what you like, you can't stop me. None of you can. You can't even kill me. There's a copy of my mind on its way to Mars as we speak, and a new body waiting for me ashore. Nguyen will—"

"Nguyen's dead," Victoria said. "I killed him."

"You?" For the first time, the older woman seemed genuinely taken aback.

Merovech took another step towards her.

"Put the axe down, mother."

The Duchess backed up against the rail. Her nostrils quivered.

"No!" She glared around at the three of them. For a moment, Victoria thought she would let fly with the axe; but instead, evidently seeing no way out, the woman's left hand dropped to the decorative handbag slung over her right shoulder, and emerged with her fingers clutching the knobbed fruit shape of a shiny black hand grenade. She hooked a thumb through the pull-ring. "Now please, all of you put your weapons down and step away."

Merovech lowered his gun.

"You wouldn't."

Duchess Célestine's eyes were narrow slits. "What have I got to lose? I may fall here, but I will rise again. As the Empress of two worlds."

She raised the grenade and used her teeth to pull the pin from its mount.

With a cry, Merovech lunged forward, but she brought the axe around in a one-handed sweep that caught him on the left shoulder, sending him staggering sideways. The Uzi clattered from his grip.

"Idiot boy!"

Her cry galvanised Victoria. Without stopping to think, she squeezed the trigger of the pistol the Commodore had given her. It bucked in her hands. A loud bang, and the recoil almost shattered her wrists. Duchess Alyssa gave a grunt and looked down. The bullet had drilled a smoking hole through the fabric of her gown. The axe fell from her hand, and she tottered, still clutching the grenade. In Victoria's mind, Paul yelled at her to get down, but she knew she didn't have time to get away. The gangway offered nowhere to hide. The explosion would kill them all.

But then, from beside her: a streak of fur. Ack-Ack Macaque sprang forward in a flying crouch. He wrapped his long arms around the Duchess's legs and heaved upward. She screamed, and he screeched, and together they tipped over the edge of the gangway, thirty feet above the floating dock beneath.

Victoria threw herself down beside Merovech, who moaned and clutched his shoulder, thick red blood slathering his fingers. Below, the grenade exploded in mid air. The gangway convulsed beneath her, smacking against her hard enough to drive the wind from her body. She tasted blood. The roar of the blast rattled the enclosed dock, battering her senses.

And then, there was nothing but the sound of fire alarms and the smell of burning.

She lay still for a long time, hardly daring to believe she was still alive.

The monkey had saved them. But at what cost?

She turned her aching head to the edge of the walkway, and her eyes caught sight of something brown wrapped around the chrome rail. She got to her feet, every inch of her body complaining bitterly, and struggled over to it.

Hanging by his tail, Ack-Ack Macaque dangled above the smoking black remains of a splintered, burning pontoon, his crumpled cigar still wedged between his teeth. Thirty feet below, gown shredded by the explosion, the Duchess lay face-down in the water.

"You're alive!"

He glared up at her with his one good eye. With his cuts and scrapes, he looked like something from a taxidermist's nightmare.

"Yeah. So, quit gawping and help me up."

She reached for his outstretched hand.

"I thought, for a moment, that you were—"

"Me too." He rolled the end of the cigar around in his mouth. "But, you know, once you've fallen out of a few trees, it turns out you get to be pretty good at catching yourself."

With her thighs braced against the rail, she gave a heave. She helped Ack-Ack Macaque onto the gangway, and they both flopped down onto their knees, panting. From her jacket pocket, her phone rang. On the fourth ring, she pulled it out and answered it. The call was from Julie.

"Is Merovech there? Is he all right?"

Victoria glanced at the boy lying a few feet from her, still clutching his shoulder.

"He will be. What's going on? Have we captured the ship?"

"Yes, but—" Julie's voice faltered. Victoria could hear her breath rasping on the other end of the line. "I have some bad news."

Victoria felt cold inside.

"What is it?"

"It's the Commodore." Julie's voice dropped to a hoarse whisper. "He's dead."

CHAPTER THIRTY-NINE
ALL THE MYRIAD COUNTRIES STRETCHED BENEATH

As DAWN BROKE over the Channel, clear and cold, Victoria stood on the rubberised helipad atop the *Tereshkova*'s central hull, looking out over the sea. There would be no stick fighting practice this morning: she had her right arm in a sling and, beneath the loose woollen jersey she now wore, extensive bandaging to hold her ribs in place.

In her left hand, she gripped the Commodore's bloodstained tunic. One of the stewards had given it to her, along with an envelope addressed to her in the old man's handwriting.

Injured as he was, the Commodore had finally been killed while capturing the *Maraldi*'s bridge: shot through the heart at point blank range, by a man already skewered on the tip of his cutlass.

Her godfather's body now lay beneath a sheet in the *Tereshkova*'s infirmary, awaiting burial at sea.

She draped the jacket over the rail, and reread the letter.

My dearest Victoria, it began. *I have no children of my own, and no wife. Therefore, in the event of my death, it is my fondest wish that you become sole beneficiary of my estate— including ownership of the* Tereshkova. *My lawyers will be in touch to discuss the details. In the meantime, please take care of the old girl.*

The end of the letter contained all the command codes and bank account numbers she would need to operate the old airship, and was signed with an ornate, and unreadable, flourish.

The paper flapped in the breeze. She folded it in half, and slipped it into the back pocket of her jeans. Then she reached out and touched the medals pinned to the breast of the stained tunic.

"Goodbye, old friend."

Overnight, the airship had been partially patched. Another skyliner had arrived, and had donated part of its helium reserves to re-inflate a few of the *Tereshkova*'s newly-repaired gas bags. The sabotaged engine had been examined and declared safe, the bomb having failed to crack the reactor housing. And now, the skyliner loomed over the water, still listing slightly to starboard but otherwise buoyant, a couple of hundred metres from the damaged liner.

Looking across at the dazzling white ziggurat-like terraces of the *Maraldi*, Victoria saw where the upper stories had borne the brunt of the *Tereshkova*'s impact: smashed windows; snapped aerials; a broken funnel. The liner wouldn't be going anywhere under her own steam for a while, and would be towed back to Portsmouth as soon as a hastily-despatched aircraft carrier arrived to take her passengers aboard.

Victoria planned to limp the *Tereshkova* back to Heathrow for repairs.

The wind blew in from the south-west, fresh with the promise of a new morning. Behind her, the sun climbed higher in the eastern sky, throwing her shadow across the fabric of the hull.

"It looks as if it's going to be a nice day," she said.

Floating in the air before her, Paul's image smiled.

"You know," he said, "for a while back there, I didn't think we were going to make it."

Victoria wriggled her fingers. Her arm felt stiff in its sling.

"Me neither." But when the Commodore's men had found her sitting on the gangway, watching the monkey trying to stem Merovech's axe wound with rolled up folds of his own clothing, they'd brought the news she hadn't dared hope for: that the British fleet had turned around, and was sailing for home with no shots fired. The holocaust for which she'd been bracing herself had been averted. At least, for today.

Now, standing on the helipad, she felt desolate and desiccated, as if every drop of fear and despair had been wrung from her.

"So," Paul asked, scratching his bearded chin. "What now?"

Victoria turned and peered into the east, using her hand to shade her eyes from the sun's orange glare.

"I don't know. If the repairs hold long enough to reach Heathrow, I might stay here, on the *Tereshkova*." She patted the pocket containing the Commodore's letter. "It is mine now, after all."

Paul shuffled his trainers on an invisible floor. "I meant, what now for you and me? Where do we go from here?"

"I guess that depends on how long you last before you start to fragment. The longest I ever heard of a back-up being run was six months."

He looked sheepish. "Do you think you could put up with me for that long?"

Victoria pursed her lips.

"Perhaps." She wouldn't admit it, but she'd started to get used to having him around, and she didn't like the idea of losing him. Too much had been lost already, and she didn't want to go back to being lonely and alone.

"If we do this," she said, "we're going to have to come up with a few ground rules. I like your company, but I need my privacy, if you know what I'm saying?"

Paul held up his hands. "Oh, absolutely. Anything you want." He grinned. "And who knows what will happen in six months? If I'm lucky, I might get an android body, after all. Then you'll never get rid of me."

Victoria pantomimed a shudder.

"What a horrible thought."

She started hobbling back towards the hatchway. As she drew close, it opened, and Merovech appeared, with Julie in tow, her weight braced against a crutch.

The young King looked tired. He also had his arm in a sling, and an extensively bandaged shoulder; but he'd taken the time to shave and change. She looked down at the red military jacket he wore.

"It's one of the Commodore's," he said. "Julie didn't think you'd mind."

Victoria smiled. "It suits you."

Merovech stuck his lip out, clearly unconvinced.

"You have to address the nation," Julie told him. "If you are going to be the king, you need to look the part."

He took her hand in his. For a moment, they looked into each other's eyes. Then Merovech turned back to Victoria.

"And how are you?"

Victoria blew air through her cheeks. "Oh, you know. Look like shit, feel like shit."

He grinned.

"Well, you'll be pleased to know that we have all the members of the Undying cult detained. At least, the ones who were on the *Maraldi* last night. As for the rest, we have their names from my mother's files, and the police can deal with them."

Victoria looked around. "Where's the monkey?"

Julie cleared her throat.

"He is down in the lounge, eating bananas and drinking daiquiris with the press. They cannot get enough of him and, frankly, I think he likes the attention. He is already talking about suing Céleste for the copyright to his image."

"I hope he's got a good lawyer."

Merovech shook his head. "He won't need one. With my mother dead, her share of the company passes to me. And it's a controlling interest, so I can do whatever I like."

"Well, you are the king."

His young face darkened, like a cloud passing across the sun.

"For now, anyway." He took her hand. "Thank you, Victoria. You've done so much, I can't begin to—"

"Ah, *c'est rien.*"

"No, I'm serious. If there's anything I can do, just say the word. How about a knighthood? A stately home? Something like that?"

Victoria laughed, and gently extricated her fingers from his grip.

"I don't think so." She turned to look back along the length of the hull, towards the airship's tail. "I have a place here now."

At that moment, Ack-Ack Macaque stuck his dishevelled head through the stairwell hatch. His fur looked patchy and ragged; he had a few new scars around his muzzle; and safety pins held the sleeve of his jacket in place. K8 had fashioned him a new eye patch from gauze, and he'd bummed half a dozen cigars from the assembled reporters.

"Hey," he said. "What are you all doing up here? You're missing all the fun."

Victoria held up her hand, warding him away.

"We've all had more than enough 'fun' for one day, thank you."

"Then what'cha doing?"

"We're getting ready to leave."

The monkey pulled himself up onto the helipad and lit a cigar. K8 followed him out, blinking in the sunlight.

"In that case," he said, "we're coming with you."

"What about the cameras?" Victoria asked. "What about your fans?"

Ack-Ack Macaque stuck his bottom lip out. "I'm not cut out for stardom. I'm a pilot." He blew smoke at the clear dawn sky. "And, with the old man gone, and his pilot injured, I'm guessing you could do with someone to fly this tub for you? Am I right?"

"Can you fly an airship?"

Ack-Ack Macaque cracked his knuckles.

"I can fly anything." His face dropped into a simian scowl. "I've got a hell of a lot I need to figure out. This will keep me out of trouble while I decide what I'm going to do with the rest of my life. And besides, there's a whole world out there that I never knew existed. I'd like to see some of it."

"And K8?"

"Well, we'll need a navigator, won't we?" Ack-Ack Macaque scratched his cheek. "From what I can see, most of this ship's run by computer, and she can do anything with them." He grinned proudly. "The girl's a goddamn genius."

Victoria's hand fell to her side.

"Okay then, it's settled. Welcome to the crew, Monsieur Macaque. And you, K8. We set sail in an hour."

The monkey touched leathery fingers to his brow in salute.

"Much obliged, skip. What's our heading?"

"First London, for repairs. After that, we'll play it by ear."

Merovech laced his fingers in Julie's, and looked at the three of them. "Where do you think you'll go?"

Ack-Ack Macaque scratched his belly. Even battered and scorched, he looked ready for another adventure, and Victoria knew for certain that, with him at the wheel, life on board the *Tereshkova* would never be dull.

She watched as he turned and grinned into the wind, his yellow eye scanning the far horizon, taking in the cloud-flecked cobalt dome of the sky, and all the myriad countries stretched beneath.

He took a pull on his cigar.

"Everywhere," he said.

THE END

EXTRAS

ACK-ACK MACAQUE FIRST lumbered his way into my consciousness some time in 2006, and I still have no idea where he came from. One day, I simply found myself repeating his name, over and over and over again, like a tune I couldn't get out of my head.

Ack-Ack Macaque. Everything else came from those four syllables. Catchy and deceptively simple, unpacking them demanded I come up with a world in which a monkey could credibly pilot a fighter plane.

About a year later, the following short story appeared in the September 2007 issue of Interzone, the long-running UK fiction magazine. Writing of it on his website, the novelist and comics writer Warren Ellis memorably described it as: "The commercialisation of a web animation into some diseased Max Headroom as metaphor for the wreckage of a fucked-up relationship."

I like that description.

As 'Ack-Ack Macaque' was only my second fiction sale to Interzone, I was both surprised and delighted when the magazine's readers voted it as their favourite story of the year.

Delighted, and a little stunned. You see, as a twenty-something creative writing student in the early 1990s, I'd dreamt wistfully of publication in Interzone. To have something I'd written finally appear in its pages, and then to have it so wholeheartedly endorsed by its readership, seemed more than I could ever have hoped for.

Pleased and encouraged by this response, I included the story in my first collection, The Last Reef (Elastic Press, 2008), and moved on. I wrote some more stories, and a couple of novels. But that monkey wouldn't leave me alone: he wanted more adventures; he wanted to get out into the world and cause mayhem; and he wanted to see his ugly mug on the front cover of a book.

So, when Jon Oliver at Solaris asked if I had a book I wanted to write, Ack-Ack Macaque was right there waiting, puffing on a huge cigar, a stupid grin plastered across his grizzled face.

"I knew you'd be back," he said. And he was right. I'd never quite shaken him off. I probably never will.

But now, as he rides off into the sunset at the end of his first novel-length adventure, let's look back five years, to that September 2007 issue of Interzone, and the short story that started it all.

This was his first public appearance; these were his first baby steps into the world; and I hope you enjoy them.

Gareth L. Powell
Bristol, July 2012

ACK-ACK MACAQUE
Gareth L. Powell

I SPENT THE first three months of last year living with a half-Japanese girl called Tori in a split-level flat above a butcher's shop on Gloucester Road. The flat was more mine than hers. We didn't have much furniture. We slept on a mattress in the attic, beneath four skylights. There were movie posters on the walls, spider plants and glass jars of dried pasta by the kitchen window. I kept a portable typewriter on the table and there were takeaway menus and yellowing taxi cards pinned to a corkboard by the front door. On a still night, music came from the Internet café across the street.

Tori had her laptop set up by the front window. She wrote and drew a web-based anime about a radioactive short-tailed monkey called Ack-Ack Macaque. He had an anti-aircraft gun and a patch over one eye. He had a cult online following. She spent hours hunched over each frame, fingers tapping on the mouse pad.

I used to sit there, watching her. I kept the kettle hot, kept the sweet tea coming. She used to wear my brushed cotton shirts and mutter under her breath.

We had sex all the time. One night, after we rolled apart, I told her I loved her. She just kind of shrugged; she was restless, eager to get back to her animation.

"Thanks," she said.

She had shiny brown eyes and a thick black ponytail. She was shorter than me and wore combat trousers and skater t-shirts. Her left arm bore the twisted pink scar of a teenage motor scooter accident.

We used to laugh. We shared a sense of humour. I thought that we got each other, on so many levels. We were both into red wine and tapas. We liked the same films, listened to the same music. We stayed up late into the night, talking and drinking.

And then, one day in March, she walked out on me.

And I decided to slash my wrists.

I'VE NO IDEA why I took it so hard. I don't even know if I meant to succeed. I drank half a bottle of cheap vodka from the corner shop, and then I took a kitchen knife from the drawer and made three cuts across each wrist. The first was easy, but by the second my hands had started to shake. The welling blood made the plastic knife handle slippery and my eyes were watering from the stinging pain. Nevertheless, within minutes, I was bleeding heavily. I dropped the knife in the bathroom sink and staggered downstairs.

Her note was still on the kitchen table, where she'd left it. It was full of clichés: she felt I'd been stifling her; she'd met someone else; she hadn't meant to, but she hoped I'd understand.

She hoped we could still be friends.

I picked up the phone. She answered on the fifth ring.

"I've cut my wrists," I said.

She didn't believe me; she hung up.

It was four-thirty on a damp and overcast Saturday afternoon. I felt restless; the flat was too quiet and I needed cigarettes. I picked up my coat and went downstairs. Outside, it was blisteringly cold; a bitter wind blew, and the sky looked bruised.

"TWENTY SILK CUT, please."

The middle-aged woman in the corner shop looked at me over her thick glasses. She wore a yellow sari and lots of mascara.

"Are you all right, love?"

She pushed the cigarettes across the counter. I forced a smile and handed her a stained tenner. She held it between finger and thumb.

She said, "Is this blood?"

I shrugged. I felt faint. Something cold and prickly seemed to be crawling up my legs. My wrists were still bleeding; my sleeves were soaked and sticky. Bright red splatters adorned the toes of my grubby white trainers.

She looked me up and down, and curled her lip. She shuffled to the rear of the shop and pulled back a bead curtain, revealing a flight of dingy wooden stairs that led up into the apartment above.

"Sanjit!" she screeched. "Call an ambulance!"

ACK-ACK MACAQUE rides through the red wartime sky in the Akron, a gold-plated airship towed by twelve hundred skeletal oxen. With his motley crew, he's the scourge of the Luftwaffe, a defender of all things right and decent.

Between them, they've notched up more confirmed kills than anyone else in the European theatre. They've pretty much cleared the Kaiser's planes from the sky; all except those of the squadron belonging to the diabolical Baron Von Richter-Scale.

They've tracked each other from the Baltic Sea to the Mediterranean and back. Countless times, they've crossed swords in the skies above the battlefields and trenches of Northern Europe, but to no avail.

"You'll never stop me, monkey boy!" cackles the Baron.

THEY KEPT ME in hospital for three days. When I got out, I tried to stay indoors. I took a leave of absence from work. My bandaged wrists began to scab over. The cuts were black and flaky. The stitches itched. I became self-conscious. I began to regret what I'd done. When I ventured out for food, I tried to hide the bandages. I felt no one understood; no one saw the red, raw mess that I'd become.

Not even Tori.

"I did it for you," I said.

She hung up, as always. But before she did, in the background, I heard Josh, her new boyfriend, rattling pans in the kitchen.

I'd heard that he was the marketing director of an up-and-coming software company based in a converted warehouse by the docks. He liked to cook Thai food. He wore a lot of denim and drove an Audi.

I went to see him at his office.

"You don't understand her work," I said.

He took a deep breath. He scratched his forehead. He wouldn't look at my hands; the sight of my bandages embarrassed him.

"The Manga monkey thing?" he said. "I think that's great but, you know, there's so much more potential there."

I raised my eyebrows.

"Ack-Ack Macaque's a fucking classic," I replied.

He shook his head slowly. He looked tired, almost disappointed by my lack of vision.

"It's a one joke thing," he said. He offered me a seat, but I shook my head.

"We're developing the whole concept," he continued. "We're going to flesh it out, make it the basis for a whole product range. It's going to be huge."

He tapped a web address into his desktop, and turned the screen my way. An animated picture of the monkey's face appeared, eye patch and all.

"See this? It's a virtual online simulation that kids can interact with."

I stared at it in horror. It wasn't the character I knew and loved. They'd lost the edginess, made it cute, given it a large, puppy dog eye and a goofy grin. All the sharp edges were gone.

Josh rattled a few keys. "If you type in a question, it responds; it's great. We've given it the ability to learn from its mistakes, to make its answers more convincing. It's just like talking to a real person."

I closed my eyes. I could hear the self-assurance in his voice, his unshakable self-belief. I knew right then that nothing I could say would sway him. I had no way to get through to him. He was messing up everything I loved–my relationship with Tori, and my favourite anime character–and I was powerless in the face of his confidence. My throat began to close up. Breathing became a ragged effort. The walls of the office seemed to crowd in on me. I fell into a chair and burst into embarrassed sobs.

When I looked up, angrily wiping my eyes on my sleeve, he was watching me.

"You need to get some counselling," he said.

I TOOK TO wearing sunglasses when I went out. I had a paperback copy of *The Invisible Man* on my bookshelves and I spent a lot of time looking at the bandaged face on the cover.

April came and went. Ashamed and restless, I left the city and went back to the dismal Welsh market town where I'd grown up. I hid for a couple of months in a terraced bed and breakfast near the railway station. At night, the passing trains made the sash windows shake. By day, rain pattered off the roof and dripped from the gutters. Grey mist streaked the hills above the town, where gorse bushes huddled in the bracken like a sleeping army.

I'd come seeking comfort and familiarity but discovered instead the kind of notoriety you only find in a small community. I'd become an outsider, a novelty. The tiniest details of my daily activities were a constant source of fascination to my elderly neighbours. They were desperate to know why I wore bandages on my arms; they were like sharks circling, scenting something in the water. They'd contrive to meet me by the front door so they could ask how I was. They'd skirt around a hundred unspoken questions, hoping to glean a scrap of scandal. Even in a town where half the adult population seemed to exhibit one kind of debilitating medical condition or another, I stood out.

The truth was, I didn't really need the bandages any more. But they were comforting, somehow. And I wasn't ready to give them up.

Every Friday night, I called Tori from the payphone at the end of the street, by the river.

"I miss you," I said.

I pressed the receiver against my ear, listening to her breathe. And then I went back to my empty little room and drank myself to sleep.

MEANWHILE, ACK-ACK Macaque went from strength to strength. He got his own animated Saturday morning TV series. Pundits were even talking about a movie. By August, the wisecracking monkey was everywhere. And the public still couldn't get enough of him. They bought his obnoxious image on t-shirts and calendars. There were breakfast cereals, screensavers, ring tones and lunchboxes. His inane catchphrases entered the language. You could hardly go anywhere without hearing some joker squeak out: "Everybody loves the monkey."

My blood ran cold every time I heard it.

It was my phrase; she'd picked it up from me. It was something I used to say all the time, back when we lived together, when we were happy. It was one of our private jokes, one of the ways I used to make her laugh. I couldn't believe she'd recycled it. I couldn't believe she was using it to make money.

And it hurt to hear it shouted in the street by kids who only knew the cute cartoon version. They had no idea how good the original anime series had been, how important. They didn't care about its irony or satire–they just revelled in the sanitised slapstick of the new episodes.

I caught the early train back to Bristol. I wanted to confront her. I wanted to let her know how betrayed I felt. But then, as I watched the full moon set over the flooded Severn Estuary, I caught my reflection in the carriage window.

I'd already tried to kill myself. What else could I do?

WHEN WE PULLED in at Bristol Parkway, I stumbled out onto the station forecourt in the orange-lit dawn chill. The sky in the east was dirty grey. The pavements were wet; the taxis sat with their heaters running.

After a few moments of indecision, I started walking. I walked all the way to Tori's new bed-sit. It was September and there was rain in the air. I saw a fox investigating some black rubbish sacks outside a kebab shop. It moved more like a cat than a dog, and it watched me warily as I passed.

THE AKRON CARRIES half a dozen propeller-driven biplanes. They're launched and recovered using a trapeze that can be raised and lowered from a hangar in the floor of the airship. Ack-Ack uses them to fly solo scouting missions, deep into enemy territory, searching for the Baron's lair.

Today, he's got a passenger.

"He's gotta be here somewhere," shouts Lola Lush over the roar of the Rolls Royce engine. Her pink silk scarf flaps in the wind. She's a plucky American reporter with red lips and dark, wavy hair. But Ack-Ack doesn't reply. He's flying the plane with his feet while he peels a banana. He's wearing a thick flight jacket and a leather cap.

Below them, the moonlight glints off a thousand steam-driven Allied tanks. Like huge tracked battleships, they forge relentlessly forward, through the mud, toward the German lines. Black clouds shot with sparks belch from their gothic smoke stacks. In the morning, they'll fall on Paris, driving the enemy hordes from the city.

THE STREETLIGHTS ON her road were out. She opened the door as if she'd been expecting me. She looked pale and dishevelled in an old silk dressing gown. She'd been crying; her eyes were bloodshot and puffy.

"Oh, Andy." She threw her arms around my neck and rubbed her face into my chest. Her fingers were like talons.

I took her in and sat her down. I made her a cup of tea and waited patiently as she tried to talk.

Each time, she got as far as my name, and then broke down again.

"He's left me," she sobbed.

I held her as her shoulders shook. She cried like a child, with no restraint or dignity.

I went to her room and filled a carrier bag with clothes. Then I took her back to my flat, the one we used to share, and put her to bed in the attic, beneath the skylights. The room smelled stale because I'd been away so long.

Lying on her side beneath the duvet, she curled her arms around her drawn-up knees. She looked small and vulnerable, skinnier than I remembered.

"Andy?" she whispered.

"Yes, love?"

She licked her lips. "What do your arms look like, under the bandages?"

I flinched away, embarrassed. She pushed her cheek into the pillow and started to cry again.

"I'm so sorry," she sniffed. "I'm so sorry for making you feel like this."

I left her there and went down to the kitchen. I made coffee and sat at the kitchen table, in front of the dusty typewriter. Outside, another wet morning dawned.

I lit a cigarette and turned on the television, with the volume low. There wasn't much on. Several channels were running test cards and the rest were given over to confused news reports. After a couple of minutes, I turned it off.

At a quarter past six, her mobile rang. I picked it up. It was Josh and he sounded rough.

"I've got to talk to her," he said. He sounded surprised to hear my voice.

"No way."

I was standing by the window; rain fell from an angry sky.

"It's about the monkey," he said. "There's a problem with it."

I snorted. He'd screwed Tori out of her rights to the character. As soon as it started bringing in serious money, he'd dumped her.

I said, "Go to hell, Josh."

I turned the phone off and left it by the kettle. Out on the street, a police siren tore by, blue lights flashing.

I mashed out my cigarette and went for a shower.

Tori came downstairs as I took my bandages off. I think the phone must've woken her. I tried to turn away, but she put a hand on my arm. She saw the raised, red scars. She reached up and brushed my cheek. Her eyes were sad and her chest seemed hollow. She'd been crying again.

"You're beautiful," she said. "You've suffered, and it's made you beautiful."

THERE WASN'T ANY food in the house. I went down to the shop on the corner but it was closed. The Internet café over the road was open, but empty. All the monitors displayed error messages.

The girl at the counter sold me tea and sandwiches to take out.

"I think the main server's down," she said.

*   *   *

WHEN I GOT back to the flat, I found Tori curled on the sofa, watching an episode of the animated Ack-Ack Macaque series on DVD. She wore a towel and struggled with a comb. I took it from her and ran it gently through her wet hair, teasing out the knots. The skin on her shoulders smelled of soap.

"I don't like the guy they got in to do Baron Von Richter-Scale's voice," she said.

"Too American?"

"Too whiny."

I finished untangling her and handed the comb back.

"Why are you watching it?" I asked. She shrugged, her attention fixed on the screen.

"There's nothing else on."

"I bought sandwiches."

"I'm not hungry."

I handed her a plastic cup of tea. "Drink this, at least."

She took it and levered up the lid. She sniffed the steam. I went out into the kitchen and lit another cigarette. My hands were shaking.

When I got off the train last night, I'd been expecting a confrontation. I'd been preparing myself for a fight. And now all that unused anger was sloshing around, looking for an outlet.

I stared at the film posters on the walls. I sorted through the pile of mail that had accumulated during my absence. I stood at the window and watched the rain.

"This isn't fair," I said, at last.

I scratched irritably at my bandages. When I looked up, Tori stood in the doorway, still wrapped in the towel. She held out her arm. The old scar from the scooter accident looked like a twisted claw mark in her olive skin.

"We're both damaged," she said.

* * *

ABOUT AN HOUR later, the intercom buzzed. It was Josh.

"Please, you've got to let me in," he said. His voice was hoarse; he sounded scared.

I hung up.

He pressed the buzzer again. He started pounding on the door. I looked across at Tori and said, "It's your decision."

She bit her lip. Then she closed her eyes and nodded.

"Let him in."

HE LOOKED A mess. He wore a denim shirt and white Nike jogging bottoms under a flapping khaki trench coat. His hair was wild, spiky with yesterday's gel, and he kept clenching and unclenching his fists.

"It's the fucking monkey," he said.

Tori sucked her teeth. "What about it?" She was dressed now, in blue cargo pants and a black vest.

"Haven't you been watching the news?" He lunged forward and snatched the remote from the coffee table. Many of the cable channels were messy with interference. Some of the smaller ones were off the air altogether. The BBC was still broadcasting, but the sound was patchy. We saw footage of burning buildings, riots, and looting. Troops were on the streets of Berlin, Munich and Paris.

I asked: "What's this?"

He looked at me with bloodshot eyes. "It's the monkey," he replied.

WE SAT TOGETHER on the sofa, watching the disaster unfold. And as each station sputtered and died, we flicked on to the next. When the last picture faded, I passed around the cigarettes. Josh took one, Tori declined. Out in the street, we heard more sirens.

"You remember the online simulation? When we designed it, we didn't anticipate the level of response," he said.

I leaned forward, offering him a light.

"So, what happened?"

He puffed his Silk Cut into life and sat back in a swirl of smoke. He looked desperately tired.

"There were literally thousands of people on the site at any one time. They played games with it, tried to catch it out with trick questions. It was learning at a fantastic rate."

"Go on," I said.

"Well, it wasn't designed for that kind of intensity. It was developing faster than we'd anticipated. It started trawling other websites for information, raiding databases. It got everywhere."

Tori walked over to the TV. She stood in front of it, shifting her weight from one foot to the other. "So, why hasn't this happened before? They've had similar programs in the States for months. Why's this one gone wrong?"

He shook his head. "Those were mostly on academic sites. None of them had to contend with the kind of hit rates we were seeing."

"So, what happened?" I asked.

He looked miserable. "I guess it eventually reached some critical level of complexity. Two days ago, it vanished into cyberspace, and it's been causing trouble ever since."

I thought about the error messages on the monitors in the café, and the disrupted TV stations. I sucked in a lungful of smoke.

"Everybody loves the monkey," I said.

A HANDFUL OF local and national radio stations were still broadcasting. Over the next hour, we listened as the entity formerly known as Ack-Ack Macaque took down the Deutsche Bank. It wiped billions off the German stock exchange and sent the international currency markets into freefall.

"It's asserting itself," Josh said. "It's flexing its muscles."

Tori sat on the bottom of the stairs that led up to the attic. Her head rested against the banister.

"How could you let this happen?" she asked.

Josh surged to his feet, coat flapping. He bent over her, fists squeezed tight. She leaned back, nervous. He seemed to be struggling to say something.

He gave up. He let out a frustrated cry, turned his back and stalked over to the window. Tori closed her eyes. I went over and knelt before her. I put a hand on her shoulder; she reached up and gripped it.

I said, "Are you okay?"

She glanced past me, at Josh. "I don't know," she said.

THEY ENGAGE THE Baron's planes in the skies over France. There's no mistaking the Baron's blue Fokker D.VII with its skull and crossed-bones motif.

The Akron launches its fighters and, within seconds, the sky's a confusing tangle of weaving aircraft.

In the lead plane, Ack-Ack Macaque stands up in his cockpit, blasting away with his handheld cannon. His yellow teeth are bared, clamped around the angry red glow of his cigar.

In the front seat, Lola Lush uses her camera's tripod to swipe at the black-clad ninjas that leap at them from the enemy planes. Showers of spinning shurikens clatter against the wings and tail.

The Baron's blue Fokker dives toward them out of the sun, on a collision course. His machine guns punch holes through their engine cowling. Hot oil squirts back over the fuselage. Lola curses.

Ack-Ack drops back into his seat and wipes his goggles. He seizes the joystick. If this is a game of chicken, he's not going to be the first to flinch. He spits his oily cigar over the side of the plane and wipes his mouth on his hairy arm. He snarls: "Okay, you bastard. This time we finish it."

THE FIRST TWO planes to crash were Lufthansa airliners, and they went down almost simultaneously, one over the Atlantic and the other on approach to Heathrow. The third was a German military transport that flew into the ground near Kiev.

Most of the radio reports were vague, or contradictory. The only confirmed details came from the Heathrow crash, which they were blaming on a computer glitch at air traffic control. We listened in silence, stunned at the number of casualties.

"There's a pattern here," I said.

Josh turned to face us. He seemed calmer but his eyes glistened.

"Where?"

"Lufthansa. The Deutsche Bank. The Berlin stock exchange..." I counted them off on my fingers.

Tori stood up and started pacing. She said, "It must think it really is Ack-Ack Macaque."

Josh looked blank. "Okay. But why's it causing planes to crash?"

Tori stopped pacing. "Have you ever actually *watched* the original series?"

He shrugged. "I looked at it, but I still don't get the connection."

I reached for a cigarette. "He's looking for someone," I said.

"Who?"

"His arch-enemy, the German air ace Baron Von Richter-Scale."

Tori stopped pacing. She said, "That's why all those planes were German. He's trying to shoot down the Baron. It's what he does in every episode."

Josh went pale.

"But we based his behaviour on those shows."

I said, "I hope you've got a good lawyer."

He looked indignant. "This isn't my fault."

"But you own him, you launched the software. You're the one they're going to come after."

I blew smoke in his direction. "It serves you right for stealing the copyright."

Tori shushed us.

"It's too late for that," she said.

The TV had come back on. Someone, somewhere had managed to lash together a news report. There was no sound, only jerky, amateur footage shot on mobile phones. It showed two airliners colliding over Strasbourg, a cargo plane ditching in the Med, near Crete. Several airports were burning.

And then it shifted to pictures of computer screens in offices, schools, and control towers around the world. All of them showed the same grinning monkey's face.

I pushed past Josh and opened the window. Even from here, I could see the same face on the monitors in the café across the road. A thick pall of black smoke came from the city centre. Sirens howled. People were out in the street, looking frightened.

I turned back slowly and looked Tori in the eye. I started unwinding my bandages, letting them fall to the floor in dirty white loops.

I said, "I don't care about any of this. I just want you back."

She bit her lip. Her hand went to her own scar. She opened and closed her mouth several times. She looked at the TV, and then dropped her eyes.

"I want you too," she said.

THE BARON'S BURNING plane hits the hillside and explodes. Lola Lush cheers and waves a fist over her head, but Ack-Ack Macaque says nothing. He circles back over the burning wreck and waggles his wings in salute to his fallen foe. And then he pulls back hard on the joystick and his rattling old plane leaps skyward, high over the rolling hills and fields of the French countryside.

Ahead, the Akron stands against the sunset like a long, black cigar. Its skeletal oxen paw the air, anxious to get underway.

Lola's lips are red and full; her cheeks are flushed. She shouts: "What are you gonna do now?"

He pushes up his goggles and gives her a toothy grin. The air war may be over, but he knows he'll never be out of work. The top brass will always want something shot out of the sky.

"When we get back, I'm going to give you the night of your young life," he says, "and then in the morning, I'm going to go out and find myself another war."

ACK-ACKNOWLEDGEMENTS

I'D LIKE TO thank the crew at Solaris Books for their support, especially Jon Oliver, Michael Molcher, David Moore, and Ben Smith. Also, Jetse de Vries and Andy Cox, for publishing the original Ack-Ack Macaque short story in *Interzone*. Jake Murray, for the awesome cover illustration. My family, for their unflagging belief and encouragement. Justin Pickard, for making me consider all the repercussions of setting a story in an alternate timeframe. My sister, Rebecca, for reading the first draft, and for helping me with French grammar and translation (any errors or omissions are my own, not hers). Gemma Morgan, for providing the reference photo of Hong Kong harbour. Emma Dmitriev, for sending me a handy list of Russian swearwords. My agent, John Jarrold, for his support. And, most of all, my wife Becky, for keeping me going when the outlook looked bleak and the hill too steep to climb; for giving me as much writing time as she could; for reading and commenting on the first draft; and, without whom, none of this would have been possible.

My heartfelt thanks to you all.

US ISBN: 978-1-907992-09-4 • $7.99 // UK ISBN: 978-1-907992-08-7 • £7.99

'A cliché it may be, but there really is something for everyone here... an ideal bait to tempt those who only read novels to climb over the short fiction fence'
Interzone on The Solaris Book of New Science Fiction

THE NEW SOLARIS BOOK
OF SCIENCE FICTION

SOLARIS RISING

EDITED BY
IAN WHATES

Alastair Reynolds
Peter F. Hamilton
Stephen Baxter
Ian McDonald
Paul di Filippo
Ken Macleod
Adam Roberts
Pat Cadigan

Solaris Rising presents nineteen stories of the very highest calibre from some of the most accomplished authors in the genre, proving just how varied and dynamic science fiction can be. From strange goings on in the present to explorations of bizarre futures, from drug-induced tragedy to time-hopping serial killers, from crucial choices in deepest space to a ravaged Earth under alien thrall, from gritty other worlds to surreal other realms, Solaris Rising delivers a broad spectrum of experiences and excitements, showcasing the genre at its very best.

'What, then, are Solaris publishing? On the basis of this anthology, quite a wide-ranging selection of SF, some of it very good indeed'
– *SF Site on The Solaris Book of New Science Fiction*

 WWW.SOLARISBOOKS.COM

Follow us on Twitter! www.twitter.com/solarisbooks

US ISBN: 978-1-78108-056-6 • $8.99 // UK ISBN: 978-1-78108-055-9 • £7.99

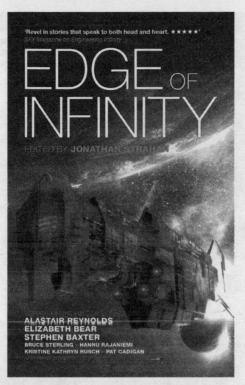

Edge of Infinity is an exhilarating new SF anthology that looks at the next giant leap for humankind: the leap from our home world out into the Solar System. From the eerie transformations in Pat Cadigan's "The Girl-Thing Who Went Out for Sushi" to the frontier spirit of Sandra McDonald and Stephen D. Covey's "The Road to NPS," and from the grandiose vision of Alastair Reynolds' "Vainglory" to the workaday familiarity of Kristine Kathryn Rusch's "Safety Tests," the thirteen stories in this anthology span the whole of the human condition in their race to colonise Earth's nearest neighbours.

Featuring stories by Hannu Rajaniemi, Alastair Reynolds, James S. A. Corey, John Barnes, Stephen Baxter, Kristine Kathryn Rusch, Elizabeth Bear, Pat Cadigan, Gwyneth Jones, Paul McAuley, Sandra McDonald, Stephen D. Covey, An Owomoyela, and Bruce Sterling, *Edge of Infinity* is hard SF adventure at its best and most exhilarating.

US ISBN: 978-1-78108-001-6 • £8.99 // UK ISBN: 978-1-78108-002-3 • UK £7.99

The aliens are here, all around us. They always have been. And now, one by one, they're destroying our cities.

Dodge Mercer deals in identities, which is fine until the day he deals the wrong identity and clan war breaks out. Hope Burren has no identity, and no past, struggling with a relentless choir of voices filling her head.

In a world where nothing is as it seems, where humans are segregated and aliens can sing realities and tear worlds apart, Dodge and Hope lead a ragged band of survivors in a search for the rumoured sanctuary of Harmony, and what may be the only hope for humankind.

 WWW.SOLARISBOOKS.COM

Follow us on Twitter! www.twitter.com/solarisbooks

"Keith Brooke's prose achieves a rare honesty and clarity, his characters always real people, his situations intriguing and often moving." — **Jeff VanderMeer**

KEITH BROOKE

THE ACCORD

"...some of the best science fiction to be found anywhere." – **Sci Fi Weekly**

UK: 978-1-84416-710-4 US: 978-1-84416-589-6

SOLARIS SCIENCE FICTION

US ISBN: 978-1-907992-85-8 • £8.99 // UK ISBN: 978-1-907992-84-1 • UK £7.99

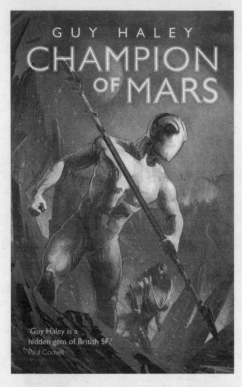

In the far future, Mars is dying a second time. The Final War of men and spirits is beginning. In a last bid for peace, disgraced champion Yoechakenon Val Mora and his spirit lover Kaibeli are set free from the Arena to find the long-missing Librarian of Mars, the only hope to save mankind.

In the near future, Dr Holland, a scientist running from a painful past, joins the Mars colonisation effort, cataloguing the remnants of Mars' biosphere before it is swept away by the terraforming programme.

When an artefact is discovered deep in the caverns of the red planet, the company Holland works for interferes, leading to tragedy. The consequences ripple throughout time, affecting Holland's present, the distant days of Yoechakanon, and the eras that bridge the aeons between.